Weeping Willows Dance

Gemini Press
Brooklyn, New York
2001

Weeping Willows Dance

This novel is a work of fiction based on a true story. Special permission granted to the author by the main character. Some names, characters, places and incidents are true, while others are the product of the author's imagination.

Gemini Press. 321Autumn Lane, Stroudsburg, PA 18360
Copyright © 2001 by Gloria Mallette

Gemini Press
321Autumn Lane
Stroudsburg, PA 18360

gempress@aol.com

ISBN: 0-9678789-1-8
Library of Congress Catalogue Card Number: 2001129079

Cover Design: Marion Designs
Copy Editor: Chandra Sparks Taylor

First Gemini Press Printing; May, 2001
Third Printing; March, 2005

Printed in the U.S.A.

Dedication

Mozelle, my beloved grandmother, you will always be in our hearts and in our fondest memories. From the moment you told me that you built your house with your own hands, I knew that your story had to be told. If we, your children, were lucky enough to inherit even a smidgen of your convictions and your courage, we are blessed ten times over.

Cora, my beloved mother, you left us oh so long ago, but we came to know you because of the love of your mother, Mozelle. We, your children, pray that we have done you proud.

Kandance, your sweet little voice and your angelic face is imprinted on our minds. You were wise in the Lord beyond your years.

JaMichael, your smile lit up the hearts of all that knew you.

Acknowledgments

Aunt Jimmie, thank you for the annual tradition of celebrating the long life of Mozelle, and for showing her that her love and sacrifices for her children were not in vain.

Aunt Ann, thank you for selflessly giving of your time six days a week to make sure that Mozelle was safe and wanted for nothing. We celebrate your life and give thanks to God for bringing you through.

Brother, Sylvia, and Douglas, thank you for staying close to Mozelle. She never had to wonder where her children were.

A special thanks to all the people of Gadsden, Alabama who came out on Sunday, December 10, 2000, to show their love for a noble woman.

Other books by the author.

Shades of Jade
When We Practice to Deceive

One

1929

Fried burned hair smothered the greasy smell of mouth-watering fried pork chops and homemade buttermilk biscuits, filling the hot kitchen with a stomach-wrenching stench. The pork chops and biscuits had tasted good, but the smell of burned hair was the reason Mozelle wasn't ever straightening her own. It reminded her of the smell of singed chicken feathers. Besides, if Alfreda, Ruth, and Sister weren't burning their hair, they were burning their ears or their necks. That was another reason not to put a hot comb to her hair. Two nappy plaits on either side of her head would have to do. And poor Mama, she couldn't keep her hair dry enough to straighten. Sweat poured from her head and face down onto her chest like she'd been working out in the field under the blistering sun all day. It was only nine o'clock in the morning. Mama, as was her usual, had been up since five o'clock cooking breakfast, ironing clothes, plaiting hair, and wiping crusty sleep out of the corner of the youngins' eyes with a rag, trying her best to get everybody ready for church on time. Mozelle didn't have to work as hard as her mama, although all the big children helped out with the youngins, but Mama had to have her hands in everything. It wasn't done right if she didn't touch it herself. Mama would be the last one dressed, and she wouldn't be sitting down all day except for in church and after supper.

Daddy sat out on the front porch drawing on his old hand-carved pipe dressed in his Sunday-go-to-meeting faded black suit with his new black Stetson cocked to one side of his near-bald head. He was proud of that hat; he well ought to be. It took him two years to save for it—two cents a week out of his sharecropping money. Pennies that Mama said could've bought more flour or rice or beans. Mama only said that one time to Daddy outright, after that, she kept it to herself, though she never would look at that hat. That's because Daddy hushed her up right off when he said that that hat was the first new thing he'd bought for himself in twenty years. Truth to tell, he was most likely right. With twelve youngins to feed, it was a wonder he saved the two pennies a week at all. If Mama hadn't had a hard time giving birth to Tulie, Daddy might've had twelve more mouths to feed.

Mama would've laid down and had more babies if she could've; she seemed to like having lots of babies in the house. She took Beulah's two when Beulah went off to Atlanta to find work. That was more than a year ago. While Mama didn't mind having all those babies around, Mozelle did. Not one of them babies come out of her belly, yet all the time she had to change nasty diapers or pick up a crying baby—there was always a baby on her hip, or on somebody's hip. Only thing she hadn't done was suckle them babies, and she planned on never, ever suckling a baby because she was never, ever going to have any. Too much work.

"Flo, y'all c'mon now," William called to her from the front porch.

Earl opened the screen door. "Mama, Daddy say y'all c'mon. He say he don't want us'n to be late for church."

"Mozelle, you and Alfreda take them youngins that's ready and start on down the road. Ruth, you stay and go on with me. Earl, tell Daddy U'ma catch up with y'all down the road."

"Yessum."

That's the way it was every Sunday. Mama coming into church awhile after they'd been there, always with a youngin in her arms and a youngin or two holding on to her skirt tail. She'd take her seat in front of Mozelle, Ruth and Alfreda, all the while wiping sweat off her face with a washrag.

"Ruth, that man over yonder keep lookin' at us," Alfreda whispered, nudging Ruth in the side.

"I know. Ain't he good-lookin'?"

Alfreda sighed. "Yeah, he mighty good-lookin'. Don't you think so, Mozelle?"

"I ain't lookin' at no man, and y'all best hush up befo' Daddy hear y'all."

Leaning across Alfreda's lap, Ruth whispered, "It look to

me like he lookin' at you, Mozelle."

"He ain't," she said, though she was a mite curious. She shifted her eyes and stole a peek. Their eyes met. He nodded. Right quick, she looked back at the front of the church, her neck stiff as a plank.

"I told you so," Ruth said gleefully. "Look, now he smilin' at you."

Mozelle turned her head ever so slightly and glanced over at the handsome dark-skinned man with the slicked-back wavy hair sitting on the aisle. He winked at her. She quickly turned back and looked straight ahead at Reverend Macaroy. Her heart was fluttering like the wings of a butterfly.

"I told you so," Ruth said again, looking at Mozelle, grinning. "Who is he?"

Mozelle shrugged. She really didn't care.

"U'm the oldest," Alfreda said, pouting. "He supposed to be lookin' at me."

Mozelle agreed. "I wish he *was* lookin' at you."

"I wish he was lookin' at me," Ruth said.

"U'ma tell Mama," Mozelle threatened. "You only fourteen. You too young for anybody to be lookin' at."

"You ain't grown neither, you just fifteen."

"That's still older than you."

"He look too old for both of y'all," Alfreda said.

"Y'all hush up back there," Florence whispered, looking back at her daughters over her right shoulder.

Mozelle, Ruth, and Alfreda hushed up right away. Florence turned back around in her seat. Mozelle looked straight ahead at Reverend Macaroy. He was preaching to raise the roof. He was pacing. He was wiping the sweat off his round, shiny face and the spit out of his mouth with a big white handkerchief, all at the same time. Nasty. That always made her cringe. Reverend Macaroy was at that point in his sermon where his voice started getting raspy, yet his words came out like he was singing a song. When he got to sounding like that, the whole congregation would rejoice.

Although Reverend Macaroy was wiping spit all over his face, Mozelle liked him just the same. He was a fire-and-brimstone preacher. He always got a rise out of his congregation, her included. That he could do better than most any other preacher. Almost everybody in church was either saying "amen" or "preach." Reverend Macaroy baptized her when she was five years old, and she had gotten the Holy Ghost when she was ten because of his preaching. She liked hearing his whole sermon, which was why she didn't like sitting next to Ruth and Alfreda. All they ever did was talk about other people in church and try to get boys to look at them. They were too grown for their own good.

"He sittin' next to Alice Hilman," Ruth whispered to Alfreda. "You know, he kinda look like her, don't he? You reckon they kin?"

"He sho'nuff is. He her brother. She told me the other day he was comin' for a spell. If'n that's him, he from Alabama."

Florence glared back at Alfreda. "If'n I gots to tell y'all one mo' time to hush up, U'ma have y'alls' daddy wear y'all out when we get home."

Mozelle quickly shook her head, "It wasn't me, Mama."

"I said, hush up," Florence said, giving Mozelle a warning glare before turning around again in her seat.

Mozelle looked around Florence's head toward the front of the church where William Douglas sat rigidly with the rest of the deacons. He was nodding in agreement with whatever Reverend Macaroy was saying. She certainly didn't want him to beat her with the razor strap he kept on a nail on the back of the front door at home. He hung it there because he said he wanted them all to see it on their way out of the house. That way they were reminded to behave themselves on the outside. William never put up with them acting out around other folks, and they never did—not anymore. That's because at one time or other, they'd all felt the cutting sting of that strap, and Mozelle had no intention of ever feeling that sting again. She folded her hands in her lap and again looked straight ahead. Ruth snickered behind her hands while Alfreda looked over at the good-looking stranger—he was looking straight ahead, too.

Mozelle didn't like that the stranger had winked at her. She didn't care how good-looking he was; she didn't want him winking at her. She had made it her business to stay away from boys, not to mention men, because she did not want a beau. Having a beau meant smooching, then necking, then sneaking into the woodshed, and then having to get married because your daddy made you, either before you made a baby or because a baby was on the way. She didn't want to get married. She didn't want no babies. Ever. She wanted to be an old maid. She would never be a sharecropper's wife like her mama.

Florence Douglas had twelve babies—six boys, six girls. All she ever did was birth babies and work hard raising them. She took care of her house, she took care of her husband, she worked in the field, and she washed white folks' dirty clothes. But as far back as Mozelle could remember, there was always a baby in the house. If it wasn't her mama's baby, it was one of her sisters' or brothers' babies. Being the fifth oldest, she had to work just as hard as her mama and sisters raising babies that weren't hers. This would never be her life. She dreamed of working and earning her own money to live on—just her, by herself. She would even buy a car and drive from town to town, a free woman. There would be no husband to tell her she couldn't do what she wanted; there would be no babies to keep her from doing what she wanted. Soon as she turned eighteen, she was hitting the road.

The service was ending. Everybody in church was holding hands. Reverend Macaroy was giving the benediction. Mozelle was determined to not look again at the man who winked at her. Alfreda, on the other hand, couldn't stop looking at him. She kept smiling, hoping that he'd pay her some attention. When the last amen was said, Mozelle dropped her sisters' hands and pushed her way out of the church. At the door, she had turned back just in time to see Alfreda, smiling, walk over to Alice Hilman and the winker. Stepping outside the church, Mozelle waited for her mama. If she didn't have to help take some of the youngins home, she would have run on ahead.

Under the late June sun, the walk home was slow and easy. The youngins ran off ahead of Florence and William. Mozelle walked as fast as she could, trying to stay way ahead of Randell Tate, but every time she dared to look back, he never seemed that far behind. She felt like he was staring a hole in her back. She knew he was watching her because when Alice Hilman introduced him to Florence and William as her brother, Randell shook William's hand and looked over his head and smiled at her. Mozelle felt like her heart actually stopped. His smile made her feel woozy. And when his eyes twinkled when he smiled, she stared stupidly at him. She knew she was staring, and she struggled to pull her eyes away, but she couldn't. He was smiling at her, showing his pretty even white teeth. They were as white as his skin was black. She could tell by the way he kept touching his tie knot that he knew he had the attention of all the womenfolk, Alfreda in particular, but he kept looking at her, making her feel uneasy. She had to get away from his twinkling eyes. She grabbed the hands of three-year-old Millie and two-year-old Roy and started for home, running ahead of everybody else. Mozelle felt like she was running for her life.

Two

In her dreams, Mozelle could not run away from Randell Tate. He was always right in front of her. He would not let her sleep in peace. She could not rid her mind of his smile or the way he looked at her. She woke up tired, but strangely tingly in her most private place. It shamed her. All throughout the day while she did her chores, again thoughts of Randell would not leave her be. Backing out of the henhouse after taking a basketful of eggs, she said to herself, "Soon as I take these eggs to Mama, I gots to pray on this." Mama was making sugar cookies for Alfreda's birthday—she was eighteen today. Birthdays were the only time they got sugar cookies, which was often since it was always somebody's birthday.

"Who you talkin' to?" Ruth asked, coming up behind Mozelle.

"Myself."

"You touched?"

"Is you?" she asked, closing the henhouse door, making sure that it was latched. Daddy didn't like the hens roaming around in the yard dropping eggs and walking off; said he'd make them eat the egg, shell and all, if he found one egg in the dirt. Jim was the only one, so far, who'd eaten raw eggs—three of them— shell and all. For two days he stayed in the outhouse.

"You in a mood, huh?" Ruth asked.

Mozelle turned her back on her. She didn't want Ruth to see in her face that she was bothered.

Ruth went around to stand in front of Mozelle. "You been in a mood since Sunday. What's wrong with you?"

"Nothing. Jest least me be."

Ruth looked hard into Mozelle's eyes. She squeezed her own eyes into slits. "Ooo!"

Again, Mozelle turned her back to Ruth. "Ruth! U'ma tell
Mama on you. You best leave me be."
    Ruth danced around Mozelle. "I know what's wrong with
you."
    Mozelle suddenly grabbed a chunk of Ruth's skin on her
upper arm and pinched her hard.
    "Ouch!"
    "Leave me be befo' I beat you up."
    Yanking her arm free, Ruth rubbed her arm hard. "Hell's
bells, Mozelle. I was only funnin' you."
    "Well, I ain't in a mood for funnin', and if'n you say *hell*
again, U'ma tell Daddy."
    "Well, you hurt me," Ruth said, pouting.
    "Well, you was botherin' me."
    "I ain't playin' with you no mo'."
    "Good."
    Ruth started to walk off, but she abruptly turned around.
"Mama say c'mon with them there eggs. And then she want me
'n you 'n Alfreda to go take Miss Lulamae and Miss Alcott they
wash."
    "U'ma go wash my feet first. Take these eggs to Mama."
Mozelle pushed the basket of eggs into Ruth's hands and started
across the yard to the well, dragging her feet in the dirt along the
way. Washing her feet after being in the henhouse was a must.
Like all of her brothers and sisters, she went barefoot, except
when she went to church. Nothing ever irritated her or hurt her
feet—not rocks, not splinters, not even the hot Royston, Georgia
clay. Just nasty chicken droppings. She hated that nasty squishy
feel, which was why she was glad rounding up the eggs was Jim's
chore. He didn't care what stuck under his feet. Just now he was
out in the field picking tomatoes and cucumbers with Daddy and
the other boys.
    Soon as she bent over the well, Mozelle was surrounded by
chirping, grabbing youngins. "Y'all best go on away from me,"
she said, shooing them away. They didn't leave her be until she
started hitting them on their tails. Laughing, they ran off.
Sometimes, they were so irritating, especially when they used her
to hide behind in their games of hide and seek.
    Finally alone, she drew a half bucket of water from the well
and carried it over to the wobbly wooden chair against the woodshed. She sat down, her back to the sun. She first rubbed each

foot with a handful of dry dirt; then poured cool water over them to rinse them. That done, she raised her left leg and rested her foot on her right thigh. Her faded dress hung between her thighs as she bent over to examine her big toenail. All of her toenails needed clipping, but the big toenail was worst of all. It was thick and dark. She never understood why. She hated looking at it. She started to stand when suddenly a long shadow fell over her.

"Leave me be," she said, thinking that Ruth had come back. Although the shadow remained, not a word was spoken.

"I ain't playin' with you."

"Hey, little girl," a man's voice, deep and throaty said.

Mozelle froze.

Randell Tate slowly circled Mozelle and stood close in front of her.

She couldn't move. She looked up at him. He was smiling his white-tooth smile that made his eyes twinkle. She was in trouble—again, she couldn't look away. Her cheeks felt like they were on fire. Randell looked down at her legs. She saw where his eyes rested. A warm throbbing sensation surged between her thighs. She sprang up off the wobbly chair so fast that when she stood and realized how close she was to him, she stepped back, stumbling into the chair. She would have fallen except for Randell catching her by the arm and pulling her up against his chest, holding her to his body. Her breath left her. Excepting her daddy when she was a little girl, she had never been up against a man's chest before. Randell's was hard. She inhaled his sweet muskiness. A powerful surge of blood shot through her heart. It skipped a beat. Suddenly, she was as hot as a yam cooking in embers. She thought she would faint. Her knees went weak under her.

"Ooooo! What y'all doin'?" Ruth asked, running up behind Randell.

Mozelle pulled herself out of his grasp; she stumbled backward into the chair, falling onto her tail end anyway. Ruth laughed, and so did all the youngins, making her feel silly.

Smiling, Randell put out his hand to help her up.

Mozelle ignored his hand. Choosing instead to scoot over onto her left side and leap up off the ground on her own.

"Look what you did!" she accused, brushing the mud off her dress. She was wearing one of the four dresses that was hers alone that she had besides her Sunday-go-to-meeting dress. She didn't like getting any of them too dirty because she didn't like washing them all the time—it made them look all the more worn out. She patched them as they needed it, and this one had needed it a lot.

"Sorry, Miss Mozelle," Randell said smoothly. "I didn't mean to scare you."

"You didn't scare me," she said, meaning it. What he did was confuse her. She was feeling things she had never felt before. "What you doin' back here anyhow?"

Randell touched his tie knot. "Just come a calling," he said, grinning.

"On who?" Ruth asked, nudging Mozelle, putting her in a worse mood.

"On your nice family. Your daddy said I was welcome, and nobody was out front."

"How come you got on your Sunday-go-to-meetin' clothes?" Ruth asked.

He smiled at Mozelle. "These my everyday clothes."

She looked him over. He was long and lean. His white shirt was pressed and neatly tucked inside his brown britches. His brown shoes were dusty, but she could see that they weren't raggedy or run over. He definitely was not a sharecropper. His hands were as smooth-looking as his face. His nails looked better than hers.

Elvin, who had been standing quietly behind Ruth and Mozelle, stepped forward. "How come you got a tie and a white shirt on? You a doctor?"

"Nah, boy. I always wear a tie and a white shirt," Randell answered, again touching his tie knot.

"How come?"

"Because I like to look good," he said, winking at Mozelle.

"Ooo," Ruth said, giggling behind her hand.

Again, Mozelle's heart fluttered, but she was taken aback that he would flirt with her, out in the open, right in front of everybody. Embarrassed, she took off running toward the house, just as Florence came out onto the back porch.

Florence stood with one hand on her hip and the other shielding her eyes from the late-day sun. "Howdy," she called out to Randell.

Mozelle leaped up the one step onto the porch and scooted past Florence into the house.

Randell Tate's long stride brought him quickly over to the porch. The children ran up behind him, circling him, touching him. Randell tried to not make a show of pushing their dirty hands off him, but he did step away from them.

"How do, ma'am?" he asked, standing stiffly below Florence in the yard. "Mr. Douglas said I could come a calling."

"Then sit a spell and have a cool drink," she said, showing him to a white-washed, straight-back wooden chair on the porch. "I can't offer you nothin' but water."

"That'll do just fine," he said, sitting down. He opened the button on his jacket.

The children started sitting down at Randell's feet. He crossed his legs.

"What I tell y'all 'bout sittin' under grown folks?" Florence asked. "Go play befo' I put a switch to y'all's behind."

All seven of youngins got up. They jumped off the porch and ran out into the yard, laughing.

Randell brushed at the dust on his pants leg.

"My husband is out yonder in the field, Mr. Tate. He'll be comin' in for supper any time now. You welcome to sup with us."

"Thank you kindly, ma'am."

"How long you be visitin' Alice?"

"About a month."

"That's right nice," Florence said, going over to the screen door. "Alfreda, bring Mr. Tate a cool drink of water."

"Please, ma'am, call me Randell."

Florence nodded that she would.

Mozelle stood behind the door listening. As soon as Florence stepped into the house, she asked, "Mama, how come Daddy ask him over here?"

"Never you mind, Missy. You 'n Ruth 'n Sister take them there clothes to Miss Lulamae and Miss Alcott."

"Ain't Alfreda comin', too?"

"Mozelle, do like I tell ya befo' I gives you what fo'."

Smiling smugly, Alfreda sauntered past Mozelle carrying a tin cup of water.

Florence lightly shoved Ruth. "Y'all go on now. It's gettin' late."

"Where Sister?" Ruth asked.

"Sister down the road a piece at Miss Louise. Y'all stop off and get her."

"She always down there," Mozelle said, starting out of the kitchen.

"That's 'cause she's sweet on Billy Joe," Ruth said.

Together the two of them left the house through the front door carrying two overstuffed burlap bags of clean clothes. Mozelle was glad to be leaving. Ruth, of course, wanted to stay. "I think he here callin' on Alfreda."

"I don't care," Mozelle said, though she was curious. If it was Alfreda he was calling on, then all the better. He wouldn't be bothering her. As it was, she did not like that her heart kept fluttering whenever he looked at her, or that she felt weak and there was a warm tingly surge between her thighs when she was up against his chest. She was still tingling. Maybe this tingling was what Alfreda had been trying to explain to her. This must be how she felt whenever she was around that Crawford boy before he moved to Mississippi. Maybe Alfreda had her eyes on Randell Tate now. Maybe that's how come Mama told her to fetch him some water; maybe he was calling on Alfreda. Daddy had said just this morning that Alfreda was a woman; it was time she married. To him, that meant one less mouth to feed. Well, better Alfreda than her. No man was going to have to feed her—she was going to get her own job. She was going to feed her own self when time came.

The burlap bags were empty. Mozelle had a dollar in change in her hand. Mama would use it to buy flour, cornmeal, sugar, and dry beans.

Randell was still there. He was sitting out on the back porch with William. Alfreda was sitting at the table talking to Florence. The sweet smell of sugar cookies filled the five-room house.

"Mama, Alfreda ain't done nothin' all day," Ruth whined.

"That's cause it's her birthday."

"Y'all tryin' to marry her off, ain't y'all?" Sister asked. "She a ol' maid, ain't she?"

"I ain't no ol' maid!"

"Go sit down 'n eat your supper," Florence said, slapping Sister across the butt. "Mozelle, you 'n Ruth, too."

Everybody had eaten except the three of them, and they were hungry. They sat down and ate their fried chicken, white rice and gravy, snap beans, and corn bread.

Jim came inside. "Mama, when we gon' eat them sugar cookies?"

"When y'alls' daddy is ready," she said. Florence began massaging her sore gums with her fingers to ease the pain from her rotting teeth.

"What they talkin' 'bout out there?" Alfreda asked Jim.

"Mr. Tate asked Daddy if'n he can call on Mozelle," he answered, leaning over the platter of sugar cookies and inhaling their sweet vanilla smell.

Mozelle choked on her corn bread.

Alfreda jumped up out of her chair and went to stand next to Florence. "Mama, he tellin' a story!"

"I is not."

"Jim heared it wrong, Alfreda. Randell come a callin' on you," Florence said.

Folding her arms under her full bosom, Alfreda stood looking down at Mozelle. "You can't have 'em."

"I don't want 'em," she said, sipping water from a preserve jar to wash down the suddenly dry corn bread in her mouth.

"I knowed he wanted Mozelle," Ruth said. "He look at her funny."

"He don't want me," Mozelle said feebly, though she couldn't deny that he did look at her funny.

"That's right, he don't want you," Alfreda said. "It's me he come a callin' on."

"Good. 'Cause I don't want 'em," Mozelle said. "And Alfreda, I don't know what you wants with 'em. You got three beaus already."

"Yeah," Sister agreed, "'Ceptin' none of them wants to marry her."

Alfreda was hurt. "Mama, they do, too, want to marry me. I jest don't wants to marry them. Mama, make them leave me be."

Watching his sisters, Jim shook his head. "U'm glad I ain't a girl. Alfreda, you wants to get married that bad?"

"Oh, you shut up!" Alfreda, shouted.

"Y'all stop botherin' Alfreda," Florence said, still massaging her gums.

Ruth got her back up. "Mama, Alfreda the one—"

"Mozelle!" William bellowed. "Get yaself out here, girl."

Her heart leaped into her throat. She gulped. She looked

anxiously at Florence.

"Mama!" Alfreda cried, throwing her arms around Florence's neck and sobbing.

Florence cringed when Alfreda's head hit up against her jaw. She groaned from the pain.

"I told y'all," Jim said, pinching a piece of sugar cookie and tossing it into his mouth.

"Mozelle, you hear me callin' you, girl?"

Dropping her spoon, her heart thumping in her chest, Mozelle whined, "Mama, I don't wants to go out there."

Alfreda cried all the harder.

Florence patted Alfreda on the back like she did when she was a baby needing to be burped. "Mozelle, do like your daddy say."

"But, Mama—"

"Mozelle, don't make me holler for you again," William threatened.

She stomped her foot. She looked to her mama for help, and getting none, she got up on rubbery legs. She wanted to run the other way, but she had to obey her daddy. With her mouth so dry she could hardly swallow, she walked out onto the back porch.

Three

Mozelle felt trapped. There was not one nook or cranny in the house to hide in to be by herself. She would have gone outside if it wasn't raining so hard. All the youngins were making noise and getting on her nerves, Alfreda was acting nasty and not talking to her, and Ruth kept asking her questions about Randell and whether or not she was nervous about getting married tomorrow. How many times did she have to say that she wasn't nervous? She wasn't even scared. Fact of the matter was, she was excited. Florence and William weren't though. They had been arguing on and off all day, all week about her marrying Randell. They were arguing now. She hated that she had to stay cooped up in the house with them talking about her like she wasn't there. All she could do was sit, listen, and pray for tomorrow to come quick.

"If'n you didn't want her to marry 'em, you had no business lettin' him court her," Florence said. "What you think was gon' happen in the end?"

"You sayin' it's my fault?"

"Well, William, when that boy asked for Mozelle's hand, you oughta said no. So, I reckon you is the blame."

William pointed his finger in Florence's face. "Watch what you say to me, woman."

Florence gave William one of her "you wrong" looks and went quietly over to the fireplace.

Mozelle hid her face in her hands. *Please let them stop, Lord.* She didn't want her folks fighting over her getting married. Her daddy was real mean when he was riled, and he didn't much care what he said when he was riled. He wasn't one for beating on her mama, but he could say some nasty things that would make her cry, and her mama's tears were akin to an angel's tears of sorrow.

Florence picked up the poker and stoked the fire in the fireplace, pushing the ashes aside. It wasn't her way to fight with William, but she was mad. She tossed a log onto the fire and stood rubbing her hands together, watching the fire blaze. William wasn't through. "You her mama. You coulda told her to stay away from that boy."

"How you say that?" Florence asked, turning to face William. "Since when I can tell any of these youngins to do somethin' contrary to what you tells 'em? When you seen that Randell didn't want Alfreda, you let 'em have Mozelle. You the one that coulda stopped 'em."

"Well, I—" William shrugged his shoulders. There was nothing he could say to defend himself. Florence was right. He had only looked at the fact that he had to get one hungry mouth out of his house. Just that it was supposed to be Alfreda. She was the laziest of all his children. She never did do her goodly share of work.

Florence pointed at Mozelle. "That child too young for a man like Randell—he been out in the world. He least twenty-five years old. That child ain't nothin' but a fifteen-year-old girl."

Mozelle hadn't even thought about Randell being older than her, only about the way he made her feel.

"I ain't makin' her marry that boy," William defended. "She the one wants to marry."

"That, too," Florence said, turning on Mozelle. "How come you all of a sudden wants to marry? You useta say you was gon' be a ol' maid."

She looked sheepishly up at Florence. "I loves him, Mama, 'n ain't Daddy older than you?"

"That's different. I was twenty when me 'n your daddy marry, 'n your daddy wasn't no Dapper Dan."

"What's a Dapper Dan?"

"That's how come you ain't got no business marryin'," William said. "You don't know what you marryin'."

Mozelle looked down at her hands. She did feel stupid, but that was only because she didn't know what a Dapper Dan was. Whatever it was, it couldn't be all bad. Randell was real sweet to her.

"Mozelle, you useta say you ain't want no man. How come you changed your mind? Could be he got roots on you? Mayhaps that's how come you changed your mind?"

"No, Mama. That ain't how come." Fact of the matter was, she didn't understand it herself. Could be that Randell put something on her, because marrying him was all she thought about. From the first time he held her hand, she was smitten. Since the first kiss, it seemed like something warm went from his body to hers. He had stirred up feelings in her body that she never knew she had. Whenever he took her in his arms, she felt like she had died and gone to heaven. She knew they were meant to be together because even their names almost sounded alike—Mozelle, Randell. She couldn't wait until tomorrow when she would become Mrs. Randell Tate.

"I want you to hold off marryin' 'em," Florence said. "I asked the Lord to show me he's a good man. He ain't showed me yet."

"He is a good man, Mama."

"Child, in my bones, I know he ain't nice and gentlemanly as he put out. No man can be like that for real 'n no woman ain't catched him befo' now. I got a bad feelin' about that city-talkin' boy."

"I know how come he ain't been catched," Alfreda said, sitting down on her mama's bed. "Alice say he ain't never want a houseful of snotty-nose youngins. She say when a woman goes to talkin' about marryin', Randell up and leave her. She say he say children ain't nothin' but bloodsuckers."

Florence stoked the fire one more time. She leaned the poke against the wall. "The bible say 'Be fruitful 'n multiply.' If Randell don't want children, he ain't got no business marryin'."

"Mozelle got a hard head," William said, filling his pipe.

Mozelle glared at Alfreda. The hateful look on Alfreda's face got to her. "Alfreda, you need to mind your own business. I ain't never want no children neither, but I can change my mind if'n I wants to. Randell ask me to marry him. That mean he want children with me, not you," she said, sneering at her. "You jest a jealous ol' maid."

"Jealous! You ain't nothin' to be jealous of. You ain't—"

"Hush up! Both of y'all," Florence ordered.

"Mama, she say—"

"Your mama done told y'all to hush up," William said sternly. "Now hold your tongue, Alfreda. I don't wants to hear another word from neither one of y'all."

Angrily sticking out her bottom lip, Alfreda stomped her foot and folded her arms high up on her chest.

Mozelle folded her arms, too, but that's about all she did. She didn't want her mama or her daddy to get mad enough at her to outright forbid her from marrying Randell. Neither one had flat-out said no—yet.

"Now, Mozelle," Florence said, "folks make mistakes all the time. You 'bout to make a big one, and time got a way of tellin' how big that mistake is gon' be. Mark my word, Missy, that boy gon' show his true self after while, 'n you ain't gon' like it."

"Mama, if'n Randell wasn't true, if he wasn't a good man, I'da knowed it by now."

"How? You ain't knowed him but three months."

"That ain't no time, Mozelle," William said, lighting his pipe, drawing on it deeply.

"It's a plenty time for me, Daddy."

"That's 'cause you still wet behind the ears."

"But, Daddy, I got to know Randell. He—"

"Mozelle, you know what bother me 'bout that boy?" William asked.

"What, Daddy?"

"It bother me the way he smilin' all the time. I ain't never knowed a righteous man smile all the time."

"Me, neither," Florence agreed.

"That's his way, Daddy."

William shook his head. "Ain't no grown man got no business grinning all the time. 'Nother thing. How he make a livin'? I asked him, and he say he work in the steel mill, but there ain't no steel mill here. So I reckon he ain't got no job."

"He work, Daddy. He gots money all the time."

"Child, you don't know what he done did to get that money," Florence said. "He ain't got no job here in Royston."

"He paint folks' houses sometimes. He get paid good."

William's eyes widened. "He told me that, but I ain't never seen him do nothin.' In fact, the boy ain't got the hands of a man that work in the steel mill, and he ain't got the clothes of a painter. How he paint with a white shirt and a tie on?"

Mozelle sighed heavily. "He don't paint with no tie on, Daddy, 'n you know he's goin' back 'n forth to Alabama. He work over in Jacksonville."

"That's what he say. How he wound up in Jacksonville, anyhow? Ain't his people from Elberton?"

"He say he left home when he was twelve and walked till he felt like stoppin'. He stop in Jacksonville."

"Who he stay with?"

"Nobody. He say he stayed in a graveyard at night."

"Well, how come he did a stupid thing like that?" William asked.

"Daddy, it wasn't stupid. Randell say he stayed in the graveyard at night 'cause nobody was gon' bother him there."

William thought about it. He nodded his approval.

"That ain't somethin' U'm ever gon' do," Florence said. "Too scary."

"Randell only did that, Mama, 'til he got a job and could afford to get hisself a room."

"Well, then," William said. "I reckon he's been a man since he was twelve. I got out on my own when I was thirteen."

For the first time, Mozelle was starting to feel like her daddy just might see something in Randell he liked.

"Well, Mozelle, since he been a man long as me, he ought not have to take his wife to live with his sister. She got a houseful of youngins herself. If'n he was a man, he'd have a house for you befo' he marry you."

"Daddy, he gon' buy me a house."

"When?"

"Soon as he figure out where we gon' live."

"Tell the boy, stop shucking around 'n take the damn money out his pocket 'n build you a house down on Peachtree Road. The land been up for sale goin' on two years now."

"Daddy, I don't know—"

William slapped the top of the table. "U'm done talkin'. Randell ain't no boy; he's a man. If'n he can't buy you a house, then he ain't no good."

Tears threatened, but Mozelle wasn't about to let her daddy see that he upset her. "Daddy, you wouldn't be against Randell if'n he was marryin' Alfreda," she said, tearing anyhow.

"That's 'cause Alfreda know how to handle a man like Randell. You don't," William said matter-of-factly.

"But, Daddy, jest 'cause I ain't never been with a boy befo' don't mean that I can't take care of myself."

William puffed on his pipe and blew the pungent smell of

burned corn and hickory into the room. Mozelle coughed and screwed up her nose. Alfreda covered her nose and her mouth with her hand.

Florence seemed to not notice the smoke or the smell. "A hard head make a soft tail, Mozelle. You gon' find out how hard it is to make do in this here world. It ain't easy, child."

"Don't tell her nothin', Flo. She'll learn the hard way," William said. "What I wants to know is what that city boy want with a country girl like Mozelle, 'n just the same, I wants to know what she want with him? Y'all ain't got nothin' in common."

"Daddy, I loves 'em, 'n he loves me," she defended, now really annoyed that her folks were giving her such a hard time. "Daddy, you talked to Randell befo' any of us. How come you ain't asked him what he wants with me?"

"Girl, don't you go sassin' me. You'll get married tomorra with welts on your tail."

Mozelle sat back right quick. She had only gotten a beating one time in her life, and she remembered well the painful stinging of the razor strap. No, she wasn't going to sass her daddy again. She folded her hands in her lap.

William narrowed his gaze on her. "Come to think 'bout it, Mozelle, your mama's right. You ain't never had no use for no boy befo' now, 'n ain't no boy ever come a callin' on you either. How come you all hot to marry all of a sudden?"

Alfreda, sitting cross-legged on the bed, snickered. "'Cause she a tomboy, and she scared ain't nobody else gon' want to marry her."

Mozelle glared at Alfreda. "U'm gettin' married befo' you though, ain't I?"

"Mama, Benton woulda married me if'n—"

"I don't wants to hear 'bout that," William said impatiently. "I done told both y'all to hush up 'bout that. Alfreda, go see what them youngins doing back there makin' all that fuss."

Starting out of the room, Alfreda squinted her eyes threateningly at Mozelle and put up her fist to show her that she was going to beat her up.

William saw her. "Come here, Alfreda."

Knowing that she was in trouble, Alfreda was timid as she went over to William. When she got within an arm's length, William reached over and finger-popped her on the arm.

"Ouch!" she squealed, grabbing her arm, rubbing it hard to

quiet the harsh sting.

Mozelle smirked at Alfreda who sucked her teeth and rolled her eyes at her before stomping out of the room holding on to her arm.

Florence looked over at Ruth. She had been quiet but her eyes and ears were wide open. "You go on, too. I done told you 'bout listenin' to grown folks talk."

"Mama, Mozelle ain't grown folk."

"She gon' be if'n she marryin' tomorra," William said. "Now do like your mama say befo' I gives you what fo', too."

Ruth cut her eyes at Mozelle and left the room. She didn't go far. Mozelle could see the hem of Ruth's dress sticking out from behind the door. Plain old nosy, that's what she was.

Florence sat down at the table across from Mozelle. "Listen, child. Randell is older than you. He gon' treat you like you his child," she said, shyly glancing over at William and then lowering her eyes. "Menfolk do that most times anyhow, 'specially when they takes a child bride."

"What's that suppose to mean?" William asked, eyeing Florence. "I ain't never treat you like no child."

"Mama, Randell ain't never—"

"Shush, girl. U'm talkin' to your mama."

Sighing, Florence raised her eyes. "William, U'm just tellin' Mozelle that she best wait and grow up first. That's all I mean."

William studied Florence's face for a minute. What he was looking for in her eyes, in her expression, Mozelle didn't know, but it had to be something that only the two of them knew about.

"Flo, Mozelle think she grown. Let her go on and do what grown folks do."

"Daddy, y'all ain't got to worry 'bout me. Randell's gon' take good care of me."

"We'll see," Florence said, rubbing her gums through her cheek. "You ain't got to be in such a hurry lessen you ain't told us somethin'."

Florence and William both were looking at her in that way that kinfolk look when they want to know if you did something you wasn't supposed to be doing.

"Mama! Randell ain't never touch me the wrong way. He court me the good 'n proper way."

"Well, then you—"

"Flo, don't tell her nothin' no mo'. She ain't listenin' to what we say. Mozelle was always stubborn as a ol' mule," William said, laying his pipe on its side in the tin lid on the table. He placed both his hands down flat on the table. "She wants to marry, let her. I jest want her to remember one thing though: when she marry Randell Tate, she best stay married to 'em for life. She can't come out her marriage like she come out of school. Somethin' go wrong, she don't ever got to go back to school, but she got to go back to her husband. That's final."

A tinge of fear crept into Mozelle's heart. She used to like going to school but everytime she had to stop going because she had to help out on the farm, she fell farther and farther behind. Going back wasn't easy. She stopped going altogether when she was twelve. Her mama had wanted her to go back, but she didn't like that she couldn't read as good as the eight-year-olds. She felt stupid and just decided to not go back. But Randell wasn't like going to school. He was going to be her husband. She was never going to fall behind in what she had to learn about being his wife.

She looked into her daddy's old, tired eyes. He looked like he'd seen the troubles of the world through those eyes. Is that why he made marrying for life sound like her life was going to be over the minute she said "I do?"

"My granny useta say," William began, "'You make yaself a hard bed, you turn over that much more often.' Time will tell, Mozelle, how many times you gots to turn over to get comfortable."

Florence began to tear. "William, I don't want my child to have to find out the hard way."

"Well, Flo, sometime that's the onliest way."

"Mozelle, you for certain this what you wants to do?"

"Yessum."

"Be real certain, child, 'cause once you marry Randell, you got to stay with him the rest of your livelong days. You understand me?"

"Yes, ma'am."

"Well, sa," William said, pushing himself up from the table. "U'm done talkin'. We'll go on down to the courthouse tomorra 'n sign for you to marry. Down the line a piece when it come time to say I told you so, U'm gon be right here to say I told you so."

Again tears welled up in Mozelle's eyes.

"Can I go to the courthouse, too?" Ruth asked from the

doorway.

"If'n I wasn't so tired, Ruth," William said, "I'd tan your nosy hide. Get back there. Ain't none of y'all goin'."

Ruth jumped back behind the door.

Behind William's back, Florence looked steadily but angrily at him.

Mozelle could almost tell what her mama was thinking. Sometimes, her daddy treated her mama like she was one of the children. Maybe if her mama had it to do all over again, she might not have married her daddy; maybe she might not have had all those babies. But her mama was never going to say such a thing out loud. She was going to hold her tongue and watch her marry Randell without saying a hateful word against him. That was just her way. In that way, her daddy and her mama were alike. They were going to let her live her own life and make her own mistakes, but they were going to be ready to say, "I told you so." But she wasn't making a mistake, and she would argue no more to defend her desire to marry Randell.

She sat and watched her daddy pull off his dusty, run-over work boots, his coveralls, and his shirt. Everything he dropped onto the floor would be picked up by her mama as soon as she got up from the table. He kept on his baggy old long johns and crawled into his bed near the front door. He would make his *X* for her like he said, then wait for her to come running back home crying. He would have to wait forever. She was going to stay married to Randell until the day she died. No matter what.

Four

Long before the old red rooster crowed, and long before her daddy opened his eyes, Mozelle had been awake waiting anxiously for her wedding day to begin. She had tiptoed out of the house to the backyard and started a fire under the iron pot. She had filled it with water for her bath from the well. In the kitchen, behind a blanket draped from the door across to a nail on the wall, sitting in a big tin tub, she scrubbed certain areas of her body more than once, because those were the areas she was sure Randell would concern himself with after they were married. Though she was still a virgin, there was some things she knew without being told. Most things she knew because Alfreda told her. Soon she'd learn for herself.

It was the longest bath she'd ever taken without being told to hurry up and get out. At least this time she got to use the bath water first. Slipping down into the water, her knees up to her chest, she imagined that Randell must have been with other women before her. What if he didn't like being with her? What if he didn't like her body? Until now, she hadn't worried whether a man found her pretty or whether her body was shapely. It just never mattered. She touched her titties; they were firm and soft. Alfreda always teased her about how little they were, even for a tomboy. Hopefully, Randell didn't think they were too little. She absentmindedly stroked her titties.

"Thinking about Randell, huh?"

"Mama!" she said, quickly dropping her hands from her titties. She started to sit up but then scooted back down into the water, quickly covering herself up with her washrag. Water splashed over the sides onto the floor. It had been years since her mama had seen her butt naked.

"Humph," Florence said, with a little chuckle. "You 'bout

ready to get out, ain't you?"

"Yessum. U'm gettin' out now."

Florence didn't bother to turn away. She continued to look down at Mozelle.

Mozelle was quite embarrassed. She held the washrag over her titties as she reached cautiously across to the chair near the tub. She took hold of her dress and yanked on it, bringing it, balled up, against her wet body. It annoyed her that her mama wouldn't turn around.

"Child, stop actin' simple. Your dress is gettin' wet. Get yaself out that water and dry off."

"But, Mama, it ain't proper for me to be standin' butt naked in front of you."

"Child, I done seen all y'all naked. Y'all all come outta me naked as a plucked chicken."

"But, Mama—"

"Mozelle, I ain't got time for you actin' silly. I ain't surprised about nothin' you tryin' to hide. I got all you got and mo'."

"Oh, Mama," she said, standing quickly and drying herself off with her small washrag. Now she did feel simple. She stepped out of the tub onto the bare plank floor, wetting it more.

Florence went over to the wood-burning stove and pulled open the door. Bending down, she checked the fire Mozelle had started, before closing the door again and turning back to her. "U'm glad you up early, Mozelle. I been thinkin' about last night. You gon' marry Randell today. You ain't gon' be no child no 'mo. You gon be his wife. I pray to God he treat you right, but if'n he don't, that's 'tween him 'n you. If'n he treat you good, that's 'tween him 'n you, too. You understand me?"

With her dress thrown over her wet body, Mozelle pulled on her bloomers. "Yessum."

"My mama told me when I married your daddy, it ain't fittin' for a wife to talk outside her door to nobody 'bout her husband, not even to her mama. It ain't nobody's business what go on in your house. Besides, nobody want to hear your troubles, they got they own."

"I ain't gon' have to talk to nobody about Randell, Mama. He gon' always be good to me."

Florence shook her head. "No tellin' what's behind a man's eyes or what's in his heart, or what his intention is when he's courtin' you. When you marry Randell, you marry him for keeps.

There ain't no turnin' back."

Mozelle wasn't taking to heart anything her mama said about Randell treating her bad. He'd already promised that he'd always do good by her. Far as she could see, there was nothing for her to worry about. Her folks just didn't want her to marry right now because she was only fifteen.

"You go on 'n wake them other youngins."

"Yessum." She started to walk away but turned back. "Mama, would you straighten my hair?"

The drive to the courthouse in her daddy's old Model T was quiet. From the time William rolled out of bed, he clamped his jaws tight as a dog with a bone. He never said a word. No matter how she felt about it, Florence had to see her child get married, but she, too, was quiet and stared at the road ahead. Mozelle felt like crying. This was supposed to be a happy day. She had been on this same road going to a funeral just a month ago, and even then, folks looked like they were in a much better mood.

She married Randell with just her mama and daddy there to say that it was so.

It wasn't until after the short ceremony and Randell handed her the marriage license, that she saw that he was born March 15, 1892. When she saw her own date of birth of March 22, 1914, at first she was glad that their birthdays were in the same month, another sign that they were meant to be. However, it was the difference in the years that surprised her. Even with her little bit of schooling, off and on, she knew enough to know that there was a big difference between 1892 and 1914. Closing her eyes, she did the figuring in her head. When she opened them, she stared at Randell. She couldn't believe it. Nobody had ever asked him how old he was. Both her mama and daddy thought he was about twenty-five. She could never tell them that he was thirty-seven.

Mozelle quickly folded the marriage license and slipped it inside her dress pocket—just in case her daddy wanted to look at it. He couldn't read, but he could do figuring. Her mama couldn't read nor do figuring, so her, she wasn't worried about. Her daddy was older than her mama by twelve years, but surely they both would have a fit if they knew that the difference in years between her and Randell was almost twice theirs. To Mozelle, it didn't matter that Randell was twenty-two years older, she loved him just the same. Fact of the matter was, it made sense to her that because Randell was that much older, that he would take better care of her than any boy her own age. Her daddy should appreciate that. But just in case he didn't, she was keeping her mouth shut.

There was no party, there were no presents. What she got from Randell was a thin gold ring. That's all she wanted. Her daddy drove them from the courthouse to Alice's house. He let them out down on the road; he didn't bother to drive up to the house. Florence handed her a small bundle tied with twine. It was all she owned in the world.

"Well, daughter," William said, looking straight at the road ahead, "you got what you wanted. You married now. From now on, you belongs to your husband."

Mozelle, her head lowered, glanced shyly at Randell. She wondered, didn't Randell now belong to her just as she belonged to him?

Standing behind Mozelle, Randell didn't bend his back to look into the car at William. "Like I said, Mr. Douglas, I'm gon' take real good care of your daughter."

"U'm reckonin' you gon' do just that," William said. He gripped the steering wheel tightly.

Mozelle bent down to look past her daddy to her mama. "Bye, Mama. U'm gon' come 'n see y'all."

"Child, come on 'round here so I can talk to you," Florence said.

Scooting around the back of the car, Mozelle went to stand on the other side of the car. "Yes, Mama."

Florence spoke softly. "Mozelle, that ring on your finger say you belong to Randell now. You do like he say."

"Yessum."

"Don't you go actin' all stubborn like you do."

"No, ma'am."

"Child, keep me and your daddy proud of you. Don't ever go steppin' out on your husband."

"No, ma'am. I ain't never gon' do that."

"You best not. It's a sin. You stay with your husband through thick and thin. You hear me?"

"Yessum," she said, suddenly feeling that the plain shiny gold wedding band on her finger felt a little snug. She twisted on it as her folks drove off. She stayed looking after them until she could no longer see the car through the cloud of dust way down the road. A single tear slid down her cheek. Her daddy hadn't even bothered to say good-bye.

Randell went to Mozelle, he put his arm around her waist. "Let's go inside."

Mozelle clung to her bundle as she let Randell take her up the road toward the house. Until a minute ago, the thought of a new life with the man she loved had not frightened her; but now that her folks had gone back home without her, she felt like a little girl under the weight of Randell's heavy arm on her shoulder. What if her folks were right? What if she wasn't ready to be Randell's wife?

"C'mon, baby, smile," Randell said, knocking at his sister Alice's door.

Alice opened it with a flourish. "Welcome, sister-in-law," she said, stepping back for Mozelle to come inside. Just as she started inside, two of Alice's boys ran past her out of the house.

"Y'all come back here. Say howdy to y'all's new auntie," Alice said.

"Hey!" they both shouted, still running.

"Hey," Mozelle said back at them. She started inside.

"Hold up," Randell said, taking Mozelle's bundle from her and tossing it to the ground. "U'm supposed to carry you in."

"You a married lady now," Alice said, hugging her. "My brother best treat you right, else he gon' answer to me."

"U'ma always treat my baby right," he said, scooping Mozelle up in his arms.

Suddenly she had no doubts. She was ready. She giggled.

Randell carried Mozelle into the house.

She giggled again.

Alice brought in Mozelle's bundle and handed it to Randell.

"Congratulations," Alice's husband, Herb, said from across the room. "See if'n y'all can stay married long as me 'n Alice."

"We will. Right now, we got something to do," Randell said, carrying Mozelle through the two front rooms to the back of the house where there was a double bed waiting for them in the small room he had been staying in since he came back to Royston.

"Y'all bet' not make no baby back there," Alice called to them. "My six more than a plenty in this house."

"You 'n Herb best remember that," Randell said, kicking

the door closed with his foot. He dropped the bundle on the floor and carried Mozelle over to the bed and set her down on it. Suddenly she felt like she was about to swoon. It wasn't even hot outside, but it seemed hot in the room. She was use to the heat that came from the sun, it was the heat that was coming off of Randell that she wasn't use to. When she was in his arms, it seemed like his skin was on fire, yet not a bead of sweat dampened his forehead or upper lip. That same heat was smothering in his eyes as he looked at her now. Fanning herself with her hand, she pretended to look around, but she could not focus on a thing.

Randell took off his jacket and hung it on the back of the chair near the window. He unknotted his tie and slipped it from around his neck. Holding on to the tie, he unbuttoned his shirt, took it off, and hung it neatly on a wooden clothes hanger. He draped the tie around the hanger collar. He took off his undershirt. All the while his eyes never left Mozelle's face.

Try as she might, Mozelle could not keep her eyes off of him either. She was weak. This was why she was married to him now. He took her strength just by looking at her and left her with no will of her own. She fixed her gaze on his smooth, hairless chest to keep from looking either up or down.

"Hey, baby girl," he said low and deep. He puckered his lips at her.

She giggled into her hands.

Randell unbuckled his belt. He began zipping down his britches. "Daddy got something real special for his baby girl."

A nervous little giggle escaped from her when Randell stepped out of his britches and she saw the outline of what he had for her through his drawers. She quickly looked away. She knew very well what married folks did. Her mama and daddy did it all the time at night, real quiet like when they thought they were sleeping. While Alfreda always giggled when she heard her daddy grunt and make hissing sounds, she always felt embarrassed because she felt like she wasn't supposed to hear something so private.

Once his britches were hung neatly on the hanger under his shirt, Randell dropped his drawers and stood in front of Mozelle naked and proud. He stepped in closer to her—only a foot of air separated them.

Mozelle couldn't help but look. She couldn't help but feel a little afraid but was all the more amazed at what her eyes beheld. She kept looking while she twisted nervously on the hem of her Sunday dress. She had never seen such a thing; none of her brothers had anything like this.

Randell reached down and pulled her up off the bed. He drew her up against his chest. He hugged her tight.

She felt him, hard and hot, throbbing against her. It seemed her cotton dress was as thin as a spider's web—it was like it was not there. She thought she would drop to her knees, her legs were so weak. But he held her so tight and so close, she felt like she was becoming part of him. She started to hug him back but dropped her arms when she realized that she was about to hug his naked body. This she had never done before, and before she had never felt a man's hardness against her stomach. Her heart was pounding in her chest, but something else was throbbing between her thighs. Her breathing was shallow; she started to sweat.

Randell held Mozelle against him while he unbuttoned the four buttons on the back of her dress. That done, he reached down and gathered the skirt of her dress up in his big hands and pulled it up over her waist.

She let him.

"Raise your arms over your head."

She did.

The dress came off her body so smoothly she almost didn't feel it except it covered her face for a mere second. She stood before him naked except for her faded bloomers. Her mama was never able to buy her or any of her sisters brassieres or slips from the store. If they got them at all, they were already worn by the white folks her mama washed for. Almost as an afterthought, Mozelle quickly raised her arms to cover her titties.

Randell gently pulled her arms away, placing them down to her side. "I like 'em firm and little like this," he said.

Her cheeks grew hotter.

He took both titties in his own hands, stroking them. He felt their softness before he dropped to his knees and kissed each of her hard nipples. She shivered with pleasure. When Randell buried his face between her titties and eased his hand up between her thighs, she dropped her head back. While what he was doing to her felt sinful, it felt good. She couldn't help but moan with pleasure. What she was feeling was like nothing she'd ever felt before. It was sweet. Real sweet.

Five

Mozelle knew the day they got married that Randell had to leave her behind to go back to Jacksonville. Now that he had been gone twenty-one days, her body actually ached from missing him. Before he left, he told Alice to keep her in the house. He said he didn't want other menfolk looking at his baby. Knowing that he cared so much for her made Mozelle feel special. Though he didn't have to worry about other menfolk looking at her, she wouldn't see them if they did. She would never want any other man but him. That's why she had no problem staying around the house cleaning, cooking, and helping Alice with her children.

On the thirty-sixth day, Randell came home. He brought with him everything he owned.

"There ain't no reason to go back to Jacksonville," he told her after pleasuring her. "The work done dried up in the mill. They done let everybody go. I don't know what U'm gon' do."

"You can paint folks' houses, can't you?"

"Folks ain't got no money to spend on painting, Mozelle. They need what little money they got to buy food. They say we in a depression."

"That's what everybody talkin' about in church. What we gon' do?" she asked, laying her head in the crook of his arm.

"We'll stay here a spell 'n see if I can pick up work."

"You can pick cotton."

"Mozelle, I ain't picking no cotton. I been working in the steel mill and painting 'cause I ain't never liked working in the field like a slave. My daddy 'n mama come out of slavery hateful of picking cotton. I ain't never seen my daddy cry except when he talked about being a slave and picking cotton."

"My granddaddy was a slave in Mississippi," Mozelle said. "My daddy told us that my granddaddy was sold away from his folks when he was thirteen. That's how my daddy come to be born in Georgia after slavery. My daddy had seven uncles he never laid eyes on, and maybe hundreds of cousins he never got to see. He said my granddaddy looked for them all his life."

"He never heard tell who they was sold to?"

"He never did."

"That's another reason I ain't picking cotton," Randell said. White folks sold off a lot of cotton-picking niggers. They might see me out there picking cotton and forget they don't own me. Have me sold off before I can straighten my back."

"Oh, Randell, they can't do that," she said. "Can they?"

"Mozelle, you kinda naive, ain't you?"

She didn't know what that word *naive* meant, but she wasn't whatever it was. She started to let it go but it bothered her. "Randell, what—?"

"Don't ask. I got more important things to worry about. I got to make me some money."

"If'n we don't pick cotton, what else we gon' do?"

"I be damned if I know."

Looking at her wedding band, Mozelle raised her hand. It had tarnished a bit since Randell put it on her finger, but that was because she never took it off—even scrubbed clothes with lye soap with it on. "You can sell off my ring. If'n you clean it, it'll shine like new."

"Girl," he said dryly, "I couldn't bring back the shine on that ring even if I had a tub of lard to rub on it."

Sitting up in bed, she looked from her dull gray ring to Randell's dull black eyes. Like her ring, the twinkle in his eyes all of a sudden faded. That had to be because he was worried about how he was going to make money to put in his pocket. But the ring. "How come my ring ain't gon' shine no mo'?"

"You sho'nuff young, ain't you, Mozelle? That ring was made of fool's gold."

Her heart sank: she stared at the ring.

"Ain't nobody gon' pay five cents for that. It ain't real gold."

Her eyes slowly filled with tears. She had been so proud of her ring—the first piece of jewelry she ever owned. Lots of times she held out her hand to look at it. She had never taken it off because she had been afraid of losing it, and she hadn't worried when it dulled and turned gray, she figured it could be cleaned up.

"Don't go getting yourself all worked up. There ain't no difference between gold 'n silver 'cept silver is better. White folk swear they rich 'cause they got silver forks 'n spoons 'n teapots. Now you got a little piece of silver of your own."

Wiping her eyes dry, she pressed her lips together. It wasn't so much that her ring was silver that bothered her, it was that she thought that Randell had given her a gold ring. She felt like he had lied, like he had deceived her. "How come you didn't give me a silver ring in the first place? I wouldn't've mind."

Randell turned on his side away from her. "Be grateful you got anything. Now, shut down the lamp 'n go on to sleep. I gotta get up early in the morning."

She stared at his naked back. Unlike his face, his back was covered with lots of blackheads and scratch marks. Maybe she ought to be grateful, after all. It wasn't unusual for menfolk to borrow a ring for the marriage ceremony and then later take it off their wives' fingers and give it back to whomever they borrowed it from. That's what happened to Beulah. Now she didn't have a ring or a husband.

"Randell, I like my ring jest fine."

"Girl, go on to sleep."

She leaned toward the kerosene lamp sitting on the chair next to the bed. Lifting the glass cover, she blew out the flame, lowered the cover, and then lay down again. From the sound of Randell's breathing, she knew that he was already asleep. She eased closer to him. She pressed her body along the lines of his long, hard, warm body. She purred. It wasn't the ring that was important; it was being Randell's wife. Snuggling up under her husband, she closed her eyes and smiled.

Six

By noon, Mozelle had a job picking cotton. It was the only job she could get. She used to help her mama wash clothes for white folks, but there wasn't much washing to do. White folks were washing their own clothes.

After long hours of backbreaking bending to pull the cotton off its branch, she could hardly stand erect. At the end of a long day, when she brought home a dollar and twenty-five cents, and bleeding fingertips, it hardly seemed worth it. At thirty-five cents a hundred pounds, she knew she would never make enough money to eat well or help buy the land down on Peachtree Road.

Randell made do with his hammer, fixing up around town for whatever change folks could spare. Though he couldn't make the kind of money he was use to filling up his pockets with, he still refused to pick cotton.

It was six months before Mozelle went home to see her folks. She could hardly believe how much the farm had dried up. Her daddy couldn't afford to buy seed, and the family had eaten practically all the farm animals. Her feelings were hurt when her mama told her that Alfreda had married Eugene Johnson and was living down the road a piece. She was just on the other side of town, yet nobody had bothered to send word to her. They acted like she wasn't part of the family anymore. She didn't even know that her mama was suffering more from her painful bleeding gums. Most all of her teeth had fallen out, and those that reminded were loose. Her mama said it was hard to eat anything that wasn't soft, but since there wasn't much to eat anyhow, what she did eat was usually mashed. Her daddy wasn't making enough money to send her mama to a doctor, and her mama was scared that her body was going to be poisoned by her own mouth. For some time she had been getting raw pus-filled boils on her gums that broke open and seeped back into her body.

"Mama, how come y'all ain't told me about Alfreda, and how come somebody didn't come and tell me how bad off you was?"

"Alfreda run off and married that Johnson boy. We didn't know right off. And I wasn't gon' put my worry on you, child. There ain't nothin' you can do about my teeth," she said, gently rubbing her gums through her cheek.

The fact that Mozelle knew that her mama was right didn't make her feel any better about not being able to give her money to send her to a doctor. She didn't dare ask Randell for money, he was bitter as it was that he was broke like everybody else.

After two years of living with Alice, what little work Randell had been able to find dried up altogether. His smile had long since dried up when he couldn't pull a handful of dollar bills out of his pocket. He thought there might be work down in Elberton where his other sister, Bernice, still lived. He was sure she was better off than Alice and would have plenty of room for them in her house. When they left Royston, she felt like she was saying good-bye forever to her folks. She didn't want to leave, but her mama told her that her place was at her husband's side, no matter where that was. There had never been a question that she would not go with Randell, but she wasn't happy about it. If he had picked cotton, they might've been able to stay.

Like so many that had to take to the road in search of work or a place to live, they got to Elberton by hitching a ride on the back of a train. They were packed in cars like herds of cattle bound for market. The smell of animal waste was suffocating, and Mozelle was sure the dried brown stains she sat on were manure. She felt dirty, but with Randell's arms around her and her head resting on his chest listening to his heartbeat, she would have sat in a whole lot worse to be with him. After all, it wasn't his fault that the Depression had come.

When they got to Bernice's house, Randell's hope was dashed. Bernice was worse off than Alice. Randell hadn't seen her in years so he didn't know that she was barely able to feed the three children that were still at home. Fact of the matter was, her and her children were near starving. Her husband had left her to go try his luck up north, but she hadn't heard from him in more than a year. What little money she and her children made picking cotton wasn't enough to feed them and pay the rent on their four-room house. In the end, Randell decided they had to stay and help her out. Bernice put them in the room on the side of the house with a fireplace, which is where Mozelle was to do her cooking.

Mozelle wound up in the cotton field bent over and hungry; Randell wound up in the cotton field bent over and bitter. He wouldn't work in the same field with her and wouldn't give her a reason why. Between the two of them, they brought home less than three dollars most days. Mozelle handed her pay over to Randell because he said she had to. He said he needed it to pay the rent. There were days they couldn't afford to buy anything to eat. When she couldn't take the hunger pangs gnawing at her gut, she took to eating handfuls of red dirt she scraped off the side of a hill nearby. It was tasteless, it was dry, it was like eating flour. She used her spit to wet the dirt enough to go down. Back at home, she took her fill of water from the well until the hunger pangs died down. A bellyful of dirt was the only way she could sleep at night; and for a brief moment, the only way she could forget that the next day wasn't going to be any different from the day before. If Randell was hungry, she never knew. He never complained. She never knew if he took his fill of dirt. She was grateful that they hadn't lost Bernice's house—at least they weren't outdoors. Just up the road a piece, the Wilkinses were sleeping under a makeshift tent alongside the road.

Barely a month passed before Randell started coming home drunk. Mozelle first wondered why he didn't spend the money on food, but her first thought was quickly pushed aside when she saw how nasty he was to her. That scared her. Even without the whiskey he had been saying mean things out of spite. The drinking made him even nastier. That's when he hated what his life had become. She understood that. Randell hated having to wear big, loose-fitting, dirty coveralls. He hated that the dirt from the fields got under his fingernails. And mostly, he hated that the dirt in the fields got into his hair and mixed with the sweat and made him look like he was a slave. That's what he kept saying. After work he'd scrub himself raw trying to wash away the dirt that clung to him. He'd put on clean dress britches, a white shirt and tie. At first, dressed up with nowhere to go just added to his bitterness. That was until he found somewhere to go that he wouldn't take her. He started treating her like he was mad at her—no longer talking, no longer loving. That was until he was ready to pleasure her. But she sensed it was out of need that he touched her and not out of love. There were no more little kisses on her titties; no longer did his hands gently stroke that private place that pleased her and made her weak for him. Now he was rough. Now he hurt her without concern. She no longer enjoyed laying down with him, but she had to. She was his wife.

What she feared most, happened. She was pregnant. A baby was the last thing in the world she wanted, but what she was most afraid of was what Randell would do. They were on hard times, and he was bitter about that. And, too, she remembered what Alfreda said about Randell not wanting children. What if that was true?

She waited until Randell had to go to the outhouse and followed him. They would be alone there. She told him through the closed door.

Randell was as quiet as a church mouse.

"Randell, you hear me? U'm havin' a baby."

The door suddenly flew open. Randell came storming out. "I ain't got no money to be feeding no bloodsucker." He angrily did up his britches. "U'm telling you now, Mozelle, if I can't pay the midwife to cut the bastard outta your belly, I'll cut it out my damn self."

Stunned by his words, she clutched her belly. She started feeling queasy.

"Don't stand there looking at me like you a loon."

"Randell, this your baby you talkin' 'bout," she said, trying to look him in the eyes. She wanted to see if the man who courted her was anywhere inside the eyes of this man.

Randell turned away from her and walked over to the well.

She followed him. "I ain't never want no children neither," she said. "But I do now 'cause I love you and it's us that made this baby. That make it special, don't it? Don't you want our baby?"

He looked her dead in the eye. "Hell no!"

Gawking at him, she drew a breath and held it. Alfreda's words rushed back at her. It was all true.

"Tell me something, Mozelle," he said coolly. "How do you know it's my baby?"

"How you say somethin' like that 'bout me? I ain't never laid up with nobody but you, Randell."

"I don't know that for sure."

A wounded, pitiful cry erupted from her throat.

Randell was unmoved. "Cry all you want. I ain't saying nothing's mine 'til I know for sure."

She didn't know what to think about that because nobody could tell what a baby looked like when it was still in the mama's belly. Mozelle looked hard at Randell. She saw in his eyes that he wasn't fooling. In fact, nothing about him said that he was fooling with her. There was no bend in his back. He held himself tall and erect, high above her, his jaws tight, his lips frozen in a sneer.

"Randell, I was pure; I was a virgin when you married me. You know that."

"Far as I know, you could've been with somebody besides me since. I ain't with you all day."

Tears spilled from her eyes. "God is gon' punish you for denyin' your own. He gon' strike you down."

Randell slapped her—hard—snapping her head back, stunning her into silence. Mozelle fell backward against the well. Randell flung himself on top of her, pushing her backward until her head was over the well. The pain in her back was so intense, she couldn't scream. Thinking that he was going to break her back or push her over if she kept trying to get up, she clawed frantically for the edge of the well wall. Gripping it, she held her body rigid. But then Randell grabbed her around the neck and started choking her.

"You trying to put a curse on me, girl! I'll kill you befo' your God can hold up His little finger."

In her struggle to breathe, to pull herself up, she prayed for God to help her. Randell's crushing fingers around her throat were not only cutting off her air, making her lungs feel like they would surely burst, but her head was pounding. It seemed her eyes would pop right out of her head.

"Woman, talk against me one more time, I'll put you in your grave," he said, pushing himself off Mozelle's throat.

She grunted painfully.

Randell left her bent backward over the well wall gasping for air, feeling like she was about to lose her hold on the wall and on her life. She looked up at the sky. The stark whiteness of the clouds and brightness of the sun near blinded her as she searched the sky. Where was God? Why didn't He help her? As soon as those questions came to her mind, she regretted them. She knew that God was there. He kept Randell from killing her. Getting a stronger grip on the well wall, she painfully pulled herself up. She was shaky. Her head and back hurt just as much as her throat. She didn't know what part of her body to rub first—her head, her throat, her back. She started to cough, so it was her neck that she rubbed. Her throat was dry and scratchy. Randell could have choked her to death. Swallowing, trying to wet and soothe her throat, she looked around to see where he had gone. He was walking down the road toward town. God forgive her, but she prayed that he would never come back. She was scared of him and could not stop shaking. What her mama said had come back to haunt her. "He ain't nice and gentlemanly like he put out."

Hurtful tears washed over her face. She could not cry aloud, her throat hurt too bad. She turned toward the house and there, on the porch, stood Bernice, staring at her with eyes as cold as a snake. Mozelle quickly snatched up the hem of her dress and dried her face.

"Bernice," she whined, "I didn't do nothin'. How come Randell hurt me like that?"

Bernice sneered and spit on the ground. She turned on her heels and started back into the house.

Mozelle sank to the ground. "Oh, God. What U'm gon' do?"

With her back up against the well wall she cried into her hands. She was all alone. There was no one she could turn to. No one. Suddenly she heard a tapping. Somewhere behind her, high overhead, she heard a woodpecker pecking on a tree trunk. It was probably the same one that came every afternoon. She stopped crying to listen. She knew that that bird was going to peck at that tree until it got what it wanted. It wasn't going to leave until it did, and it wasn't going to ask another soul to help it get what it wanted out of that tree. Like her, that woodpecker was on its own. She had to find her own way, and she was going to have to keep her hurt to herself. Like her Mama said, "Nobody wants to hear your troubles, everybody got their own troubles." She cried all the harder.

Randell didn't come back home. Although she had prayed that he wouldn't come home, all night she worried about where he could be. She got up before dawn, like always, and hopped on the truck with Bernice, her children, and the other workers going to the cotton field. By mid-morning she felt sick. She thought it was probably because she hadn't eaten, until she went to stand up straight. A sharp, painful cramp gripped her belly. Something gushed out of her body; she felt wet between her thighs. Squatting down right quick, she hid among the cotton bushes and lifted the front of her dress. She pulled aside the seat of her bloomers. Blood poured out of her into the dry earth. The cramps kept gripping her and would not let her go. She wanted to throw up and was about to when suddenly she felt something solid gush from within her. She shrieked when big, dark blobs plopped onto the ground.

"You all right over there?" a woman's voice called to Mozelle.

Biting down on her knuckles to keep from crying out, Mozelle made herself say, "I cut my hand real bad, that's all."

"Everybody get cut bad now and then," the woman said.

Mozelle studied the bloody mass that had emptied from her body. In the middle of the thick dark blobs of blood was a pink-ish lump. It was about the size of her thumb. It didn't look like a baby, but somehow she knew that it was her baby.

"Lord a mercy," she said softly. She could not believe what lay at her feet. With her finger, she touched it to see if it would move. It felt mushy. It didn't move, it was dead. Her baby had died in her. It hadn't even had a chance to grow, to be born, to live. She began to weep softly. Her tears bathed her poor baby on the ground under her.

Looking around to make sure that no one was close by, Mozelle dug into the soft earth with her fingers and made a tiny, shallow grave. She pushed the blood, the blobs, the baby into the grave. She covered it all with the dirt she walked on. Painful spasms tore at her belly and her heart. She closed her eyes and quietly prayed over the tiny grave. "Dear Lord, U'ma shameful sinner. If'n U'm the cause of my baby droppin' from my belly 'cause I use to say I don't want no children, please forgive me. If'n my baby got a soul, Lord, please take it to Your kingdom on high. Amen."

Again, a powerful cramp gripped her belly. Gritting her teeth, Mozelle lowered her head to her knees. More blood and dark red blobs pushed from her body. Letting them drop to the ground, this, too, she buried. There was no way she was going to be able to keep working. Still squatting, she reached under her dress and eased her bloody bloomers down her thighs and legs to the ground. They were soaked. She wanted to bury them, too, but she only had four good pair to her name. They would have to be washed, but she couldn't carry them home like that, soaked with blood. Dropping them to the ground, she began rubbing them into the dirt until the dirt soaked up most of the wetness. She took off her head rag, tied it around the soiled, stained bloomers into a tight ball, and dropped it down into the front of her shirt, which was tied at her waist. It would not fall out.

She hated to have to tear her already torn skirt, but she tore a big plug out of the bottom on the side. She laid it flat on the ground. Reaching into her sack, she took out two handfuls of raw cotton, lay them on the rag, and overlapped the rag over the cotton. Then she stuffed the padded rag between her thighs, snug against her body. She could only hope that it would keep the blood from running down her legs. Standing slowly, she made sure that the rag would not drop. It was thick and lumpy. It was uncomfortable. She looked around. No one was looking at her. Everyone else was bent down, hard at work, trying to pick enough cotton so that they could eat. Taking a moment more, with her foot, Mozelle covered up any traces of blood on the ground with dirt. That done, she managed to drag her half-filled sack over to the loading truck.

The straw boss glanced around at her. "This bag ain't full up."

"No, sa. I can't do no mo' today."

"If'n you don't finish out the day, I can't pay you."

She looked at her sack. A painful spasm made her touch her stomach. She looked at the straw boss; he was waiting for her to decide. She had no choice. Pain or not, discomfort or not, she had to get paid. There was no food in the house, and Randell would be mad if she came home empty-handed. Bernice was going to be mad, too. She was working somewhere out in the field. Bernice needed her to help keep a roof over her children's head. If they got put out, Randell was going to blame her.

Mozelle turned and dragged her sack back to where she left off, though she was careful to not step on her baby's grave. Keeping her thighs pressed together, she bent back to her task. Her gait was awkward but she did what she had to. Her pain wasn't just in her belly, it was also in her heart. She cried without sound, but her tears sprinkled the earth.

Mozelle got paid.

After getting off the truck, she went straight to the well and drew some water. She secretly washed her bloomers and hid them behind the outhouse to dry. The lye soap had gotten the blood out good. The bleeding and cramps had stopped, but she still wore the cotton rag bunched up between her thighs.

Randell didn't come home until she was laid down for the night. He lay down beside her, his arm heavy atop her stomach. He nestled his face in the crook of her neck. He smelled of whiskey and a sweet scent she couldn't rightly identify.

"I lost our baby," she said.

"That's best for now," he said, pulling her closer. He kissed her on the neck.

She wanted to wipe away his kiss but dared not. "Randell, how come you so mean to me?"

The sound of him snoring was his only answer.

She tried to pull away from him. She couldn't. She was pent down by the weight of his body. Like a rabbit, she was trapped. She couldn't even turn her body to get comfortable. She realized then that her bed was indeed hard.

Seven

For a man who didn't want children, Randell wouldn't take no for an answer when she tried to keep him off top of her. It didn't matter to him that she didn't want to do it or that she was afraid that she might get pregnant. All he cared about was getting his own pleasure.

"I ain't gon' do it hard. Just lay back."

"What's gon' happen if'n we make another baby?"

"We ain't," he said, trying to force her thighs apart with his knees.

She squeezed her thighs tighter. "But Randell, I don't want to."

"Mozelle, you my wife. I can have you anytime I want to. Now you stop giving me a hard time and do like I say."

As much as she didn't want to, she did as she was told. She lay back and let up on the tightness in her thighs, letting Randell have his way. She knew that it was Randell's right as her husband to have her any time he wanted, but it made her feel worse off than a slave girl. It didn't help any that he grunted louder than he ever did, making her worry that Bernice and her children could hear them. One of them, Patsy, was the age Mozelle was when she married Randell. Now that Mozelle was nearly eighteen, fifteen seemed so young. Back on her wedding day, she didn't quite understand what her mama was talking about her being so young. She understood it now.

Randell never mentioned the baby she lost or what had happened to it. Instead, he started watching her closely. He must have really believed that some other man knocked her up, because when she got a job as a cook at the Buckeye Cafe, he made sure he showed up there to let the menfolk know that she was married to him. He would hug her and say out loud, "You're my woman. I better not find another man sniffing after you."

It was humiliating that he kept doing stupid things like that. He expected her to come straight home from work when he himself wasn't coming straight home. And he had Bernice snooping over her shoulder. Bernice told Randell whenever Mozelle was a minute late. The few times she was late getting home, Randell beat her with a switch like she was a child. Worse than the beatings, it was upsetting to see Bernice looking on, nodding her approval, making her hate her more and more. Hours later, Randell would have his way with her blistered body. It didn't make her feel any better when he said that he was doing what was best for her. She didn't see exactly how he was doing that. When he slept, he held on to her like he did on their wedding night. Back then, he used to say that he loved her, and she believed him. Now, he didn't say much about love, and if he did, she didn't know if she'd believe him. She didn't understand why he was treating her the way he was. Which was why, most of the time, she didn't know how to feel about him. He had changed. He was staying out more and more and drinking heavier, not caring that she was hungry.

It was hunger that made her say what was on her mind. "Randell, maybe we can buy some food befo' you go off drinkin'."

"I do what I want with my money. You want more food, make more money."

When she made a nickel more, he took that, too. She stopped trying to make more. It wasn't doing her any good.

Randell's hold on her life was choking her just as his hands had once done around her throat. There was no opportunity for her to meet other folks, no opportunity to get away. She was sorely missing her own family. Her need to see them grew stronger each and every day that Randell left her home alone. He wasn't pleasant company when he was around, but he was company nonetheless. He didn't pay her any mind when she told him that she was as lonely as a body could be. He could care less. Once in a while she went to church—if Randell let her; but after church she didn't linger.

She had no close or distant friends that looked in on her or that she could go calling on. The only folks she knew were folks she saw in the cafe, and she was too busy there to sit down and talk. That suited Randell just fine—he didn't want her around other folks outside of his family. But what was the use of that? Bernice never made out like she liked her. She was nothing like Alice. Mozelle got on just fine with Alice, they didn't have a bad word between them. White Bernice was cold to her and stayed clear of her and must have told her children to do the same. None, except for Evamae, gave her the time of day.

Evamae was an itty-bitty twelve-year-old who seemed to like being around Mozelle. In fact, it was Evamae who told her that she noticed that she was going to the outhouse a lot more. Four months had passed since she lost her baby, and it wasn't until she thought about it that she realized that she hadn't had to go on the rag for nearly as long. She sent Evamae into the house to fetch her comb so that she could sneak off to the outhouse. Alone in the stale, pungent near darkness, she lifted her skirt and felt her stomach. She was surprised that there was a little fullness there. It was not from eating, because she surely didn't eat much of anything. As skinny as she was, it could only mean that she was knocked up again.

"Oh, God, don't let it be," she pleaded softly. Fear of what Randell was going to do to her brought tears to her eyes. She hugged her belly. If there was a new baby growing inside her, she had to protect it. She didn't want to see another one of her babies pour from her body into the dirt under her feet. "Lord, if it's Your will that I hold this baby, let it be. U'm puttin' my baby in Your hands, Lord. Please help Randell accept his baby, Lord." When she walked out of the outhouse into the light of day, she knew that this baby would live.

She was scared. When she laid down with Randell, she kept her secret to herself. She really did want this baby, but she feared that if she couldn't get anything to eat, her baby wouldn't either. She began hoarding scraps from the cafe—eating anything left on a plate. Still, she didn't put on too much noticeable weight, her full-skirted, loose-fitting dresses hid her tiny belly. God was good, she never got sick—she was able to go to work every day. Falling asleep in the middle of the day on the floor in the corner of the kitchen was about as telltale as her pregnancy got. She was beginning to feel good about having her baby. It would be somebody for her to love, somebody to love her back.

Randell still took his pleasuring. Though by what she figured was her seventh month, he took notice of her ripening body. "You filling out right nice, ain't you? But you getting a bit too fat."

Nervous, she said, "U'm the same."

"Nah. Your belly's filled out, and your titties are rounder," he said, palming them.

It was a good thing her titties were his favorite thing to touch—when he touched her at all. He never rubbed her body anymore or he would have guessed then and there. Two weeks later when he caught her washing her body in the corner of their room, he did guess. Her stomach had all of a sudden popped out. She quickly pulled on her dress.

"I told you I don't want no baby," he said, shoving her up against the wall, holding her there with his arm.

Scared, she sobbed, "I didn't know I was carryin'."

"You lying heifer. You knew you was carrying," he said, spraying her face with his spit. "It ain't mine anyhow. You tell that bastard you laid down with that I ain't feeding his bastard."

She figured it was best not to say anything. As long as he didn't hit, her she could take his hateful words; they would not kill her baby. Then he drew back his fist to hit her.

"Please, Randell, don't hit me," she cried, holding on to her stomach.

He held his fist to her face, pressing hard against her left cheek. "I ain't never gon' say this is my baby," he said, releasing her roughly and storming out of the house.

Trembling, Mozelle tried to catch her breath.

"Mozelle, you all right?" Evamae asked, walking timidly into the room, her hands cupped to her mouth.

Still up against the wall, Mozelle tenderly stroked her belly. "U'm jest fine."

"Uncle Randell ought not a done that."

Mozelle said nothing as she picked up the wash basin to take it outdoors to empty. Her hands shook so badly, the water sloshed over, splashing onto the floor.

"I'll pour it out," Evamae said, taking the basin from her. "Mozelle, you want some mo' water?"

Shaking her head no, Mozelle sat down on the bed. Slowly rubbing her stomach, she closed her eyes. "Lord, help Randell be 'ceptin' of his baby; 'n thank you, Lord, for holdin' back his hand. Amen." Her baby moved inside her belly. She patted her belly. Alfreda's words four years ago again reminded her that Randell did not want children. She could never tell Alfreda that she was right.

Randell wasn't there when the midwife pulled Cora, puny and
limp, from Mozelle's belly. He wasn't there when she saw that
her baby's fingers and toes were crooked. When he did come
home, Bernice told him about Cora before Mozelle could. He
would look at neither Cora or her as he took a blanket and lay it
on the floor in front of the fireplace. He slept there. When Cora
cried, he yelled out, "Hush her up!"

A month after Cora was born, Mozelle lost her job at the
cafe because Cora had colic and kept up too much of a fuss in the
kitchen. There was no one to leave her with. She had to go back
to picking cotton with Cora tied to her chest. Randell came and
went for weeks without talking to Mozelle, except to ask for her
pay. As much as she didn't want to, she gave it to him. Lord
knows, if she wasn't suckling Cora, she didn't know how she
would have fed her, but her baby needed more. Cora was such a
tiny little thing, and Mozelle's milk alone wasn't helping her to
grow. She just wasn't making enough milk.

Mozelle kept trying to nurse her baby and prayed that every
drop of milk would make Cora strong. But eight months had
come and gone, and Cora had grown very little. Her cries were
weak and so were her movements. Mozelle knew that she had to
do something or her baby would die. She had to start feeding
Cora solid food. That's all there was to it. So when she got paid,
she kept half of her pay–one dollar and fifty cents.

Randell counted the change. "Where's the rest?"

"I gots to feed my baby."

"Use your tittie. I want my money."

She lifted Cora higher on her chest. "My milk ain't enough
no mo'. I gots to feed her solid food."

"That ain't my problem. I want my money."

"Randell, I ain't standin' by and lettin' my baby die," she
said, forgetting that she was afraid of him. "I gots to feed her."

Randell's jaw went to work grinding his teeth while he
balled up his fists and glared bitterly at Mozelle.

"If you gon' hit me, go 'head. But U'm still gon' feed my
baby."

Randell raised his fist and drew it back.

Mozelle didn't flinch. She lifted her chin away from Cora's

head and squared her shoulders.

"Goddamnit! Mozelle, don't try me." Randell turned abruptly and walked out of the house, slamming the door behind him.

The noise from the slamming door didn't make Cora cry, but Mozelle could have sworn that Cora smiled at her. Or was that gas?

With the money, Mozelle bought milk, eggs, lard, grits, flour, and cornmeal. She kept part of the money for another day. It didn't take long before Cora started filling out. It did Mozelle's heart good to see her baby gaining weight. Randell was mad at her and stayed gone days at a time, explaining nothing when he turned up was his way. Bernice must have taken pity on Cora, out of nowhere she gave Mozelle the baby clothes she kept in a cedar trunk. From Bernice, Mozelle didn't expect this and saw it as her chance to talk to her.

"How come Randell act like he do?" she asked.

"He was jest fine 'til you went and got yourself knocked up."

Mozelle picked up the shirt she had been scrubbing out of the wash tub.

"Well, he the one that got me that way."

"That might be, but you knowed after the first time that Randell didn't want no baby. You shoulda got rid of it."

"I ain't got no money to get rid of no baby, 'n I wouldn't've done it if'n I did. If Randell didn't want no baby, he should not a laid up with me. A baby gon' be made if'n he sex me."

Bernice set the empty water bucket on top of the well wall. "Look, Mozelle. Long as I can remember, Randell ain't never want no babies. He said womenfolk use babies to hog-tie a man, then sap him of his strength by makin' him work hisself to death. That's what he said Mama did to Daddy. He always said if he knocked up a girl, he was gon' get her fixed. Far as I know, that's what he always did."

"Randell got girls fixed?"

"Now, don't go askin' me nothin' like that 'cause I ain't gon' tell you nothin' Randell don't want you to know."

"But I got to know—"

"You ain't got to know nothin', Mozelle. If Randell want you to know somethin', he'll tell you hisself," Bernice said, coldly. "I jest don't understand how he come about marryin' you. He wasn't never gon' get married. What you do to make him marry you?"

"I ain't done nothin'. He come after me."

"I don't believe that. He ain't never liked little ol' country girls."

"Well, he liked me enough to marry me."

"You musta done somethin', but then, it ain't none of my business. Y'all in it now. Anyhow, fill up this bucket 'n go scrub down the front room."

"U'm busy right now," Mozelle said, hunching back over the scrub board. She scrubbed hard on Randell's shirt. She was wrong for thinking that Bernice might be understanding when she hadn't been friendly in all this time. In fact, Bernice treated her like one of her children, ordering her to do whatever she wanted her to do. Most times Mozelle did what she was told, but she wasn't about to stop what she was doing just like that. Besides, Bernice had girls old enough to be scrubbing their own floor.

"Mozelle, you do like I say. Go scrub down that front room."

She closed her ears to Bernice. She didn't look up from the scrub board. Her back was sore from picking cotton all day, and it was sorer still from washing the few clothes she, Randell, and Cora had. The last thing she wanted to do was get down on her hands and knees and scrub floors.

"U'm talkin' to you, Miss Mozelle."

Ignoring Bernice, she concentrated on dunking the white shirt in the washtub to rinse it. She wrung it out. She she threw it across the clothesline.

Bernice went over to the shirt, yanked it off the line and threw it to the ground.

"What you do that fo'?" Mozelle snatched the shirt up off the ground and threw it back into the washtub.

Bernice planted her hands on her narrow hips. "When I talk to you, girl, you pay 'tention to me."

"U'ma grown woman, Bernice. I ain't got to pay 'tention to you."

"If'n you wasn't married to my brother, I'da put you outta my house a long time ago. I don't like you."

That hurt her. "How come you so hateful to me, Bernice? What I ever do to you?"

"I don't like your kind," she said, moving closer to Mozelle.

Mozelle took a step back. "What's my kind?"

"You a loose woman."

Her eyes popped wide open. The only loose woman she knew about back in Royston had seven children by four different men, no husband, and lots of menfolk coming and going from her house all times of day and night. Everybody talked about her and the talk was that menfolk gave her lots of money.

"I ain't no loose woman."

"Yes, you is. That's the only kind of woman my brother know."

"Well, I ain't one. Randell ain't never give me a dime to be with him. He ain't even give me money to feed his own baby."

"That's 'cause it ain't his baby."

Everything that came out of Bernice's mouth was vile. "You a hateful woman, Bernice," Mozelle said, feeling badly. "I ain't been nothin' but good to you and your children. Y'all eat when I don't. How can you take my money 'n hate me just the same?"

"That ain't your money. Randell give me that money."

"That's my money he give you."

"Well, you ain't doin' me no favor. You 'n your bastard livin' in my house just the same."

Mozelle glanced over at Cora laying on her back on the blanket with her toes in her mouth. Evamae had stopped playing with Cora and was standing, staring at Bernice.

"My baby ain't no bastard, she got a daddy."

"Not my brother."

Mozelle grabbed the shirt up out of the water. She angrily dunked it to rinse the dirt off of it. "You a hateful old woman to talk 'bout your own kin like that."

Bernice pointed at Cora. "That ain't no kin of mine."

"Mama," Evamae said, picking up Cora and cradling her. "Mozelle ain't did nothin' bad."

Bernice cut her eyes over at Evamae. "You hush your mouth befo' I whop your tail. And put that baby down—you ain't her mama."

Evamae looked at Mozelle and back at Bernice. She made no move to put Cora down.

Bernice smirked. "I got a mind to tell Randell you was

talkin' to Dudley Carter out in the field today."

"We was talkin' 'bout boll weevils and how they useta eat up all the cotton."

"Liar."

Mozelle let the shirt slip back into the tub. "You just mad he wasn't talkin' to you."

"You nappy-headed heifer! I ain't no hoe like you."

"You can call me all the ugly names you want, Bernice. I don't care. But I know somethin' 'bout you. I know how come your man ain't never come back home. You is a hateful, mean, ugly woman."

"You nasty heifer!" Bernice spat, rushing at Mozelle like she was going to hit her.

Stepping back real quick, Mozelle started drying her hands on the front of her dress.

"Mama! Mama, don't hit Mozelle!" Evamae screamed.

Bernice glanced over at Evamae, then back at the scour on Mozelle's face. She backed down. "I got a hankerin' to slap your face on the other side of your head."

"You hit me, U'ma hit you back," she said, balling up her fists. She was scared, but she wasn't about to be beat on by Randell and his sister, too. Fighting with Alfreda and play-fighting with her brothers had taught her well how to defend herself. "U'm tired of you treatin' me bad, Bernice. You go 'head, hit me. See what I do."

"Mama, y'all 'bout to fight?" Jolene asked excitedly, running out into the yard.

Bernice didn't answer Jolene or look at her; she was busy sneering at Mozelle.

Mozelle's nails dug into the palms of her hands—the stinging pain kept her hands from shaking. She was aware of the quiet that settled around her. Her only concern was that if they did start fighting, that they didn't hurt Cora. She had to trust that Evamae would protect her baby.

"Child, I wouldn't dirty my hands on the likes of you," Bernice said. She turned abruptly and strutted away in a huff.

Jolene stuck her tongue out at Mozelle before she rushed to catch up with Bernice.

As much as she wanted to say something ugly back to Bernice, Mozelle held her tongue. She didn't want to upset Evamae. Her, she liked. Jolene, though, was another matter.

Jolene was like Bernice—hateful. She picked at Evamae all the time. She looked over at Bernice just as she rushed into the house, slamming the door behind her and Jolene. No, she didn't like either one of them.

"Evamae, is my baby all right?"

"She all right," Evamae answered, sitting down again on the blanket with Cora. "My mama ought not be mean to you like that."

"I reckon she can't help herself." Again she grabbed the same white shirt out of the tub. She angrily thrust and dragged it up and down the scrub board until the muscle in her lower back knotted up. She ignored the pain.

Jolene skipped back out into the yard. "Evamae, Mama want you."

"In a minute."

"She want you *now.*"

Evamae continued to sit. She sighed and rolled her eyes. "In a minute."

"U'ma tell Mama on you," Jolene said, but she waited.

Letting go of the shirt, Mozelle straightened up. She tried to rub the knot out of her back. She could almost feel Bernice's eyes on her from behind the dirty windowpane. So she stared hard at the window, hoping that Bernice could see that she hated her just as much. She never thought she could hate anybody, but Bernice brought those feelings out of her. It was just as well that how they felt about each other was out in the open. Now she understood why Bernice was always so eager to tell Randell if she was a minute late. Maybe Bernice was hateful to her because she was missing her husband. Then again, maybe it was like she said: Maybe Bernice's husband stayed gone because she was so hateful. Couldn't Bernice see that she was not a loose woman? Couldn't she tell that she was a God-fearing woman?

Taking the shirt out of the water and wringing it out, she hung it back on the clothesline just as Randell came around the side of the house.

She swallowed hard. "Hey," she said, trying to sound calm.

Randell didn't return the greeting.

Jolene and Evamae watched Randell as he walked up to the well, drew a bucket of water and poured it into the wash basin.

"Gimme the soap."

Taking the lye soap off the scrub board, Mozelle handed it

to him and stood back.

Randell took off his coveralls and shirt, dropping them to the ground. He stood in his drawers, the least bit concerned that Jolene and Evamae were looking at him. He went about scrubbing the dried sweat and dirt off his face, his neck, his arms, his chest, and his underarms. He picked under his nails with his knife, getting out the dirt from the cotton field. That done, he scrubbed his legs and feet.

Jolene and Evamae watched Randell's every move.

"Damn dirt," he said, drying his hands and arms on Mozelle's wet dress hanging on the clothesline.

She sucked her teeth barely loud enough for him to hear. Although faded and washed out, that was her one good dress.

Leaving the lye soap and rag in the dirty water, Randell glanced at Mozelle. "Go fetch my brown trousers 'n white shirt."

"Randell, I got to talk to you."

"I said, go fetch my clean clothes. I was feeling downright dirty in those slave clothes."

"Can I talk to you after I fetch your clothes?" she asked, wringing her hands anxiously.

Randell grabbed up his dirty coveralls and threw them at Mozelle. "Get!"

Flinching, she stepped back. The heavy coveralls dropped to the ground at her feet. Something else for her to wash. Turning abruptly on her heels, she started running toward the house.

"And don't forget my tie."

Inside the house, Mozelle rushed past Bernice standing at the potbelly stove stirring in a big pot. She quickly grabbed Randell's shirt, trousers, and tie and ran back out into the yard. She held on to the shirt and tie while Randell put on his trousers.

"Randell, can we get our own house? I can pick more cotton to pay the rent."

"Gal, what you talking about?" he asked, taking his shirt from her and putting it on.

"Well, if we had our own place to stay, we—"

"We're staying right here," he said, snatching his tie from her hand. "Where's my money?"

"I got it," she said, pulling out the rag she had stuffed under her left tittie. Unrolling it, she took out one dollar in coins and handed it to him.

"Randell, we ain't never stayed by ourself. We—"

"This all you made?" he asked, holding the coins in his open hands out to her.

"Yes," she lied.

"Damn. You need to pick more cotton, Mozelle, just to give me my money. You ain't never gon' make enough money to pay rent."

She felt empty. The sweet, intense love she used to have for him had left her completely. "Randell, how come you ask my daddy for my hand if'n you was gon' treat me bad?"

"I treat you better then you deserve," he said, dropping the money into his pocket.

If he had slapped her face, it would not have hurt her more. She bit down on her lip.

"Uncle Randell," Jolene said. "Mozelle was 'bout to fight Mama."

"Hush your mouth, Jolene!" Evamae said.

Without warning, Randell turned on Mozelle. He grabbed one of her long plaits, yanking it hard. The pain was brutal. She thought he would pull a plug out of her scalp.

He snarled, "You hit my sister?"

"No, Uncle Randell!" Evamae shouted. "Mozelle didn't hit Mama."

"You hurtin' my head," Mozelle cried, trying to hold her hair to her head to ease the pain.

Tightening his grip on her hair, he slapped her repeatedly over her head and face with his other hand. "Heifer, you don't lay your hand on my sister. I'll kill your black ass."

"She didn't hit Mama, Uncle Randell!"

Randell wasn't listening to Evamae.

Cowering, while still trying to press her head into his hand, Mozelle cried, "I didn't hit her."

"She didn't hit me but she sass me," Bernice said strolling up to them.

Randell yanked on Mozelle's hair. "You sass my sister, heifer?"

Mozelle clawed at Randell's hand, trying desperately to free her plait.

Tugging harder on her hair, Randell let her scratch up his hand. "Don't you know I'll kill you?"

Mozelle began squealing like a scalded pig. The piercing pain in her scalp was blinding. She was about to black out when

Cora's crying pulled her back to consciousness.

"Don't you be sassing my sister. You ain't nothing! You ain't nobody! You hear me? You ain't nobody but a backwoods, dumb country girl!" He suddenly let go of her hair and brutally pushed her head away from his body.

Mozelle fell in a heap to the ground.

"You better shut up that bastard before I whop her black ass, too!"

Oh, God. She couldn't let him touch Cora. Although her head was killing her, Mozelle got up on her knees. She started crawling over to Cora, but Randell again grabbed on to the same plait and yanked her back to him. *God, the pain.* Mozelle grabbed ahold of her head and Randell's hand, trying to keep him from pulling her hair. She cowered from the pain shooting through her head and neck. She cowered, too, from his rage. She had never known such rage. Not even from her own daddy.

"Heifer, tell my sister you sorry!"

"U'm sorry," she whimpered immediately, hoping that he would let her go.

Instead, Randell shoved her to the ground onto her tail bone. He still held on to her hair. The pain was unbearable, but she strained to look over at Evamae trying her best to quiet Cora down.

"Randell, I didn't hear her say she was sorry," Bernice said. She folded her arms across her chest and looked down at Mozelle like she was covered in manure.

"Bernice didn't hear you. Speak up," Randell said, pulling Mozelle's head back so that she looked up at Bernice.

"U'm sorry!" she croaked.

Randell pulled his hand out of Mozelle's tangled hair, hurting her more. "Get away from me," he ordered.

Bernice hawked. She spat on the ground. "You shoulda not marry that trash."

"I sho shouldn't've."

Mozelle lay on the ground trying to figure out how she had been so fooled by Randell's charm. If she could have, she would have beat her own self for not listening to her mama and daddy.

"Bernice, next time she sass you, U'ma put her six feet under," Randell said, picking up his tie from the ground. He shook it off before he put it around his neck. With his toe, he kicked Mozelle on the bottom of her foot. "Get your sorry ass up and get my supper."

"Wait a minute," Bernice said, nodding her head toward Evamae. "You tell that hoe that Evamae ain't helpin' her with her bastard no mo'."

"You hear what she say?"

With her eyes closed, Mozelle nodded. Her head was killing her.

"Mama, I wanna play with Cora," Evamae said, laying Cora back on the blanket.

"Girl, don't make me take a switch to you."

Pushing out her bottom lip, Evamae turned away from Bernice and walking past Jolene, shoved her hard, forcing her to stumble backward.

"Mama!"

"Evamae! Girl, you gettin' too big for your britches!"

Evamae took off running, with Jolene chasing behind her.

Refusing to cry, Mozelle crawled away from Randell before she could manage to get to her feet. She lifted Cora up off the blanket and clutched her to her heart. She ran off into the house, away from Randell and away from Bernice.

Lord, give me the strength to fight back.

Eight

In four years, twice more, Mozelle got pregnant. Her babies grew in her womb and were born, but twice more they died. Maybe the Lord knew best to take the poor souls—by herself she could hardly feed Cora. Cora was four but she was small for her age. Her misshapen hands and feet were more apparent the older she got. One more reason for Randell to deny her. She couldn't use all of her little fingers—they were stiff and crooked. Her toes, too, were crooked, and her feet turned out slightly to the side, making it hard for her to walk without waddling.

Mozelle couldn't afford to buy the special shoes Cora needed, so she wrapped her feet and ankles tightly with rags to give her some support.

Randell said Cora was cursed. Mozelle might've believed him, except she knew that her baby didn't grow right in her womb because she didn't have nourishing food to feed her. Cora had starved before she saw the light of day, and, poor thing, it was no better for her now. The only time they got something other than corn mush, beans, grits, or pan biscuits, was when Mozelle went to white folks' farms and chopped cotton in exchange for food—sometimes white pototoes, sometimes salt pork, sometimes flour, sometimes fish. She had no lard to fry the fish in and learned to like it plain boiled. When she could get white potatoes, they gobbled them up boiled with no salt. Sometimes a farmer would let her take home leftover bits of skin off of a hog. Now, that's when they ate good—she fried the skins up crisp and used the grease they made to season her beans or to sop her biscuits.

Every day she prayed. Every day she asked God to ease her burdens. As she saw it, Randell was her heaviest burden. Now and then she overheard talk about him in the cotton field. She had guessed all along that he was whoring around, she just didn't know for sure. The many nights he stayed away from home, she knew he had to be sleeping somewhere, she just didn't know with whom. She was twenty-three before she realized that the different scents she smelled on him when he came home and got on top of her, were the scents of other women. Much worse than that, he would leave home with her money, come back with nothing, and selfishly eat what little food she had. That angered her because he didn't care that he was taking food from Cora. He didn't care if Cora had a full belly or not.

"Where's my supper?" Randell asked, coming home late, well after his single slice of fatback and boiled potatoes had cooled.

"There ain't no supper," she lied, bending and placing a log in the fireplace, hoping that he wouldn't see the tin plate hidden under the dishrag on the table.

Randell sat down in the straight chair on the side of the bed. He began unbuttoning his shirt. "Woman, you best get me something to eat."

Using a log, she slowly stoked the fire. The crackling flames held her gaze. The warmth of the fire seemed cool compared to the torrid heat that had been building inside her for so long. She didn't see how come she had to feed Randell, wash his clothes, give him her money, take his fist upside her head, and live with his cheating, too. Her mama didn't say she had to live with him cheating on her. And what if he was giving her hard-earned money to another woman? That she couldn't abide.

"You oughta had the hoe you was pleasurin' get your supper," she said, straightening up and turning away from the fire to look at him directly.

"What you say?"

Stoned-faced, she looked at him. Randell was staring at her like he couldn't believe what she had said. She didn't believe it herself.

"You sassing me, woman?"

There was no fear in her heart. She looked him straight in the eye. "U'm tellin' you, Randell. U'm tired of you takin' me for a fool. I ain't standin' for it no mo'."

"Woman, you don't talk to me like that," he said, getting up off the chair. "Don't you know I'll kill you?"

"Not if I kill you first."

For a startled moment, frozen by her angry black eyes, Randell gaped at Mozelle.

She felt like she was on the battlefield for the Lord; like she was ready to fight with the devil himself. She felt strong. Her strength was a long time in coming, but she was ready. She did not lower her eyes. Her wrathful stare challenged the evil that was in Randell, and he knew it.

He wasn't accustomed to her not backing down. "Heifer, I know you wanna die!" He started at her.

With the log she stoked the fire with still in her hand, she charged at him. "*Aaaaaaah!*"

Randell stopped, cold in his tracks, but Mozelle was on him. With both hands holding the log, she angrily struck out at him. Randell threw up his arms to ward off the blows, but she hit his arms so hard that he couldn't keep them up. She whopped him upside his head, on his face, on his shoulders, his chest, anywhere at all was her target. Neither his screams or his threats to kill her deterred her. She felt like the mighty hand of God was in her hands. She struck Randell as many times and more for every one time he had hit her. She thought about how often she had to eat dirt or let her baby go hungry or picked cotton until her fingers and heart bled knowing that although she was working, she still couldn't afford to buy food to feed Cora or herself.

Randell tried desperately to block the frantic blows. He couldn't. Mozelle was all over him. He howled. He ran around the room, ducking and cowering from her attack. He dropped to the floor and tried to get under the bed, but he couldn't fit and got stuck. Mozelle seized the moment and beat him across his backside. Randell scrambled from under the bed and sprang up off the floor. He bolted for the door and grabbed the knob. Mozelle ran right up on him and kept pounding him on his back and shoulders. Never mind the splinters she got in her hands.

Randell took the blows while he fumbled with the loose doorknob. He couldn't get the door open. "Ouch! Goddamnit, woman! You done lost your mind!"

"You right. I been out my mind for a long time for lettin' you beat on me and take my hard-earned money and give it to your hoes whilst my baby went hungry. You ain't doin' it no mo', 'cause U'ma crack your cheatin' head wide open for the buzzards to feed on."

From the other side of the door, Bernice shouted, "Mozelle, you stop beatin' on my brother!"

"You get the hell away from my door befo' I come out there and beat you, too!"

"Don't you threaten me, Mozelle! This is my house. Randell!"

"Bernice, she done plum lost her mind!" he shouted, still fumbling with the doorknob that just turned and turned in his hand. He flinched from the blows. "Open the door! I can't open it from this side."

Mozelle felt like she couldn't stop beating him even though ugly bruises on the side of his face were beginning to bleed.

"Mama. . .Mama," Cora cried from the far corner of the room next to the chifforobe.

She had forgotten about her child. She hadn't even heard her crying, nor had she realized that her arms had grown tired. Suddenly the log weighed heavy in her hands. She felt like she had been chopping a mound of firewood. Her arms dropped. She stopped beating Randell. Stepping cautiously away from him, she said as sweetly as she could to Cora, "Stop crying, baby. Mama'll be with you in a minute." Her arms were awfully tired but she raised them and held the log like a bat, ready to strike Randell if he turned on her.

Giving the door one might yank, Randell pulled the door open. Bernice was standing outside the door. "Don't you be hittin' on my brother, you crazy woman!"

Randell stood shoulder to shoulder with his sister. "Goddamnit, Mozelle! U'ma whop your crazy ass!"

Mozelle drew back her arm to throw the log at his head. She almost laughed when his eyes bugged and his mouth dropped open, but nothing about him was funny. She threw the log.

Randell quickly pulled the door shut, slamming it loudly.

The log crashed against the door and fell. Pieces of bark scattered on the floor. Oh, how she wished it was Randel's brain scattered there. There wasn't a time she could call to mind where she wanted to hurt another living soul. She fought with her sisters and brothers, but she never wanted to hurt them. She had always had a hard time watching when her daddy slaughtered a pig or wrung a chicken's neck, mainly it was the blood that turned her stomach, but the squealing, thrashing animals upset her most. Lord forgive her, but she'd gladly watch Randell bleed to death if that log had hit him and split his head open.

Exhausted, she stood staring at the door, wondering if Randell would burst back through it. Her chest was heaving, the vein in her neck pulsed rapidly, she could hear it thumping in her ear. Panting, she waited with her fists balled up. If he came back, she'd beat him like he beat her. Not until she heard the outer door slam did she relax her hands. Going over to Cora, she lifted her into her arms and carried her to the bed. She started to climb in with her, when she thought, what if Randell came back while she was sleeping? She needed to know when he came back. Looking around the room, her eyes fell on the big wooden chair next to the window. She put Cora down on the bed and went and took hold of the chair, dragging it over to the door. She wedged the back of it, tight, under the doorknob. Now she would know if Randell tried to come in.

Randell didn't come back that night. The first few hours, as tired as she was, Mozelle couldn't close her eyes for fear of what Randell might do if he came back. But when her eyelids felt as heavy as the log she had wielded, she dropped off to sleep. It was the first night in a long time that her sleep was that sweet and that comfortable. Maybe it was because she was bone-tired, or maybe it was because she had stood up to Randell. She slept good all the same.

"Who you think you is, beatin' on my brother?" Bernice asked Mozelle the instant she stepped outside her room.

"You best leave me be, Bernice," she warned. She held tight on to Cora's hand. "U'm sho tired of you lookin' down your nose at me, U'm tired of Randell beatin' on me, and U'm tired of him takin' my money 'n givin' it to you 'n his hoes whilst me 'n my baby go hungry. I ain't givin' him no mo' my money, and if'n he put his hands on me again, U'ma break them."

Evamae and Jolene stood behind Bernice. Bernice pushed them back. "I ain't gon' have you carryin' on like—"

"You ain't gon' have me carryin' on like what? Like I don't wants to be beat down like a stray dog?"

"You can get outta my house, missy."

"Oh, I guess I can stay if'n I sit still and let Randell beat on me, right?"

"No, I don't want you here at all."

"Let me tell you somethin'," she said, stepping in closer to Bernice, making Bernice draw back. "I don't bother nobody. I done tried real hard to get you to like me, but I don't think you can 'cause I don't think you like your own self."

"I like myself jest fine, but I ain't gotta ever like you."

"No, you don't. But you gots ta stay outta my business. You got lots to say 'bout me fightin' back, but you ain't never got nothin' to say when Randell was beatin' on me like a dog. You stand by 'n watch him beat on me like I ain't God's child. Now, I done asked God to give me the strength to fight back, and He done finally give me the mind to do it. I ain't gon' tell Him I don't want the strength He done give me. U'm warnin' you, Bernice, you and Randell best leave me be from now on."

"I ain't scared of you, Mozelle. You a nobody, jest like my brother say. I wish to God he'd a married Gail instead of you."

Mozelle had never heard that name before and was stumped

for minute. Given Randell's age, she knew there had to be some-body before her, but until she heard a name, she hadn't troubled herself about it. And truth to tell, she wished that he had married that Gail woman, too, then he would not have come around to destroy her life.

"You know somethin', Bernice? Randell coulda married you for all I care. Y'all both evil."

"What you sayin' about me and my brother!"

"Jest what you think U'm sayin'," she said, opening the door and walking out of the house, taking Cora with her. She did-n't bother to look back. She already knew that Bernice's face was all screwed up.

From that day on, Bernice treated her like she was grown and didn't tell her what to do anymore. There were no more nasty remarks about her or Cora, though Bernice kept Evamae away from her, which was too bad. Mozelle had no one else besides Cora to talk to.

Randell stayed away from her, too. He kept calling her crazy, but that was all right. As long as he didn't put his hands on her, his words couldn't hurt her. She couldn't believe that he had-n't tried to get back at her. Thinking back, she should have gone after him the first time he put his hands around her throat. But how was she to know that her husband would be the one that hurt her most? Now that she knew, she was going to make sure that Randell never treated her that bad again.

Starting the next day, she kept all of her own hard-earned money. If Randell bought anything home to eat, he ate it himself. Yet, he still expected her to have his supper ready. Just to keep from arguing with him, if there was anything left, she let him have it, but she didn't plan on saving anything for him. At times, he berated her for it, but he didn't lay a hand on her. Two months later, the one time he looked like he might, she warned him, "If'n I got to fight you again, U'ma try with all my might to kill you. I don't care if I die tryin'."

Randell hit the wall with his fist. "U'm sorry I ever laid eyes on you."

"Randell, you can't be no sorrier than me."

He stomped out of the house, leaving her grateful to God that she didn't have to fight, but she meant every word she said— she would die trying to kill him. This wasn't the way she was brought up, she was brought up in the church. More than anything, she hated that she had to fight her own husband, but if this was the only way to keep Cora and herself safe and fed, then she was going to fight.

Nine

1938

Mozelle lived in such misery, she couldn't take it another day. In the spring, she took Cora, without telling Randell—not that he'd care, and hitched a ride with a traveling preacher back to Royston. Her mama smothered Cora with hugs and tender kisses. Mama said she understood about Cora's hands and feet— they had gone hungry, too. Mozelle wanted to tell her about her three lost babies but decided against it, she might end up telling too much if she got started.

Daddy kept asking, "He treatin' you right?"

It was easier to say, "Yes, Daddy," than it was to hear him say, "I told you so." They were only just words and couldn't hurt her, but they were hard to take. As much as she wanted to tell him that she was not just visiting, that she wanted to stay, she could not muster the courage. It didn't help any that her folks were just as bad off as her and Randell. Besides, there wasn't any room for another body. Three of her brothers and their families were living in the house taking care of Mama and Daddy both. Daddy wasn't doing too good; he couldn't work the fields anymore. His male organs were swollen and painful, making it difficult for him to walk sometimes. And Mama was sick most of the time from her rotten teeth and red swollen gums. Mozelle could see that her folks had grown old. They were wasting away. For all their troubles, Mozelle couldn't stay and be a part of their burden.

Of course, there was Alfreda. Maybe she could stay a spell with her. She went off to see her and her four children. At first

Alfreda was happy to see her, but from the start, they didn't get along. Alfreda fussed about everything she did or didn't do right in her house. She put the scrub board back the wrong way, Alfreda fussed about that. That was such a small thing, but every small thing turned into a big fuss. By the end of the second week, they were arguing like they did when they were children, especially when she couldn't take Alfreda always asking about Randell.

"No, y'all wasn't right," Mozelle said defensively. "For one thing, we got one baby, so far."

"Well, it don't look like he takin' too good a care of her. She look like a pickaninny."

That hurt her. "No, she don't."

"She sho'nuff do. I ain't never had to put my girls in sack dresses, and you been wearing the same ol' two dresses since you got here."

She had hoped that nobody would notice. "Well, Alfreda, if Eugene Johnson's daddy's family didn't own this here farm, you'd be bad off just like me."

"Not me. I'd die befo' I put a sack on any of my children's back. That husband of yours ain't worth spit like daddy said. I know his type, Mozelle. He the kind of man that spend his money on loose women. U'm glad he married you 'stead of me."

Mozelle couldn't dispute a single word. It would have been too hard to try and defend the lie she would have to tell to make Randell look good. It was easier to pack up and leave Alfreda's house, easier to go back to Elberton, back to Randell. For years, thoughts of leaving Randell and going back home had always been on her mind, but she now knew for sure that there was no home to go back to. Whether Randell treated her right or not, she was going to have to stay put like her mama told her to. To her surprise, Randell acted like he was glad to see her and Cora. He gave Cora a handful of peppermints. That was the first time he'd given her anything. And that night he pleasured Mozelle like he did the day they got married. It made her think that going away for a while was the best thing she could have done, although not much else changed. Randell didn't hug her anymore just because, so her knees no longer went weak, and her heart no longer went *pitter-pat* when she saw him coming. Still, at night it felt good when she let him pleasure her. She loved every minute of his touch, and when she thought about it, considering the fact that he didn't do anything else for her, pleasuring her was the least he could do. She needed some affection.

Randie was born the second week in December 1939. The old midwife that delivered her was nearly blind and told Mozelle that she had a boy. It was two days before Mozelle was well enough to examine her baby herself, whom she had already named Randell Junior, and saw that Junior was a girl. Randell Junior was changed to Randie. Again, she had to close her mind to Randell's denial of his child; though she overheard him ask Bernice, "Don't she know how to make boys?" He left the house and stayed gone for four days. Again he wasn't there when she needed him.

Three days after Randie was born, her brother, Jim, came from Royston to tell Mozelle that her daddy had died. He was already buried, already with God. Mozelle cried, more because she had lied to her daddy about how she was getting on with Randell than because he had died. But Jim wasn't fooled by her lie. He could see that she wasn't all right like she had said when she was home. Randell was nowhere to be seen, and she couldn't offer Jim a bite to eat, not even a leftover biscuit.

Jim looked at the empty shelf where food should have been. "Ain't nobody doing good right now, Mozelle, but your husband oughta be able to put food on the table for you and your babies. It ain't like you got ten children."

"Don't worry about me, Jim. U'ma be jest fine," she said, hating that he had seen the truth and might go back home and tell it. "I eat. I jest ain't bought nothin' today."

Jim eyed her like he didn't believe her. "Alfreda told Mama and Daddy that you was worst off than you made out."

"U'm gon' beat Alfreda's tail when I see her again," she said halfheartedly.

Jim chuckled. "Mozelle, of all the girls, you was always the tough one. You useta fight like you was supposed to be a boy.

Remember what Daddy useta say 'bout you?"

"Well, Daddy useta say a lot of things 'bout me," she said, feeling terrible inside. "He said I was stubborn."

"Yeah. And he said you had more grit than all of us. I useta hate when he said that 'cause that meant that I wasn't as strong as you."

"That's not true, Jim. You was stronger than me."

"U'm 'bout equal, Mozelle. I do all right by my family considerin' the time we's all in, but U'm worried 'bout how you gettin' on."

"Don't worry 'bout me, Jim. U'm jest fine."

"That's what you say, Mozelle, but I can see with my own eyes that you ain't."

Feeling shame, she lowered her head. They all knew. Her daddy had gone to his grave knowing how bad off she really was.

"Mozelle, Daddy said you'd chew on rusty nails befo' you'd admit you was wrong about marryin' Randell. He was right, wasn't he?"

Her eyes filled with tears.

"Mozelle, don't let Randell beat you down. If you can't make it, c'mon back home. You can stay with me and Lena."

"I can't."

Sighing deeply, Jim started digging down into his pocket. "I can't make you do what you don't want to, Mozelle, but I hope you still got a lot of grit in you like Daddy said. U'ma go on back home, but I want you to take this," he said, handing her five single dollar bills. "Buy some food for you and Cora."

As much as she wanted to, she couldn't even say no. She didn't tarry in his arms longer than a few seconds for fear of losing her will to not crawl back home.

When Randell came home a day after Jim left, she didn't bother to tell him about her daddy, though nosy Bernice told him about Jim being there. She could have saved her breath because Randell didn't even ask why, but she asked him, "Where you stay when you don't come home?"

He said right off. "I be down at the all-night cafe drinking with Walt Williams, and other menfolk."

Since she never went to the cafe, she didn't know if he was telling the truth, though she doubted it. She let it go—no use fighting over something she could do nothing about. She wasn't going down there to stand in his shadow.

A few days later she was sitting outside nursing Randie when Walt Williams strolled into the yard looking for Randell.

"I don't know where he got off to," she said, thinking that if anybody knew, Walt would. "You ain't seen him?"

"Naw," he said, ogling her exposed tittie.

Mozelle closed her dress over Randie's head, covering herself up.

Walt squatted down in front of her a few feet away. "You look right pretty feeding your baby."

She didn't know what to say to that. "You want me to tell Randell you come by?"

"I can most likely tell him myself, I know where he is."

She peered down at him good. "If you know where he is, how come you come lookin' for him?"

"Thought I'd give you a holler," he said, smiling at her.

Oh, this didn't sound right. His smile wasn't true, it was too devilish. She squinted at him. "You ain't never give me a holler befo'."

"I always wanted to, but you being married to Randell 'n all," he said, picking up a little stick and scratching in the dirt. "I wasn't raised to talk to another man's wife."

Feeling uneasy, Mozelle got up out of her chair with Randie still suckling. "U'm still Randell's wife. This here his baby suckin' on me. What you want with me?"

Walt slowly stood. He wasn't but a head taller than Mozelle, so he didn't have to stoop down to look her in the eye. "I want to be your man."

Mozelle's mouth opened but nothing came out. She backed away from him. "I ain't no hoe."

Walt spread his arms out to her. "That's how come U'm talking to you, I know you ain't. I been watching you out in the field for a long time, you too good for the likes of Randell Tate. Like right now, he down the road a piece at Jeanette Mooney's house in bed with her."

As shocking as that news was, Mozelle was more amazed that Walt told it to her as easy as he would tell her that it was a nice day.

"It ain't right," he said. "Mozelle, I can take care of you and your babies like you deserve."

For a befuddled second, Mozelle stared at him. Walt had to be crazy if he thought she was trifling like Randell. "Walt, you right. I is a good woman. My daddy would turn over in his grave if I stepped out on Randell. Now, you get," she said, pointing past him.

"Wait, Mozelle, Randell ain't been a good husband to you. Do your daddy know that?"

Quickly picking up a stick bigger than the one he had been scratching in the dirt with, Mozelle raised it threateningly. "I don't care 'bout what Randell do. My mama said a married woman don't got no business steppin' out on her husband. And I ain't. Now, you *get*!"

"I didn't mean no disrespect."

Mozelle turned her back on Walt and raced into the house, slamming the door behind her. Hurriedly, she put Randie down on the mat on the floor in her room and told Cora to watch her. Going back to the door she peeked outside. Walt Williams was on his way. Without missing a beat, she bolted out of the house. Jeanette Mooney lived a little ways down the road with her twelve-year-old daughter and her mama. She recalled seeing her in church a handful of times over the years. They nodded at each other maybe twice. This time when she nodded at her, it wasn't going to be in church or friendly, and if Randell was in her bed, she and Randell were going to be sorry.

Mozelle got to the Mooney house out of breath. No one was outside. She listened at the front door. It was quiet. She peered through the window, the front room was empty. Like a thief in the night, she stole around to the back door. Nothing. Just as she started to walk away, she heard Randell's voice.

"C'mon, baby, do your big daddy again."

Mozelle burst through the unlocked back door. "You

lowlife bastard!"

Straddled atop Randell, Jeanette screamed.

Seeing Mozelle, Randell shoved Jeanette off. He leaped straight up off the bed, landing flat on his feet. "I wasn't doing nothing!"

"Man! You naked as a new born baby."

"Yeah, but I wasn't—"

"Randell! You a lyin' bastard. I caught you doin' it. You a liar," she spat, rushing at him.

Leaping up on the bed, Randell ran across it to the other side of the room. He snatched up his clothes off the chair.

Mozelle charged around the bed at him. Cornering him, she pounded wildly at him with her fists. "U'm gon' kill you!"

Without flinching, Randell took the blows while he struggled to pull on his britches. He got them on and with one mighty shove, he pushed Mozelle out of his way. He ran headlong for the door.

"Randell!" Jeanette screamed, trying to hide her naked body under the covers. "Get her outta my house!"

Randell never stopped running.

Mozelle started to run behind him but stopped at the foot of Jeanette's bed instead. "I ain't goin' nowhere 'til I whop your ass."

"Randell!"

"He can't hear you. He's gone," she said, snatching the covers out of Jeanette's grasp, exposing her naked body.

Jeanette jumped off the bed and ran for the open door. Mozelle grabbed her by her hair, snatching her back. She flung her so hard that Jeanette slammed into the wall, bounced off it and fell to the floor with a dull thud. Right away Jeanette started trying to crawl away. But Mozelle wasn't going to let her get away; she wasn't through with her. She threw herself on top of Jeanette's back and straddling her, grabbed her right arm and wrung it up behind her back, pushing it high, almost up to her shoulder.

Jeanette's screams were ear-splitting.

"Hush up!"

"You breakin' my arm!"

"U'ma break it for sure if you don't hush up."

"Let me loose!"

Mozelle pushed Jeanette's arm higher up her back, making her scream louder. "The next time you and my husband lay up together, it's gon be side-by-side in a grave."

"I ain't gon' lay with him no mo'. I swear befo' God."

"You bet' not," Mozelle said. She pushed Jeanette's arm harder for good measure.

Jeanette howled.

Mozelle left Jeanette, whimpering, crumpled up on the floor with her arm still behind her back. She ran all the way back home to find Randell in bed playing possum. Cora and Randie were both on the mat asleep. She rushed over to the bed and started beating Randell in the stomach and chest.

He grabbed hold of Mozelle's wrists, clamping down hard on them so that she couldn't move. "Woman, you sho'nuff done lost your damn mind!" he said, pushing his way from under the cover and off the bed.

She wouldn't let the pain in her wrists stop her. She struggled hard to free herself. She wanted to kill him. Truth to tell, she really did feel like she'd lost her mind because she couldn't stop herself. She kept trying to get loose. She tried to bite his hand.

Randell shook Mozelle off of him so that she wouldn't bite him, but he was afraid to let go of her. "What's wrong with you?"

Unable to pull out of his grasp and breathing hard, her chest heaving, she said, "If I ever catch you on top that hoe or any hoe again, U'ma cut that thang off and feed it to the 'gators. Now let loose of me!"

His grip tightened. "What I tell you 'bout threatening me? I'll break you like a twig."

Mozelle's fingertips began to tingle. She realized that she was no match for him. "Randell, you stronger then me, but you sleep harder then me."

Randell's eyes batted rapidly. He knew damn well what she meant. He pushed off on her, releasing her wrists at the same time. "You ain't gon' do nothing to me," he said, the uncertainty in his voice belying the words he spoke.

"If you don't think so, you go on and sex her again," she said, wiping the sweat off her face with the hem of her skirt. Her heart wasn't beating so fast anymore.

"Woman, I ain't gon' stand still for you threatening me and hitting on me. U'ma man; I'll do what I want."

"Keep doin' what you want, Randell, you gon' be a geldin' as sure as U'm standin' here."

Randell grabbed his crotch. "You crazy."

She tried to calm down. "Randell, in ten years I ain't knowed nothin' but misery. I know how come I gots to stay, but you ain't gots to stay with me. I wants to know how come you ain't run off with one of your hoes?"

Strolling over to the fireplace, Randell ran his hand slowly over the top of his head. His processed waves didn't move.

Mozelle suddenly felt calm. "Randell, you can go on 'bout your business. You don't gots to stay with me. You go on."

"I ain't goin' nowhere," he said, his back to Mozelle.

"I want you to go, Randell. You don't want me, and I don't want you."

He shook his head. "Mozelle, let me tell you about my daddy."

"What fo'? You ain't bothered to tell me nothin' 'bout him befo'."

"Woman, why don't you just listen to what I got to say?"

She huffed and folded her arms.

Randell waited to see if Mozelle would say anything else. When she didn't, he turned away from her. "My daddy stayed with my mama all his life, through thick 'n thin. He told me when he was a boy on a slave plantation, he saw lots of menfolk sold off from their womenfolk, and lots of children sold off from their mamas and daddies. He said that was one of the worst things white folks ever did to colored folks—broke up lots of families. He told me, if I ever take a wife, I better stay with her 'til my last breath, and that's what I intend to do."

"So you stayin' with me 'cause you got to?"

"That's right, 'cause I got to. But my daddy said, too, that if my nature rise and it need satisfying, and my wife can't do right by me, then get myself a outside woman."

Her arms dropped. "You sayin' it's my fault you hoe around? That I ain't satisfyin' you?"

"Mozelle, you wasn't but a girl when I married you. You ain't never been woman enough for me."

Her nose stung. "Then how come you marry me, Randell? You knowed I wasn't but a girl when you lay eyes on me. How come you asked my daddy to let you marry me?"

"Look, I took you over a lot of women. You ought to be right proud."

"Well, I ain't, there ain't nothin' prideful in misery. Randell, if you knew that I wasn't never gon' satisfy you, then how come you wanted me to be your wife?"

"Because you was a pretty little thing, and I figured you had never been touched."

She stared at him. "That's the reason?"

"That's right, but you ain't a pretty little thing no more. Not since you started getting knocked up. You don't look the same to me. You oughta be glad U'm going out to get satisfied."

Alfreda's words rushed into Mozelle's mind. If she could lay down and die, she would, but she had Cora and Randie to take care of. Her eyes welled up. She had to get away from Randell. She needed fresh air. She started toward the door.

"Don't go acting like I hurt your feelings. You oughta be grateful I ain't pestering you all the time."

She stopped walking. "You keep tellin' me what I oughta be. I guess I oughta be happy that my husband is sleepin' with other women, and I oughta be glad you spend my money on them, too."

"See, there you go. I do what I want with my money. See, Mozelle, you just don't understand. I'm a man with a strong nature. One woman can't ever satisfy me," he said, sitting down on the edge of bed. "For that reason alone, I ain't never wanted to be bothered with a wife. That's how come it took me so long to take a wife. Believe me, U'm sorry I ever got married."

"Randell, you ain't no sorrier than me. You ain't had no

business askin' me to marry you, if you wasn't gon' treat me right. I was jest fine till you come along struttin' and grinnin'. I wish to God, you never come into church that day."

"Can't take back yesterday, Mozelle."

She hated his attitude. "You right, Randell. Ain't no one woman ever gon' satisfy you. You like a dog in heat. 'Stead of your daddy tellin' you to step out on your wife, he shoulda told you to be good to your wife," she said. Her chest was tight with her anger. She watched Randell lay back on the bed. "You get out my bed with your hoe's scent on you."

"I ain't studin' you," he said sleepily.

She rushed over to the fireplace and grabbed a log.

Randell bolted up off the bed. He grabbed his britches. "You crazy out your mind," he said, yanking on his britches. He plopped down in the chair. "I ain't got time for this stupidness."

She glared angrily at him though she was mad at herself for not being woman enough to keep her man at home.

Ten

1940

In September, Mozelle packed up Cora and Randie's sack dresses eagerly when Randell decided that he wanted to go back to Royston. For him, the work had dried up in Elberton, and they couldn't wait around for another cotton-picking season. Bernice had found herself a boyfriend old enough to be her daddy whom she let move in with her. There was talk in church about them living together, but Bernice didn't care—she needed a man for reasons other than money. Randell couldn't help her with those needs, and Bernice didn't need Randell around when he let it be known that he didn't like Nathaniel Lawson. He called Nathaniel an old slickster because he said that he was out to live off his sister. Wasn't that the pot calling the kettle black? Hadn't Randell taken the little bit of money she made for himself? He hadn't given a dang about her, Cora or Randie.

As for Bernice, other than a roof over her head, which she was renting, she didn't have a pot to piss in. At least Nathaniel made enough fixing on old cars and pickup trucks to get by on. That was something that a lot of menfolk around town didn't know how to do. Bernice was lucky to catch herself a man at all, as nasty as she was. Most likely, Randell was jealous he couldn't do the kind of work Nathaniel did, which was probably why he picked up and moved them out soon as Nathaniel moved in.

It was a blessing in disguise for Mozelle. She was glad to leave Bernice and Elberton behind, and happy to be close by her family again. The bad part was they didn't get their own place;

they moved back in with Alice. Alice and her husband were making do by selling vegetables.

It was Alice who told Mozelle that her mama had moved to North Carolina to live with Ruth and her family. It was Jim who told her how poor her mama was faring. Most days she was down with fever and infection. Although Mozelle wanted to go to her mama in Statesville, she couldn't afford to. She had no money, and she didn't want to be on the road trying to hitch a ride with eight-year-old Cora and one-year-old Randie. All she could do was call on the Lord. She prayed day and night that her mama wasn't suffering too badly.

Randell didn't like what he found in Royston—the same work conditions he left behind in Elberton. Everybody he used to know had gone up north to New York City or Detroit to find work, but Randell was sure that he could get a job in the steel mill in Jacksonville, especially since he had worked there before. That's when he started talking about leaving Georgia altogether.

Mozelle had no argument against moving to Alabama. Fact of the matter was, moving to Alabama meant that none of Randell's family would be there for him to move in on. She could finally have her own house. If there was work in the mill for her, too, it was all the more reason to go, but they couldn't afford to go right away, they had no money.

It took three months of doing odd jobs for pennies for Randell to get up the money for his train ticket. When he was ready to go, he went ahead, alone, to find a place for them to live. It was eight weeks before he sent her and Cora's train tickets. She didn't need a ticket for Randie. It was Mozelle's first time on a train as a real passenger. She was just as excited as Cora, except she didn't stay up on her knees most of the way with her nose pressed to the window. She sat like a lady was supposed to, prim and proper, looking out at the passing countryside. Randie slept all the way to Piedmont.

Carrying Randie and two small bundles of clothes, Mozelle stepped off the train behind Cora. Randell was nowhere to be seen. After four hours of sitting on the hard wooden bench inside the station house, she was worried that something terrible might have happened to him. She had no way of finding out if he was all right. It didn't help a bit that she and Cora both were hungry. Thank God Randie was still taking her milk. The darkness she saw through the window choked Mozelle with fear. What if Randell did not come? What was she going to do? She had no money to get back to Royston, no money to go on to Jacksonville, and no money to get a room in Piedmont. Oh, God. She had told Randell more than a handful of times that he could leave her. What if he had done just that? She looked down at Randie asleep in her arms. Cora was stretched out on the bench. What was she going to do? She couldn't feed her children. She didn't know anyone to go to.

"God, please, show me what to do," she prayed quietly to herself.

"Miss? We've noticed you sitting here for some time now. Can we help you?"

She opened her eyes and looked up. Standing before her were two women and a man. The three of them looked like they were wearing their Sunday-go-to-meeting clothes. The woman wearing a pearl necklace and matching earrings asked, "Is someone meeting you?"

Mozelle stared at the woman's jewelry. She had only seen something that pretty on the pastor's wife in Royston. She had long since dropped her own, so-called gold wedding band down the well at Bernice's house.

"Miss?" the man asked. "You waiting for someone?"

"Yessa. My husband, Randell Tate," she answered, pulling her eyes away from the jewelry.

"Did he say what time he would be here?"

"He was supposed to meet the train," she said, looking around the room, "but he ain't come yet."

"Perhaps he was detained unintentionally," the younger woman said.

Mozelle had never heard such fine talk from colored folk before, and for a minute, she was about to pretend that she knew what *detained* meant, but she realized that it might be too important a word to ignore. "What do *detained unintentionally* mean?"

"It means, perhaps something unavoidable, that he had no control over, got in the way of him getting here to meet you," the man answered.

"Oh," she said.

"Ma'am, my name is Miss Verna Poindexter," the younger woman said. "This is Mrs. Niecy Scott and Mr. Windom Butler."

"How do," she said. "U'm Mozelle Tate, and these here my girls, Cora and Randie."

"Mrs. Tate, we're members of the Rugged Cross Baptist Church here in Piedmont. We come here to meet the train to offer assistance to those getting off who might need our help," Mr. Butler said.

"That's right neighborly of y'all."

"Can we help you? Are you and your children hungry?" Mrs. Scott asked, watching Cora stir, beginning to wake up.

"If it ain't puttin' y'all out, we could use a bite to eat."

"It's our pleasure to share our blessing of God's bounty with you," Mr. Butler said.

"God bless y'all."

"After you eat, perhaps we can take you to your husband. Is he staying here in Piedmont?"

"I think he's up the road a piece in Jacksonville. He told me the train don't go to Jacksonville. That's how come I got off here."

"He's right. He might have been delayed on the road trying to get here," Miss Poindexter said. "We can put you and your children up for the night. In the morning we can drive you on to Jacksonville. It's not that far."

"I declare. That's right kind of y'all," Mozelle said, relieved. Inside she was thanking God for answering her prayers so quickly.

Mrs. Scott reached out to take Cora's hand. "Come, child," she said. "Mrs. Tate, where's your home?"

"Royston, Georgia."

"My people come from Atlanta," she said, helping Cora to stand.

Mr. Butler took the bundles while Mrs. Scott, holding on to

Cora's hand, led the way outside to the car. Mr. Butler drove them to Mrs. Scott's house. There they were fed fried chicken, collard greens, rice, and corn bread. There was sweet creamy banana pudding for dessert, and milk a plenty for Randie and Cora. Mozelle couldn't help but notice the little smile on Cora's lips the whole time she was eating. Eating good food and plenty of it was worth a smile; she smiled herself.

"Mrs. Scott, ma'am, you got any children?"

"I had a little girl. She died of consumption when she was two. It wasn't God's will that I have another child."

"U'm sorry," Mozelle said.

"Don't be. I'm all right with my God. We've talked. He's given me other blessings," she said, smiling.

Mozelle nodded in agreement. "Praise the Lord."

"Yes, praise the Lord," Mrs. Scott said. "Mrs. Tate, why don't we put your babies to bed? They're about to fall off."

Mrs. Scott took them to a spare bedroom where, together, she and Mozelle undressed Cora and Randie and put them to bed.

Looking around the white room, Mozelle was in awe. "Is you rich?"

"No, not at all. Me and my husband have land that we rent out well over twenty years now. My husband keeps a small country store in town. We've done well for ourselves, but we're not rich."

"You own this house, too?"

"Sure do," Mrs. Scott answered, tucking the covers around Cora.

Mozelle looked at the pretty white lace curtains at the three windows. "I declare. I ain't seen no colored folks do good like you in all my life,"

"Mrs. Tate, if you don't mind my asking, how old are you?"

"Twenty-six my last birthday."

"You're still young yet. In time, you can get all you want and more."

"I can't 'magine that."

"Imagine it, Mrs. Tate. You have to be able to imagine what you want before you can go after what you want."

"I ain't never heard that before."

"It's true. How do you know what you want if you don't put it in your mind first?"

"That right?"

"Sure is. Times are bad right now, but in time, Mrs. Tate, you'll see lots more colored folks owning their own land and doing well. When you get a chance, buy yourself a piece of land. Build yourself a house on your land for your children. That land is yours, not some landowner's somewhere. You see, Mrs. Tate, landowners can throw you off their land and out of their houses if you don't pay them their rent. You can live in their houses for fifty years, and they will still kick you out. All the money you paid out in those fifty years belongs to the landlord. You don't even own a handful of his dirt."

What Mrs. Scott said was true. "My daddy was a share-cropper."

"Then you know what I'm talking about."

"Yes, ma'am."

"Good. You see, Mrs. Tate, if you pay out money for fifty years for your own land, build on it, live on it, maybe even rent some of it out if you want, you can make money with your land. The land is yours. You are the landowner. What you see growing there is yours. Just pay your taxes every year, you'll be fine."

Mozelle was beginning to imagine herself a landowner. "U'm gon' own me a piece of land one day," she said, looking over at her sleeping children. She wanted for them all that she never had.

Long after Mrs. Scott left her alone, Mozelle lay nestled in the coziness of the clean-smelling soft bed next to Cora and Randie. It would be a blessing to be able to one day build a house on her own land. She didn't know how she would do it, but she felt that one day, with God's help, she would. When sleep claimed her completely, she dreamed that it had already come to be.

On the way to Jacksonville, in search of Randell, the realness of not owning her own land made her lose hope. She didn't see how she could ever get enough money to buy a piece of land. Right now, she only prayed that she could find Randell; that he had a place for them to stay. A roof over her head was all she could hope for. But after being in a colored person's house as nice as Mrs. Scott's, she knew that it was possible to live better, she just didn't know how to make it her reality. As a child in her daddy's sharecropper's shack, sleeping like a sardine in a can with eleven sisters and brothers in four beds; then living in a room in Randell's sisters' homes since she was fifteen, she wanted—no needed—another way to live out the rest of her life for herself and for her children. If it meant working harder to earn more money so that she could save just a penny of it toward buying her land, she would do that. If Randell didn't help, she would not beg him. She would do it alone.

By the time she stepped out of Mr. Butler's car in Jacksonville, she was determined to start her new life toward one end—owning her own land.

"Do you know where Mr. Tate is staying?" Mrs. Scott asked.

"No, ma'am, I don't," she answered, holding on to Randie who was trying to climb back into the car. Looking around the town, she scooped Randie up into her arms. If she hadn't traveled to get here, she would've sworn she was still in Royston. The air smelled the same, the stores looked the same, and the people looked no different from the folks back home. They looked just as poor.

"Perhaps we should ask someone if they know Mr. Tate," Mrs. Scott suggested.

"Somebody oughta know him," she said. "He been livin' in Jacksonville on and off 'bout twenty-five years."

"In that case, I'll ask in there," Mr. Butler said, going off toward the general store.

Mrs. Scott looked around. "I hope we didn't pass him on the road to Piedmont."

"I hope not, too," Mozelle said. "Though, if'n he here, could be he's workin' this time of day."

"Mama," Cora began, looking up at Mozelle sadly, "maybe Daddy don't want us here. That could be how come he ain't meet the train."

"Your daddy want us here, baby. He sent the tickets, didn't he?"

Cora looked down at the ground. "Yes, Mama," she said softly.

"Of course your daddy wants you here," Mrs. Scott said, patting Cora gently on the back. "Don't worry, dear, we'll find him. See, here comes Mr. Butler now."

Cora looked up. She didn't smile.

"One of the gentlemen in the store said we should check the cafe at the end of the road," he said, nodding in that direction.

"Cora, why don't we walk down there and see," Mrs. Scott said.

"If'n y'all don't mine," Mozelle said, looking at Mrs. Scott. "I'll go take a look-see myself." If Randell was in there drunk, she didn't want them to see him act out.

"Oh, of course. We'll wait here."

Cora started off behind Mozelle.

"No, baby, you stay here with Mrs. Scott and Mr. Butler. Mama's comin' right back."

Cora looked as if she was about to cry, but she stopped walking. Mrs. Scott gently pulled her back, and with one hand on her shoulder, began gently twirling one of her long braids around her fingers.

Still carrying Randie on her hip, Mozelle walked off down the road toward the cafe. She wanted Randell to be there because she didn't want to hold Mr. Butler and Mrs. Scott any longer than she had to. On the other hand, she prayed that he was at work.

Pushing open the door, she stepped inside the cafe. She looked around the room for a minute before she lay eyes on him. He was sitting on a stool hugged up with a big-butt woman who was giggling loudly. Randell was kissing and nibbling on her ear.

Her own ears got hot. "Randell Tate!"

He jumped though he did not turn around

"I shoulda known what you'd be doin'. You just ain't no

good."

Randell turned slowly, just his head, and looked over his right shoulder right at Mozelle.

The woman nudged Randell. "Who's that?"

He faced forward.

Mozelle shifted Randie on her hip. She walked over to Randell. Standing behind him, she fixed her eyes on the woman. "U'm his wife."

The woman shoved Randell, almost pushing him off the stool. "You lowlife bastard. You told me you wasn't married."

Randell picked up his glass. He gulped down the shot of whiskey that was left.

"Randell, say hey to your baby girl," Mozelle said.

Randie took one long look at the back of Randell's head before she threw herself against Mozelle's chest, clinging to her neck.

"You know, Mrs. Tate, U'm tired of meeting up with triflin' lowlifes," the woman said, sliding down off the stool. "U'm glad U'm not his wife."

Randell watched the woman's swaying hips as she walked over to another stool farther down and sat down next to another man. Randell smirked at her when she glanced back at him and rolled her eyes. He only looked at Mozelle when she jabbed him in the back with her finger.

"Don't do that," he snarled, adjusting his tie.

"You ain't never gon' do right, is you?"

"That's what you say," he answered coolly.

"U'm sick of this, Randell. You was suppose to meet us in Piedmont."

"You got here, didn't you."

"Not on our own!" she snapped. "Randell, you shoulda been at the train to meet us."

He got up off the stool and started for the door. "I forgot and that's that. C'mon outta here, embarrassing me in front of my friends," he said, leaving the cafe.

For the first time, she noticed that everyone in the cafe was looking at her. Not one of the three women there looked as bad as she did. She couldn't believe that women put on good clothes to come to a cafe to sit up with a bunch of drinking men. But, then, the truth was, she did know why these women came to the cafe. They came for the men and what they could get out of them. This wasn't the place for her. Mozelle switched Randie to her other hip and backed out of the cafe. She stepped outside just as Randell was starting to cross the road.

"Randell!"

"Come on!" he shouted back.

She stayed put. "Randell!"

Angrily, he whirled around. "What?"

"I got to get Cora and our stuff."

"I ain't got no time to be fooling around with you, Mozelle. Hurry up."

"Then come help me!"

Randell huffed impatiently. "Woman, I ain't got time for this. Where's your stuff?"

Mozelle glared at him. "You look a here, Randell Tate. I come here 'cause you said we could start a new life. A better life. Now, we in this together. I ain't gon' beg you to be nice to me."

"Woman, I ain't got time for your whining. All I need to know is where your stuff is, nothing more."

God forgive her. Looking at Randell standing in the middle of the road, Mozelle found herself wishing that a car would come down the road and run him down. Better still, she wished that he'd fall through a hole in the ground never to be seen again. Either way, she'd be free.

"Randell, one of these here days, U'ma get free of you and—"

"Woman, you ain't never going nowhere, and no other man is gonna want your country ass, either."

"Your friend, Walt Williams, wanted me."

Randell began walking back toward Mozelle. "What you talking about?"

"Mrs. Tate, is this your husband?" Mr. Butler asked. He and Mrs. Scott were walking up to Mozelle. Mr. Butler was carrying her bundles and Mrs. Scott was holding onto Cora's hand.

Randell folded his arms high across his chest and looked down at Mr. Butler.

"Yessa. This my husband, Randell Tate," Mozelle said, praying that neither Mr. Butler nor Mrs. Scott had seen or heard Randell show out, or even overheard her being ugly.

"Glad to meet you, Mr. Tate," Mr. Butler said, extending his hand to Randell. "You have a right nice family."

Randell seemed reluctant, at first, but he finally shook Mr. Butler's hand.

"Hey, Daddy," Cora said, shyly looking up at Randell.

Randell took the bundle out of Mr. Butler's hands. "We gotta get going," he said. He turned and walked off across the road without a thank you to Mr. Butler or Mrs. Scott, or a glance at Cora.

Mozelle gently stroked Cora's cheek. She hated that Randell always ignored Cora, making her child sadder than she was. Mrs. Scott and Mr. Butler both had puzzled looks on their faces when Mozelle looked timidly back at them. She felt so ashamed. "Thank you for being kind to me and my children."

"It was our pleasure, but are you going to be all right," Mrs. Scott asked. "Is there something we can do to—"

"Mozelle!"

"U'm gon' be jest fine, Mrs. Scott. Mr. Butler, thank you for bringin' us all this way. God bless you."

"You're quite welcome, Mrs. Tate, and God bless you and your children."

"Thank you, sa. Say bye, Cora," Mozelle said.

"Bye," Cora said, softly.

"Thank you," Mozelle said again, rushing across the road behind Randell, trying to catch up to him. She didn't want to cry, so she didn't look back at the folks that had treated her so kind. She didn't want to see in their eyes what they were thinking about her having a husband like Randell Tate. She was ashamed of him, and she was ashamed of herself for letting his smile take away her dreams.

Randell took them to a single room in a boardinghouse. The four of them slept in a double bed after eating a meal of neck bones, black-eyed peas, and corn bread. Randell never did ask her again about Walt Williams. In the morning, they took a bus up to Gadsden. It didn't make sense to her that he was going to be working in Jacksonville but living in Gadsden. Randell would not answer her when she asked him how come they couldn't stay in Jacksonville with him. In fact, he acted like he was mad at her for even coming to Alabama and had very few words to say to her. Nothing was any different between them.

Eleven

Five dollars a week paid for their two rooms in the back of Kenny and Elvira Singletary's house on Sixth Street. Randell paid up two weeks rent, just in case he might not be able to come up with the money one week. The Singletary's granddaughter, Hannah, was company for Cora while Cora looked after Randie. Mozelle went out every day looking for work. Being new in town and not knowing a living soul in Gadsden, she had no luck finding a wage-earning job. After a while, she fell back on the work her mama used to do—washing clothes. Like in Royston, white folks in Gadsden with a dime to spare wanted somebody else to wash their clothes. Thank God, or else Mozelle would not have had any money at all. She scrubbed big bundles of clothes for fifty cents a bundle, and she was grateful for that. Mrs. Singletary was good enough to let her use her black iron pot and clotheslines out back.

Randell took the bus every day back to Jacksonville to work in the steel mill. With the little money he gave Mozelle and the pennies she earned, she was barely able to feed herself, Cora, and Randie. That's why she cried when she realized eight weeks later that she was pregnant again. God knows she didn't need another baby. She had no way of making a good life for the two children she had. With another mouth to feed, she didn't see how she was ever going to get the money to buy her land.

Essie was born in the spring of 1941 when Cora was nine years old and could help Mozelle out most by tending to her sisters. Of course Randell was his usual denying self and went off to Jacksonville. He said he had a job painting a house and didn't know when he'd be back. After a week had come and gone,

Mozelle figured that he was probably doing more than painting. After the second week, she was sure he was gone for good. No word came from him or about him. As much as she wanted him gone, she needed him to pay the rent. It angered her that it didn't matter to Randell that she couldn't pay the five-dollar rent, or feed her babies. With the passing days went the food. That's when, like a beggar, she walked miles to knock at the doors of any white family that she could find, asking if she could wash their clothes. No one turned her down, and she was grateful for that. She scrubbed so many clothes, her raw, dry hands cracked and bled. She walked everywhere, not one nickel went on bus fare. Instead of money, from two of the white ladies she washed for, she got a five-pound sack of flour, a dozen eggs, a bag of black-eyed peas, and a sack of cornmeal. It was worth more than the dollar she would have been paid.

As much as she could, she avoided running into the Singletarys. On bare feet, she crept around the house thinking that if they didn't hear her, they wouldn't think about her and the money she owed. But by the end of the fourth week, she couldn't keep Essie and Randie quiet. If an empty belly can make a grown man cry, Lord knows an empty belly was what was making her babies holler. Randie and Essie cried an awful lot, while Cora, use to being hungry, tried to comfort them both. The shrill crying was a constant reminder to Mr. Singletary that he wasn't getting paid his rent. Mozelle could hear him fussing at Mrs. Singletary about wanting to put her out, but Mrs. Singletary would say, "The Lord will rebuke us if we put those babies outdoors." Being a God-fearing man was the only thing that kept Mr. Singletary from putting them out. But he was not neighborly when he saw her. He stopped speaking altogether. Again, Mozelle felt ashamed but there was nothing she could do about paying Mr. Singletary his rent. She kept apologizing to Mrs. Singletary for not having the rent money, but to her own ears, it was annoying to hear over and over. Plenty of days she wished she could simply cry and be taken care of like a baby. Then, too, there were plenty of days she wished that she was fifteen again.

When Mrs. Singletary finally told her that she could stay

until Randell got back, but then they would have to move out, she knew then that it was only a matter of days before Mr. Singletary put his foot down and put her outdoors. She was awake most nights, unable to sleep, praying that Randell would come back with money in his pockets. Five weeks after he left, he came back.

"I'm home!"

Out in the backyard, bent over the scrub board, Mozelle heard Randell's voice. She kept scrubbing on the white sheet in her hands.

Randell came out of the house and eased up behind Mozelle and slipped his arms around her waist. "Hey, baby girl," he said, kissing Mozelle at the nape of her neck.

"Don't *hey* me," she said, pushing him away and showing him Essie, asleep on an old blanket on the ground. "Say *hey* to your baby."

"Don't get me started," he said, going back indoors.

Even from the back she could see that Randell was wearing new clothes and new shoes. She quickly dried her hands on the front of her dress and followed behind him. He was opening up the large brown sack he had set on the bed. As usual, it was his clothes that concerned him, not his children. He didn't look at Essie when he was outdoors, neither did he ask where Cora or Randie were or even if they were all right. He carried the sack over to his trunk in the corner of the room. She watched him carefully lay his new clothes out like they were as fine as gold. He made her skin crawl.

"Randell, is that all you care 'bout?"

He ignored her.

"You been gone for five weeks. Where you been?"

"I told you were I was going. That's where I was."

She rushed at him. "You a selfish man, Randell Tate. While you was in Jacksonville hoin' and buyin' fancy clothes, we was starvin' and gettin' ready to be put outdoors."

"You know how to wash clothes, don't you?"

She gritted her teeth. "That's what I been doin'. What money I made wasn't enough, and you know it. You makes good enough money to feed your babies and keep a roof over they heads. We got to leave here because you ain't paid a cent of rent. Cora need special shoes to walk right, but you go buy clothes for yourself so you can look pretty for your hoes. I don't even own a pretty dress to my name, just three rags to cover my body."

Randell loosened his tie. "Woman, if you don't get from up in my face about my money, I'll break your goddamn neck."

She gritted her teeth harder. She knew good and well that it wasn't fitting for them to be fighting in Mrs. Singletary's house. She lowered her voice. "I hate you."

Randell sneered. "See, you the reason I stay gone. Everytime I come home, you carry on about what I ain't doing. That's how come I don't do nothing. What the hell, I can't never satisfy you anyhow. Maybe if you didn't bitch so much, I'd stay home more and feed you and your ugly babies."

Clinching her fists, she could feel her chest tighten. Essie was a beautiful baby, just as beautiful as Cora and Randie had been. How could Randell call his own ugly?

"Randell," she said sweetly, "I got somethin' for you."

"You ain't got nothing for me."

"Yessa, I do," she said, sauntering over to the stove. She picked up the iron skillet.

Randell watched Mozelle pick up the skillet. He snatched his tie from around his neck and started wrapping it around his right hand. He then balled his fist up around it. They faced off.

She was breathing deeply. She tightened her grip on the skillet. "I ain't the cause of you being triflin', Randell. You tri-flin' 'cause you was weaned by the devil hisself. It's in your blood."

"Heifer, you talking about my mother?"

"If she was the devil, I am."

Randell clinched his teeth. "Don't you talk about my moth-er, my mother is dead. You—"

"Any man who talk ugly about his own ain't got nothin' but the devil in 'em. You ain't no good, Randell."

Raising his wrapped fist, Randell sneered, "I am going to beat your black ass."

Mozelle swallowed to wet her suddenly dry throat. She hefted the heavy skillet. She could feel the years of crusty rust on the handle of the black skillet. She wondered if she bursted Randell's skull with it and got blood all over it, would she ever want to cook in it again?

They glared at each other. Neither one flinched.

"Mama!" Cora said, rushing into the room from the front of the house. Randie toddled close behind her. Cora stopped dead in her tracks when she saw Randell. She looked at his raised fists. Her eyes cut to the raised skillet in Mozelle's hand. She ran to Mozelle.

"Mama," she said, tugging on Mozelle's arm, trying to pull her out of the room, while tears rolled down her cheeks. "Miss Singletary want you."

"Tell her U'ma be there in a little bit."

"Mama, she want you *now*. Please, Mama, c'mon now."

Mozelle could feel the trembling in Cora's hands on her arm. She glimpsed the tears streaming down Cora's cheeks. It made her feel bad that once again Cora was witness to their fighting. She didn't want this to keep being a part of her children's lives. Glaring at Randell, trying to tell him with her eyes that he better not try her, she lowered her arm and started backing slowly out of the room. She kept her eyes fixed on him until she couldn't see him anymore.

Randell dropped his fists. "Crazy heifer." He took out a cigarette, lit it, and moseyed on out the back door.

Out in the front room Cora was still holding on to Mozelle's arm. "Mama, please don't fight Daddy no mo'. He might hurt you."

"Don't worry, baby. Your daddy ain't never gon' hurt me," she said. "Go look after your sisters. U'm gon' go see what Mrs. Singletary want."

She found Mrs. Singletary sitting in her front room. "You want me, ma'am?"

"I know you having a hard time, Mozelle, and I don't want to add to your troubles, but I can't have arguing in my house."

"U'm sorry, ma'am. We won't be arguin' no mo'. It won't

happen again."

"That's just it, Mozelle. There won't be another time for it to happen again. You ain't paid rent for some time now."

"I know, ma'am, but my husband's back now, and he—"

"Mozelle, Mr. Singletary want y'all to move on. He don't let tenants stay on this long that ain't paid rent."

It wasn't like she didn't know that she was going to have to move on, Mozelle just didn't think it would be the very moment Randell came back. "We don't have nowhere to go."

"U'm sorry, Mozelle," Mrs. Singletary said sadly.

She had to try. "You been good folks for lettin' me and my children stay 'til now. U'ma be gone befo' the end of the week."

"U'm sorry but you got to leave today."

Mozelle's heart sank. "Mrs. Singletary, U'm sorry for not being able to pay Mr. Singletary his rent. We'll be gone in a little bit, we ain't got much to pack. U'm sorry," she said again, rushing out of the room before she cried.

Within twenty minutes her three bundles were packed, including the wet sheets. Her children were ready, too. They sat on the bed, waiting. She wasn't waiting for Randell to come back, she was trying to figure out where to go. With no money, the only place that was free was the roadside under a tree beneath God's darkening sky. Oh, why hadn't she listened? Her life wasn't supposed to be this hard. Randell promised her he'd be good to her, he promised her a house. His promises were lies.

Cora touched Mozelle lightly on her thigh. "Mama, I can wash clothes."

"Cora, our clothes already washed."

"Not our clothes, Mama, white folks' clothes."

For the tiniest minute she looked into the eyes of her sweet big-hearted daughter. Cora had her daddy's eyes and much of his looks. Thank God, she didn't have his ways. Cora didn't have a selfish bone in her little body. She would give her last bite of bread to Randie; and as hard and as painful as it was for her to draw up her hands, she was willing to scrub clothes.

"Mama, I can give you the money to pay the rent, then Daddy don't gotta come back. We won't need him no mo'."

Mozelle's heavy heart melted. God truly blessed her with Cora. Putting her arm around Cora's small shoulders, she hugged her tightly and kissed her on the forehead. Then she quickly stood up. "Thank you, baby, but U'ma take care of us. Don't you worry."

It wasn't right that her child was willing to do what her daddy wouldn't. Mozelle looked over at Randell's steamer trunk filled with his fancy clothes and shoes. The more she looked at it the madder she got. He treated his precious clothes better than he treated her or his children. He always pressed his white shirts and creased his britches himself because he said she didn't do it right. That was just fine. Ironing was one less thing she had to do for him, especially since she hated his clothes. She felt like setting fire to them. Maybe she could do that right. She went over to the trunk. For one long minute, she stood over it. The idea of setting Randell's clothes on fire got better and better. Suddenly, she grabbed one of the leather side handles and dragged the trunk across the room toward the back door.

Cora slid off the bed. "Want me to help you, Mama?"

"No, baby. You stay here and look after your sisters. U'ma be out in the backyard."

Grunting, Mozelle dragged the trunk out into the yard. She got her breath and started back into the house for the matches.

"I'll take the trunk," Randell said behind Mozelle, startling her. "You carry the rest."

Mozelle, hid her hands behind her back. "Where we goin'?" she asked, trying to sound normal even though her heart was thumping.

"We got a room over on Spruce Street on the west side."

"We needs more then a room. We got three children now. I don't want to live crowded up like in my daddy's house."

"We can't get more than a room right now, Mozelle. Let's go," Randell said, picking up his trunk.

"We could get bigger if'n you didn't look out for jest yourself," she said, not knowing for sure if he heard her or not. "Cora, you take Randie's hand and that little bundle for Mama."

"Yes, Mama," Cora said, picking up the bundle and taking

Randie's hand. The bundle was about as big as Cora was as she dragged it behind her out the door.

Mozelle tied Essie to her chest with a threadbare sheet wrapped around her own body before she picked up the two larger bundles. They left without saying good-bye to Mrs. Singletary or her children. Mozelle was too embarrassed.

The Hamiltons on Spruce Street were old; old as anyone Mozelle had ever seen. Mr. Hamilton's black skin looked like scraggly old hide, while Mrs. Hamilton was bent over and skinny and looked like she might break in two. They were renting out their large single room on the side of their three-room house to make ends meet.

After they were settled in, Mozelle pulled Randell outdoors. She didn't know how much the rent was, and she didn't want to know. She just wanted to know that it was going to be paid.

"Soon as I get me a job that pay me enough money to feed my children and pay my rent, you can stay gone for good."

"I told you, I ain't going nowhere."

"Yes, you is—someday. Until then, you best pay the rent like you is suppose to."

"Gal, you don't tell me what I best do."

"I done said all U'm I gon' say," she said, turning abruptly and going back into house, leaving Randell outside cussing and calling her ugly names. She didn't care, as long as the rent got paid.

A year and a half since coming to Gadsden, she finally got a job as a cook at the Country Kitchen Cafe. Her pay was nine dollars a week. It was more money than she ever made at any one time. The first thing she did with her pay was buy food and a secondhand dress for herself and clothes for her children from the church rummage sale. She wanted to buy Cora a pair of special shoes to support her crippled feet, but she couldn't afford the seven dollars they would cost brand-new. It would have helped if she could have taken leftovers from the cafe once in a while, but Mr. Peterson took them himself—it was his cafe. Besides that, he counted every bean, every biscuit, every grain of rice, and knew whose mouth it went into. That is, except what went into Mozelle's mouth. When the smell of the cooking food overwhelmed her senses, and no one was watching, she would jam a spoonful of whatever she was cooking into her mouth to calm the nagging hunger pangs in her stomach. She burned her tongue so often at first, it was stinging all the time. After a while, like her fingers from turning frying chicken and pork chops, her tongue grew numb and indifferent to heat. Most days, she left work, well fed. She was even starting to put on weight.

She thanked God for her job and for Mrs. Hamilton for looking after her girls while she worked.

A month later Randell left his job in Jacksonville for a job in the pipe factory in Gadsden. He never would say why he changed jobs, he just did. After his work was done at the factory, he took on painting work on the side. Right away, he got a big painting job out at the Trueblood plantation. He was painting the whole house so his pockets were always full, yet he gave Mozelle not a dime to buy food but the rent he did pay. He could have at least bought shoes for Cora, but he looked at Mozelle like she had lost her mind when she asked for the money for the shoes. But that was all right. She didn't get upset. If Randell wasn't willing to do right on his own, she was going to make him do right against his will. A week after he started painting the Trueblood house, she called on Mrs. Trueblood. Of course, she made sure, first, that Randell was through for the day. She hid down the road behind a big maple and watched him go by. He was way out of sight when she went and knocked on the freshly painted white back door.

"Please, ma'am, U'm sorry to bother you. U'm the painter's wife."

"Well, he's gone for the day."

"Yes, I know. If you'll pardon me, ma'am, I needs to ask somethin' of you for my child."

"Is there trouble with your child?" Mrs. Trueblood asked, stepping out of the house onto the back porch. She left the door behind her open.

"Yessum. My Cora need special shoes so she can walk better. Her feet hurt bad sometime 'less I wrap them tight with rags. When she was littler that helped a bit, but now she be ten soon, and the bigger she grow, the harder it be for her to walk. It hurt my heart to see her hurtin' so."

"Well, what is it you want me to do?" Mrs. Trueblood asked, leading Mozelle over to the side of the porch where she sat down on one of the three large white wooden chairs. She did not offer Mozelle a seat.

Mozelle stood. "Well, ma'am, the shoes cost seven dollars. I ain't askin' you to buy them," she said quickly, "I know my husband earns enough money paintin' your house to pay for the shoes, but he won't."

"Why not?"

"It ain't important to him, ma'am. That's jest how he is. I want my husband to pay for Cora's shoes, but I needs to get the money from him befo' he get his pay. Though it don't need to be all at once."

"Oh, I see," Mrs. Trueblood said, thoughtfully.

"Ma'am, I don't mean for you to tell a tale, but if'n you could tell my husband that his pay is one dollar less, he won't miss the dollar he don't get."

Mrs. Trueblood was pensive.

Mozelle could see the uncertainty in Mrs. Trueblood's face. Maybe she was wrong to come. She started backing away. "Ma'am, U'm sorry to bother you with my trouble. I won't—"

"Well, I guess I can take a dollar from your husband's pay every week until I take seven dollars. I don't see no harm."

Mozelle stopped. She couldn't believe it. "Yessum, that'll help."

Mrs. Trueblood stood. "I'll tell your husband that I can only pay him twenty-four dollars a week for a while. I'm sure he won't quit over a dollar less."

"Thank you, ma'am," Mozelle said gratefully. Again starting to back away.

"Any time I can help, I'll be glad to."

"Thank you, ma'am." Mozelle went home with a lighter heart.

Mrs. Trueblood kept her word. The first week Randell complained about the missing dollar from his wages, Mozelle acted like she was concerned, all the while wishing that she could get a dollar or two of his pay every week. Between his two jobs, Randell was making lots of money. He kept paying the rent on time and surprise of surprises, he bought mints and chewing gum home for Cora and Randie. Still, he wouldn't spend a cent on real food, yet he ate just as much, if not more, of the food she bought. Every now and then when he wanted it, he bought a quart of milk or orange juice. The problem was, he drank every drop himself while Cora and Randie watched. That was a mean thing to do, but Randell didn't see anything wrong with it.

"You a mean, selfish old man," Mozelle said, swollen with anger.

"Woman, leave me alone."

"How can you drink orange juice in front of your children and not give them a drop?"

"Look, I pay the rent, and that's enough. I ain't about to kill myself trying to feed nobody but myself."

"I don't know how a man that ain't got no heart can make babies. Them your children!"

"That's what you say," he said snidely, lighting up a cigarette. "I say, mama's baby, daddy's maybe."

She wanted to smash the lit end of the cigarette in his face. "U'm tired of you callin' me a hoe. One of these days—"

"Save your breath," he said, getting up and walking out of the house.

Grimacing, she balled up her fists and shook them at the door. She prayed that God would let her live to see one of "these days." Randell had to reap what he was sowing. It wasn't right that a mean, selfish man could do such ugly things to his children and live, while good folk dropped dead every day. Randell went through life like he had not a care in the world. At the end of each week when he got paid, he sometimes went back to Jacksonville or somewhere in Gadsden she didn't know about. On Sunday afternoons when he came back, he was usually crying broke with his lying self, and cussing at her for no good reason except to be nasty.

Of course, she knew that he had been laid up with some woman who he spent his money on. Day-to-day, walking on the road, she never knew when she was looking into the face of one of his whores, which irritated her because more than likely his whore would be better dressed than she was. That was bad enough but she was use to not having much of anything, but it bothered her that she didn't have a brassiere. She didn't feel good about not wearing a brassiere. The last one she had, she had washed and worn until it was threadbare and stringy. She had held it together with safety pins and knots tied into the shoulder straps. In the end, it fell apart like dried-out paper. When she was a young girl, she could go without a brassiere. But unlike when she was a young girl when her titties were small and firm, they now hung heavy and low almost to her stomach. It shamed her to know that they moved when she walked and that people could see them move. Truth be told, she was in need of everything to clothe herself properly. She had worn holes in her old black work shoes from walking the four miles to and from work. Now that she was grown, she couldn't go barefooted. Mornings before she left home and afternoons before she left work, she had to cut pieces of pasteboard to put inside her shoes. If she could have worn a pair of Randell's six pairs of shoes, she would have. They were much too big for her. What she needed for herself would have to wait; what her children needed came first.

Still, as full grown as she was, she had only three dresses to work in, and only one good dress to wear to church. She had taken to going to three different churches on alternating Sundays so that no one church congregation saw her in the same dress two Sundays straight. Of course that wasn't something Randell had to bother himself with, he took his well-dressed hypocritical self to Mt. Sinai on the Sundays when he happened to be home and he wasn't hung-over from the night before. Reverend Witherspoon thought Randell was the very pillar of the church. That's because Randell always put paper money in the offering plate. He was probably the only man in church who could do that; most every-body else put in change—probably because they took care of their families first. It had been a long while since Mozelle had been to Mt. Sinai; it had been too hard to say amen whenever Reverend Witherspoon praised Randell for being a good and righteous man. Made her sick to her stomach. When she saw the two of them talking like they were buddies, she made up her mind to not come back to Mt. Sinai. For all she knew, Reverend Witherspoon was running around town whoring with Randell. She figured if Reverend Witherspoon was a spiritual man, he should have recognized that Randell was not. Her mama use to say that the biggest hypocrite in church was the preacher. Until now, Mozelle didn't know what that meant.

Seven weeks later she went back to Mrs. Trueblood and picked up the seven dollars. Cora's special shoes were ready two weeks later. Cora had to get use to their stiffness, and while she still walked a little awkwardly, the shoes worked better than rags. They were made a size bigger to allow Cora's feet to grow, but Mozelle was already thinking about when she'd have to buy another pair. As it was, it worried her that Randie might well need special shoes, too. She was barely three, and although her little feet were not as bad off as Cora's, some of her toes and a few of her fingers were a little crooked, and she was knock-kneed. Thank God she was walking okay.

Many a day, Mozelle wished that she could live her life over. She would have lived it as she dreamed it as a child—as an old maid, free of men and children. Now that she had children, she loved them more than her own self. It was for them that her eyes opened and that her feet hit the floor every morning, but she'd be lying if she didn't admit, at least to herself, that she wished that they had never been born—not into the life she was giving them. The fact that she had not been able to provide better for them worried her most, and the way her life was going, she didn't think she ever could.

Twelve

1942

There was a war going on and she was pregnant again. Lord knows, if there was a way she could stop getting pregnant, she would gladly do whatever it took. Randell Junior came along a year and a half after Essie, and Mozelle cried as much for herself as for her baby. Her eleven-dollar-a-week wages were going to be spread even thinner. Randell didn't deny his son. In fact, he was the one who said that his son ought to be named after him. That didn't set too good with Cora. She started right off calling Junior, Brother. It stuck.

Mozelle had no stomach for Randell's pleasuring, but she did as she was supposed to. As much as she tried to stop laying down with him altogether, making up excuses when she could, she still needed him to pay the rent. She never gave in easy, though. Randell would pester her and not let her sleep until her thighs reluctantly opened. Sadly, before, during, and just after he pleasured her was the only time Randell was halfway decent to her. That's when he promised to buy her land. That's when she allowed herself to be lulled into a false sense of hope that he would do right. But always, the harsh reality that comes with daylight hardened Randell's heart and cleared the cobwebs out of Mozelle's head. She got where she didn't bother to remind Randell of what he promised; he always denied that he ever made such a promise.

Randell knew that she couldn't leave him or put him out, so he kept whoring around. Long as he paid the rent, she didn't much care. The nights he stayed out no longer bothered her, in fact, that's when she slept best. That is until a barrage of knocks at the door in the middle of the night awakened her out of a deep sleep. The woman at the door looked scared; she looked beat up. Mozelle did not know her.

"Miss Tate, you gotta come and get Randell befo' my husband kill him!"

"Let him," Mozelle said, trying to close the door in the woman's swollen, bruised face.

Sticking her foot in the door to keep it open, the woman pleaded, "Please, you gotta come. Randell is tore-down drunk. My husband gon' kill him for sure."

"Good. Now get your foot out my door befo' I break it."

"Mama," Cora said from behind Mozelle, "I'll tend to the babies."

Mozelle looked back at Cora's sad puppy-dog eyes. No matter that Randell did not do for her, no matter that Randell did not claim her, Cora did not want anyone to kill her daddy. Mozelle didn't feel that way, but to put Cora's mind at ease, she quickly put her clothes back on. For good measure, she slid Randell's straight razor into her pocket before she rushed out of the house. When they got to the woman's house, Randell was cussing and swinging at the woman's husband—a man equal in size—with one hand and trying to pull up his britches with the other hand. Randell's shirt was half on, his britches kept falling down around his knees, and there was blood on Randell's face and hands. His eyes were swollen almost shut. The woman's husband's face didn't have a mark on it.

Mozelle took hold of Randell's arm and tried to pull him out of the house.

He pushed her off him. He swung at her.

Mozelle ducked. "Randell, you ain't that drunk. You bet' not hit me," she warned, grabbing onto his arm again.

Randell jerked his arm free. "Woman, don't be pulling on me! I ain't no horse."

"Randell, I ain't got time to be messin' with you. Let's go."

"I don't need you to take me nowhere. I can get home on

my own." Bending down, Randell pulled up his britches and fumbled to zip them up. Mozelle slapped his hand aside and zipped them up herself. Randell stood swaying, squinting down at her like he was trying to focus.

"If I catch him with my wife again," the man said, "U'ma kill him." He looked over to where his wife was squeezed up into a corner of the room. "U'm gon' beat your black ass."

"Baby, U'm sorry. I didn't mean—"

The man rushed at his wife, scaring her. She shrieked. He grabbed up a fistful of her dress at the neck. "Emma Jean, shut your lying mouth! I oughta put my foot up your ass. No. I oughta put you out my house on your ass. Woman, how you do another man in my bed?"

The woman hushed up tight as a clam though her eyes were wild with fear.

Mozelle couldn't tell by Emma Jean's frantic eyes which was more frightening to her—being put outdoors or getting her behind beat.

"Lady," the man said, talking to Mozelle but looking at his wife, "get that junkyard dog out of my house. *Now.*"

"U'ma do that, Mister. But next time, jest kill him. You'd be doin' me a favor," she said, wanting to get out of there herself. She hated that she had to be there at all. The room smelled of anger, blood, sweat, and musky sex. She was disgusted. No, she was never going to apologize for Randell. He was dead wrong for laying up with the man's wife in the man's own bed, just like this Emma Jean was wrong to lay up with him. They were both low. Funny thing was, Emma Jean was the whore that Randell accused her of being. Lord, if she could kill Randell herself and live with it and be right with God, she would.

"If he stay in my sight a minute longer, I jest might kill him," the man said.

Mozelle snatched Randell by the arm and started pulling him toward the door.

"What you doing? Let go of me!"

Her hold on him tightened. "Randell, if you know what's good for you, you'd get your drunk tail on home."

"I ain't goin' home 'til U'm good 'n ready," he slurred. He lurched forward, falling against Mozelle, knocking her off balance. She quickly steadied herself. Randell seemed to notice her for the first time. "Just a doggone minute! Mozelle, didn't I tell you you bet' not come after me ever again? You a hardheaded woman. My mama said a hardhead make a soft ass. U'ma whop your hardheaded ass." He drew back his fist to hit her.

Mozelle whipped out the straight razor and dragged it across Randell's naked chest. She didn't cut him deep, but blood poured out before Randell realized that he was cut.

Emma Jean screamed. "You cut him!"

"You cut me!" Randell shrieked, holding on to his chest with both his hands.

From where she stood, Emma Jean searched around the room until she saw what she wanted. She started to go to the chair for the white towel draped on the back. Her husband grabbed her and shoved her so hard that she was thrown into the chair. She and the chair both hit the floor.

"Stay your ass away from him," the man snarled. He then turned to Randell. "I hope he die."

"U'm bleedin'! U'm gon' die!"

Mozelle pushed Randell, stumbling and clutching his chest, out of the front door into the moonlit night. "Randell, you fifty-one years old 'n you goin' around actin' like a wild dog in heat," she said, pocketing the razor.

"U'ma kill you!" he said, turning on her.

She yanked out the razor. It felt sticky in her hand. When she had brought it with her, she didn't know whom she would have to protect herself from. She should have known that the only threat to her life always came from the man she married.

Glimpsing the razor in her hand, Randell backed up but he looked steadily into Mozelle's face. Whatever he saw there, made him turn away from her and walk off. He stumbled home, crying that she cut him and that he was going to die. He didn't. For two days he stayed in bed whining about it though. Mozelle figured it wasn't that bad or he would have died and freed her. She would make do. If she had to work from the time the sun came up until the moment the moon waned, she would. She'd had enough.

To spite her, Randell stopped paying rent but he wouldn't leave. She tried to find more work, but couldn't. She couldn't pay the full rent with what she was earning and keep her children fed, too, so three weeks later they were put outdoors again. But as she expected, Randell didn't much like being outdoors himself, so he searched all afternoon and well past sundown for a place. They made their way in the dark over to Willow Street. This time it was two rooms they unpacked in. In two years they had lived in six different places in somebody else's house. She was tired of being in somebody else's house, always being put out because of Randell's trifling ways. She might've been better off if he had been able to go fight in the war. At least his pay would have come every month, and she would not have had to put up with him. Too bad, at fifty-one, he was too old to join the Army, though he was not too old to get a good job. He left the pipe factory and went to work for Goodyear.

Randell's pay was better but his attitude wasn't. Holding the rent money over her head, he started demanding that she have water already hot for him in the washtub for his bath when he got in and his dinner on the table. After working in the cafe all day, she wanted to be able to take a bath, dress up, and go somewhere to sit up, too—or in Randell's case, lay up with people and while away the evening hours. In all her life, Mozelle had never been able to while away even a minute of her time. When she came home, she had to cook and feed her children and Randell, too. He never ate when the food was ready. He'd come in late and make her get up out of bed to heat up his food again. That always irked her because she was bone-tired as it was. Some nights they argued about it. That was, until she got tired of arguing and took to leaving the food in a pot sitting in the ashes. That didn't work out but a day. Randell wanted her to get up and serve the food to him. Most nights she did it so as not to wake the children; other times she did it because it was easier than not.

If it wasn't for Cora, Mozelle didn't know how she would have made it from day to day. Sweet as a baby lamb, Cora never whined about helping out with the babies. Instinctively, Cora did what had to be done. If she could have suckled the babies, Cora probably would have done that, too. There were times Mozelle wished that she could have sent Cora to school, but she couldn't afford the pencil and paper, and Cora's clothes were too raggedy. The threadbare cotton dresses she wore weren't pretty, but again Cora didn't complain. That's why, when Cora turned eleven, Mozelle took the little change she had set aside for a rainy day and bought flour, sugar, milk, and eggs to make pan-fried sugar cookies, like her mama used to. The sparkle in Cora's eyes, the smile on her lips when she took her first bite were well worth it. Mozelle's eyes watered.

"Thank you, Mama," Cora said, hugging her.

Mozelle kissed her child on the cheek and hugged her tight. If she could have given Cora the world, she would have. The door opened, ending their embrace. Randell came into the room. He looked tired.

"You early," she said.

He glanced at her and nodded.

"Hey, Daddy," Cora said, smiling.

Randell didn't bother to look Cora's way, but he did say "Hey" back.

Sadly, Mozelle shook her head. It broke her heart to see that hurt look replace the sparkle in Cora's eyes. Cora took three cookies. She went over to where Randie sat on the floor with Essie pulling straw out of the broom, and shared her cookies with them.

Randell sat down and started taking off his work shoes.

"It's Cora's birthday," Mozelle said.

Dropping his shoe to the floor, Randell glanced over at her. "How old is she?"

"'Leven."

Cora gave her usual shy glance to Randell.

Randell leaned to one side and started digging down inside his pocket. Pulling out a handful of change, he held his hand out to Cora. "Come here, girl."

Cora looked first at Mozelle. Mozelle nodded. Only then did Cora get up off the floor. She went timidly over to Randell's outstretched hand. Her eyes fixed on the many coins he held out to her.

"Take what you want," he said.

Cora's eyes widened but then she quickly looked at him suspiciously. "You foolin'?"

"Go on before I change my mind."

She quickly picked out a quarter with her thumb and middle finger. Looking at him, she cupped the quarter in both her hands and started backing away.

"Is that all you want?"

Cora looked over at Mozelle.

Mozelle again nodded. "Take another one." She wanted to say, "Take it all."

Cora stepped back up to her daddy. She started to pick up another quarter, but stopped and looked into Randell's eyes. Neither blinked. It was as if they were looking at each other for the first time. Randell studied Cora's face and smiled. Cora studied her daddy's face but no smile curled her lips. Her jaw was set. With her right hand, she dragged all of the coins into her left hand, dropping some of them onto the floor.

Randell threw back his head and laughed.

Mozelle smiled to herself.

Cora hurriedly carried her money to the table and put it down. Then she ran back to Randell, picked the rest of the coins up off the floor at his feet, and took the money to her pile of coins on the table.

Still laughing, Randell said, "The little heifer got more than you use to make picking cotton in a week."

Mozelle glared at him but turned away before Cora saw her. This was Cora's day. She wouldn't spoil it by arguing.

"I'm going to take my bath," Randell said, standing up. "I want my supper when I come back." He went off into the back room to take his bath.

"Mama."

"Yes, baby."

"This your money."

"Your daddy give you that money," Mozelle said, taking

Brother, who had fallen asleep while suckling from her nipple and laying him across her lap. She closed her dress.

"No, Mama, I got this money for you. You needs it to pay the rent."

Her heart swelled. It didn't surprise her that Cora, too, was tired of being put outdoors. "Thank you, baby. Put it in the tin under the bed."

Cora got the tin from under the bed and filled it with the change that she did not count.

"If you wanna give your daddy one of your cookies, you can."

"Yessum."

"Mozelle!" Randell shouted.

She looked toward the back room. "What you want?"

"Get in here!"

She didn't like the sound of Randell's voice—she wasn't rushing in there to get into an argument with him. "In a minute," she said. She stood slowly so that she wouldn't wake Brother.

"Woman, get in here, *now*! There's something on me."

Something in his voice scared her. In fact, he sounded scared himself. She quickly put Brother down on the bed and rushed into the back room where Randell was standing butt naked in the washtub. He was scrubbing his body hard.

She froze when she saw the terror in his eyes.

"Look at my arm! What's that on me?" he asked, pointing at small white spots on his arms and chest. He turned his hands. The spots were there, too.

She went up to him; she stared at the spots. "Ain't it paint?"

"I ain't been painting in more than a month," he said, taking the lye soap and rubbing it directly onto his arm until it foamed a little. He scrubbed again with the rag. The spots were still there when he splashed water on his arm.

Mozelle scrapped at some of the tiny spots with her fingernail. They did not flake off. "They part of your skin," she said, amazed. She stepped back and looked at Randell's body. The white spots were small but against his dark skin, they stood out.

"How come they all of a sudden come on you?"

"I didn't notice them 'til now. They on my face, too?"

She studied his face. "Just a bit on your neck. Maybe you got chicken pox."

"Grown men don't get chicken pox."

"They sho'nuff do if they ain't never had it befo'."

"Well, I did."

"It don't look like chicken pox, anyhow," she said, stepping farther away from him. "Lord a mercy, is it catchin'?"

Practically jumping out of the tub, Randell splashed water all over the floor. Mozelle jumped back even farther, her feet got splashed anyway. Randell snatched his drawers off the chair and pulled them on without drying off.

Beginning to feel itchy, Mozelle started wiping her fingers on her dress. "Lord a mercy, Randell. What we gon' do if you got the leprosy?"

"I ain't got no leprosy!" he barked, dressing quickly.

"Where you goin'?"

"U'm gon' find me a doctor," he said, rushing out of the house, carrying his shoes in his hands, his white shirt flying open behind him.

Mozelle stood at the door watching Randell run up the road. He was probably going to catch a bus to town, but as scared as he was, if no bus was coming quick enough, he'd probably run all the way there. Maybe even barefooted. She had never seen Randell Tate go anywhere barefooted or with his clothes messed up. Going back over to the tub, she dragged it, sloshing water and all to the door. Lifting up one end, she emptied it outside on the ground. She then pushed the tub itself out behind the bathwater. She would scald it out later. God knows what those spots were. Taking Randell's towel, Mozelle sopped up the water from the floor. That, too, was thrown outside on top of the tub. That, too, she would scald.

"Lord, please don't let me have what he got," she prayed, pulling off her clothes to examine her own body. Wherever she could see, she studied. There was nothing discoloring anywhere on her skin that she could see. After she put back on her clothes, she got down on her knees. "Lord, what is this Randell got?"

Thirteen

Hours later, Randell came home. He was still upset and still spotted. His head was hanging as low as his spirit. Mozelle hadn't seen him so somber in all their years of marriage, except maybe when he had to pick cotton. His face was drained of color; he looked ashy.

"What the doctor say it is?" she asked.

Randell slumped down into the chair near the fireplace. "He say it come from the paint. I don't believe him," he said, extending his arm out toward the fire to examine it in the light of the flames. "U'm gon' find me another doctor. This is 1943, somebody oughta be able to tell me what this is. I know it ain't paint."

"Well, Randell, it could be some paint stayed on your skin too long and burned into it," she said, sitting up in bed.

"The doctor said something like that, but I been painting all my life. I know other men who been painting all their life, too. I ain't never know paint to do nothing like this."

"Well, me neither. Did the doctor give you medicine?"

"Naw. He said since I don't feel sick, he don't have to give me nothing. He said it might clear up on its own. Mozelle, I ain't sure about that. What is this on me?"

She almost felt sorry for him. "Randell, I don't know. You never noticed it befo' now?"

"No."

"Well then, I jest don't know. You want your supper?"

"Naw," he said, turning away from the fireplace. "U'm going to bed."

She watched him, his shoulders slumped, come slowly to the bed. She was so use to seeing him walk tall and proud, that she almost didn't recognize the scared old man before her. Until now, she had never seen Randell's true age in his face. He was old and suddenly not as good-looking as he used to be. She frowned. Randell sat on his side of the bed, untied his shoes, and dropped them to the floor. As he slipped out of his clothes, he dropped them to the floor, too. She knew then that he was worried for sure. His clothes never touched the floor. And, too, his staying home and going to bed early without his supper was not like him. He climbed into bed and sighed deeply as he turned to face the wall. He appeared to go off to sleep, but Mozelle wasn't sure. She didn't know what to say to him.

She almost wanted to point a finger at him and say, "God is punishing you." But she kept still; God was having his say. He was finally showing His displeasure with Randell. Only a little part of her felt sorry for him, but then, she could feel sorry for a mangy old dog. It was a shame that it took little white spots to keep him home with his family. But didn't her mama used to say that all sick birds come home to roost? Randell was home because none of his whores was going to take care of him.

Wouldn't it be his comeuppance if he caught something from all those whores he had laid up with? That's what he got for going around always in heat. As for herself, she had better stop laying up with him. Lord knows, she didn't want to catch what he had. It didn't help a bit that she had to worry about whether or not she was already pregnant. She had been feeling that old familiar way she felt when she was pregnant—sleepy and hungry all the time. She worked through her sleepiness and ignored her hunger. She was used to her stomach growling through the worst of times, and after the first few times, it would stop on its own because it knew it wasn't going to be fed. But she was worried all the same. Her womb had been as ripe as a watermelon seed since Randie was born. In fact she was scared every time Randell touched her. If she was pregnant again, she didn't know what she was going to do. She wasn't going to be able to manage another baby—it was just too hard. As she drifted off to sleep, she prayed that she was not pregnant and that if Randell was sick, that she wouldn't have to wait on him hand and foot.

Those little white spots put the fear of God into Randell. When he came in from work, he stayed in. Most times he stayed to himself in whatever room the children weren't in. If they bothered him, he snapped at them, scaring them into a fit of tears. Mozelle did her best to keep them out of his way. It didn't help that Randell wasn't sleeping much. That was probably what made him more ornery than he normally was. Sometimes Randell sat for hours looking at his outstretched arms or at his body through the bureau looking glass. If he wasn't doing that, he sat around moping or rubbing calamine lotion all over his body, making himself white all over. In the morning, before going to work, he washed himself off.

Visits to three different doctors didn't give Randell any relief. None knew for sure what caused the spots, but they all said he was fine. Yet, some of the spots had spread into bigger spots. His neck and face started spotting white, too, and there, they were more noticeable. They seemed whiter. That really upset Randell. He was always vain about his "smooth pretty black skin." He couldn't wear his collar high enough to hide his neck and face. He joked once about wearing a hood like the Klan to hide behind. Neither one of them laughed about that. If anybody asked Randell about the spots, he never mentioned it to Mozelle. In fact, he stopped talking to her about them altogether.

She didn't have to talk to Randell to know that he was scared. His being scared was good for her though. When he did talk, he talked to her right nice like before the children came along. He even started giving her money from his pay to buy food. Maybe spotting him like a pinto was God's way of making him do right. She didn't mind having the tub ready for him when he got in from work, even scrubbing his back was nice—like it used to be. She knelt alongside and slowly scrubbed his back. Randell purred like a old fat tabby.

"When I first saw you," he said, dropping his head to his chest so that Mozelle could wash his shoulders and neck, "you was so pretty."

That surprised her. "You ain't told me that in a long time."

He raised his head. "That ain't something a man gotta say to a woman. The fact that I looked at you meant I thought you was pretty. But it wasn't just that you was pretty, Mozelle, you put me in mind of a girl I useta know back when I was a boy in Elberton. You got her eyes and cheekbones."

She dropped the washrag into the water. If he didn't think she needed to hear him say that she was pretty, then what made him think she needed to hear him say that she reminded him of another woman?

"Don't stop," he said. "It feel good."

Pursing her lips, Mozelle felt down in the water for the rag. Finding it, she slapped it onto his back. This time she scrubbed harder.

Randellflexed his back muscles. "There you go acting all jealous. I knew that gal long before you was even born."

If that was true, then the woman had to be just as old as Randell now, and from what Mozelle could see, he liked women a whole lot younger than thirty. "So who was this girl you useta know back in Elberton?"

"Who? Gail?"

"Gail?"

"Yeah. Useta be with her all the time. She was. . .special."

Remembering that Gail was the name of the girl that Bernice mentioned years ago, Mozelle asked, "How come you didn't marry Gail?"

Randell sat up taller. He splashed some water on his chest and on each of his arms.

She didn't think he'd answer her.

He cleared his throat. "The war came. It was 1914. While I was away in the Army, she up and married somebody else."

Mozelle knew she was pushing it, but, "Randell, how come you didn't marry her yaself before you joined up?"

"Never you mind."

"Fine. You don't have to tell me nothin'. She let the washrag slip down into the water. "U'm finished."

"Rub my back some more. It felt good."

"Jest for a minute," she said. She began rubbing his back. Randell sighed long and deep. She wished that he had married Gail, then he would not have been free to marry her.

As if he heard Mozelle's thoughts, Randell said, "I was gonna marry Gail after I got back, but she couldn't wait. Claim she was knocked up with my baby."

Startled, Mozelle stopped massaging his back. "She got a baby for you?"

"Her daddy said she was shaming the family. He made her marry some boy that was sweet on her."

"You got a grown child? Was he born in 1914, like me?"

"Yeah."

"I declare."

"The boy got himself killed a few years back over in Jacksonville."

"Lordy. How did he get killed?"

"One morning they found him dead in a alley. Somebody shot his head almost clear off his body. And nobody know nothing."

"My God," was all Mozelle could say. Randell's son had been just as old as her, and even though she felt bad that he had gotten killed, she couldn't help but feel a little jealous, a little angry. Randell had never told her that he had a son, and that son was by a woman that he wanted to marry. "Randell, where's his mama?"

"In Jacksonville."

She sprang up off the floor. "That how come you didn't want me livin' in Jacksonville?"

Randell turned and looked up at Mozelle standing behind him. "It ain't what you're thinking. I ain't been with Gail. She's married."

"That ain't never stopped you," she said, drying her hands on the front of her dress. "That's how come you kept goin' back to Jacksonville, ain't it?"

"See that. Mozelle, you all wrong now. I told you I was working, and I was."

"I don't believe you, Randell. You tell so many tales."

"I ain't lying. Look, all that stuff happened about thirty years ago. I don't know nothing about Gail no more."

"Well, you—"

"Look, that's in the past. I got other troubles on my mind. I was thinking about seeing a hoodoo woman about these spots. What do you think?"

The best Mozelle could do was shrug her shoulders. If he didn't want to talk about that Gail woman anymore, then fine. She really didn't care. Though she still wondered about all those times he stayed over in Jacksonville. "My daddy useta say, 'if what hoodoo folk do ain't done in God's name, then it's the devil's work.' If'n it was me, I wouldn't mess with no hoodoo woman." She had nothing more to say on the matter. She went off to see what her children were doing.

Randell went looking for a hoodoo woman. It didn't take long for a snaggletooth old man at the bottom of Elm Road to tell Randell about Mama Divine down in the meadow. Twice he went to her to get the smelly green stuff that looked like mud that he spread all over his body. He wouldn't tell Mozelle what it was he was using, and she doubted whether he knew for sure what it was himself. It smelled like cow dung to her. When that didn't work, Mama Divine gave him some smelly bitter brown potion to drink. Randell drank that for about a week until he got tired of running to the outhouse. Nothing worked. In the end, Mama Divine told him that somebody had put a hex on him that she couldn't remove unless she knew who it was. That day Randell came running home and pointed the finger at Mozelle.

He penned her up against the wall with his arm pressed up against her chest. "Heifer, you put a hex on me?"

Mozelle tried to push him off her. "I don't know nothin' about puttin' no hex on nobody. If I did, I wouldn't've spot you white, I'da made your peter draw up and fall off. But I wouldn't do that neither; the Lord would smite me for goin' to the devil."

Randell let go of her after he thought about it. "Well, somebody put a hex on me. Mama Divine say that's how come her potion ain't working."

"It wasn't me. You best go 'n figure out who else you done wronged."

If Randell had somebody in mind, he never said so. He stopped going to see Mama Divine; he called her crazy. Mozelle tried to get him to go to church for the laying on of hands by Reverend Witherspoon, but he wouldn't go. Probably afraid it would get around town that he was cursed.

Friday afternoon, two months after Randell first saw the spots, he said, "The hell with it. If U'm turning white, I may as well live with it. I ain't never seen white people drop dead from being white."

He sat down at the table, pulled out a roll of bills from his billfold, counted out one hundred and fifty dollars in front of Mozelle, and then put every single bill back into his pocket. She wanted desperately to ask for some of it, but dared not. It would be begging. She figured the reason he had so much money in the first place was because he hadn't been spending it on his whores.

"I been stuck in this house too long," he said. "U'm going out."

He left without so much as a backward glance. Mozelle took a deep breath. She didn't know if she was relieved that he was gone or if she was afraid that Randell was most likely going back to his old self. The coming home early; the staying in all night was over. She was not going to wait up for him. No telling what time he was going to find his way home.

Fourteen

Lord, how much harder was her bed going to get? Again, she was pregnant. Again, having to face it, having to accept it, numbed her and filled her with guilt. Her nights were sleepless. Mozelle tossed and turned on her lumpy mattress, unable, most nights, to close her eyes. When Randell noticed her swelling belly, he cursed her and left the house. He came home nine days later with the musky smell of other women clinging to his body. Seemed they didn't mind the spots, but that was just fine with Mozelle—she was glad he wasn't pestering her. He turned a blind eye to her and said nothing about the baby she would bring into the world in four months time. Randell went about his business living like he didn't have a care. Even when he was laid off at Goodyear, he landed on his feet like an old cat that gave his tail to the world to kiss. Randell got a job a week later at the cement factory. Mozelle never knew what kind of work he did on his jobs—he wouldn't talk about it with her. As long as he was getting paid, he had no complaint. And she had no complaint about him, as long as he kept paying the rent.

There was nothing loving between her and Randell although they kept on living together. They had an understanding that that was just the way it was going to be. It was Cora who didn't understand.

"Mama, Daddy ain't never been nice to you. How come you keep laying down with him?"

"U'm his wife." What else could she say? She knew what she had to do as Randell's wife, but how could she explain to her child what being a wife meant?

"Mama, can't you tell Daddy to stop giving you babies?"

She thought for a moment. "Cora, when I married your daddy before God, I promised to honor and obey him. I got to do whatever he want me to do 'cause U'm his wife."

Cora looked at her innocently. "Mama, you don't do everythin' Daddy want you to do. He don't want you to fight him, but you do."

"That's different," she said, knowing full well that she wasn't supposed to be fighting Randell. "U'm protecting myself."

"Daddy ought not hit on you, Mama."

"No, he ought not."

Cora was pensive. "Mama, Daddy won't pay the rent if you don't lay—"

"Cora, grown folks' things betwixt me and your daddy, you won't understand 'til you grown yourself. I don't want you to worry 'bout me."

"Okay, Mama," Cora said, softly. For a minute she was deep in thought. "Mama, I hate Daddy."

So did she, but Mozelle didn't want Cora carrying hate in her soul. "Cora, the Lord want you to love your daddy. Don't you want to go to heaven one day?"

"Yessum."

"Then you have to keep love in your heart for everybody, 'pecially your daddy and mama. The Good Book say you got to honor your father and mother. That mean you got to love your daddy equal like you love me. That's what the Lord want us all to do."

Cora lowered her head. "U'm sorry, Mama."

"That's all right, baby. You ain't got nothin' to be sorry for. Your daddy the one that oughta be sorry. He got to learn to be a better daddy. But, Cora, you go on and love him anyhow. Can you do that for Mama?"

"Yes, Mama."

Mozelle felt like she was a hypocrite. In her own soul, she hated Randell, but she had to teach Cora to be different from herself. Her anger with Randell should not be Cora's anger. That wouldn't be right.

Mozelle's mama kept coming to her in her dreams. The dream was always the same—her mama was the midwife tending her. When her baby was pulled out of her belly, it was a girl. When she reached out for her baby, her mama cradled her protectively in her arms and shook her head no. Then her mama turned and walked out of the house, taking the baby with her. For that baby Mozelle cried. She cried herself awake. She touched her belly. Her baby was still there. It had only been a dream. She dried her eyes. The dream bothered her though. Maybe something was wrong with her mama. No word had come from Ruth in a long time. Mozelle could only pray that everything was all right.

A day later, it was time. Mozelle sent Cora for the midwife. She was scared. Scared because her baby had been still in her belly all morning. It was the dream that stayed on her mind when the midwife pulled her baby girl from her. She was as limp as a dead chicken. Her baby didn't cry when she was smacked on the bottom. She was alive, but barely. Two hours later, before her baby could even be called by her name, she died. Mabel was buried far out in the backyard a foot from the blackberry bush. The telegram Mozelle was half expecting came. Her mama, too, had died. The doctor said her body was full of fever and poison from her teeth and gums. Like in the dream, Mozelle cried. Her poor baby had not truly seen the light of day, while her mama had seen the light of many a day. For her mama, Mozelle cried because she hadn't seen her in such a long time. Though she was heartbroken, she was comforted somehow in knowing that her mama was taking her baby to heaven with her, and neither would know pain nor sorry from that day on. Mabel would never know what it was to be hungry.

Some days Mozelle asked God if her life on earth was ever going to get easier. She knew better than to question Him, and she knew that He wouldn't laden her with more than her shoulders could bear, but she wondered how much more she was expected to bear. Every time she had to pack up her children to find another shack to call home, it made her heart bleed.

When the war ended in 1945, she couldn't rejoice like so many in Gadsden, mainly because she didn't know a thing about the war overseas. Her war was at home in Gadsden. The day the war ended was the day she found out that, again, Randell had gone back on his word. He had stopped paying the rent. While he was gone, God knows where, they were thrown out into the night. Only after she begged Mr. Otis did he let her leave her bundles on his back porch while she went in search of a place to stay. If it wasn't for the light of the moon, her and her children would have walked the road alone in complete darkness. Mozelle carried Essie on her hip while she held on to Randie's hand.

"Cora, I know you tired of carryin' Brother, but try to keep up, baby."

"U'm tryin', Mama," Cora said, sounding winded.

"God," Mozelle said, looking up at the sky, "how come my children got to suffer for my mistake? Being poor is a heavy cross to bear, Lord. Havin' no roof over my head and four children to feed nothin' to but flour cakes and mush is a cryin' shame. Lord, have You forgotten your humble servant? I know You know what's best, Lord, but I need a place to call my own so my children don't have to be put outdoors time and again, or have to curl up on the cold wood floor to sleep. It ain't fittin' that they got to suffer 'cause they got a sinful, triflin' daddy. Please, Lord, help us to get where we goin' even though we don't know where we gon' end up."

"Mama, where is us goin'?" Randie asked.

"Shush, child. U'm talkin' to the Lord."

Randie whimpered. "U'm tired, Mama."

"Hush up, I said!" Mozelle was tired herself, but she was not going to give in to the weakness of her body, and she was not going to let her children give in either.

Randie's six-year-old legs were having a hard time keeping up with her mama's long stride. She stumbled. She fell.

Mozelle pulled Randie up by the arm. "You gots to keep up, Randie. I can't carry you."

Randie whined. She started to cry.

Mozelle regretted scolding Randie. It wasn't Randie's fault that they were out there on the road in the dark. She slowed down a bit.

"Randie, baby, please stop cryin'. U'ma get you somethin' to eat soon as I can."

Randie stopped crying but she didn't stop whimpering.

"Lord, Lord, Lord. It pains me to see my children hungry. I know I can do better for them, Lord, but I need you to show me how. Show me how I can get me some land and build my children a house. I don't ever want to have to walk these long, dark roads at night again. Please, Lord, hear my prayer and see us through this night. Amen." She glanced back at Cora. "C'mon now."

"Mama, U'm 'bout tuckered out," Cora said, breathlessly, "When we gon' get to where we goin?'"

The church up ahead seemed to appear out of the darkness. "It's just a little ways up the road to the church. If Reverend Woodrow let us stay the night in the back, U'm surely gon find us a place to stay in the mornin.'"

"Mama, can we eat somethin' at the church?" Cora asked.

"I hope so, child. Jest keep up with Mama a little bit longer."

"Okay," Cora said softly, switching Brother to her other slim hip. "Mama, is Daddy gon' know where we at?"

"Let's not think 'bout your daddy right now," Mozelle answered. Her anger only grew when she thought about Randell.

Reverend Woodrow took them in. He fed them and gave them a place to sleep in the back of the church on the pews. For even that, Mozelle was grateful. Two days later Randell showed up at the cafe.

"I rented us a house all to ourselves down on Plum Street. What's more, I paid up three months rent."

Until he said that, Mozelle was about to tell him to go on his way and leave her be forever, but sleeping on those hard pews in church had left her achy and tired. And, too, her children shouldn't be living like bums. The truth was, she wasn't making enough money to go it alone without Randell.

"A whole house?" she asked cautiously.

"Yep. You got all the rooms you ever wanted."

"How many?"

"Five."

"It's gon' be jest us?"

"Just us. I'm gonna make the rent every month. I promise."

"Don't be lyin' to me, Randell."

He raised his right hand. "As God is my witness, U'm gon' make the rent every month."

Knowing that he had her, Randell started out of the cafe, and like she'd done so many times before, she followed behind him.

Fifteen

1948

It had been three years since the war ended. To Mozelle, it seemed like life was getting better for lots of folks in Gadsden. The problem was, she didn't see how her life was getting any better. True enough, Randell had kept his word; he kept the rent paid up. But the five-room house they called home down in the valley on Plum Street wasn't fit for hogs. The house was all but falling down around them, but Mozelle didn't complain—they had a roof, although leaky, over their heads. They used the furniture that had been left behind—a rusty old squeaky iron bed with a torn dirty stained mattress, a rickety old table and two wobbly chairs, and a six-drawer bureau. From yard sales, she bought two secondhand beds for the children. The best part of all, was that they lived in the house all by themselves and, at times, Mozelle felt like it was her house. It was only when the landlord came to the house to collect his rent from Randell that she was reminded that it wasn't.

One good thing about living down in the valley was the branch that ran past the front of the house on its way down into the woods. In fact, they were only a few yards from the woods themselves. The branch was pretty to look at—the water sparkled as it washed over the rocks. Mozelle remembered the first day she saw the branch. The first thing she did was get down on her knees and scoop up some of its sparkling water with both hands to taste its cool sweetness. On many a hot, sweaty day, the chilren splashed around in the low waters of the branch while

Mozelle sat on the edge and cooled her feet. The only thing that changed its beauty was the heavy rains that came in the spring, overflowing it, flooding out the road on the other side, making it impossible for a car to come down into the valley close to the house. The water was waist-high on Mozelle and practically over her children's heads, but that was when they wanted most to play in it. That was when they made out like they were swimming. None of them knew exactly how to swim, and at first Mozelle worried that one of them might drown. Thank God they were good about keeping their heads above water. They must have learned that from her.

Then there were the pretty green weeping willow trees, fat and full like well-fed hogs. They were everywhere—off the road, near the branch, around in back of the house, and hundreds more throughout the woods. They shaded everything that lay beneath them, and the slightest breeze moved their long, drooping branches in a lazy, swaying kind of way. Though the branches didn't look too strong, they were. Essie and Brother liked wrapping them around their hands and swinging back and forth. Their hands might bare the marks of the branches wrapped too tightly, but rarely did a branch ever break under their weight. Mozelle could hear them laughing late into the evening. Their laughter brought joy to her heart. Her children were playing as children ought to, and she was pleased that they were as happy as she was to be living down in the valley. The weeping willow trees filled the valley with life and an airiness that on a hot summer day was like the breath of God taming the heat that baked the Alabama soil. Mozelle had never seen so many weeping willow trees in her life and saw it as a sign that someday soon her life would be as bountiful.

The valley was welcoming after a hard day of work. It was mighty peaceful, like living way out in the country. It reminded her of living on the farm with her family when she was a child. That was so long ago. Down in the valley, there were only two other houses besides the one they lived in. Rosa Lewis and her four children lived at the foot of the road, and the Clays, who had ten children, had a big spread far back behind the house Mozelle rented. Everybody stayed to themselves on their own land. Sitting out on the front porch at the end of the day, Mozelle enjoyed looking out across the branch up at the spread of hilly land covered with trees and pretty wildflowers of yellows, reds, purples, and orange that rose high above the road. Finally, Mozelle felt like her children had a home, but it still wasn't their land.

After seven years, her job at the cafe was not paying a dime more than before the war, though Mr. Peterson was a bit more generous with leftovers. Randell paid the rent but that was all he did. He was still spending his money on himself and his whores. He brought himself an old black Studebaker and even took the time to teach her how to drive it, though he wouldn't let her ride in it or drive it on her own. She never understood why Randell wasted his time teaching her to drive. She still had to walk the two and a half miles to and from the cafe while he still came and went as he saw fit in his car. Mozelle didn't care about what he was doing or where he was doing it, she was just glad that he paid the rent and that his nature for her was weak. The few times that he bothered her until she had to lay down with him, she prayed hard and long that they didn't make another baby. As it was, feeding growing children was harder than feeding babies, but she had had enough of babies, too.

If it wasn't for Cora taking care of the little ones, washing their clothes and cooking their supper, Mozelle didn't know how she would have made it with the long hours she worked in the cafe. Cora was a little thing still, small for fifteen, but that didn't stop her from working harder than any girl twice her size. When she got in from work, Cora was always there with a smile and a hug, ready to give her a bite to eat. It was like Cora was taking care of them all.

Since they had been living down in the valley across the way from Rosa Lewis and her four children, Cora had become smitten with Rosa's oldest boy, Henry Jackson. Henry didn't live with his mama—he lived down in Greenville with his daddy's family—but he came often to visit. Henry was taken with Cora. He asked permission to court Cora two days after meeting her.

Mozelle was glad that Henry, like most people who knew Cora, saw her tender soul and sweet disposition, not her crooked fingers and turned-around hands and feet.

Henry hadn't too long come home from the Army. He was twenty-six years old, just eight years younger than Mozelle, but to her, Henry Jackson was a boy. The few times they had talked, she felt like she could be his mother. Her life with Randell made her feel years older than her thirty-four years. The eleven-year difference between Henry and Cora did concern her; she didn't want Cora to walk in her footsteps. But then, she saw that Henry wasn't acting worldly like Randell; he didn't seem to be sniffing behind every skirt tail he saw. He seemed to be a simple country boy. He was thinking about moving to Gadsden and getting a job in the pipe factory. He could support a wife if it came to that. If Cora did marry Henry, it would be all right with her—she already liked Henry's mother. Though at times it aggravated Mozelle when Rosa didn't want to talk about anything but how much she wanted her husband to come back home. Rosa hadn't heard from Atticus in the six years since he left Alabama to find work up north. When she was feeling low, that was mostly all that Rosa talked about. Poor old soul, she didn't know how lucky she was. If Atticus could leave her like that, and she was doing just fine raising her children all by herself, she didn't need him. If Mozelle could raise her children by herself and keep a roof over their heads, Randell could leave and never come back. It would be an answer to her prayers. Of course it didn't look like her prayer would ever be answered, so she didn't dwell on it. She went on her way, day by day, worrying only about her children.

Still Cora stayed on her mind most. Mozelle didn't know if she was going to be able to let go of Cora. Cora had been her baby for seven years before anyone else come along, and even though she was almost grown, she was still her baby. If Cora never wanted to marry, she wouldn't have to. Cora could stay with her for life. Fact of the matter was, she would rather that Cora never got married if she had to live with a man who was anything like her daddy. So far, in the seven months they had been courting, Henry had been a perfect gentleman. Most nights he and Cora sat out on the front porch on milk crates talking. The most Mozelle had seen him do was hold Cora's hand. None of this, however, was lost on her. She remembered how sweet Randell had been when he had courted her. There was nothing he did that told that there was another side to him. She prayed that Henry was as nice as he put out, because Cora's little face lit up every time she saw him. Mozelle sensed that the courting might well lead to them marrying, and it would hurt her to her heart if Henry hurt her baby and stole her light.

At work, she said to Mr. Peterson, whose own daughter had just gotten married, "Well, it's just a matter of time befo' my baby, Cora, marry, too."

"Mozelle, Cora ain't no baby no more if she courting already," Mr. Peterson said, taking money from the cash box, folding it, and stuffing it into his front pocket.

Mozelle started back toward the kitchen. "That's sho'nuff true."

"Hold up a minute, Mozelle. I been meaning to talk to you all morning."

She didn't stop walking. "Can we talk whilst I peel potatoes?" she asked, pushing open the door to the kitchen.

"Sho can," Mr. Peterson said, following behind her.

Going into the kitchen, Mozelle sat down at the heavy wooden table in the center of the room and picked up the knife. She then picked up the white potato she had left half peeled when she went out front to meet with the insurance man. Sometimes he came to the house, sometimes he came to the cafe, but once a month he came to collect her two dollars for the life insurance and burial policies she took out for herself and her children.

Mr. Peterson sat down across from her. He rested his big fleshy arms on the table. "Mozelle, your cooking just about the best in these here parts."

"Well, thank you, sa."

"Yes, ma'am. 'Cause of you, lots of people come back here to eat. You been with me a long time, and if I could live with myself without feeling guilty, I'd keep you cooking for me 'til the day I die."

Dropping the peeled potato in the pot of cold water sitting in front of her on the table, Mozelle put down the knife and looked at Mr. Peterson. She didn't quite understand what he was coming around to saying but she was starting to feel afraid.

"You ain't studin' about lettin' me go, is you?"

"Not 'cause I want to," he said, interlocking his fingers and resting his hands on the table.

Mozelle stood abruptly. "Mr. Peterson, what I do wrong? Please, sa, don't let me go! I'll do better. Just you tell me what I gots to do."

"Mozelle, settle down. You ain't done nothing wrong. Just sit down and let me talk to you for a minute."

She started wiping her hands on her apron. She didn't want to sit. "Mr. Peterson, I needs my job. I—"

"Mozelle—"

"I got young ones at home, Mr. Peterson. I can't be without work. I—"

"Mozelle!" Mr. Peterson shouted.

Startled by his booming voice, Mozelle jumped. Her heart was beating a mile a minute.

"Mozelle, sit down. I can't talk to you if you won't let me get a word in edgewise."

Reluctantly, she sat down again. Her back was straight, her eyes unblinking as she waited anxiously to hear why Mr. Peterson was letting her go. Losing this job was her worst nightmare come true. She felt like she was going to be sick.

"Now, Mozelle, I know it ain't my business, and I ain't never said nothing, but I know about your husband."

Stunned, she stared at him. She had forgotten that she had left her bundles at the cafe one of the nights that she was put outdoors.

"Mozelle, folks talk. That's how I know your husband don't do right by you and your children."

Ashamed, Mozelle lowered her head. For so long she thought only her past landlords and Randell's whores knew about his trifling ways. It never occurred to her that folks with eyes that didn't seem to be noticing her could see that Randell was no

good. They had to see, too, that she was suffering. Her old faded
dresses and broken-down shoes probably told on her more than
the gossipy words spoken by the landlords or Randell's whores.
Mozelle never gave a thought to Mr. Peterson being concerned
about what was going on in her life. He had never said a word to
her, and she never talked out of turn about her personal life. What
she knew about him, was that he was a God-fearing family man,
and now that Mr. Peterson knew the truth about Randell, he might
not want her in his cafe.

"Mozelle, I ain't trying to get in your business or nothing,
and I hate to lose you."

Again, she stood. "Then how come you lettin' me go, Mr.
Peterson? I do my work. I can do more if you want me to."

"I got to let you go, it's for the best."

Tears emptied from her eyes. She began wringing her
hands. "My God. What U'm gon' do?"

"Mozelle, settle down. You don't understand. Let me—"

"My children—"

"Land sakes alive! Mozelle! Let me talk!"

The tightness in her throat nearly choking her, she fought to
not shame herself by crying like a baby. Looking at Mr. Peterson,
she was about to lose that fight. She didn't know why he was letting her go when she had worked so hard for him. She lowered
her eyes, and as she slowly sat down again, she studied the many
jagged cut marks in the top of the wooden table from cutting
everything from onions to chicken to ribs. Years from now, no
one would ever know that she had made some of those cuts. That
she had even been there. Shaking her head, she wondered what
was going to happen to her and her children now.

"Mozelle," Mr. Peterson said, lowering his own head, trying to get her to look up at him. "You need more money then I
can pay. If I could pay you more, I would. I just can't."

She looked up into his eyes. "Mr. Peterson, I been makin'
do jest fine with what you pay me."

"Making do ain't enough, Mozelle. You need more in order
to do better for yourself. This I know, so I won't be right with
God if I keep you on here."

That she didn't understand. "How you gon' be right with God if you let me go?"

"Well, Mozelle, God got a plan. My brother, Carlton, work over in Alabama City at the Dwight Cotton Mill. He told me they was hiring. I asked him to put in a word for you, and he did. He say you start Monday morning."

Mozelle's mouth slowly dropped open.

"The hours are from seven in the morning 'til four in the afternoon. The pay is forty-five dollars a week."

Stunned, Mozelle stared at Mr. Peterson. Forty-five dollars a week! "What you say?"

"Forty-five dollars a week."

Surely she was dreaming. Forty-five dollars a week was more money than she had ever dreamed of making on any job, and picking cotton was the last thing she ever wanted to do again in life. But if that's what she had to do to make that kind of money, she'd bend her back and drag a big old heavy scratchy sack behind her filled with cotton, while her pricked fingers dripped blood into the earth and dirty sweat glued her clothes to her body making her smell as musty as any man.

Mr. Peterson waited for Mozelle to take in what he'd said.

"Forty-five dollars a week?" she asked again. "Is you foolin' me?"

"I swear before God," Mr. Peterson said, raising his right hand. "Mozelle, if I could pay you that, I would. I know you can use that kind of money."

Her eyes widened. "I sho'nuff can. Mr. Peterson, I ain't never made forty-five dollars a week in all my life."

"You can now," Mr. Peterson said, leaning back in his chair.

"God be praised," Mozelle said prayerfully. The top on the pot boiling on the stove jiggled, drawing her attention. Quickly getting to her feet, she stepped around the fifty-pound bag of potatoes standing next to her chair. She rushed to the stove. Using the dishrag, she lifted the heavy cast-iron top off the pot. She picked up the serving spoon and stirred the big pot of boiling string beans. God knows she could use every penny of that forty-five dollars a week. She wouldn't have to depend on Randell to keep a roof over her children's heads anymore.

"Oh, and Mozelle. Just in case you wondering, you won't be picking cotton."

"I won't?" she asked, putting the pot top back on. She left the rag on top. She felt that old fear that lived with her so long creep back up on her. Besides washing clothes, cooking, and picking cotton, there wasn't much else she could do, and none of those jobs ever paid her forty-five dollars a week. She hoped she could do whatever the job was, but for the time being, she was too afraid to ask what she would be doing. Using the same spoon, she scraped the bottom of a second pot filled with brown gravy and pork chops to make sure the gravy wasn't sticking. She set the spoon down on the counter before going back to the table.

"Don't you want to know what you'll be doing?"

"Well, it don't much matter."

"I guess not, but, Mozelle, you'll be working inside the mill with other womenfolk winding cloth on the bolts after it's been dyed and dried."

"I ain't never done that befo'."

"There ain't nothing to winding cloth," Mr. Peterson said, getting up from the table. "Don't trouble yourself worrying about it. Them white folk gon' show you how to do it the first day."

Mozelle breathed a sigh of relief. "I can't thank you enough, Mr. Peterson," she said, wrapping her apron around her hands. "But you only got one cook now. What you gon' do if'n I leave?"

"Another cook's coming on Monday. As much as I hate to let you go, I know it's the right thing to do. You finish out the day, I'll see you get a little extra in your pay."

"U'm real grateful to you, sa. I don't know if I can ever thank you enough," she said, walking toward him.

Mr. Peterson reached out and took both Mozelle's hands in his. "Just say 'hey' to my brother, Carlton, if you see him."

"I will," Mozelle said eagerly. "Thank you."

Mr. Peterson let go of her hands and left the kitchen.

Mozelle pressed her clasped hands to her chin and closed her eyes.

Sixteen

Mozelle couldn't help herself. The giggles that burst from within her throat surprised even her. She couldn't stop them. Every time she giggled out loud, she covered her mouth with her hand to squelch them. Then she'd glance around to see who might have heard her. Lord knows she didn't want folks to think she was crazy. Those folks that walked the same dusty road as her greeted her with big neighborly "how dos." She always answered "how do" back with a big smile and a gracious nod. But, Lord, if she could tell them all that for the first time in her life that she had forty-three dollars at one time pent to the inside of her dress pocket, that she was about to feed her children more than corn bread made without eggs and fatback and beans, they would understand her joy. The first thing she was going to buy was a bunch of collard greens. She was going to cook up a mess of greens for Cora. They would all eat some, but it was for Cora that she would cook them for dinner Sunday. Cora had liked collard greens since the one time she ate them at Mrs. Scott's house in Piedmont. More than a handful of times Cora talked about eating those sweet greens. Mozelle smiled just remembering how Cora mushed her golden corn bread and greens together on her plate with her fingers before practically sticking her whole hand in her mouth. It didn't matter how crooked her little fingers were, Cora didn't leave one green speck on her plate. Mozelle had shown Cora how to eat them that way, like she had been shown by her mama when she was a little girl. For the longest time Cora didn't know that uncooked collard greens grew as big, wide green leaves; she thought they grew in little pieces. That was until she saw a farmer on the side of the road selling them and wanted to know what they were. The child couldn't believe it, even after Mozelle explained to her that greens had to be cut down. As much as she wanted to buy a bunch of greens for Cora then, Mozelle couldn't, it would have been a tease. What she might have been able to afford would have cooked down to just a cupful, definitely not enough to feed six people.

Mozelle glanced back over her left shoulder when she heard the motor of the bus from Alabama City coming up the road behind her. The bus slowed as it got closer. The balls of her feet were sore from rubbing against the hole coming through the piece of pasteboard in her shoe. Yet, she waved the driver on. A cloud of bellowing dust was left behind to blind and choke her. She fanned at her nose and eyes until the dust cleared away. Not a nickel of her first week's pay was going to be wasted on bus fare. Every penny was needed for food, shoes, and clothes for her children. That was, if she could find secondhand clothes cheap enough. It was time her girls stopped wearing dresses cut from flour sacks or even thin, threadbare cotton dresses. Randie, Essie, and Brother all needed clothes for school, and Cora needed something prettier to court Henry in. What Mozelle could afford to buy still wouldn't be as nice as the clothes Katie Dennis' children wore, but anything would be better than what they were use to.

She got back to Gadsden later than usual because she had to wait in line to get paid. She made it before Mr. Frankle closed the Piggly Wiggly. She was tired, but not too tired to pick out food that she had never been able to buy for herself or her children. Mozelle's heart actually beat faster when she picked out a whole chicken, two pounds of neckbones, and six pig knuckles. Her fingers trembled when she paid the sixteen dollars for all that she bought. Proudly she walked the last half a mile home hugging her three bags of grocery to her chest. Besides the chicken, neckbones, and pig knuckles, she carried a slab of fatback and two bags each of black-eyed peas, red beans, and pinto beans. She had five pounds of rice, two bags of cornmeal, five-pound sacks of flour and sugar, a tub of lard, a dozen eggs, a can of baking soda, a box of salt, and a small bag of peppermints. She bought so much, she almost couldn't manage, but she did. It was a burden she didn't mind struggling under. The only thing she didn't buy were the collard greens. They could be bought on Saturday.

Mozelle held on tighter to her bags when she started down the sloping dirt road into the valley. Almost at a trot, she pounded down the road. Halfway down, she saw right away that Randell's black Studebaker was not parked in front of the house. For that she was grateful. She didn't want him to see all the food she bought. He would surely eat a bellyful and spoil her good feeling.

Cora met Mozelle at the door. "Mama, is this all our food?"

"Every bit of it," she answered, letting Cora take one of the bags. Randie and Essie gathered around them, pulling at the bags trying to see what was inside. Mozelle didn't let them hold her back as she went on into the kitchen. She set her bags on the table. Cora did the same. Mozelle stepped back out of the way while Cora and Randie quickly emptied them.

Cora was eager. "Mama, can we cook the chicken now?"

Looking at the pot on the stove, she asked Cora, "Didn't you cook the corn bread and butter beans for supper?"

"Yessum, but Mama, can we fry the chicken anyhow?"

"Ain't y'all ate already?"

Cora frowned. "Yessum."

Taking the bag of peppermints off the table, Mozelle opened it and poured some out onto the table. Randie, Essie, and Brother snatched up every last piece.

"Y'all jest take one apiece."

The three of them held on tighter to the candy in their hands.

"Y'all hear me?"

"Aw, Mama," Randie said. "Can't we have two pieces right now?"

"No. If y'all eat it all now, y'all won't have any the rest of the week, and I won't buy y'all anymore."

They didn't have to think about that. One by one, Randie, Essie, and Brother put almost all of the candy back on the table. They each held on to one piece of peppermint. "Y'all can have one apiece every day. Cora, don't you want a piece?"

Cora shook her head. "No, ma'am."

She hated telling Cora that she couldn't fry the chicken, and when she saw the tears in her eyes, it hurt her to her heart. "Cora, this food got to keep us 'til I get paid the end of next week. I know you ain't hungry, 'cause y'all already ate supper."

"Then when we gon' fry the chicken?"

"Sunday."

"Not tomorra, Mama?"

"Cora, if you can wait 'til Sunday, tomorra U'ma give you some money to go buy some collard greens."

Cora's eyes suddenly brightened. "Collard greens?"

She nodded.

"Mama, can I cook them?"

"Sho'nuff can. You can use a piece of neckbone to season them, too."

Cora threw her arms around Mozelle's neck. "Thank you, Mama." Excited, she pulled away from Mozelle. "Want me to put the food up, Mama?"

"Yes, baby," she said, going over to the wood-burning stove. Touching it, she checked to see if it was still warm. It was cold. It didn't matter, she would eat her supper cold. She opened the pot to see how much of the beans were left for her. Not much. "Did y'all daddy come home and eat?"

"Yessum," Randie answered. "He cleaned up and left soon as he was through."

"Mama," Cora said, "you want me to put the chicken 'n neckbones 'n pig knuckles in the icebox?" She held the meats, still wrapped, to her chest.

"Yes, baby."

The rusty old icebox was in the house when they moved in. They never had anything to keep inside it other than milk, which didn't sit for long. Mozelle liked drinking ice water, so she let the ice man bring a block of ice three times a week for ten cents.

"I'll open it," Randie said, running over to the icebox.

"I wanna open it," Brother said, running over to the icebox, too, and grabbing the handle, trying to push Randie out of the way.

"Mama, look what he doin'," Randie said.

"Boy, get over here befo' I whop your tail," Mozelle threatened, taking the pot to the table. She poured cold butter beans onto her chipped plate over the last square of corn bread. With her spoon she scraped out the last bean. She sat down at the table on a wire milk crate; it was stronger than the chair she usually used. "Brother, what I say?"

Pouting, Brother bumped Randie once more before going back to the table. Randie ignored him and pulled open the door for Cora to put the meat inside on the bottom shelf.

"Take them there eggs and put them in there, too," Mozelle said.

Essie quickly picked up the eggs and took them to Cora. Cora put them on the top shelf. Still holding on to the door, Randie pushed it closed. The latch on the handle clicked. Cora touched the side of the icebox.

"Mama, reckon the chicken'll keep 'til Sunday?"

Looking up from her plate of beans, Mozelle waited until she chewed up the food in her mouth before she said, "It's jest one day. At the cafe, food keep longer than two days in the icebox."

Cora sat down on the floor in front of the icebox.

"Mama, Brother hittin' on me," Randie said.

"Randie, you, Essie, and Brother 'bout ready to go to bed, ain't y'all?"

"It ain't dark outside yet, Mama," Essie said.

"It's dark as it gon' get. Y'all go on and lay down so I can get to sleep, too. U'm plumb tuckered out."

"Ahh, Mama," Essie and Brother both whined.

"Y'all hear Mama," Cora said. "Y'all pick up that candy paper off the floor and go lay down like Mama say."

Ignoring Cora, Essie looked at Mozelle. Mozelle didn't look up. Essie pouted. Cora pointed at the empty candy wrapper. Essie swiped up her candy wrapper off the floor. Then sucking her teeth, she rushed out of the kitchen behind Randie.

Brother picked up his paper, too, but he glared at Cora. "Mama, Cora always actin' like she our mama."

Mozelle glanced over at Cora still sitting on the floor, her back against the icebox. She smiled at her and Cora smiled back. There was a special bond between them that she didn't share with her other children. Cora was her firstborn. The child that she held closest to her heart when she realized that she really was all alone in the world. If it were not for Cora, she would not have been able to take care of the other children. Cora did not give birth to her brother and sisters, but she just about raised them. Cora spent more time with them than Mozelle ever did or could, and now that she worked in Alabama City, her workday was even longer because of the six miles she had to walk there and back. It was because of Cora that she could go to work and stay all day without worry. Maybe that was why Cora seemed so much older than girls her own age.

"Brother," Mozelle began, "Cora is your big sister. When I ain't here, she do for you and your sisters like a mama, and even when I is here, you best listen to Cora. I can't go to work and earn money to feed y'all without her, you understand me?"

Cora slowly slipped her tongue out at Brother.

Brother angrily stuck his tongue back out at her.

Mozelle saw him. She had not seen Cora. "Boy, U'm gon' tan your hide."

"Mama, Cora stuck her tongue at me first."

Cora smiled innocently.

Mozelle could tell by the mischievous twinkle in Cora's eyes that she had done something, but she saw no cause to scold her. Cora was a good girl. "Brother, U'm plumb tuckered out. I ain't got the strength to tangle with you tonight."

"But, Mama, Cora—"

"Brother, 'nuff said. Go to bed."

Still glaring over at Cora, Brother stuck out his lower lip and stomped his foot. "Doggone it!"

"Boy! U'ma wash your mouth out with lye soap if I hear you swearin' again. You hear me?"

Brother stuck his lip way out and stomped his foot.

"Don't you stomp your foot at me. You want me to tan your tail?"

"But, Mama, you ain't sayin' nothin' to Cora. She—"

"Brother, don't you make me have to get up off this crate."

Folding his arms tight, Brother pushed his narrow shoulders all the way up to his ears. He clinched his jaw while his eyes welled up and overflowed.

As tired as she was, Mozelle didn't have the strength to whip him. "Brother, you tryin' me, boy. Go on to bed befo' I give you somethin' to cry about."

Brother abruptly left the kitchen without saying good night.

Mozelle looked at Cora. The twinkle was gone. "He been givin' you a hard time?"

"No, ma'am. The worst he do is go off in the woods when I tell him not to. He jest a boy, that's all, but he's not bad."

Mozelle turned back to her plate.

"Mama, I gots to tell you somethin'."

"Then tell me, child," Mozelle said, finishing up the last piece of corn bread wet with bean juice on her plate. She licked the spoon.

Cora got up off the floor. She went over to the table and took Mozelle's empty plate and the pot over to the sink.

Watching Cora start to wash the plate, Mozelle asked, "What you got ta tell me?"

Cora let the plate sink into the pot of stagnant dishwater. She turned back to face Mozelle. "Henry done ask me to marry him."

Though she had long dreaded that this day would come, Mozelle had expected it but not this soon. Henry was talking a lot more about staying in Gadsden.

"Mama? That all right with you?"

"Do you want to marry him?"

"Yessum."

"Are you sure?"

"Yessum."

"You reckon you ready to be mama to your own children?"

"Yessum. I want lots of children."

"Oh, Lord, child. Is you sure that's what you want?"

"Yessum."

Mozelle felt like crying all of a sudden. She began to rub on the back of her neck. Out of nowhere, it just tightened up on her.

"Mama, I won't be goin' away from you. U'ma be close by."

The tightness in her neck was moving up the back of her head. Mozelle rubbed harder. "Cora, U'm makin' mo' money now, and Brother's in school. You can go on to school with him if you wants to."

"Mama, U'm too old to be sittin' up in first grade," Cora said, going back to stand next to Mozelle. She gently took Mozelle's hand off her neck and began to rub it for her. "Mama, don't worry. U'ma be jest fine with Henry."

Sighing, Mozelle wished that she could forbid Cora from marrying, but she knew that it wouldn't work, it didn't work with her. And there was no use arguing about it, that didn't work with her either. "I guess you gon' be gettin' married then," she said sadly.

"When Henry ask you, Mama, you gon' say yes?"

"If that's what you want."

Cora kissed her on the cheek. "Thank you, Mama."

She took Cora's hand. "I want you to promise me something."

"Anything, Mama."

"Cora, don't you ever let him hit you."

Cora looked a little startled. "Henry won't hit me, Mama."

"If he do, I wants to know. You hear me?"

"Yessum."

"And you see to it that he feed you and your babies from the start," she said, squeezing her hand.

"Mama, you don't have to worry about me. Henry ain't like Daddy."

Mozelle patted Cora's hand. "Men got a way of changin', Cora. And truth to tell, some men ain't true when they courtin' a young girl. After you marry, Henry best treat you gooder then as he do now."

"He will, Mama."

"If he don't, Cora, you come back home. Don't ever be

shame to come back home. You hear me?"

"Yes, Mama."

"You go lay down. U'ma wash up the dishes."

Cora gave Mozelle just a hint of a smile before she left the kitchen. Mozelle got up slowly off the milk crate and rubbed the back of her thighs where the metal had pressed into her flesh, making her thighs itch. She went to the sink but stood staring at nothing. God, as much as she had known that it was bound to happen, she had hoped that Cora would not have wanted to get married for a while yet.

"Lord, please look after my child," she prayed. "Please don't let her know the kind of sufferin' her daddy done cause me."

"Mama?"

Mozelle turned around to see Cora standing in the doorway.

"Mama, a long time ago when I was little and we went to visit Grandma and Granddaddy in Georgia, did you wish that you coulda stayed?"

Mozelle nodded.

Cora appeared to be thinking. "Daddy ain't never been good to you, huh?"

Mozelle put down the pot. "The first three years we was married, he was."

"That's befo' I come along."

She nodded again.

"So. . .Mama. . .Daddy, Daddy started treatin' you bad after I was born."

The sadness in Cora's voice and the hurt in her eyes was painful.

"Cora, don't you go thinkin' you at fault for how your daddy treat me. Your daddy got ways that ain't like a lot of men-folk."

"So what do that mean, Mama? I seen Daddy treat other folks good."

"That's 'cause those folks ain't his family. Cora, I don't think your daddy trust hisself to be part of a family. I think he's scared to let hisself care too much about his children."

"That don't make sense, Mama. Ain't a daddy suppose to love his children jest as much as a mama do?"

"Well, sa. He suppose to, but your daddy probably scared if he love all y'all too much, he might lose a part of hisself."

Shaking her head, Cora frowned.

Mozelle could see that she was confusing Cora. "Baby, I know it's hard to understand your daddy, I ain't quite got a handle on understanding him myself. What I know about your daddy is that he's a selfish man, and a selfish man can only love hisself."

Thinking about that, Cora nodded. "Yeah, I guess that's how Daddy is."

"And he ain't never gon' change. He selfish to his bones."

"Mama, your daddy wasn't like that, was he?"

"Oh, no. My daddy was different. He was strict on us children, but he was good to my mama. He didn't beat on her, and he made sure there was food in the house. My daddy made sure we was fed befo' his ownself. And my mama never had to worry 'bout my daddy steppin' out on her with loose women. Cora, your granddaddy was a good man."

"That's good, Mama. U'm glad you got good memories of your daddy."

Mozelle was glad herself, but it saddened her that Cora was never going to be able to say that about Randell. He hadn't ever so much as given her a pat on the head.

"Mama, you think Henry is gon' be a good daddy?"

"Is you worryin' about Henry? He say somethin' to make you think he ain't gon' do right by his children?"

"No, Mama, Henry ain't did nothin' bad. Fact is, I think Henry is gon' do right by me and by the children we have. Truth is, I was jest tryin' to figure out if Daddy ever loved you," she said, turning slowly and going into the back room.

For a minute Mozelle had to wonder about that herself. She picked up the pot again and started scrubbing it with the dingy old dishrag. Randell never did say that he loved her—not that she could recall. If her memory served her right, what Randell had said was that she belonged to him. In a way, she used to think it meant the same as saying that he loved her. When she was young and foolish, she mistook those words to mean that he loved her. How wrong she was. Again she put down the pot. She draped the wet dishrag over the front of the sink. She didn't feel like washing dishes. She left the kitchen.

Sitting on the edge of the bed, she dug down in her bosom and pulled out her money. She counted it—twenty-seven dollars. When she got paid, she had asked for twenty-five dollars in one-dollar bills so that she could feel like she had even more than she had. Nobody told her she had to pay taxes, something she had never done before, so she was a little upset that they kept two dollars. She spread the money out on the bed in front of her like a fan. She looked at it. Considering that she had already bought food, what she had left was a lot of money. If all those ones were ten-dollar bills, she would really have a lot of money. But she didn't, and none of it was hers to keep. She had to pay the sixteen dollars a month for the rent. When Randell found out that she was working at the cotton mill, he stopped paying the rent. She didn't bother to argue with him about it, she was just going to pay it. She was tired of having to pick up and move out in the middle of the night.

She put aside four dollars toward the month's rent. All the children needed shoes, except for Cora. Her shoes were holding up. Soon her shoes would be Henry's concern. Mozelle put aside fifteen dollars more for shoes for the other children and for herself. They all couldn't get shoes at the same time, but if she was lucky, she could find a bargain for herself in the secondhand shop. Lord knows she needed a pair shoes, but brand-new shoes for herself would have to wait. Eight single dollars lay in front of her. Five dollars could buy a respectable dress for Cora to get married in. If there was anything left after she gave Cora fifty cents to buy collard greens for Sunday's supper, she could get what she wanted most for herself—a brassiere. She looked down at herself. She hefted her titties. They were heavy. Yes. First thing in the morning she was going into town. She was going to buy herself a brassiere. Fifty cents should be enough.

Two dollars lay alone. She stared at them. Picking them up, she rubbed them with her thumb. Buying land was still something she wanted to do. Maybe she could save one dollar every week. Maybe a single dollar could be her salvation. Getting up off the bed, she went into the dimly moonlit kitchen. Opening the cupboard she immediately saw what she was looking for—a medium size glass preserve jar with a top on it. Opening it, Mozelle dropped the dollar inside and screwed the top back on. Now, where to hide it? She looked around the kitchen. Although the kitchen was the one place Randell never stayed in but a minute to eat, the cupboard was not a safe place. She didn't want to take the chance that he'd go looking for something in there and come upon her money.

She was about to walk out of the room when the floorboard underfoot squeaked. She looked down at the floor. Her eyes cut to the corner near the window. The first time she scrubbed the floor on her knees after moving into the house, she had discovered that a short plank had been nailed down with just one nail in the corner. It stuck up on one end and moved if it was walked on.

Taking her butcher knife off the sink, Mozelle tiptoed over to the corner. Down on her knees, she tapped on the plank with the knife before prying it up. It came up easily. She had not lit the kerosene lamp. It was too dark to see how deep the space was, so she eased the jar down into the hole until it would go no farther. She carefully placed the plank over the opening. The jar was low enough for the plank to almost fall back in place. It stuck up where the protruding nail hit the floor beam. Mozelle sprang to her feet and got her black cast-iron skillet and banged twice on the head of the nail, driving it back into the beam flat to the floor.

"Mama, is that you knockin'?" Cora called out.

"It's me. U'm done now. Go on to sleep."

"Nightie night, Mama."

"Nightie night," she answered back. Mozelle set the skillet down quietly on the stove, then tiptoed back to her room. She gathered her money, tied it back up in her money rag, and put it under the mattress near the head of the bed on the side where she slept. Thoughts of all that she would buy filled her mind as she lay her head down. When she finally drifted off to sleep, she dreamed about buying her land.

Seventeen

Out of the door—bright and early. Mozelle stood with her children outside of the only shoe store in town. The doors were still locked. With their hands cupped around their faces, they all peered through the glass at the six pairs of brown and black leather shoes in the window. Randie would get the first pair of shoes.

"Mama, can I get penny loafers?" Randie asked. "Faye Dennis got a pair."

"No. They don't tie up."

"That's how come I want 'em."

"That's how come you ain't gettin' 'em. You need more support for your feet."

"My feet ain't bad like Cora's."

"No they ain't, but you need somethin' better then loafers."

"Please, Mama."

Mozelle shook her head. She didn't think she had to worry about how the shoes looked as long as they were new and wore good. "Randie, do you got pennies to put in penny loafers?"

Randie started to answer, but then she shook her head.

"Well then. When you got pennies that you don't need to buy food with, that's when you can buy loafers."

Randie frowned. She went back to peering through the store window at the shoes.

"Mama, U'm gon' get new shoes, too?" Essie asked.

"Not this time. Mama gon' buy you a pair of shoes next week."

Essie's bottom lip shot out. "I want new shoes, too."

"If'n you don't be still, you won't get none next week either."

Essie hushed up right quick.

Mozelle rubbed her eyes. She was still sleepy. As much as she hated to get up so early on her day off, she had gotten up when Randell got up, which was before dawn. She didn't know what time he had crawled into bed next to her—she had slept sounder than a cricket in daylight. They hadn't said a word between them in a handful of days, and that was all right with her. He left the house in white coveralls, which meant he had a painting job somewhere.

"Mama, when U'm gon' get a new pair shoes?" Brother asked.

"Another time," she said, not wanting to promise him exactly when. If she could, she would buy new shoes for all her children. None of them, except for Cora, had ever had a new pair of shoes before. If she could get a good price, she just might buy Essie a pair. If she did, Essie was only going to wear the shoes to school and church. Other than that, like the others, she could go barefoot. They did that all the time anyhow.

Mr. Mitchell suddenly appeared at the door, unlocking it from the inside. He pulled it open for them to come in.

Mozelle led the way. "Mornin', Mr. Mitchell."

"Mornin'," he replied, holding the door open. "Y'all right early this morning, Mozelle. Cora need another pair of shoes?"

"Oh, no sa," she said, glancing first at Cora, who was holding Brother's hand, and then at Randie and Essie. The sparkle in their eyes that told of their excitement belied their straight faces and the stiff way they stood. "In time, I hope to buy new shoes for everybody 'ceptin' Cora, if I can."

Mr. Mitchell arched his brow. "That's a lot of money for you, ain't it?"

She nodded. "Yessa. That's how come U'm buyin' jest for Randie and maybe Essie today. Do you got somethin' reasonable?"

"Sho do," he said, looking down at Randie's bare, dusty feet.

"Your girl can't be putting her dirty feet in my new shoes now."

"Oh, no sa. I got me a rag," Mozelle said, pulling out a rag from the brown bag she carried. "If I can get some water I'll clean her feet good."

"Some water out back," Mr. Mitchell said, pointing to the door at the back of the store.

"C'mon, Randie," Mozelle said, going toward the back door. "Cora, y'all stay put now."

"Yes, Mama."

Mozelle darn near scrubbed Randie's feet raw, but when she was done, Randie slipped into a pair of brand-new black-and-white Oxford tie-ups. They were a size bigger so that Randie wouldn't grow out of them too soon.

"How much them shoes?" Mozelle asked.

"Six dollars. They made out of fine leather."

That was about what she expected but she didn't want to pay that much. "Mr. Mitchell, sa, will you take less?"

Mr. Mitchell was looking at Essie's feet. "You want shoes for her, too?"

"Well, sa, you got some reasonable?"

"Sho do. I'll let you take those Oxfords for five dollars and fifty cents."

"Thank you, sa," Mozelle said, grateful. Every penny counted.

"Now I got me some shoes that ain't been picked up by a customer. They look to be the size your girl wear. If they fit, I can let you have them for three dollars."

"That's jest fine," Mozelle said, hoping that Essie's feet would fit into the shoes.

Mr. Mitchell went off to the back room to get the shoes, Mozelle cleaned Essie's feet just as she had done Randie's. The brown leather shoes were a little wide and, like Randie's shoes, a size bigger, but Mozelle didn't mind that. Randie's feet would grow. Essie wanted to wear her shoes homes, while Randie placed her Oxfords neatly back inside the box and hugged them to her chest. Looking at her children's beaming faces, Mozelle's heart swelled with pride. Finally, she was going to be able to do something for them. Brother was sullen and quiet but she didn't pay him any mind. He would get shoes next time. It felt good to think that there would be a next time. Mozelle sent the children out of the store with Cora while she counted out eight dollars and fifty cents to pay for their shoes. It felt good to be able to do that, too.

"Mozelle, you looking to work on Saturday?" Mr. Mitchell asked, taking the money.

Surprised, she answered, "Why sho," without even knowing what the work was. She wasn't turning down anything that paid her.

"My wife's looking for a girl to clean the house on Saturdays. If you interested, you can go on over to the house and tell Mrs. Mitchell I sent you."

"Well, thank you, sa," Mozelle said. "When's the best time to go?"

"Anytime after ten would be fine. U'ma give you my street number where I live," he said, writing on a piece of paper. "Mrs. Mitchell will tell you what the pay is."

"Thank you, sa," Mozelle said, taking the piece of paper he tore off the edge of the brown wrapping paper on the counter. She slipped it down inside her dress pocket without looking at it. She had time. Besides, it didn't matter where the house was, she was going to take the job if Mrs. Mitchell wanted her. As soon as she stepped outside of the shoe store, she glanced upward. "Thank You, Lord."

"You thanked the Lord for Randie and Essie's shoes?" Brother asked.

"Sho did, and for Mr. Mitchell for offerin' me another job."

"Mama," Cora said, "how you gon' do another job after workin' hard all day?"

"This job cleanin' Mr. Mitchell's house on Saturday. I can do that easy."

"But, Mama, you be so tired at the end of the week, I feel bad to see you so tired. I wish I could get me a job and help you."

"You do a lot to help me every day," she said. "Right now

I need you to take the children home for me."

"You goin' to work now?" Randie asked.

"Dependin'. U'ma go see if Miss Mitchell want me first. Cora, you take this here dollar 'n buy some greens," Mozelle said. "Pick some pretty ones."

Cora smiled, "I will, Mama, but how I know they pretty?"

"If they ain't got a lot of holes, no brown spots, 'n they green all over, then they pretty. And if there's any change left, get some apples. U'm gon' make us a apple pies."

"Oh, Mama," Cora said excitedly.

"Randie, you, Essie, and Brother go on with Cora. After y'all buy the greens and apples, y'all go on home, and stay there. Y'all hear me? Brother, you stay outta them woods."

"Mama, I ain't goin' in the woods."

"You make sure you don't or you ain't gon' get no apple pie. You hear me?"

Brother shuffled his foot in the dirt and didn't look at Mozelle. "Yessum."

Knowing that Brother most likely would not stay out of the woods, Mozelle gave him a solid slap on his behind and a gentle shove to get him going. She didn't hit him hard but he said, "Ouch," anyway. Mozelle watched the children cross the road before she went on down to the dry-goods store. It took her less time to pick out a white-collared pink-flowered cotton dress for Cora than it took for her to be measured and fitted for a brassiere. Her titties had gotten bigger with each baby she suckled. Sometimes they hurt from hanging so heavy to her stomach. When the shopkeeper gave her the big harness-looking white cotton brassiere, Mozelle would have laughed if she had a sense of humor. Instead she shook her head and said, "I declare."

Alone in the back room she struggled to hook the little eyelets on the brassiere across her back. It was awkward, it was something she wasn't use to doing. Her fingers fumbled. Her arms ached from being twisted up behind her back too long. Beads of sweat popped out on her forehead before she finally hooked the last eyelet. She was breathing heavily. The brassiere was tight. The pressure she felt on her shoulders, against her chest and around her back was not altogether too uncomfortable, but it would take some getting use to. Once she adjusted herself inside the brassiere, Mozelle stood looking at herself in the mirror. She turned from side to side. Her titties pointed out like hunting dogs pointing at game.

"I declare," she said again. With her dress back on, she looked at the way her titties stuck her dress out high in front. Clearly she could see the imprint in her dress where they used to hang. That, she tried to flatten out. With her titties out of the way, she could halfway see a waist. Her figure really didn't look all that bad. Of course, it would have been nice if she could have bought a brand-new dress for herself. Shaking her head, she shook that thought right out of her head. That would be a while yet.

"That'll be four dollars for the dress and one dollar for the brassiere," the shop owner said.

"Will you take less?"

"That's the price, ma'am."

"I know, sa, but will you take less?"

The shop owner looked steadily at Mozelle while he mulled over her question.

"I'd 'preciate it, sa."

"Twenty-five cent less, and nothing more."

"Thank you kindly, sa." Mozelle smiled when she paid him the money. She walked out of the store carrying Cora's new dress in a brown bag and proudly wearing her new brassiere. She never felt so good in her life. She nodded good day to all whose eye she caught. Reaching inside her pocket, she checked the address. She wasn't that far from Hickory Street. She squared her shoulders, and with a smile on her face, she walked like that all the way to Mrs. Mitchell's spacious, well-furnished house. At the kitchen table, she sat tall and straight when Mrs. Mitchell said she could have the job starting the following Saturday.

"I want you to start at eight o'clock in the morning and finish up by two. Is that a problem for you?"

"No, ma'am. I can be here right on time."

Mrs. Mitchell palmed the big knot of gray hair on the top of her head. "The only thing I fuss about is my lace curtains. They in all five bedrooms and in the front sitting room," she said, smoothing back a strain of stray hair from her forehead.

Mozelle remembered seeing the curtains in the front room when she was shown through the house.

"They're English lace, you know," Mrs. Mitchell said.

Though she didn't know English lace from any other lace, Mozelle nodded like she knew. What came to mind was Mrs. Scott's lace curtains over in Piedmont.

"I like my curtains white as the clouds in the sky. The sunlight looks right pretty shining through white lace curtains, don't you think?"

Mozelle nodded. In her house the sunlight or the blackness of night came straight through naked windowpanes. The one set of faded curtains hanging up to the window in her bedroom were shredded pieces of old cloth left in the house by people probably long ago dead. She had carefully washed and hung them back because she couldn't replace them with anything better.

"I just hate how the sun turn my curtains yellow. I got special wash powder for them. My last girl washed my curtains every other Saturday, and put them back up before she left for the day. She did most of her heavy cleaning every other Saturday, too. Can you do that?"

"Yes, ma'am."

"Well good. Mozelle, I'll see you next Saturday then," Mrs. Mitchell said, getting up from the table.

"Yes, ma'am." Mozelle picked up her bag with Cora's dress inside it off the floor as she got to her feet. Mrs. Mitchell showed her out through the back door and closed the door. Mozelle didn't know how much she was going to make and was hesitant to knock on the door to find out. Whatever it was, it would do. She started to step off the porch when the door suddenly opened again.

"By the way, I can pay you ten dollars for the day."

"Thank you, ma'am."

Mozelle walked quickly around the side of the house back to the road before she dared to shout, "Thank you, Lord!" Ten dollars more a week! Surely her cup runneth over. There was so much she could do with ten more dollars—clothes, food, her land. This was truly a blessing from God. Washing clothes and scrubbing floors was easy work. There wasn't going to be anything hard or tiring about dusting and polishing all the pretty fine furniture she saw in that house.

Of course, Mozelle knew that most white folk lived rich like that from when she was a child in Royston. She could tell that from the kitchens of the white folks whose wash she picked up for her mama. She didn't blame Mrs. Mitchell in the least for wanting to keep her lace curtains pretty and white. Maybe one day Mozelle could own something as pretty. With ten dollars more, she might just get her land after all. She sang "Count Your Blessings" all the way home.

Cora graced Sunday's supper of crispy fried chicken, fluffy white rice, corn bread that tasted like cake, and collard greens sweetened with a heavy touch of sugar. The food was so good, they were all licking their fingers and saying "M'm" every time they took a bite. The pan-fried apple pie were just as good as the meal. Mozelle enjoyed the smiles on her children's faces just as much as she enjoyed her meal. This was the way it was supposed to be.

Eighteen

1949

Cora and Henry were married seven months after they first started courting and a month before Cora's sixteenth birthday in March. Cora tried to look all grown up. Mozelle straightened and curled her hair, but that didn't help much. Cora was a pretty little thing in her new dress; she looked like she was about twelve. That's because she was standing next to Henry with his chubby self. He liked to eat, which made Mozelle feel all the better about Cora marrying him. At least there would be food in the house.

Randell didn't see fit to show up at the courthouse to give Cora away. He wasn't missed. Mozelle was there to do what Randell wouldn't—she gave Henry Cora's hand. Truth to tell, she secretly respected Randell for that. Him acting like a daddy one day would never make up for the sixteen years he wasn't.

The night Cora got married, Randell came home early. He was in a good mood. He gave candy to the children, fifty dollars to Mozelle, and for the first time in years, he pestered her until she gave in and let him sex her. She didn't want to; it was the fifty dollars along with him reminding her that she was his wife that made her feel obliged. She lay still under him, pressing her lips together while Randell grunted and sweated atop her. Being with him in this way was different now. Nothing like when they got married. Now, she didn't like the feel of his body on her or inside her. The hotness of his breath on her neck irritated her. Randell got his fill and dropped off to sleep. She got up and cleaned herself up. She didn't know how she was going to live out the rest of her life like this. Lying back in bed next to him, her mind would not let her rest for thinking about Cora's first night with Henry. She prayed that he was gentle with her and would be just as good to her twenty years down the line.

Cora and Henry settled into their own house up over the hill on Short Vine Street. Randell took a shine to Henry like he hadn't taken to his own children. Maybe it was because Henry was a full-grown man. Sometimes Randell went out with Henry after work. Neither Cora or Mozelle liked that because Henry got where he wouldn't tell Cora anything about where they went. In fact, Henry starting telling Cora, "A woman ain't got no business studin' in a man's business." That could only mean that he was paying attention to how Randell was going about being a bad husband. Mozelle didn't like that either. She didn't step aside and let Cora marry Henry to be mistreated. She started praying that Henry wasn't following in Randell's footsteps all the way, because she wasn't of a mind to let him hurt Cora and do anything about it. What she'd do, Mozelle wasn't sure, but Cora was never going to be miserable like her—not if she could help it. As it was, Cora had suffered through and seen enough of her daddy's meanness. His not showing up at the courthouse was just one more example of that.

Mozelle missed Cora being at home. Every day after work she stopped by Cora's house to pick up the children. From her back door down in the valley, she could look up over the hill and see Cora's kitchen window. Cora didn't have a backyard because the back of her house sat on stilts high up off the ground. The lush green hill that it sat on sloped down into the valley over the Clays' farm spread. On that hill behind Cora's house there were two peach trees from which Cora picked the fattest, juiciest mouthwatering peaches Mozelle had ever had. She and Cora made sweet, tasty cobblers from those peaches. When the seasons changed, at Cora's front door, the big pecan tree across the road dropped plump pecans on her porch and on the road. Mozelle saw that as a sign that Cora would never go hungry. God was making sure of that.

Henry kept his word—he didn't make Cora go out to work. With the little money he saved before they got married, he was able to buy a bed and a kitchen table and chairs. Cora kept her plank floors washed, her three-room house neat and tidy, and her husband fed. She ate collard greens as often as she could buy them, which was every Friday when Henry got paid. Cora was happy. That's why it was no surprise, two months later, when Cora said, "Mama, U'm pregnant." Mozelle hugged her child, but she couldn't share in her happiness. She had only that morning discovered that she was pregnant, too. It had been seven years since Brother was born, and she had been believing that her body, at thirty-five, was done with making babies. What's more, she figured that Randell should've been all dried up—he was fifty-seven years old. It was a cruel joke. She was supposed to be done making babies. Fact of the matter was, she had been getting the vapors and thought that she might be going through the change. She knew it was possible because Rosa told her that she went through the change before she was forty, and that women weren't supposed to get pregnant after that. How wrong she was.

"U'm gon' have a baby, too," Mozelle told Cora, after making sure that the children were outdoors playing.

Cora inhaled sharply. "Oh, Mama, no."

"I know."

"You said you didn't want no mo' babies."

"I don't."

"Then, Mama, how come you keep lettin' Daddy. . .you know. . .?"

She shook her head. "Cora, I don't let your daddy 'cause I want to, I let him 'cause I got to."

Cora looked befuddled. "How come?"

"'Cause U'm still his wife, and I ain't out the woods all the way."

"But, Mama."

Mozelle slumped in her chair. "Cora, I ain't set with my money in a way that I won't ever need your daddy again. One day I hope to be. That's how come for now, I got to be with him when he want me to."

"When you get set, Mama, you gon' leave Daddy?"

Mozelle worried over that question because she knew the answer was one she did not want to give.

Her mama's silence and downcast eyes answered Cora's question. "Mama, I don't understand. Daddy ain't never been good to you. How come you won't leave him when you get set?"

"Cora, my mama told me to never leave my husband. I married your daddy for life. I can't leave him."

"But that ain't what you told me when I married Henry. Didn't I marry Henry for life?"

"No, Cora, you married Henry for as long as he's good to you. If he ain't good to you, you got a home to come back to. I want you to remember that."

Cora seemed to relax. "Yessum, but, what about you, Mama? You been miserable with Daddy all your life."

Wasn't that the truth? Sitting back, Mozelle started rubbing away the stiffness in her shoulder. "I pray that your daddy up and leave me one day. When he do, he won't be comin' back. I won't let him come back. Then I won't be miserable no mo'. But for now," she said, beginning to tear, "U'm gon' be havin' a baby I ain't got no business havin'."

Cora went and stood alongside Mozelle. She cradled her head against her budding bosom. "It's gon' be all right, Mama. We gon' have our babies together."

"Cora, it ain't fittin' for a woman to be 'pectin' along with her own child."

"I seen Miss Clay 'n Shelly carryin' they baby at the same time. It ain't nothin' to be shame of. Ain't nobody gon' talk."

"It ain't 'cause of talk U'm ashamed. U'm shame of myself 'cause I ain't got no business gettin' laid up with another baby by your daddy. I don't know what U'm gon' do. U'm tryin' to do better for the children I got. How U'm gon' do that with another baby in my arms?"

Cora put her arm around Mozelle's shoulders. "U'ma help you with your baby, Mama. You ain't gon' be by yourself."

Wiping the tears from her cheeks with both hands, Mozelle

looked up at Cora. "You gon' have your own baby and a husband to tend to. You gon' have lots to do in your own house."

"Mama," Cora said, pulling a chair out from the table. She sat. "I can still take care of your baby while you at work. I takes care the other children after they get in from school by myself 'n they older now. I helped you with all of them when they was babies, didn't I?"

Remembering Cora carrying babies bigger than her own little body in her arms, Mozelle smiled. "You sho did, and it wasn't easy. Me and you, we went through some hard times together, Cora, and you ain't never complain one time. You was my little angel, my little helper, my saving grace," she said, her heart filled to the brim and overflowed with her love for her child. She lay her hand on Cora's knee and gently squeezed it.

"I'd do anything for you, Mama. U'ma take care of your baby like it's mine."

"I know that, Cora. But, you know your daddy ain't gon' like me havin' another baby."

"Don't go worryin' yourself about Daddy. He ain't never liked you havin' no baby from me on down. Anyhow, he ain't gon' give you none of his money to help you out. You gon' make do like you always do, without him."

"That's just it, Cora. U'm tired of makin' do. U'm just about startin' to do better. Another baby gon' set me back. I don't know when U'm gon' get my land now." Again tears slipped down her cheeks.

"I told you, Mama, don't worry. You gon' get your land. U'm gon' help you if'n I can and U'm gon' pray on it," Cora said. She slipped out of her chair down onto the floor at Mozelle's feet and lay her head on her lap like she used to when she was getting her hair plaited.

Mozelle began to lightly stroke Cora's hair. "Thank you, baby. U'm prayin' on it, too." And she was praying hard. Another baby. Lord, was it ever going to get easy? What if she got put out of work when her baby made her so big she couldn't do her job? What was she going to do then?

"Mama, you gon' be jest fine. You'll see."

Nineteen

She didn't lose her job, but then neither did she slack up on her work. She was kept on at the cotton mill until a month before she was due. Before she left, her boss told her to call in after the baby came. Nell was born two days after Cora's boy, Junior, on a cool November day in 1949. Nell was Mozelle's first baby to be born in a hospital. A nurse in the hospital said that it was an omen that a mother and daughter had their babies so close together. She didn't say if it was a good or bad omen. Mozelle hoped that it was a good one. She needed for something good to happen. Randell said nothing bad about Nell being born, but then he didn't say anything at all. Maybe that was a good omen.

After Nell was born, Mozelle's body stayed sore for days. It wasn't like when she was young and a day later she was as strong as before. Now she was just plain tired. She couldn't afford to be tired when she needed to get back to work. Two weeks after having Nell, she went up to the general store to call the Cotton Mill to ask for her job back. Her stomach was all tied up in knots when she walked back home. Someone else was doing her job. The supervisor said he'd get word to her when something else opened up. What in the world was she going to do without her job at the mill? Her Saturday work wasn't enough to keep the rent paid. It wasn't enough to help her get her land. It wasn't nearly enough. The sixty dollars she had set aside for the time she would be out of work having Nell was dwindling. She had to ask Randell for rent money and to her surprise, he gave it to her. There was no discussion, no argument. He gave her the rent money for December. She had learned a long time ago that Randell didn't like to be asked for anything. What he gave, which was rare, on his own, it was because he wanted to and not because he had to. She hardly saw much of him anymore other than when he came home to change his clothes and to eat. All for the best.

Without her job, Mozelle felt hopeless. The ten dollars she made on Saturdays went fast after she bought food. She refused to touch her land money stashed under the kitchen floorboard. Over the past year, every time another dollar was added to the jar, she felt richer than she had ever felt in her life. Not just in dollars, but in spirit. She was beginning to feel like she was worth something. She had saved fifty dollars toward fulfilling her dream. Lord knows, she did not want to have to start from scratch if she had to spend that money now.

Her children didn't have a Christmas, though they didn't miss what they never had. They were lucky to have had something to eat, and that was because of the basket of food the church sent over. Randell paid January rent without being asked, and Mozelle gave him his dinner without any lip. By the third week in February, after calling the cotton mill for the sixth time, Mozelle started to worry that she might not get her job back. The rent for the month was past due. Randell claimed that he didn't have the money, and with March fast approaching, worrying about how she was going to pay two months rent and feed her children made Mozelle's head ache constantly. Most likely the itchy hives on her arms came from worrying, too. More than a handful of times she took the jar from its hiding place and counted every dollar, trying to decide whether to use it or not to keep a roof over their heads. In the end, each time, she'd stuff the money back inside the jar and put it back in the floor. She had to get herself a house to keep from having to be put outdoors again. She had no other choice. She had to ask Randell. Long after the children were asleep, she waited up for him, hoping and praying that he would come home and that he would be in a good mood.

It was ten-thirty when she heard his car pull up in front of the house. She started to stay seated at the table but she was too anxious to stay put. She went to the door and opened it.

He was surprised. "Something done happened?" he asked

as he went past her.

She got a whiff of the strong smell of whiskey on his breath. She screwed up her nose. "Ain't nothin' happened."

Randell turned and looked at Mozelle as she pushed the door up. She did not latch it. "Then you must want something from me," he said, going straight to the bedroom. "That's how come you waiting up for me, ain't it?"

She realized that he wasn't slurring, so he wasn't drunk. He just smelled bad and looked bad. His eyes were redder than the open belly of a sow and against his white-spotted dark skin, he looked downright evil.

She followed him into the bedroom and closed the door so as not to wake up the children. "I need you to do me a favor."

He eyed her suspiciously. "What kind of favor?"

"I need thirty-two dollars to pay rent."

Shrugging his shoulders once, Randell cut his red eyes at Mozelle in a "that's not my concern" sort of way. He smirked.

Mozelle told herself to stay calm, to not let him get her started. After all, she needed him. She waited, following his every move as he went over to the bed and sat down on the edge. He crossed his right leg over his left thigh and began to slowly untie his shoes like he had all the time in the world. She knew what he was doing. He was trying to aggravate her last nerve and he was doing just that. He made her feel like a child waiting for her daddy to have his say about something she wanted to do. Anxious, she went and stood in front of him.

He didn't look at her; he acted like she wasn't there.

Mozelle folded her arms high and tight across her chest.

Randell ignored her still. He took off both shoes. He placed his shoes side by side under the bed. He stood up, forcing Mozelle to step back while he took off his britches.

She dropped her arms and stopped tapping her foot. She wanted to scream, but she held her tongue.

"You need me now, don't you?" he said, tauntingly.

"You gon' give me the money or not?"

"I ain't got no money."

"Randell, U'ma pay you back soon as I get back to work at

the mill."

Brushing past her, he went to the closet. "You still working over at that white woman's house on Saturday?"

"Yeah."

"Then you can make ten dollars tomorrow and every Saturday for four Saturdays until you make the money you need," he said, crawling into bed. Nell stirred when he crawled in next to her, but she didn't wake up.

Standing over Randell, Mozelle's stomach churned. "I need thirty-two dollars now, Randell. In four weeks, U'm gon' need rent money for April. The money I make on Saturday I buy food with it."

"You need me now, don't you? You ain't acting all high and mighty now, is you?"

"What's that suppose to mean, Randell?"

"You ain't got your big job at the cotton mill no more."

"What big job? I don't understand what you talkin' 'bout."

"Since you went to work at that mill, you walk around like you got all the money in the world, buying shoes and clothes and stuff."

"I buy what I need to buy for our children, Randell. You don't buy them nothin'. Now you gon' give me the rent money or not?" she asked, losing the little bit of patience she had been clinging to. "If I put the ten dollars I make tomorra toward rent, the children gon' go hungry."

"That ain't my problem," he said, turning away from Mozelle.

Mozelle's throat tightened. She had expected that he would act like this, but she had hoped that he wouldn't. "Randell, please. I don't want to be put outdoors, not one more time."

He didn't stir.

"U'm beggin' you, Randell. These your children. You need to keep a roof over they heads and food in they bellies."

Randell raised his head but he didn't look back. "As far as I'm concerned, I ain't got nobody to worry about but myself. None of them children come outta my gut, they came out of yours. When my belly's full, my whole family's fed." He lay back down.

Her chest heaved. Glaring at the back of his head, Mozelle balled up her fists at her sides. "You old bastard! Them children might not've come outta your gut, but you put 'em in mine. If they hungry, it's just as much your damn problem as mine."

Randell suddenly flipped over onto his back and sat up. "I told you, heifer. . ."

"Don't call me that!"

". . .those ain't my children, and I ain't got to feed them."

Tears blurred her vision. "Randell, you can't go all your life denying your own."

"'Mama's babies, daddy's maybe,'" he said calmly.

Mozelle felt hot. Inside she was boiling. Her hands began to shake.

"Heifer, don't be looking at me like that. You don't scare me."

A piercing scream erupted from Mozelle's throat startling Nell awake. Before Randell could react, Mozelle threw herself on top of him, walloping him in the face with her fists. Nell began hollering at the top of her lungs while Mozelle's scream had turned to a fierce growl. Randell gave up trying to fend off her punches. He grabbed her wrists with both his powerful hands and thrust her off him onto the floor. She hit the floor with a loud thump. Randell kicked out from under the cover and leaped straight up out of bed. He snatched Mozelle up by the hair before she could get up off the floor on her own. Lord knows she didn't know how he managed to always get her hair wrapped around his hand.

Thrashing out at him, she screamed, "Let go of my hair!"

"U'm gon' take your head off," Randell threatened.

"Mama! Mama!" Essie called from the other side of the door.

"Leave my Mama be!" Brother shouted.

"Shut the hell up!" Randell ordered. "I'll beat both your black asses."

"Mama! Mama, you all right?"

Mozelle could hear Essie calling her. She could hear Nell

and Brother crying, but she couldn't hear herself screaming as she clawed at Randell's hands.

"Woman, I done told you I'll kill you sure as U'm breathing," Randell snarled in her face. "I ain't got to give you a damn dime if I don't want to."

God, help me, Mozelle prayed. She balled her right fist up tight and punched Randell hard in the groin. A whoosh of air escaped from him. Mozelle punched him again. He abruptly let go of her hair to clutch his groin. He dropped to his knees. Mozelle sprinted across the room to the door and yanked it wide open. It banged hard against the wall.

"Randie, get me my skillet!" she ordered.

Randie took off running.

Groaning, Randell doubled over.

Nell wailed.

"You woke up my baby," Mozelle said, wanting to jump on Randell for that alone. She had had a hard time putting Nell to sleep."

Essie and Brother held on to each other. Randie came running back with the skillet in hand. Grabbing hold to the skillet with both hands, Mozelle wielded it threateningly at Randell. He wasn't paying her any mind though. He was trying to catch his breath and pull the pain out of his groin.

"You triflin' bastard," Mozelle said, standing over him. "I wish to God I never laid eyes on you."

Randell coughed up phlegm and spit it out onto the floor. "Bi—"

"What you 'bout to call me?"

He glared up at her. "Woman, ain't nobody sorrier than me I married your poor, ugly ass."

"Then why don't you get the hell outta here! Go back to the hoe you laid up with tonight. U'm tired of you, Randell. U'm tired of you eatin' my food 'n layin' up in my bed to rest up between your hoin'. You ain't doin' nothin' for me or my children. I want you to go on 'bout your business. I want you to stay gone. I can do bad by myself. Get out!"

Still in pain, Randell got to his feet while still holding on to groin. "I ain't going nowhere."

"Well, you ain't stayin' here lessen you give me rent money. I need thirty-two dollars 'n you best give it to me or U'ma bash your no-good skull in." She raised the skillet over her head.

Randell plopped down on the bed. He slid his hand under the mattress. "I got me a gun. I'll blow your goddamn brain out."

Essie and Brother wailed.

"Mama!" Randie cried.

Mozelle didn't look at Randie. "Randie, take Essie and Brother to the back room."

"Mama, you come, too," Randie said.

"Y'all go on and do like I say," Mozelle said, not taking her eyes off Randell. Their eyes were locked in a dance of wills. "Go on, now."

Nell was hollering at the top of her little lungs, but Mozelle dared not go to her. Nell was laying too close to Randell. She wasn't worried about him harming Nell. He had never touched any of the children—not to hug them, not to hit them. Behind her, Essie and Brother's crying moved farther back in the house.

"Your gun don't scare me, Randell, and neither do you."

"You big and brave, ain't you?"

"I got God. I ain't got cause to be scared of no man, 'pecially you. Randell, you ain't doin' me 'n my children no good. I ain't lettin' you sleep in my bed or under the same roof with me no more lessen you give me some money."

Nell's crying was unending.

"I ain't got no money."

"Liar! I know you got paid today."

"All I got left is five dollars to go back and forth to work."

"You a sorry man, Randell. You ought be ashamed of yourself. If you did spend all your money, how you gon' eat if we ain't got no food."

"I can always get me something to eat."

"Yeah, I bet you can. Get the hell outta here!"

"I ain't going nowhere."

"Yes, you is. Go to your hoes, but you best give me that five dollars first."

Smirking at her, Randell continued to sit. "You gon' make me?"

Nell continued to cry.

"I done told you befo', if I got to die trying to take your life, I will."

Randell didn't take her threat lightly. He didn't move toward her. Neither batted an eye. Both were taking long, deep breaths. Mozelle adjusted the skillet to get a better grip on the handle. Randell looked from Mozelle's face to the skillet then back to her face. As if he made a decision, he suddenly stood. Mozelle flinched, raising the skillet higher. Randell snatched his britches out of the closet and dug down into the pocket. He pulled out a crumpled-up bill and threw it at her.

She let the money fall to the floor at her feet.

Randell snatched up his shoes. "I ain't going 'cause you say so; U'm going 'cause your mouth ain't gon' let me get a wink of sleep," he said, swaggering out of the room past her.

When she was sure that Randell was out of the house, Mozelle gasped, her lungs had been about to burst. She picked up the money off the floor. Uncrumpling it, she saw that it was a twenty-dollar bill. She shook her head. "Nothin' but a liar."

"Mama," Randie said, timidly.

"U'm all right," she said, going over to the bed and setting the skillet down on the floor next to the head of the bed. She lifted the mattress and slid her hand under it, searching for the gun on the springs underneath. Until Randell said it, Mozelle never even knew that he had a gun. She went all the way around the bed, looking and feeling. There was no gun. She picked up Nell and cradled her. Nell's crying didn't stop until Mozelle put her wet nipple into Nell's mouth. Mozelle sat on the bed. Now that it was quiet, it dawned on her that she had not heard the sound of Randell's car.

"Mama," Randie said again.

"Yes, child," Mozelle said, glimpsing Randie's tear-streaked face.

"Can we sleep in here with you?"

Mozelle nodded.

Randie went out into the other room. She came back with Essie and Brother.

The sight of their tear-streaked faces tore at her heart and made her even madder at Randell. "Randie, you and Essie sleep at the foot. Brother you sleep up here with me and Nell."

Randie, Brother, and Essie climbed up onto the bed. Mozelle watched her children get under the one blanket on her bed. They had seen ugly fights between her and Randell many times before, but every fight scared them just the same. It wasn't right that they had to live like that. Somehow, even if she couldn't get rid of Randell, she had to put an end to the fighting. She could remember when she was a child and the few times her mama and daddy fought, it not only scared her, it made her sick to her stomach. Days afterward, she'd still feel sick, and her folks didn't fight nearly as much or as bad as her and Randell. How her children were feeling, she could only imagine. For them, she had to do better. They deserved better. Next to her, Essie and Brother dropped off to sleep right away; Randie slumbered fitfully.

Mozelle didn't know if she was going to be able to sleep—she was too wound up. Her racing heart hadn't quieted down yet, and Nell was drawing hard on her nipple, hurting her. But it was Randell's silent engine that bothered her most. He hadn't gone anywhere. Maybe he was asleep in his car. That was fine by her as long as he didn't come back into the house. She was not up to seeing one hair on his head. When Nell had her fill, Mozelle lay next to her and in the early-morning hours she dozed.

Twenty

Randell's Studebaker was gone. The early-morning dew was the only sign that he had left after dawn—the spot where the car had sat was dry. Mozelle sent the children off to Cora's with plain boiled grits and water on their bellies. She started out early for Mrs. Mitchell's—she had a lot of cleaning to do.

Soreness in her shoulders and a pounding headache didn't keep Mozelle from getting to work on time. Heavy on her mind was the thought that the twenty dollars she got from Randell and the ten dollars she would make for the day was still two dollars shy of what she needed to pay the rent she owed, and she still needed money to feed her children for the week. She was left with no choice; she was going to have to use her land money, and she knew that once she started dipping into the jar, owning her own land would never come to be.

"Mozelle, you been looking troubled all morning," Mrs. Mitchell said. She had been watching Mozelle work hard at polishing the mahogany sideboard in the dining room. "You look like you carrying the weight of the world on your shoulders."

Bending sideward, Mozelle rubbed down the front side of the sideboard, all the while making sure that Mrs. Mitchell couldn't see her face. She didn't want her to see that she was about to cry and had been feeling that way all morning. Every time she thought she was doing better, she was always knocked back down on her tail, reminding her that the climb out of a deep hole was never easy without some help.

"Mozelle, is everything all right?"

Mozelle eased down on her knees to polish the front legs of the sideboard. At that moment her tiredness came down on her. "I guess I might be feelin' a little under the weather."

"What's ailing you?"

"Nothin' particular, ma'am. Sometimes a body get weak from carryin' more than it's able."

Mrs. Mitchell pulled a chair out from the table and sat down. "What's worrying you so?"

Mozelle poured a dab of black oil polish onto her rag. "Ma'am, I don't wants to burden you with my troubles." She began rubbing the polish into the round legs.

Mrs. Mitchell watched Mozelle rub until the wood had a brilliant shine. "They call you back to the mill yet?"

"No, ma'am."

"Is that what's troubling you?"

She realized that Mrs. Mitchell was not going to leave her be with her toubles. "Partly," she said, crawling to the side of the sideboard. She began wiping down the back leg.

"Mozelle, why don't you rest a minute? Maybe you can talk about what's ailing you."

"Mrs. Mitchell, my troubles is so heavy, I can't talk about it to my own self."

"Then you need to take a minute and talk to God about it."

"Ma'am, I talk to God all the time in my heart. When I go home, U'm gon' talk to him like U'm talkin' to you."

Mrs. Mitchell slid off her chair onto her knees. She faced her chair and bowed her head.

Surprised to see Mrs. Mitchell down on her knees, Mozelle stared at her.

"When a body's troubled, Mozelle, it don't make no sense to wait. God can hear you just as good from my house as yours. You're already down on your knees. You may as well go on over to that other chair and let's pray."

Mozelle didn't know if she ought to or not. She had never prayed with a white person before. She wasn't even sure if they prayed to the same God, considering the poor way most of them treated colored folks in general. Though she couldn't say she was ever treated wrong by white folks herself, she heard tell of folks who were lynched or run off their land. Her daddy always used to say, "Treat white folk like they is rattlers—walk wide and fast around them, and they won't bother you." Mozelle had done just that all of her life. No matter how close white folks got to her, she acted like they weren't there. On the road, she never lifted her eyes to meet theirs, and they went on their way, leaving her be. Though good folks like the Mitchells didn't seem like other white folks she heard tell of.

"Let's pray," Mrs. Mitchell urged.

What could it hurt? Mozelle lay the rag on top of the can of furniture polish before walking on her knees over to the chair next to Mrs. Mitchell. Mozelle clasped her hands together, though she didn't close her eyes all the way—she peeked.

"Lord," Mrs. Mitchell began, "we come to You burdened down with our troubles. We come as humble servants asking You to hear our prayer. Mozelle needs You, Lord, to see her through troubled waters that she don't have the strength to wade through alone."

Amazed, Mozelle felt a mite relieved hearing that Mrs. Mitchell prayed like colored folk. She closed her eyes all the way.

"Lord, we ask that You walk with Mozelle and help her to overcome her trials and tribulations."

"Yes, Lord," Mozelle heard herself say.

"Hear her plea, oh Lord."

Mrs. Mitchell stopped praying. She was quiet.

Mozelle peeked at Mrs. Mitchell. Her eyes were still closed; she appeared to be praying to herself.

"Mozelle, the Lord is waiting to hear what's troubling you."

Opening her eyes all the way, Mozelle was at a lost for anything to say. What she prayed for in her heart was that Cora had enough food to feed the children supper.

Mrs. Mitchell's eyes were still closed. "Mozelle, tell the Lord about your troubles."

Mozelle couldn't ever remember a time when she had to be told twice to talk to God. Growing up in church, she always felt that God was there for everyone, including her, but she kind of felt now like she'd called on him too much. From the time she stepped foot in Elberton, she started asking for one thing or another—mostly food and the strength to fight back. Nothing had changed in all those years, she was still asking for something—again food and the money to buy her land. God had to be tired of her begging.

"Mozelle?"

She closed her eyes. "Well, Lord, You knows my troubles. I know more people then me need Your help. I just want to thank You, Lord, for Your sweet love and for watchin' over my children. Please, Lord, show me the way to take better care of them. Amen." Her eyes popped open.

Mrs. Mitchell was looking at Mozelle with a puzzled look on her face. She made a little grunt when she pushed off on the seat of the chair to get up off her knees.

Mozelle got up off the floor easily and slid her chair back under the table. "That was right kind of you, ma'am," she said. She bent down and reached under the sideboard for the polish and rags. "I do feel loads better."

"Good. The Lord'll provide. I see you worry about your children like I still worry about mine."

"Yessum."

"My two boys both grown and got families of their own now, but I worry just the same. That's what all good mothers have in common."

"Yessum."

"Well, it's about quitting time, Mozelle. Why don't you go on now. Your pay's in the bowl in the kitchen—like always."

"Yessum. I'll jest put this rag and polish away."

"Mozelle, if you get a chance, stop off at the shoe store on Monday. Mr. Mitchell has extra shoes that people ordered but ain't never picked up. Maybe your children can wear them."

"I declare, that's mighty kind of you," Mozelle said, smiling for the first time all day—in fact, in a long time. "God bless you." She rushed home to try to be there before Mr. Hess came to collect his rent. The first thing she did was check the closet for Randell's clothes. They were still there. She had hoped that he had moved out.

The children were still up at Cora's when Mr. Hess came a half hour later. He took her thirty dollars, but looked at her sternly when he warned, "You best give me that two dollars when you give me April's rent, which better be on time. I got bills, too."

"Yessa." She was relieved that Mr. Hess had not demanded the two dollars right then and there. She watched him drive off in his shiny black Buick and saw him stop at the foot of the narrow dirt road leading up out of the valley to let the white car coming down into the valley have the way. The white car rolled slowly down the road toward the house. The driver had to be holding the brakes hard or else the car would have been moving faster. Mozelle thought it looked like Mrs. Mitchell's car and was surer the closer it got to the house. She rushed over to meet her as she drove up into the front yard.

"Ma'am? Did I forget to do somethin'?"

Mrs. Mitchell climbed out of the car. "'Course not."

"Then you need me to do somethin' for you?"

"No, Mozelle, everything's just fine."

"Then—"

"After you left the house, Mozelle, the Lord spoke to me. He said, 'Effie Louise, you go on and help Mozelle.' He told me that you needed something that I could give."

Mozelle got a chill. "I don't get your meanin', ma'am."

Mrs. Mitchell crooked her finger for Mozelle to follow her to the back of the car. They stood at the trunk. "This is for you and your children," Mrs. Mitchell said, opening the trunk.

Mozelle gasped. "My Lord." The trunk was packed with four boxes of food.

"Mozelle, the Lord led me to bring you this food to see you through until you get your job back at the mill.

"Mrs. Mitchell, ma'am, I can't take your food."

"Nonsense. Of course you can."

Mozelle wanted to drop down on her knees and throw her hands up to God and give him the glory. Lord knows she needed this food. If God talked to Mrs. Mitchell, then she could not turn down this blessing. That would be like turning her back on God.

All of a sudden Mozelle felt the pain leave her head and her heart lighten. "Thank you, ma'am, but U'm gon' pay you back."

"I don't want you to pay me back, Mozelle. U'm doing what the Lord wants me to do, and there ain't no earthly pay for doing His work."

"But how did you know I needed food?"

"Well, it stands to reason that if you're not back at the mill, that you're been coming up short."

"Thank you, ma'am," Mozelle said as the floodgates opened. With her hands pressed to her mouth, Mozelle squeezed her eyes shut and sobbed. Mrs. Mitchell touched her arm. For the minute it took for her to get hold of herself, Mozelle said over and over in her head, *Thank you, Lord. Thank you, Lord.* With all of her heart, Mozelle wanted to hug Mrs. Mitchell, but she couldn't bring herself to do that. She had never hugged a white person before. For an awkward moment they both seemed uncertain as to what to do. Then Mrs. Mitchell smiled and reached out for Mozelle. For the first time Mozelle realized that Mrs. Mitchell's eyes twinkled when she smiled and that her eyes were as green as a cabbage leaf once the outer darker leaves were peeled back. On the verge of crying, Mozelle forced a little smile, and then lifted her arms. She and Mrs. Mitchell embraced, ever so gently, like a mother and daughter comforting each other. A feeling of calm, a feeling of relief washed over Mozelle like a gentle kiss on her brow from her mother's lips.

Stepping out of their embrace, Mozelle quickly dried her eyes. "God bless you."

"I've been blessed, Mozelle. Every day of my life. If you need more—"

"No, ma'am, you done did enough," she said, bending and picking up one of the medium-size boxes with no trouble.

Mrs. Mitchell stood aside.

Mozelle quickly took the three remaining boxes out of the trunk and set them on the ground away from the car.

"Well, Mozelle, I got to get on back home. Mr. Mitchell likes me to have him a hot toddy ready when he comes in from work. He likes it real spicy. Did you know that?"

"No, ma'am." That Mozelle would not have known. She was never there when Mr. Mitchell got in from work.

"Well, he does," Mrs. Mitchell said, opening the car door. "Don't forget now, you go on over to the shoe store and get those shoes. You hear?"

"Yessum. Thank you, ma'am."

Mrs. Mitchell got into her car and started it up.

Mozelle quickly stepped forward. "Mrs. Mitchell, ma'am, how you know where I live?"

"This is Gadsden, Mozelle. Everybody knows where somebody lives and somebody knows where everybody lives. All you have to do is ask."

"I see," Mozelle said, nodding. She stepped back from the car. Long after Mrs. Mitchell's car climbed the road up out of the valley and disappeared over the top, Mozelle stood staring at the settling cloud of dust she left behind. No one could have told her that a white woman would do something like this for her. It had to be God's undying love and His love wasn't black or white. It was good.

Twenty-One

Mr. Conley marked down the date and Mozelle's payments in her policy books. "I'm glad to see you back at work."

"Thank the Lord," Mozelle said.

"How long were you out?"

"'Bout four months."

"I'm glad you were able to make up your payments."

"Yessa. I had no intention of letting my policies go," Mozelle said, not letting on that she had been scared that she would lose her insurance after missing two payments. She had been able to take the two dollars from her Saturday wages after Mrs. Mitchell bought her all that food. No, she had to keep her policies up. It was important. It would never set right with her if, God forbid, she or one of her children died and there was no policy to bury them. "Better safe than sorry," her daddy used to say. Her mama carried burial policies for each of her twelve children up until they got married. That was where Mozelle and her mama differed, she was still paying Cora's policy. She wasn't going to count on anybody to take care of her children. It was her mama who used to say that she wouldn't let any of her children lay up in a funeral parlor stinking and rotting while somebody begged and scraped up enough money to put them in the ground.

"I know we talked about it before, Mrs. Tate," Mr. Conley said, "but your husband is getting up in age now. A fifty-eight-year-old man should have burial insurance."

Mozelle shook her head. "I can't afford it," she said. With all the money Randell made, since he didn't see fit to take out a policy to cover himself, then she wasn't going to bother herself about it either. Besides, she didn't much care how long he lay up waiting to be put in the ground. What's more, if he would just leave and stay gone, it wouldn't concern her a bit if he got put in the ground at all.

"You know what's best," Mr. Conley said, handing Mozelle back her six policy books. She put them all back inside a cigar box.

Mr. Conley closed his briefcase and stood to leave. "Mrs. Tate, I'll be seeing you next month."

She stood, too. "Well, sa, long as I got my job, I should be here."

"You know what you oughta do, Mrs. Tate? Just in case you get out of work again? You oughta get yourself a piece of land and build yourself a house on it. When hard times come, you just make sure your taxes are paid up every year. That way, you and your children still have a roof over your head come hell or high water. It'll be less for you to worry about."

"Mr. Conley, I been tryin' to get me some money saved to buy me a piece of land for some time now," she said, following him out of the house. She motioned to Randie to watch Nell, who was hopefully still asleep in the back room.

Opening his car door, Mr. Conley tossed his briefcase across to the passenger seat. He was about to climb inside himself when he glanced over at the branch. "That branch remind me of when I was a boy in Mississippi. Me and my brothers spent lots of time playing at swimming and collecting rocks from the branch near our house. It was real peaceful down by that branch."

Mozelle smiled. "That's how come I like stayin' down here in the valley," she said, looking at the branch, too.

"Then why don't you buy that piece of land over yonder?" Mr. Conley asked, pointing across the branch.

Mozelle's eyes shot up at the mass of tree-covered hilly land across the way. "That's for sale?"

"That's what I hear."

"I thought it was part of the woods."

"No, ma'am. That piece there," he said, pointing again at the property across the road, "from the branch on the left, to the steps on the right, belongs to John Buford Benson. Been in his family for years. He probably never did anything with it because it ain't flat land. I hear tell he been looking to sell since last year."

Mozelle could feel herself getting excited. "Nobody bought it yet?" she asked, walking out into the yard.

"I ain't heard nothing about it."

She dared to ask, "How much he want?"

"Hear tell one hundred fifty dollars."

Her heart sank. "That's so much money. I ain't never gon' be able to save that much befo' somebody come along to buy it up."

Mr. Conley slid into his car. "I know you just got back to work, Mrs. Tate, but can you come up with any money?"

"I got me fifty dollars saved."

The car's engine roared when Mr. Conley turned the key. "I tell you what. I'll put in a word for you with Mr. Benson. He's a fair man. He sells to white folk and colored folk alike. Sold me a nice piece of property over in Anniston."

"That's right kind of you, Mr. Conley. I 'preciate it."

"Now, Mr. Benson ain't on my route, being white folk 'n all, but I see him now and then down at the office. Maybe he'll take payment on the land."

"I pray he do," Mozelle said, still looking wistfully across at the land.

"I'll call on you the minute I know something."

"Thank you, sa. U'm much obligin' to you." She didn't notice Mr. Conley driving away. Already, she could see a big house sitting far back on the hill. Of course nothing could be built until much of the land was cleared of some of the trees and the huge rocks and boulders. It would be better if it could be done before summer, before the weeds and wildflowers rushed into bloom together with the bunch of bushes blocking the lay of the land.

Suddenly, Mozelle got a hankering to stand on the land. She started walking around the branch to where it flowed under-ground under the dirt road.

"Mama, where you goin'?" Brother asked from the door-way.

"Nowhere."

"Can I go with you?"

She reached back for his hand, and together they walked onto the land. Weed and saplings were sprouting, beginning to grow tall. There were lots of rocks—big and small. Along the left side, Mozelle knew that the branch ran down from the back of the property from Spring Street, separating it from Rosa Lewis' house. Along the right side, a long row of steep stone steps led from Plum Street up to Mt. Olivet Baptist Church, sitting far back on top of the hill off Spring Street. Of course Brother had long ago discovered that. He also knew about the blackberry bushes that grew on the side of the property near the branch. He showed her the fruitless bushes. They would be ripe with berries in the summer. She couldn't begin to guess how big the property was, but it was plenty big enough to build on. Now that was another problem—money. Even if she got the land, she didn't know when she was going to be able to build a house on it. Still, she wondered how much it would cost to build a house.

While she waited for word from Mr. Conley, Mozelle must have counted the fifty dollars inside the preserve jar a hundred times. It was three weeks before he came back. Mr. Benson was willing to take fifty dollars down, and ten dollars a week for ten weeks starting the first of June for the land. Mr. Conley brought with him, from Mr. Benson, mortgage papers that Mozelle nervously signed her name to. It meant little to her that the property was fifty feet by one hundred feet. To her it looked as big as the farm she grew up on in Royston. Anxiously, she waited until Mr. Conley drove off before she threw her arms up to the sky.

"Thank You, Lord," she shouted. "Thank You for making a way for me to get my land."

Twenty-Two

Her daddy used to say, "What you don't want known, keep to yourself." Mozelle had no intention of telling Randell about her land; he had no business knowing because there would come a day when he would not be welcomed. She remembered to hide the note underneath the preserve jar under the floorboard, but she forgot to tell Brother not to tell his daddy. Brother told Randell the minute he stepped foot out of his car Sunday, just after supper. He hadn't been home since Friday morning.

"So you got yourself a piece of land."

She wanted to fall out. "It ain't mine 'til it's all paid up," she said, not looking up at him as her fingers nimbly twisted a section of Essie's hair into a neat plait on the side of her head.

"How much it cost?"

"I owe one hundred dollars. You gon' help me pay it off?"

"Woman, I ain't got no money. Besides, I wouldn't spend a dime on that hilly overgrown dirt."

Shaking her head, Mozelle smiled. She knew what Randell would say before she asked for his help.

"You must have some money you ain't told me about," he said. "How much you got?"

She went on plaiting Essie's hair. Essie began to squirm from side to side.

"Don't tell me. Just don't be asking me for anymore of my money. I ain't giving you no more."

"Then what good is you, Randell? Except for a handful of times, you ain't never give me nothin' that I ain't had to beg you for. And that's a shame."

"Don't start up with me, woman, about my money. I done

told you time and time again, I don't got to give you nothing I don't want to give you."

"Randell, you a mean, selfish old man."

"That's me, but U'ma good-looking old man," he boasted, going over to the stove.

For the life of her, Mozelle couldn't understand why Randell didn't just stay gone. That story about his daddy losing his family wasn't enough to keep him coming back when he wasn't treating his own like family. There was nothing for him under her roof. She didn't talk to him, and she didn't sleep in the same bed with him most nights. Fact of the matter was, laying in the same bed with him made her skin crawl. They lived as strangers. Most days she rarely looked him in the face. When she did, it was hard. Not only because of how she felt about him, but because the specks on his face were bigger, whiter. Even part of his lower lip was white. It was like he really was turning white. Yet, all this time she never heard him complain about feeling sick. Whatever was the cause of turning him white, wasn't killing him.

Mozelle finished Essie's hair and sent her outdoors to play with the other children. She looked at Randell hunched over his plate, shoveling spoonfuls of red kidney beans and rice into his mouth. The sight of him stuffing his face was irritating. Getting up, she went to the front window to look out at the land that one day would be hers. It looked quiet and lonely, like it was waiting for her to build on it. Somehow she planned on doing just that. She knew full well when she signed her name on the note, that the land was going to be hers alone, which meant that she alone would pay for it. Now that she was back at work, she could do it. It was just the matter of coming up with the extra money to pay somebody to build the house, to buy the wood to build the house; and whatever else was needed to run electricity and pipes. Just the idea of planning out in her head what she had to do when the land was paid for, filled her with a purpose. She wished that she could tell Mrs. Scott that she had finally bought herself a piece of land.

Leaning the side of her head against the windowpane, she prayed silently that she hadn't bitten off more than she could chew. Then out of nowhere, she knew what she had to do. Turning away from the window, she rushed back to the kitchen.

"Randell, it don't make no good sense to keep on livin' in this house payin' sixteen dollars a month rent, when I could pay on my land with that money and maybe buy wood to build the house a little at a time."

Randell took his time chewing on his food, annoying Mozelle. "Randell, you listenin' to me?"

"Where you gon' live?" he asked, finishing up his supper.

"I want to live on my land."

Randell pushed his plate off to the side. He folded his arms on the table. "Where you gon' sleep? On the ground?"

"The children 'bout doin' that now, but I want to build a house over there."

"You got money?"

"No."

"It take money to build a house, Mozelle."

"I know that," she said, taking his plate over to the sink. "Right now, it don't got to be a big fancy house. It could be a one-room shack 'til I can build the house I want."

"So, what you want from me? I can't help you."

She put her right hand on her hip and eyeballed him. "Yes, you can. Randell, I want you to get the wood to build the shack."

He eyeballed her back. "I ain't—"

Slam! She slapped the table—hard—with the palm of her hand. "I don't want to hear what you ain't got or what you can't do," she said, leaning in toward him and glaring into his eyes. "I only want to hear what you gon' do to help me get me a house built."

Randell pulled back from Mozelle. She was too close. "Look, you the one—"

"Randell, you don't do nothin' for nobody but yourself. You don't buy food but you eat. You don't pay rent, but you live in a house. U'm tellin' you, you better get the wood to build a shack, or—"

He squinted at her bitterly. "Or what?"

"You don't wants to know," she said, turning on her heels

and storming out of the kitchen. Mozelle expected him to follow behind her into the bedroom and cuss her out. He didn't. She didn't know herself what "or what" was. She only knew that if he didn't get the wood, she was going to be hard-pressed to make ends meet while trying to buy it herself. She folded her arms across her chest and flopped down on her springy, squeaky bed. Like always when she was upset, her throat tightened.

"God, please make Randell do what's right."

For three days Randell said nothing about the wood. Neither did she. On Friday, after work, Mozelle trudged down the road into the valley and was about to go on into the house when Brother called her.

"Mama, look what Daddy did," Brother said, pointing across at the property.

She looked across at her land. She did a double-take. She almost didn't see the two stacks of wood laying on the ground almost hidden by the high weeds. More surprising, was that a small section of land on the left next to the branch had been cleared. She walked onto the property into the middle of the cleared spot and stood. It was the flattest section of land off the road. Nodding her approval, she smiled. It would do just fine.

Randell was in the house when she went inside, but she saw no need to thank him. He sat still for a little while before he jumped up and started for the door mumbling, "Ungrateful heifer."

Flipping her hand at his back, she went on into the kitchen to start supper. As far as she could see, that little bit that he did wasn't nothing compared to what he should have been doing all along.

It took them two weeks of working after they got in from their jobs to build a flimsy two-room shack with no windows, no running water, and no electricity. Randell did the framing and nailing while she held the wood in place. It was the first time they ever worked together, without arguing, on anything besides making babies. They covered the dirt floor with pieces of paperboard they begged from store owners. The flat-top roof had only a layer of tar to keep the rain out. With the wood that was left over, Randell built an outhouse that she had long since hoped she would never have to use again. If a heavy breeze ever whipped up, both the shack and the outhouse would topple over. One kerosene lamp lit each room day and night because it was so dark. Thank God the weather was warm. They got away with not having a fireplace. She cooked on a small kerosene stove, and used water they hauled up from the branch. Behind her, she could hear the water washing over the rocks in the branch as it flowed down from Spring Street. From the house they took the beds, the dresser, and the table. Their only other furniture were six milk crates they used to sit on and hold clothes in. All the children slept in the back room while she and Randell slept in the front room that doubled as the kitchen.

Randell was proud of the shack he built. "I was always good with my hands," he said, looking around the room.

"It'll do for now," Mozelle said, softly, looking over at the kerosene lamp burning low in the corner of the room.

"It's going to have to do for longer than now," he said. "I ain't got no money to build nothing bigger or better."

Mozelle turned over from her side onto her back and stared up at the odd-shaped black knots in the wood overhead where the lamp sat. "Randell, how can you settle for livin' in a shack with a dirt floor?"

"I ain't settling, I just know that I can't do no better right now."

"We can do better if we want to, Randell. Look, all our married life we done lived in somebody else's house, and they all been shacks just about. I been on this earth thirty-six years, and I ain't got nothin' to show for it besides a houseful of children. I ain't gon' live in nobody else's house again. I want my own house."

"Woman, you ain't never satisfied," Randell said. He threw his legs over the side of the bed and sat up. "That's how come I don't like to do nothing for you."

"Randell, I ain't never gon' be satisfied as long as my children gotta sleep on the floor. U'm tired of sitting on milk crates instead of chairs. People got radios and televisions, and we ain't never owned nary one. I ain't gon' keep haulin' water up from the branch to drink and cook with the rest of my days."

Randell snatched his britches off the footboard. Standing up, he fumbled angrily with them before pulling them on. The metal zipper screamed when he yanked it up. Sitting down hard again, he shook the bed. Its rusty springs squealed as loud as a scalded pig all the while he was pushing his feet into his shoes and tying them up.

Nell whimpered. Mozelle gently rubbed Nell's back until she dropped back into a sound sleep.

"I told you," he said, bolting up off the bed, "I ain't got no more money." The long-sleeve shirt he snatched off a big nail on the wall, nagged and caught. "Goddamit!" There was a little tear in it, but he pulled it on anyway as he rushed to the door.

"Randell, I ain't got no money neither, but U'ma find a way to build me a better house for me 'n my children."

Randell looked back at her. "Go ask your God to show you how," he said. He yanked on the rickety door and went out into the night, leaving the door open.

Mozelle folded back the blanket. She eased up off the bed. It annoyed her that Randell always ran out whenever she said something to him he didn't like. In her bare feet, she rushed to the door, feeling the give underfoot of the paperboard into the unyielding rocky earth. Although she didn't see Randell in the darkness, she yelled to him, "Randell, you keep talkin' disrespectful about God, you gon' be sorry."

He must not have heard her because he didn't come back, and he didn't answer. She looked upward. Not a star, not a glimmer of moonlight dotted the sky. The air smelled heavily of fresh-dug moist dirt and cut grass. Until Randell turned on his engine and headlights, she hadn't seen where he had gone. Down on the road, his red taillights began moving slowly up the hill. Their brightness looked eerie in the blackness. Wherever he was running off to, Mozelle hoped that if it was to a woman, he'd get stuck in her like a old dog and have to be pulled apart, shaming them both.

The only sound she heard now was the water washing over the rocks in the branch. Not even the crickets sang. Mozelle shivered and closed the door. It swung back open on its on when she started to walk away. There was no doorknob or lock so she stuck a small piece of paperboard between the door and the doorjamb to hold the door closed. No, this was not the way she intended to keep living. She went back to bed, confident that God would keep on looking after her. He had brought her this far, He wouldn't leave her to stumble around in the darkness with no light at the end of the tunnel.

Twenty-Three

No one ever promised Mozelle that her life was going to be easy. Certainly not her mama or daddy. Their simple life of drudgery as sharecroppers didn't prepare her for the backbreaking struggle of her own life to survive. She knew that whatever she wanted out of life she was going to have to work hard for it, she just didn't think that she would have to do it alone when she had an able-bodied husband. But that was the bed she had made. So without whining or complaining, she made her way to work in Alabama City before dawn every day, worked on her feet for nine hours, then walked wearily back home another six miles before going back to pulling at the thick, deep rooted weeds and saplings to get them to release their hold on her land. The children helped pull weeds and roll the smaller rocks off to the side, while she and Henry chopped down the bigger trees with the ax he borrowed from Guy Hood's farm where Henry now worked since the pipe factory closed down in February. The one massive water oak they figured would dull the ax before the ax could make a dent in its bark, they left alone—it would make a great shade tree for the front porch. Between herself and Henry, using a plank for leverage, they were able to dislodge most of the bigger rocks and roll them to the front of the property, lining them up side by side until they stretched across the front like a fence. One of the larger rocks, that looked so much like a hassock, they rolled down to the branch to sit in the cool shadow of a weeping willow tree. That would be Mozelle's chair when she wanted to sit and relax.

Her eyes closed most nights before her head hit the pillow. Only the rain that kept up for two weeks at the end of April gave her time to rest, though she was anxious to get back to clearing her land. Realizing her dream of owning land gave her the strength to clear it, despite Randell's constant naysaying that she would never be able to afford to build a house on it. He didn't have her faith, which was why he refused to lift another finger to pull another weed. They could live in their shanty shack the rest of their livelong days, and he wouldn't have cared. Most of the time he was gone anyhow, probably laying up with some whore in a real house. That's why Mozelle couldn't let herself listen to him and lose her faith. No matter how farfetched it seemed, she had to believe that she would see her house built.

"Mozelle, you 'bout the saddest soul I ever seen," Mamie James said, biting into her biscuit and bacon sandwich. "I don't think I ever seen you smile."

Mozelle simply shrugged her shoulders and glanced around the room to see if anyone else was looking at her. No one was. She and Mamie sat far back in the corner away from everyone else.

A piece of the limp, fatty bacon hung out of Mamie's sandwich and draped between her mouth and the biscuit. Using her fingers to hold the bacon, Mamie bit down into it and pulled at it until it broke in the middle. She stuffed what was hanging out back into the biscuit.

From an old crinkled plastic bread bag Mozelle had taken from Mrs. Mitchell's kitchen, Mozelle pulled out her own greasy biscuit sandwich made with a slice of salt pork. Mamie was the first and only person she talked to at the cotton mill who knew anything about her sorrowful life with Randell. Her mama would turn over in her grave if she knew that Mozelle had talked outside her marriage. But she had to talk to somebody besides Cora. She felt like she would burst wide open from keeping all that hurt and anger shut up inside. Talking to Mamie eased the tightness in her stomach and settled her nerves. They usually found a spot on the floor off in a corner and ate their lunch together. Mamie had been trying, up until Mozelle bought her land, to get her to leave Randell and move with the children to Alabama City to be closer to the mill and her. Lord knows there were days she used to wish that she could.

"See, Mozelle, that's what I mean. You so sad, somebody tell you you sad, you take it as the gospel and don't say nothing," Mamie said, biting into her biscuit again. A few crumbs fell from her mouth onto her smock.

Mozelle nibbled on the edge of her biscuit. "I don't see no point in disputin' you. Most days, I do feel sad."

"That's because of that man you married to."

Mozelle didn't have to be told that. "Randell ain't all bad. He cleared the land and helped me build the shack."

"Well, woop-de-do for him. Mozelle, Randell shoulda bought the land, cleared the land, and built you and your children a ten-room house. He still owe you. He shoulda done a whole lot more in all the years you been married to him."

Now she felt worse than before. She glanced around the room to make sure that no one else was listening to Mamie talk about her personal problems. She couldn't tell since no one was looking back at her. She lowered her voice anyway. "Mamie, don't talk so loud. Anyhow, Randell might do better in the long run."

Mamie broke a piece of crust off of her second biscuit and popped it into her mouth. "The long run? Mozelle, how long you been married?"

"Well, he just might—"

"You foolin' yourself, Mozelle. That man ain't did right in all this time, he ain't gon' do right no time down the line. And you know something else? You gon' be sad long as you living with that old no good husband of yours. My people got a saying, 'You can't catch a baby rabbit and expect it to be a cow when it grow up.' If you waiting for Randell to change, don't waste your time, it ain't gon' happen. When you married that old man, he was the same old ugly way he is now, you just didn't see it. And him being older then you, and use to being by hisself and doing nothing for nobody but hisself, he wasn't never gon' do right by you 'cause he was already set in his ways."

Mozelle lost her appetite. She stuck her biscuit back inside the bag, tied the end, and let it lay in her lap. Crossing her legs at the ankle, she fixed her eyes on the clock high up on the wall at the end of the long room. She hated when Mamie preached to her about her life, like she didn't know how bad off she was.

"Oh, shoot. Me and my big mouth," Mamie said, touching Mozelle's left shoulder. "You mad at me, ain't you?"

"I wanna be, but I know you right."

"Then—"

"Please, Mamie. I don't wanna talk about Randell."

Mamie looked at the tense set of Mozelle's jaw. "You a good-looking woman, Mozelle, but ain't no other man gon' take notice of you. Your eyes say you seen a lot of hurt, and your eyes tell on your soul. A soul ain't got no business hurting so much, Mozelle."

Again Mozelle looked up at the clock. Their fifteen-minute lunch break seemed like an hour. The third hand on the clock stopped for a quick second at every minute mark before going on. She began counting the seconds in her head, knowing full well that Mamie was going to keep on talking until they had to go back to work. But it was her own fault. She should not have talked about her private business to begin with. She didn't need to be reminded that Randell made her life a living hell. It was just that Mamie sought her out to befriend when she went back to work. It was easy to talk to her. For the first time in her life she felt like she had a true friend, somebody besides Cora who cared about her.

"Mozelle, sometimes I worry myself thinking about you."

"Don't."

"I do though. I wonder how come you is so determined to stay with a man that stay gone."

"Mamie, please, I don't want—"

"Mozelle, a man like Randell don't care if you live under a rock with slugs or under a tree dropping pinecones. I ain't never ask you before," Mamie continued, even though Mozelle looked like she had closed her eyes and her mind to her, "and I don't mean to stick my nose where it don't belong, but since you do everything for yourself and your children anyhow, how come you still with him? Is you scared to be without a man?"

She cut her eyes at Mamie. "No. . .I. . .ain't."

"Don't be mad, Mozelle. I ain't trying to upset you or nothing, but. . .sometimes I just wonder."

Again Mozelle looked up at the clock. Ten more minutes. Mamie was watching her like she was watching the clock. She took a deep breath. "Mamie, I wish to God on high that Randell would drop dead or go on about his business. I know it's a sin to wish for somebody to die, but I always ask God to forgive me whenever I think like that, but I do want him gone."

"But how come he got to leave you? How come you can't leave him? On second thought, hell, if I was Randell I wouldn't leave you either. He don't take care of his children. He can come home and eat and change his clothes then go sex his hoes. You know what, Mozelle?"

"Mamie how come you doin' this to me?"

"I ain't the one doing anything to you, Mozelle. Randell is. You know what my mama use to say about what you been doing all these years? Fattening a frog for another snake. You ever hear that saying before?"

She had, and she didn't like it.

"Mozelle, you easy to use."

That really hurt, but after giving it some thought, Mamie was right. Randell had used her for years, and she let him. Mamie had seen that. Why hadn't she? For a minute Mozelle studied Mamie's face. Like Mozelle, Mamie had some Indian blood in her. Her high, prominent cheekbones and ruddy complexion made her look almost pure Indian. Her hair, under her head rag, was even plaited in two thick, long black braids and rested on her shoulders. Mamie's husband had died years ago, when her only child, Mary, was three years old. Mary was nineteen now and was going to school in Tuskegee. Mamie had raised her daughter with the help of her mother and father. Mamie was lucky. As for Mozelle, help from her family was something she had never known, and leaving Randell was something she could never do.

"Mamie, when I got married twenty-one years ago," Mozelle said, feeling that she owed Mamie an explanation, "my mama and daddy didn't want me to marry. They told me if I did,

I'd be sorry. My mama told me to never leave Randell, and my daddy said he couldn't wait to say he told me so."

"All folks say that, Mozelle. They say that to scare us, but that don't mean that your folks want you to stay with a sorry man."

Mozelle frowned. "It mean that a Christian woman can't leave her husband when she got his children. My mama and daddy would be 'shamed of me if I walked out."

"First of all, Mozelle, Christian women have left Christian men before, and the other way around. Second of all, your mama and daddy ain't here—they dead. Dead people don't feel no shame."

Pulling back from Mamie, Mozelle gasped.

"Well, it's the truth."

"That's blasphemy."

"No it ain't, it's the truth. See, Mozelle, my mama's people worry about what the dead think, but I worry first about what the living think 'cause they can hurt me. After that, I worry about what the Lord think 'cause I want to live in His kingdom when I die. While we on earth, the Lord want us to take care of ourselves. Fact is, God Almighty might be mad at you for staying with Randell and letting him treat you so bad."

"How you say that? God ain't mad at me."

"'Course he is. You ain't taking care of yourself."

"Yes, I is."

"No, Mozelle, you ain't. The bible say 'Thou shalt not commit adultery.' From what you say, Randell stay gone all the time. Don't you think he's somewhere doing something with somebody he ain't got no business doing? Don't you think he done committed adultery more times than you done seen the sun and the moon up in the sky?"

"I know that, but that ain't got nothing to do with me."

"Mozelle, when you know flat out what Randell's been doing, it got everything to do with you."

"But—"

"Mozelle, you know, and you stay with him. That's what I mean when I say you ain't taking care of yourself."

"But, Mamie, my mama said—"

"Forget what your mama said, Mozelle. This your life U'm talking about, not your mama's. You wasn't born in your mama's time when you had to stay with a man and suffer."

Mozelle felt like Mamie was saying something bad about her mama, but in truth she wasn't. Her life was different from her mama's mainly because Randell was so different from her daddy.

"Mozelle, you got to decide how you want to live out the rest of your life."

Tooot!

The sound of the whistle ended the lunch break. Mozelle sighed, relieved that the pressure was off. It wasn't as easy to get out of her marriage as Mamie said.

Mamie gathered her bag and pushed herself up off the floor. "Back to work."

Staring down at her run-over, scuffed old brown shoes, Mozelle continued to sit. She didn't believe that the Lord faulted her for the terrible way Randell treated her, or for keeping her wedding vow.

Standing over her, Mamie said softly, "Mozelle, you do what you got to do to build your house, but if you got to do it by yourself, you sho'nuff oughta live in it by yourself with your children."

"It ain't easy as you make out."

"If you still love the man, I guess it ain't," Mamie said. She reached down and took hold of Mozelle's arm. She helped her up off the floor.

Mozelle dusted off the backside of her dress.

"'Tween you and me, Mozelle, if Randell Tate was my husband, he woulda been fertilizing daisies a long time ago."

There was a strange look in Mamie's eyes, making Mozelle think that there was something more behind what Mamie said, but she wasn't going to pry. Together, but silently, they walked back to their workstations. Even if she wanted to, Mozelle knew that she couldn't argue against what Mamie had said. It wasn't love she felt for Randell, it was hate. The fact of the matter was, she had often thought of killing Randell herself, but she knew better. God wouldn't like it one bit. Besides, she had her children to worry about and truth to tell, she was practically living alone with her children anyhow. It made good sense that she could make it on her own without Randell, but she couldn't bring herself to leave him just yet. Maybe after the house was built.

After work, Mamie convinced her to go home with her to pick up some of her daughter's old clothes for Randie and Essie. Mamie's four-room house on Railroad Avenue was better than any Mozelle had ever lived in. All the walls were painted white except for the bedroom, which was a pretty pink. The best thing was that all of the furniture matched. There wasn't a milk crate in sight, and there was a television. It sat on the floor in a big wooden cabinet in the front room. Mrs. Mitchell had one just like it. Mozelle wanted to ask Mamie to turn it on, but didn't. She didn't want Mamie to know that she had never sat and looked at a show before. In fact, the only other colored folks in Gadsden that had a television that she knew of, were the Clays and Mr. Peterson.

By the time Mozelle left Mamie's house, she was more determined than ever to find a way to get the money she needed to build her house. She walked with her two big overstuffed bundles of clothes, one tucked under her arm, the other tied around her right shoulder with a rope, toward the bus stop. Walking six miles back to Gadsden with her bundles would tire her too much when she had work yet to do at home. A little ways down from Mamie's house, Mozelle stopped to adjust the bundle under her arm and to catch her breath. Looking around at the quiet wood-frame houses along Railroad Avenue, she was struck by the one curtainless rundown house that looked abandoned.

Setting her bundles on the ground at her feet, Mozelle stepped around them and walked up to the broken steps to the house. They looked too rickety to step on. Slowly she walked around the house. Nails here and there had long since popped out, letting a couple of planks of wood slip down or stick out at odd angles from the walls. It looked to her like the single-story house had settled badly. The walls had buckled and the broken windowpanes had shift in their frames. It would probably be easier to build a new house than to fix up this one, she thought. She tapped on the long wide planks with her knuckles. They seemed solid. The wood looked bad because the green paint on it had dried out, flaked, and peeled back off the wood. Mozelle peeked through one of the broken windows on the side of the house. The inside looked just as broken down as the outside. By the size of the large room, and by the largeness of the house outside, she guessed this was more than a three-room house.

"Afternoon, Missy."

Startled, Mozelle quickly turned around. An old man stood out on the front porch next door. He was leaning on a walking stick.

"Afternoon," she replied, guiltily.

"'Bout a eye sore, ain't it?" the old man asked, looking at the house. "Ain't nobody lived there since forty-two."

"It need a lot of fixin'."

"It been needin' fixin' for ten years now. Jest get more broke down ever year. Need to be tore down."

"The wood ain't rotten though," she said, walking through the high grass across to the old man's house. The closer she got, she saw that his right leg was shorter than his left leg by several inches. His left hip was higher than his right, making him lean awkwardly to his right side.

The old man lumbered over to a big rocking chair and eased himself down into it. Only his left foot touched the floor. He lay his walking stick across his lap. "You lookin' to buy it?" he asked.

"No, sa. U'm figurin' if I could tear it down, I could use the wood to build my own house over in Gadsden."

"I reckon the wood good 'nuff for that," the old man said. Pushing off with his left foot, he began to rock back and forth.

"Somebody own it?" Mozelle asked, standing at the bottom of the old man's steps. She wasn't going to step up onto his porch until he asked her to.

"Yep."

"You know who?"

"I reckon I do," he said, taking a piece of paper from his shirt breast pocket. He held the paper out to her. "A white man own it. Mr. Hubert Lippsett. He told me to keep this on me 'case somebody come askin'.'"

Mozelle stepped quickly up onto the porch and reached for the small piece of paper, but the old man's hand was shaking violently. Mozelle pulled her own hand back. The old man had the shakes real bad. Looking into his watery eyes, she saw that the whites were yellow. Most likely he had liver trouble like her mama's daddy. Her mama said her daddy's eyes were as yellow as a squash before he died. She said he drank rotgut like it was water because he was trying to ease the pain in his back from years of digging ditches for the county. Mozelle wondered what pain the old man was trying to quiet down.

The old man looked down at the paper in his hand. "Well, girl, you want this or not?"

"Oh, yessa," she said, taking the paper gingerly from his wrinkled old hand. She looked at it. There was a telephone number written under what she figured was Mr. Lippsett's name.

"Mr. Lippsett own lots of houses around town. Good thing he don't own mine, it might well look like that one," the old man said, pointing his walking stick at the house next door. "He ain't good 'bout fixin' on his property 'cause he rents to colored folks. If the man had the gumption God give a flea, he'd fix up 'n rent out that house, then it wouldn't be fallin' down. Can't make no money that way. You go on 'n call him though. He most likely sell to you befo' he put a penny on a pound of nails or a bucket of paint."

Mozelle began backing off the porch and down the stairs. "Thank you, sa," she said. She turned her back to stick the piece of paper down inside her brassiere.

"I'll be seein' you if'n you buy that ol' house," the old man said, beginning to rock faster in his chair.

"Yessa." Mozelle bounded over to her bundles, picked them up and half walked and half ran to the bus stop. She had no idea how much a house cost, but since that house was about to fall down, it might not cost too much. It had to be whole lot cheaper than buying new wood from the lumber yard. If she could take the wood from that house, she could start building on her house a lot sooner than she had ever hoped.

Still excited about the idea, once back in Gadsden, she stopped off at the general store to use the telephone. She started dialing the number on the paper then thought better of it. She hung up the receiver. The feeling of elation that filled her from the time she laid eyes on the house until she got back into town, faded instantly. She didn't know how to go about talking to Mr. Lippsett about buying his house. What was she supposed to say? She didn't have any money to offer him. Suddenly she didn't feel so hopeful anymore. She stuck the paper away again. Picking up her bundle of clothes, she made her way home a lot slower than she had made it to the bus stop in Alabama City.

In the last six weeks since she had started paying the ten dollars a week for her land, she had been putting aside equal amounts a week toward buying lumber. It looked like she was going to have to keep on doing that.

Two weeks passed. She couldn't get the house on Railroad Avenue off her mind. Then Mr. Conley came to collect on her policies. He used his car to lean on to write in her policy books.

"You doing a good job clearing the land, Mrs. Tate. When you reckon you gon' be ready to start building on your house?"

"It's gon' be a while yet. I ain't saved enough money to buy the lumber," she said, taking her policy books back.

Mr. Conley stood surveying the land. "When you finish clearing the land, you gon' have a nice spread here. Why don't you tell Mr. Tate to ask Mr. Morris over at the lumberyard if he'll extend him credit."

"We don't want to owe more than we can manage."

"I understand that," Mr. Conley said, opening his car door, "but lumber cost a bit of money, and unless you get it on credit, it might be a long while before you can save up for it."

"That's how come I been doing some thinkin'. Mr. Conley, I saw a ol' house over in Alabama City. Ain't nobody livin' in it. It's 'bout ready to fall down. Fact is, it can't cost a whole lot of money. Now, if I can buy that house, I can tear it down and use the wood to build my house. The only problem is, I ain't sure the owner gon' want to sell it to me."

Mr. Conley looked back at her. "That's an idea. Do you know the owner?"

"No, sa, but I got his telephone number. Though, I ain't got the guts to talk to him."

"Who is he?"

"A white man name Mr. Lippsett."

"You talking about old man Hubert T. Lippsett who own lots of houses over in Alabama City? I know that greedy old coot. I know him real good."

Mozelle began to feel hopeful. "Do you think you can talk to him for me?"

"Sho can."

The weight of the world fell off her shoulders. "I got his telephone number right here in the house," she said, excited again. She started to go to the shack.

Mr. Conley flipped open a small book he took from his jacket pocket. "I got his number right here; he sends me his new tenants to insure."

Mozelle felt like praising the Lord. "Mr. Conley, you done helped me more than you'll ever know. U'm much obliged to you."

"You can thank me by buying house insurance from me when you build your house."

"I sho will."

He smiled. "You put me in the mind of my mother, Mrs. Tate. She's dead now, God bless her soul, but she raised me and my brother and my sister all by herself. Made sure we got through school, too. My father lived in the house with us, but his dry-good store meant more to him than his family. I think he saved seventy-five percent of every penny he ever made, though we didn't live like we had a dime. We had a house and food, not lots of food, mind you, but we didn't go hungry. My mother was always wanting better for us but she didn't dare ask my father after he told her that he was saving for another depression."

Mozelle's stomach suddenly flipped. It remembered the

Depression. "Those was some hard times for lots of folks."

"I know. My mother sacrificed a lot when she didn't have to. I always hated that she died before my father did. She never got to spend any of his money. She never got to buy anything pretty for herself."

Mozelle understood that, too.

"Mrs. Tate, when my father died, me and my brother and my sister split his money and threw a big old-fashioned barbecue for all our family. We knew Daddy would turn over ten times in his grave. U'm sho sorry my mother wasn't alive to help us spend his money." A single tear slipped from Mr. Conley's left eye.

Mozelle looked away.

"Mrs. Tate, I'll do what I can to help you," he said, getting into his car.

"Thank you."

The heaviness in her chest disappeared. Mozelle felt like everything was going to be all right.

Mr. Conley not only got Mr. Lippsett to sell her the house for two hundred dollars, but he also assured Mr. Lippsett that she could be counted on to pay the twenty-five dollars a week every week on time until the house was paid up. The first payment was already due. Mozelle didn't know how she was going to do it, but she had every intention of making good on her obligation. Randell was going to have to help her—he had to. If she had to go toe-to-toe with him to get the money, she would.

"I be damned," he said, surprised. "You get what you set out to get, don't you?"

"I need you to help me pay off the land," she said, boldly.

"Well, to tell you the truth, Mozelle, I didn't see how you was going to ever get a house built on this land. Now, I gotta hand it to you. I'da never thought of buying a old house and using the wood. How much you got left to pay on the land?"

"Twenty dollars," she answered, amazed at how good Randell took the news.

He took out his wallet. "Here's twenty dollars. Pay off the

land, then you only have the house to pay for every week.."

"Th—" She almost said "thank you" but didn't think she had to say it to him for something he was supposed to be doing. With the twenty dollars off her back, she could start making the twenty-five dollar payment at the end of the week. She noticed that Randell wasn't volunteering to help with the payments but that was all right. The house was going to be hers so she would pay for it, but she was going to need help tearing down the old house.

Henry stepped right up and offered to help pull down the house and haul the wood back to Gadsden. He used the pickup truck from his job. Every day after work, he met Mozelle at the house on Railroad Avenue. Together they pulled the house apart plank by plank. As she worked, Mozelle tried to remember how each plank, how each two-by-four, how each support beam was set. It wasn't easy work. Her hands got splinters in them, she smashed every finger. By the middle of July, all of the lumber, every door, every window frame, every strip of molding, was laid out on the road in front of her property on Plum Street.

Twenty-Four

1951

She had the land, she had the wood. What Mozelle didn't have was someone to build her house. Nowhere in that hodgepodge of wood piled high and laid out in different piles according to size, did she see anything remotely resembling the structure of the house she tore down. To save her life, if she had to, she would not have been able to build a chicken coop. She didn't know where or how to begin. Only Brother and Essie knew what to do with the wood—they climbed all over it like they were climbing mountains.

For hours after work for a week, Mozelle stood looking first at the wood and then at the land. The two of them just wouldn't come together in her mind. Now that the land was cleared, it looked even more spacious, while the hill looked even steeper. If the land were flat, maybe she could try to build the house herself, but she really didn't know a thing about building a house on flat land or on the side of a hill.

Feeling overwhelmed, she skirted the mountains of wood to get to her favorite rock down by the branch. She slumped down on it, facing the wood, which blocked her view of the shack. She could hear the water running over the rocks behind her, its path certain—so unlike her. If she knew anything, she knew that the front of the house would have to be on stilts, while the back sat on top of the hill, which meant the steps leading up to the house would have to be long and steep. Just the opposite of Cora's house—the back was on stilts. God knows how she was going to build a house like that on her own.

Essie squealed when Brother fell while jumping from one pile of wood to the other. He tumbled until he stopped on a broad beam. Laughing, he got up, unhurt, and climbed back up to the top.

Closing her eyes, Mozelle rubbed her temples with her fingertips. "Y'all come down off that wood befo' y'all get hurt."

"Aaah, Mama," Brother said, standing on the highest pile.

Essie started, carefully climbing down immediately.

"What I tell you, boy? Come down off that wood before you step on a rusty nail and get lockjaw."

"What's that?"

"Never you mind. Just get your tail down, and go on and tell Randie to give y'all supper."

"I ain't hungry."

Pointing a finger at him, Mozelle said, "Boy, if I gots to tell you one mo' time to get your tail down, U'ma take one of them two-by-fours and whop you 'til the rooster crow."

Brother began running across the top of the woodpile. He stopped at the edge and looked off up the road. "Daddy's coming," he said. He jumped to the ground, landing low and flat on his feet.

Mozelle watched Brother pop up and run toward the shack. Essie went skipping behind him. They seemed to know when Randell would put up with them being around and when he wouldn't. It wasn't his payday so the children probably thought he wouldn't be coming home with candy for them. Sometimes Mozelle wondered if it bothered them that their father spent his time and money on other women and at the bag store instead of on them. They never said a word, good or bad, to her about him, but then she spent little time with them herself, working the way she did. At times she felt like she wasn't raising her own children, she was never home except on Sunday. She was working hard trying to get them a house built, and while she didn't know how she was going to do it, it would be done.

Randell was laughing even before he got out of the car. "You look really stupid sitting there with all that wood," he said.

"You think the house is gonna build itself, don't you?"

Right off she could see that he had been drinking. She was not of a mind to be around him and listen to him tear her down. She started to get up.

"Where you running off to? Don't go, stay here with your house," he said, laughing.

She sank back down on her rock. If she went into the shack he'd only follow her, and she didn't want him to show out again in front of the children. "Randell, don't start with me. U'm too tired."

He brought his foot down hard on a pile of wood, making some of the planks shift. "What you gon' do with all this wood, Mozelle?" he asked, no longer laughing. "Is it gon' stay down here on the road and rot?"

"Leave me be, Randell," she said, her tiredness coming down on her. "U'm gon' get my house built no matter what you say."

"How? Tell me how you gon' get your house built when you don't have any money?"

"Don't you worry about it. U'm gon' get it done."

"See, that's your problem, Mozelle. You a dirt poor, back-woods, uppity nigger who don't know when to stop. House builders ain't gon' take ten dollars a week to build you a house. The kind of money they want, you ain't got and ain't never gon' get. Termites gon' eat up this wood long before you get a house built out of it."

Nothing Randell said was going to draw her into another fight. Not this time. She closed her eyes and began to pray, only her lips moving.

"Go on, talk to God. Maybe He can help you," Randell said. He flipped his hand at her contemptuously. "I ain't sitting around here."

Even as he drove away, Mozelle continued to pray but now spoke out loud. "Lord, please, take Randell out of my life. I promise You, if You let me get free of him, I'll never take none other man as my husband. For the rest of my livelong days on this earth, Lord, You will be my husband. And, Lord, while I got Your ear, can You show me how to get my house built? You showed me how to get the land, you showed me how to get the wood, now, Lord, please show me how to get my house built. Amen."

Just as she opened her eyes, she heard a steady knocking sound high overhead just off the road on her property. Her ears perked. Her eyes followed the noise to a spot high up on a tree. It was a woodpecker. The last time she had seen a woodpecker was back in Elberton at Bernice's house after Randell had choked her. Maybe it was a sign, because she had never heard a woodpecker this late in the day. She watched the gray speckled bird peck for a long time on that one spot on the tree trunk. Whatever it was pecking for, it didn't stop until it got it. Then it abruptly took flight. Standing up, she watched it fly over the treetops into the woods, out of sight.

As it was every day after work, after staring at the wood helplessly for hours and still no ideas leaped into her head about how or where to begin, she gave up and went indoors. Maybe Randell was right; termites may well eat up the wood before she could use it, and that made her sick—she was paying for that wood. Suddenly she was scared that she might have made a big mistake. There was so much wood, and she didn't know what to do with it. Maybe that was why Randell said what he said; he didn't know what to do with it either. Maybe he was scared, too. He was gone now and most likely wouldn't be back that night. That was fine by her. It was for the best.

When she lay down for the night, wearily she closed her eyes with a plea, "Lord, please help me."

"*Mozelle.*"

She stirred. She didn't want to wake up.

"*Mozelle.*"

Not wanting to, she slowly opened her eyes but then had to quickly shield them with her arm. The room was bright with light. Brighter than it had ever been except before the roof was put on. She squinted down at Nell at her side; she was sound asleep.

"Randell, that you?" she asked, sitting up. "What's this light you got on?"

There was no answer. Squinting still, she looked around the room. No one was there besides her and Nell. She glanced over at the door. It was closed. The room was blindingly bright—there were no shadows. Then, without warning, the light started easing in from the corners, leaving them dark. Mozelle glanced over at the kerosene lamp. Its wick was still lit, but it's soft, low light could not have lit up the room so brightly. The darkness was beginning to fill the room again. What was this?

Her heart leaped in her chest. Pressing her hands to her bosom, Mozelle held her breath. It dawned on her that she knew who it was that was calling her name, although she had never heard his voice before. She focused on the shrinking light. It seemed to narrow in the center of the room and then slowly moved to her side of the bed. Unable to pull her eyes away from the light, she suddenly felt at peace. In her heart, she knew that God was there. He was the light that was before her. She let her hands drop onto her lap.

The light settled low on the floor alongside the bed. Leaning over the side, she looked down and was amazed. Thick charcoal-looking black lines and angles were drawn on the paperboard. Somehow she knew that it was the drawings of the layout of a house.

"Is this my house, Lord?" she asked in awe.

No answer was spoken, but she felt as if her whole being had been touched, and the answer was the warmth that embraced her. It felt like her Heavenly Father had smiled on her. And all she could do was smile back. She looked back at the drawing. She studied it. Across what looked like the front of the house were six thick, long beams that seemed to be sunk down into the ground and pointed up. The same number and size beams lay flat on top of those beams but went toward the back onto a hill. The top of the house showed lines that ran from the center peak, sloping out to the sides. On the front right side, there were sixteen steps leading from below the house to what must have been a porch that ran the width of the house. She didn't know how, but she understood

all that she saw. In her mind, she knew that six holes would have
to be dug to sink the six big support beams into the ground. Then
cement would have to be poured to hold them strong.

The light slowly dimmed. The room grew almost dark
except for the kerosene lamp still lit in the corner. Her eyelids
suddenly drooped, and she lay down on her back and stared
through sleepy eyes up at the ceiling. She could feel herself sink-
ing deep into a fog of nothingness. Closing her eyes, she
mouthed, "Thank You, Lord." She let herself fall.

Waking up with a start, Mozelle turned onto her side and looked
down at the floor. Nothing was there except the dirty paperboard—no lines, no angles. She sat up easy so as not to wake up
Nell. Her feet rested on the floor where she dreamed the drawing
of her house had been.

It was morning; the sun was up. She could see it peeking
brightly over and under the door, trying to get in. The kerosene
lamp still burned low in the corner, dimly lighting the room. She
looked again at the floor, still nothing. Yet, as clearly as she saw
the sunlight under the door, she saw the drawing of her house in
her mind. She slid off the bed onto her knees. As she offered up
a prayer of thanks to God for showing her how to build her house.
She was sure now that she could do it. Alone if she had to.

Twenty-Five

On her own, she went to the lumberyard. Mr. Morris sold her six twenty-foot beams, six twenty-four-foot beams, twelve bags of sand, and four bags of cement, all on credit. At fifteen dollars a week, she planned on paying him off in five weeks. A few of the men from the mill were willing to help her—for a small fee—build her house once Mamie told them what Mozelle was about to do. Mozelle didn't doubt that Mamie also told them about Randell. Why else would they offer to help? After she and Henry dug the six, five-feet holes spaced out six feet apart across what would be the front of her house, Tom Shott from the mill, and one of his friends, came and poured the cement foundation into the holes and positioned the support beams. They were finished by the time she got home from Mrs. Mitchell's.

Seeing the start of her house, Mozelle could barely contain her excitement. She almost shook Tom's hand right off and would have hugged him except it wasn't proper. He charged her thirty dollars for the work of which, she paid him fifteen dollars right then and promised him the last fifteen at the end of the next work week. He didn't ask her about Randell or where he was, and she volunteered nary a word.

When Randell asked her how she got the beams up, she told him, "With lots of trouble." He didn't need to know more. He'd only assume she'd slept with Tom when she hadn't. Randell didn't ask anymore questions, but he also didn't offer his help, and he didn't make her take off his old coveralls, which was good. She couldn't build the house in a dress.

A week after the foundation was properly set, Tom Shott came back with Bobby Lee Kent to connect the floor beams to the support beams. While Mozelle went on to work at Mrs. Mitchell's, they dug the floor beams right into the side of the hill. This way, the back half of the house would rest on top of the hill. With that finished, they dug a four-foot-deep trench from the road up to underneath where the kitchen and bathroom would be. Tom told her that the plumbing pipes would be laid out there later. By late afternoon, after she got back from Mrs. Mitchell's, Tom and Bobby Lee were dirty and sweaty; so were Essie and Brother from chasing each other around the beams. She had told them to go along with Randie and Nell to Cora's house, but they didn't stay, they had made their way back. Tom had put them to work fetching wood when he needed it and they were doing real good at dragging what they could up the hill. At the end of the day they all sat down and had the baloney sandwiches Cora made up for them with big jars of cool water from the branch. It was the least Mozelle could do for Tom and Bobby Lee—they were only charging her twenty dollars for digging the trench.

As the sun was going down, they were sitting on a stack of wood in the roadway looking up at the beams, talking about what had to be done next when Mozelle saw Randell's car coming over the top of the hill. The last thing she needed was for him to come home with Tom and Bobby Lee still there. No telling how he was going to act. What was he doing home anyhow on a Saturday afternoon?

Brother and Essie had seen their daddy's car, too. They were no longer playful.

Feeling jittery inside, Mozelle watched as Randell's car raced down into the valley trailing a cloud of dust behind it. It was like watching the devil come up from hell with a trail of smoke behind him. Mozelle had to get Tom and Bobby Lee on their way. She stood.

"I can lay out the floorboards myself after church tomorra and after I get in from work during the week."

"How you gon' get the wood up the hill, on top of them there beams by yourself?" Bobby Lee asked, continuing to sit.

"I got my son-in-law, Henry. If he don't get off work too late, he'll come help me. If he don't, my children can drag the wood up to me when I need them to."

"Mozelle, you're a woman. How you gon' get up there and walk on them there beams?" Tom asked, pointing up at the structure. "That ain't woman's work."

Shrugging her shoulders, Mozelle glanced anxiously at the car. It was getting closer.

Tom looked at her face and then at the approaching car. "If you wait on me, I can come back down here next Saturday and help you put down the floor."

"I can do it," she said, turning and looking as Randell's car come to an abrupt stop a little ways up the road. A thick bellowing cloud of dust surrounded him.

"Who's that?" Bobby Lee asked, shielding his eyes from the bright orange glow of the setting sun.

"That's Daddy," Brother answered. He and Essie had been quietly listening to Tom and Bobby Lee talk until now. They both started walking toward the shack.

Tom shielded his eyes, too, as he looked steadily at Randell's car. "Mozelle, if you're serious about trying to put down the floor on your own—"

"I sho am," she said, anxiously watching Randell starting to come on down the road again. He was picking up speed

"Well, then let me tell you what to do. You ought to use tenpenny flooring nails. Make sure you push the floorboards tight together before you nail them down to the beams. And get yourself a good tape measure and a level. The level's important."

Mozelle quickly nodded. "I'll do that."

The car stopped just before it hit the side of the wood pile. A huge dust ball engulfed the car and them. Mozelle covered her face to keep from breathing in the dust. Tom and Bobby Lee barely squinted their eyes. When she uncovered her face, Mozelle saw Randell leap out of the car and charge at them.

"You slut!" he slurred. "You buildin' your goddamn house on your back!"

Mozelle looked down at the ground and shook her head. Randell's words shamed her in front of men who had treated her proper and who were doing what he should have been doing.

Tom and Bobby Lee exchanged glances of disgust as they both stood in unison. It was Tom who stepped forward. "Man, you crazy?" he asked. "Ain't nan one of us sleeping with your wife. We all work at the cotton mill together. Me and Bobby Lee just helping her out."

Mozelle felt hot on her chest.

Picking up a piece of wood, Randell pointed at Tom. "Get off my property!"

"Man, we just helping out your wife. U'ma married man," Bobby Lee said, backing up but looking down and searching the pile of wood for a piece he could grab.

"That don't mean a goddamn thing!" Randell slurred.

"Not to you," Mozelle said, finding her voice. She stepped easily in-between Randell, and Tom and Bobby Lee. She planted both her hands on her hips. "This ain't your property, Randell Tate. This is my land. You best put down that wood 'cause you ain't hittin' nobody. These men ain't done nothin' wrong."

"You ain't nothing but a damn whore."

"Man, don't be talking to your wife like that! You crazy!" Tom shouted. "You got a good woman doing work you oughta be doing. If you was a man, we wouldn't have to be here at all."

Bobby Lee flipped his hand at Randell. "Don't waste your time, Tom. He's a nasty drunk."

Randell raised the wood in his hand and started for Bobby Lee.

Tom and Bobby Lee both reached for short pieces of two-by-fours.

"U'ma bust both your goddamn heads, motherf—"

"Stop it!" Mozelle screamed, thrusting her hands into Randell's chest, shoving him, knocking him to the ground. He landed hard on his tailend with a whoosh of air escaping from his mouth. The wood dropped from his hand as he fell back, hitting his head on the ground.

"I be damned," Tom said, shaking his head. "If I hadn't seen it for myself, I wouldn't've believed it. I ain't never seen a woman mow down a man like that in my life."

Mozelle jammed her hands into her pockets. If Tom only

knew. If he and Bobby Lee weren't standing right there, she would've been on top of Randell trying to beat him to death.

"If she hadn't knocked his drunk ass down, I was fixin' to," Bobby Lee said, throwing down the piece of wood he had snatched up.

Randell started throwing up.

Mozelle looked disgustedly at him. It was too bad that he was sober enough to know to turn on his side to keep from choking on his own vomit. Right away, the sour stench filled the air. She stepped back, away from him.

Tom tossed his two-by-four to the ground near Randell's thigh. "Mozelle, how a good woman like you marry a old lowlife drunk like that?"

She looked over at Tom. His face was screwed up into a mask of disgust. "He wasn't like that when we first got married," she said, knowing full well that he must have been that way all along like Mamie said. She just didn't know it. Her mama and daddy must have known something, which was why they didn't want her to marry him. She was the only one who couldn't see it.

"Tom, Bobby Lee, U'm sorry y'all had to see Randell actin' up like this."

"You ain't got nothing to be sorry for," Tom said. "But how come you stay with a man like this?"

Looking down at Randell, Mozelle frowned. He had fallen asleep with the side of his face laying in his vomit. She felt like retching herself. She looked away. "Tom, I useta know real good how come. But now, truth be told, what I useta know ain't good enough no mo'," she said. She covered her mouth and nose with her right hand. The sour stench was getting stronger. "I feel real bad that he treated y'all disrespectful. Maybe y'all best not come back down here."

Bobby Lee shook his head. "Woman, you need help building this house. You can't do it by yourself."

"U'm gon' have to. But I wanna thank y'all for helpin' me," she said, unable to look either one of them in the eye.

"Maybe we oughta go on home," Bobby Lee said, picking up his tool belt. He walked wide around Randell.

Tom picked up his bucket of tools. He touched Mozelle's arm. "If you need me to come back, you just let me know," he said. "When you ready to wire the house for electricity, I'll talk to Clavin Braxton at the mill. He'll take care of it for you."

"I 'ppreciate it," Mozelle said softly, suddenly feeling weepy that despite Randell's ugliness, Tom was still offering to help her.

"I'll see you around," Tom said. "You take it easy."

She watched him follow Bobby Lee up the road. They both lived on the west side and didn't have far to go. Bobby Lee's wife had been understanding enough to let him come, while Tom was single and never married. Mamie had told her that he had two young boys by a woman over in Huntsville. Every few months he went back to see them. Mamie thought he'd be a good man for her and a better father to her children than Randell. Fact of the matter was, a dead man was probably a better father than Randell. As to Tom becoming her man, as long as she had breath in her body, she vowed that she would never be with another living, breathing man once Randell was out of her life. Truth to tell, she was too scared to go down that road again. It wasn't in her to trust another man.

Disgusted with Randell, Mozelle began circling his drunk body. He snored loudly as he slobbered out of the corner of his mouth on to the ground. Too bad she didn't see him like that before she married him, she never would have said "I do." She stopped walking and kicked him hard on his left thigh. He didn't move. Bending, she picked up the piece of wood Tom had thrown down. Again, she looked at Randell's face. Her hate for him seemed to suffocate her. She raised the wood above her head. In her mind she could see herself smashing his face until it was a bloody mess, until he couldn't look at her like she was trash, until his mouth couldn't open to say ugly words to her ever again. Her arms began to shake, beads of sweat popped out on her forehead.

"Mama," Essie's little voice said, "don't hurt Daddy."

She had forgotten all about her children. "Oh, my Lord," she said, quickly lowering her arms and dropping the wood. It fell across Randell's chest. She hadn't seem Essie come up and stand in front of her on the other side of Randell's body. Essie's face was wet with tears. Mozelle looked around for Brother. He was standing a little ways off, looking just as scared as Essie, but he had not been crying. He looked shocked. What she had been about to do in front of her children scared even her because there was a part of her that could have killed Randell as he lay dead drunk. For that, she felt dirty. Kicking off her shoes, she snatched off her dusty, sweaty head rag and, whirling around, ran straight into the branch, and plopped down in the water up to her waist. She could feel every rock that she sat on. She scooped up handfuls of cool, clear water and splashed her face, neck, and chest. Her body temperature cooled down, and so did her rage, but her disgust with Randell didn't. Being married to him had changed who she was. She had never thought bad about anyone and, for certain, she had never hated a living soul enough to want to do harm to him. She hated Randell. She hated him for bringing out the worst part of her that was capable of wanting to kill him.

Brother and Essie came to the water's edge. They stood quietly looking down at her. Essie still looked as if she would burst out crying at the snap of a finger, while Brother's face was unreadable. Mozelle didn't know what to say to them about what they saw her about to do. Forcing herself to smile, she waved for them to come into the water. They both hesitated at first, but then Brother stepped gingerly into the branch and reached back and took Essie's hand and drew her in. They carefully lowered themselves into the water, sucking in their breaths as the cool water chilled their bottoms. With both hands, Mozelle scooped up some water and splashed them. Essie giggled softly. Brother suddenly dunked his head in the water and came up laughing. He playfully splashed Mozelle. She splashed him back.

Essie timidly waved her hands back and forth in the water, but Mozelle could see that Essie was not herself. "Essie, I don't want you to trouble yourself. Everything's gon be all right."

Looking at her feet in the water, Essie wiggled her toes.

"You all right, Mama?" Brother asked.

"I am now," she answered, flicking water at him.

Brother glanced up at Randell still laid out on the road.

"That was bad what Daddy did, wasn't it?"

Mozelle nodded.

"Mama, how come Daddy act like that?" he asked.

"I don't know, child, but I don't want you to worry over your daddy," she said. She grabbed Essie and dunked her backwards into the water like the preacher did when she was baptized. Essie came up giggling and tried to do the same to Mozelle. She couldn't until Brother helped her. They all laughed. Essie shook off her fear and started splashing and kicking in the water. Mozelle let them have their fun. That's what children were supposed to do in the summertime.

Twenty-Six

Word got around town that Mozelle was building on her own house. People, mostly menfolk, started coming down into the valley to watch. Most offered to help; all, she had to turn down because of Randell. Whether he was drunk or sober, any man he saw talking to her, he loudly accused her of being with. He shamed her mercilessly. After a while, people stopped coming around. But not Randell, he came back home at four o'clock every day to make sure menfolk stayed away. That's how evil and selfish he was—he wouldn't help, and he didn't want anyone else to help. He sat his rusty tail on a milk crate outside the shack watching her and the children working like beavers to build their house until it was too dark to see the head of a nail. Seeing him sitting there oftentime napping while they sweated, angered Mozelle to the point that she had to pretend he wasn't there at all in order to get her work done.

Scrubbing floors on her hands and knees, and bending her back and picking cotton, was nothing compared to lifting and laying down planks of wood, and hammering hundreds of nails into the floorboards. Parts of her body ached that she had never been aware of before. The bottom of her feet had always been as tough as leather from going barefooted since she was a child and took her first steps; but her toes and the balls of her feet ached from working barefoot and gripping the wood with her toes to balance herself as she crouched down to hammer. Her wrist and forearm ached from banging nails repeatedly. The back of her thighs, calves, and tail end all ached from bending over hours at a time, and so did her neck and shoulders. But when she was finished with the floor, it was laid down flatter and better than it had been

laid down in the house on Railroad Avenue. Thank goodness
Randie and Brother were eager and strong enough to drag the
wood she needed up to her, or it would have taken her longer than
two weeks to get the floor down.

At work, every day during their lunch break, Tom wanted
to know how she was coming along. Every other day, Mamie
wanted to know why she didn't throw Randell out. As badly as
Mozelle wanted him gone, she couldn't put him out. She didn't
know how to go about it. Besides, if she tried to put Randell out
of the shack he built that he was willing to live in, then he really
didn't have anywhere to go, and he would only keep coming
back. She didn't need that headache and distraction when she had
so much to do. When she told Mamie that, she didn't buy it. She
said it was hogwash and kept on pestering Mozelle about putting
Randell out, while Tom never asked her about Randell.

Tom still took the time to tell her how to frame out the walls
flat on the floor with two-by-fours. His knowledge impressed her.
The time he took to tell her how to do something gave her confi-
dence that she could see the work through to the end. Every day
she looked forward to telling him how the house was coming
along. Before she realized it, she was not only looking at Tom for
what he could do, but for who he was as a man. He was a good
man who was willing to selflessly put himself on the line to help
her. Their time together gave her a chance to get a better look at
him. He was a handsome man. He was younger and better-look-
ing than Randell, and the soft way he spoke to her and the kind
look in his eyes reminded her that she was a woman. She began
to pay attention to how she wore her hair—she cornrowed it on
the sides of her head instead of plaiting it. That was about all she
could do to make herself look better; her clothes she could do
nothing about. She found herself smiling whenever Tom was
around, though even while she was smiling, she knew that it was
wrong to let herself feel this good because of him.

Mamie didn't think it was wrong. "Mozelle, that's your
problem. You ain't never been around a man who made you feel
good about yourself."

"Sure, I have."

"Who? Your daddy?"

"Well, my daddy was a good man."

"That's just fine, but Tom ain't your daddy. If you was with him, you'd know how a real man is supposed to treat a woman."

That was the problem. It didn't take but a minute for Mozelle to see that Tom would truly know how to treat her and her children. How she was beginning to feel and think about him was unnerving. It was weighing her down with guilt. She started trying to avoid him, but that was a hard thing to do. He ate lunch in the same room she did

Tom extended his hand to Mozelle sitting on the floor. "Let me help you up."

She reached up. Their hands touched. A wave of static warmth surged into her body. She pulled back. There was a tiny flutter in the pit of her stomach.

"My Lord," she said softly.

"I know," Tom agreed.

If she didn't know better, she'd think that Tom could read her mind. If he only knew what she was thinking about him.

He smiled sweetly.

Mozelle's cheeks were suddenly warm. She lowered her eyes.

"Tom," Mamie said, reaching out for him to take her hand, "you can sho'nuff help me up off this floor."

Tom pulled Mamie to her feet and quickly turned back to Mozelle.

"*Whew!*" Mamie exclaimed. "That's the fastest I got up off this floor in a long time. Tom, we could use you every day. Ain't that right, Mozelle?"

It wasn't something she could rightly answer, seeing as how she had gotten little pulses of sweet sensations in parts of her body that only Randell had once ignited when Tom touched her hand. It was downright sinful for her body to act like that on its own with a man that wasn't even her husband.

Again, Tom reached out for Mozelle.

She was hesitant. "I can get up myself," she said, starting to do just that.

"C'mon, girl," Mamie said. "Let the man help you up. He's a gentleman."

It was like Mamie to put her on the spot. "I ain't old, you know," Mozelle said, making light of the situation. She gave Tom her hand. His lips curled into a sexy smile, mesmerizing her. She let him pull her to her feet, but he held on to her hand a mite longer than he had cause to, making her flush. His grasp was strong while his hand was warm. Suddenly she was aware of how rough her own hands were. No telling how many splinters she dug out of her skin on any given day, or how many times she banged her thumb with the hammer, or cut or scraped her skin. She eased her hand out of Tom's, though it felt like he didn't want to let go.

Mamie started to walk off. "Y'all coming?"

"In a minute," Tom said.

"U'm comin'," Mozelle said, starting to sidestep from in front of Tom to go around him, but he reached out and touched her arm.

"Can I talk to you a minute?"

Again, his touch went though her. She had to get away from him. "I got to get back to work."

"I ain't gon' keep you but a minute."

Mozelle glanced at Mamie, hoping that she'd tell her again to come on, but Mamie winked at her as she turned and started back to her workstation.

"Mozelle, I ain't gon' bite you. I just want to tell you, if you need me, you know, to help you with your house, just holler."

As much as she wanted his help, she couldn't accept it. "Thank you kindly, but U'ma be jest fine."

"That's hard work you trying to do, Mozelle. It ain't easy for a lot of men."

"Well, I ain't got no choice. U'm gon' have to do it," she said. "At least U'm gon' try."

Tom could see that he wasn't getting through to Mozelle. "Look, I know your husband don't want no menfolk around you, but if you need my help, I'll come anyhow. I ain't never been afraid of no man God put on this earth, and your husband ain't no exception. It ain't right for a woman to be building on a house and she got a man. U'm more than willing to push past him or right through him to help you."

The stinging in her nose told her that she was about to cry, while her heart and mind told her that her feelings for Tom were more than appreciation. If it was love she was feeling, it wasn't right. She turned her back to him to keep from saying, "Yes, please come help me." Those words would have meant more than asking for help on her house; they would have meant "come save me from my life with Randell." She could never say those words, it wasn't right. If only it had been Tom sitting in that church in Royston all those years ago.

Tom put his hand on Mozelle's shoulder. "You all right?"

Making sure that her eyes were dry first, she turned back to him. "U'm jest fine, Tom," she said. "Thank you for your offer, but I'll make do."

She didn't wait for him to say anything that might make her break down and cry, or make her admit that she needed his help, or in fact that she needed her husband to be like him, if not him. She rushed back to her workstation. She was glad that Mamie didn't question her about what went on between them. She probably already knew. The rest of the day, she couldn't get Tom out of her mind. It didn't seem right to think about how he might've made a better husband, in every way. It felt downright sinful, almost like she was committing adultery. In her heart, she was lusting for him. That wasn't right, it was sinful. Though she wondered what it would be like to be loved by such a man.

Tom stayed on her mind long after she picked up Essie and Brother from Cora's and started work on raising the walls of the house. Henry was there to help, too. They got one wall up, and with that done, Mozelle could finally see her house take shape. But there was so much more to do. What she needed was to be free to work full time on finishing up, but she didn't see how that would come to be. She couldn't afford to quit her job. She could only pray that God would make a way.

Thirty-Seven

The doors of the Dwight Cotton Mill were locked. The workers couldn't get in. It was the end of August, and like all the workers, Mozelle was scared. No one knew what had happened; no one knew what to do, that was until the letters came telling them all that the mill was closed down and would reopen in a few months. The blessing was that all the workers would be paid their weekly wages for the duration. Whether it was divine intervention or just the way it was supposed to be, Mozelle didn't know, but she was grateful. Every morning, eagerly, she got up before dawn and was ready to go to work on her house with the light of day. In two weeks' time, all the walls were up. She laid down her front porch and just like she saw in her dream, she had sixteen steps leading up to the porch. She couldn't get enough of standing on the porch and looking out over the valley. It was a breathtaking view.

She got Gordon Ross, who lived up behind the house on Willow Street, to build the steps for twenty-five dollars when Randell went off to work. The steps were strong and didn't creak. She painted them white along with the rest of the house. Of course, all the while she was painting, Randell criticized her. Either her brush strokes were too short or too long, or too thick or too thin. Nothing she did was right. He said he could do it ten times better, and she had no doubt that he could paint much better than she—he had been doing it for more than thirty years. She finally told him, "Do it your damn self, else shut the hell up." He shut up. She went on with her painting, even painting the floors brown.

Every room in the house was as she imagined, but it was the

indoor bathroom with a bathtub and commode that pleased her most. She didn't have the money to pay the county to connect her plumbing to the main water lines, but in time she would, and then there would be no more trips to the outhouse. It would be a while before she could afford to pay the electric company to hook up its meters and wires to tie in with the wires Clavin Braxton ran throughout the house, but everything was ready. Every one of her five rooms had real electric fixtures in the ceiling and electric outlets in the walls, also thanks to Clavin.

Word came at the end of November that the mill was reopening as the Corn Cotton Mill. That was all right with Mozelle, her house was finished. She had made her dream a reality. "Ain't it grand," she said.

All of them—Cora, Henry, Rosa Lewis and her children, Randie, Essie and Brother—stood in awe looking up at her house. Right then and there, Mozelle prayed, "Lord, You been my salvation, my strength, my hands, and my guide in building on my house. Thank You, Lord, for my family and friends that helped me. Amen."

The house was beautiful beyond what she had dreamed. Lots of folks came down into the valley to take a look and were impressed. They all said she had done a fine job. Even Tom and Bobby Lee came by, but they looked up at the house from the road. They didn't stay but a minute, but Mozelle could see that they were impressed, too. Mamie got a friend to drive her from Alabama City to see the house. She, too, was pleased and gave Mozelle a new set of dishes.

On the Friday afternoon that Henry and Cora helped her move her sparse furnishings from the shack into the house, Mozelle felt proud indeed. Her only new additions to the house, were a kitchen table she made from a piece of leftover plywood and four two-by-fours, and a used wood-burning potbelly stove Henry carted home for her. Nobody asked her why she left Randell's clothes and shoes in the shack. They already knew. When he sat and watched her build the house without lifting a finger, she had no intention of letting him move in. As far as she was concerned, he could stay in the shack or leave her property altogether.

The first night in her house, alone with her children, Mozelle slept the sweet sleep of the exhausted and the satisfied sleep of the victorious.

Mrs. Mitchell was especially happy for her when she told her that she had moved into her new house. She gave her a set of white lace curtains like those that hung at the windows of her house. All the way home, Mozelle was imagining how the curtains would look up at the front windows. She couldn't wait to get home. But the first thing she saw as she came down into the valley, was Randell's car parked on the road. She felt sick. The closer she got, she saw that he was sitting high up on her porch—shaded by the giant water oak—looking out over the valley. She could feel her blood beginning to boil. For a minute she stopped walking and asked God to help her to resist the temptation of running up those sixteen steps and grabbing Randell by the collar and throwing him over the railing to the ground twenty feet below. Clinching her jaw, she ignored him just as he ignored her. She walked past him into the house.

"Mama, Daddy told us to stay in the house," Essie said, pouting.

"Y'all go on out back 'til I get supper on."

The children raced outside, Mozelle went off to her bedroom. She stopped dead in her tracks. Standing in the far right corner of the room was a tall, dark, highly polished wardrobe. She didn't have to open the door to know that Randell's clothes were inside. Her own dresses, nine of them, were hanging from a nail behind the bedroom door.

Dropping her lace curtains onto the bed, she screamed, "No. . .no!"

A sense of panic seized her. She rushed over to the wardrobe, snatched open the door and started ripping Randell's clothes off their hangers. The children came running. So did Randell.

"What you doing to my clothes?" he shouted behind her, picking up the clothes she had thrown across the room. "Get your filthy hands off my goddamn clothes."

Angrily, Mozelle kept snatching at his pressed shirts and britches. A massive cramp gripped her heart and spread across her chest, but she wouldn't let herself give in to the pain and stop what she was doing. She began to take in big gulps of air.

Essie cried, "Mama! Mama!"

"Heifer, you mess up my clothes, you gon' pay for them!"

Throwing down the shirt in her hand, Mozelle turned around and clutched at her left breast. Her chest still heaved with rage but it pained her. She looked over at her children bunched up at the door, they were all crying except for Randie, who had her arm protectively around Essie while holding Nell in her other arm. Mozelle hated for them to see her like this—so out of control, so defeated. Backing up to the bed, she slowly sank down on it. The cramp around her heart began to ease up. She glared at Randell as he went about picking up his precious clothes.

"You a crazy-ass woman," he spat.

"Randie, y'all go on back outdoors and play for a spell," she said, breathing deeply. "U'ma get supper on in a minute."

None of them moved. They continued staring at her.

"U'm all right," she whispered.

Randie began to slowly herd Essie and Brother out of the room.

"Heifer, don't you ever put your nasty hands on my clothes again," Randell said, throwing them on the bed.

"I want you outta my house!"

"Go to hell," he said, picking up his wooden hangers.

"No, Randell. U'm gon' send you straight to hell if you don't get out of my house!"

Randell started putting his clothes back on the hangers. "That's where you're wrong, heifer, this is just as much my damn house as it is yours."

She jumped to her feet. "No the hell it ain't. You ain't bought one piece of wood and you ain't banged nary a single nail. You ain't did nothin' but sit your triflin' ass down and watch me work like a ox. Ain't nothin' here belong to you 'ceptin' that damn closet and them there clothes."

Throwing the hanger in his hand across the room, Randell

rushed at Mozelle and stood tight on her, almost knocking her back down on the bed. He started to put his hands around her throat, but she glared bullets at him, daring him. He lowered his hands, but he stood tall against her, pushing her with his chest, looming over her like a beady-eyed black possum.

She tried pushing back at him with her own body, but she couldn't budge him.

"You dumb bitch. When I married your poor black ass, whatever you owned then, which wasn't nothing, I owned. Whatever you think you own now, I own. I even own your ugly black ass."

Beginning to tremble, Mozelle could resist the push of his body no longer. She fell back onto the bed, but she sat up instantly and drew back her fist. Randell saw where she was aiming and jumped back out of her reach.

Mozelle stood. "You don't own me or what I done worked my fingers to the bone for."

"You still a backwoods Georgia slut that don't know nothing," Randell said, taking one step toward Mozelle. "A colored woman, in Alabama, don't even own her own spit outright."

"That ain't true," she said, not for certain if it was true or not. "Nobody said nothin' like that to me when I signed my name on the papers for this land."

"That don't mean a damn thing. They just figured your dumb ass knew. Besides, I paid for part of this land."

She chuckled dryly. "You talkin' about that twenty dollars you give me at the end? That ain't equal what I paid. U'm the one that paid for most all of it."

"Go ask the law, they'll tell you. Whether I paid a dime or a dollar, you can't put me off my own property. Fact is, I can throw you off if I got a mind to."

Her strength waning, Mozelle stared at him in disbelief.

"That's right, Mozelle. You don't own a damn thing."

"That's not true," she said, feebly. Was he right? Could he be right? It was true that Randell had lived in Alabama a lot longer than she had, and he certainly knew more about the law than she did, but how could she get this far and not know.

"If you don't believe me, go ask your insurance man. He know the law. He'll tell you if U'm lying."

Mozelle's shoulders began to shake. Tears spilled from her eyes.

Randell laughed. "You a stupid bitch," he said, going back over to his closet.

His hateful words meant nothing compared to him laying claim to her house and land. Randell snatched the hope that she would one day be free of him right from under her feet. What she thought she was building for herself and her children, she had built for a man lower than a snake's belly. She slowly turned and walked out of the room, out of the house. She passed her children who were huddled up together sitting quietly on the porch.

Brother stood. "Mama, where you goin'?"

She didn't turn around, nor did she answer her son, and this time, he didn't follow her as she walked down the steps that lead her out of the yard to the one thing she felt was her own with God. Her rock. Sitting down, she faced the branch. She clutched the front of her dress with both her hands and cried, "Lord, my God, why have You forsaken me so?"

Twenty-Eight

The pretty lace curtains did not go up to the windows, they went under the bed, stored away. It just didn't seem right. All the pride and joy Mozelle felt in building what she thought was her house was brutally snatched from her. Nothing irritated her more than seeing Randell coming and going and laying around as he pleased, still with no responsibility for paying any bills. The few times he tried snuggling up to her in bed closer than two spoons in a drawer, she pushed him away, choosing instead to sleep on the floor in the living room. She did nothing to make him feel welcome or comfortable. If he got anything to eat, he brought it into the house himself, which was not too often, as he went back to spending little time at home. During the week he slept there, but that was about it. That was until early spring when he started building on a small one-room shack behind the house up on the hill off Willow Street. He didn't tell her what he had in mind, and when she asked him directly what it was for, he said, "None of your damn business." It was left like that, and she didn't go back there again. Yet, she wondered if he was planning to put one of his women back there.

Two weeks after Randell started building on the shack, Brother met Mozelle down on the road to tell her, excitedly, that his daddy had opened up a store. That, she found hard to believe. A store meant that he had to put his money in something other than his clothes and his women. She went up on the hill to see for herself. Sure enough, the one-room shack was well-stocked with jars of cookies, candies, pickled pig feet and cucumbers, in addition to weenies, baloney, bread, apples, and pop.

The children were excited about the store because, once in

a while, Randell let them each get something free. It was one more thing that made him special to them. It sickened Mozelle to her stomach to hear them boast about their daddy to their friends. They weren't the least bit put out that he didn't lift a finger to put a roof over their heads, just the fact that he gave them candy put a halo over his head. It wasn't in her to remind them that it was because of their daddy they had gone hungry, slept on cold, hard floors, and had been put outdoors time and again like trash. Now that he had the store, Randell certainly could do no wrong.

He opened up his store every day after work and on the weekends. Business turned out to be pretty good; plenty of folks bought from him. Having his own store must've been good for Randell—he wasn't his usual old ornery self around the house. He took the time, once in a while, to talk to Brother and Randie. He pretty much ignored Essie and Nell, most likely because they were little. He wasn't so ugly with Mozelle either, seemed to like talking to her about how his store was coming along. After shutting down for the night, he'd come home and go to bed. Life was bearable for a change—they weren't fighting anymore.

After a time, though, like an old worm that turns, Randell went back to his old ways. Mozelle started hearing that it was women who were going into the store most. Problem with that was that Randell wasn't getting paid cash for the food he gave them. How he got paid he couldn't put in his pocket. That's why it didn't surprise Mozelle a bit when she went into the store four months later and saw that the jars were mostly empty. Randell wasn't making the money he needed to refill his jars and shelves. Six months from the day he opened, Randell boarded up his store. Good riddance for all she cared. She never saw any money from what little he made there anyhow.

Having to shut down his store seemed to bother Randell's pride. Folks around town were asking him what went wrong, and he had to tell the lie that the county shut him down. He started staying home because he was shame-faced. He was getting in her way. He wasn't humping anybody out in the street, so his nature was up. He started looking at her like he wanted to lay on top of her. Mozelle could always tell when he had an appetite for her, he'd be watching her like a circling buzzard. Every time she happened to look up, he'd be staring at her with an impish curl on his lips that put her in the mind of how it used to be between them in the early years. She found herself checking to see if a hint of her cleavage showed, or if too much of her legs showed, or if her tail stuck out in his direction when she bent over to clean. When he started offering to help out, she knew then that he was up to no good.

Mozelle felt like he was teasing her, playing a game of cat and mouse—her being the mouse. What was upsetting was that she knew better than to yield to temptation, but her body was only flesh, and at times threatened to weaken. Her hate for Randell and her fear of getting pregnant again kept her strong. As far as she was concerned, at forty, her birthing baby days were over, and so were her days of laying underneath Randell or any man, which was why she fought hard against the lustful yearnings of her body—it wanted what she didn't. Although at times thoughts of Tom warmed her blood and worried her mind, but it was Randell who came to her bed when fire surged between her thighs.

After four years of not laying down with him, the one time she looked back at him directly and didn't look away, he winked. A surprising little tingle ignited her yearning to be held, to be made love to. For weeks Randell had been playing with her—accidently brushing up against her nipples, making them hard, or holding her gaze until she flushed, or saying something nice to keep her off balance. From the start she knew what he was trying to do and didn't fall for it, but after three weeks of being seduced, she was filled with the same yearning she had felt for him when she was fifteen years old. When they finally came together, his touch, his caress, his passion were as she remembered them when she was his child-bride twenty-five years earlier. Afterward, she lay in his arms, her eyes closed, lapping up the lingering tenderness of his promises and the warmth of his touch.

"Everything's gon' be fine between us from now on," he said, gently stroking and massaging her titties.

She wanted to touch him back, but it had been so long since

their bodies came together as one, she was uncertain and didn't know how. She let one hand lay between their bodies, the other lay on her stomach. She sighed long and deep. To herself, she prayed that she hadn't made a mistake and that he was going to keep his word.

Throughout the night she slept in his arms, but the morning light brought her back to her reality. She lay trying to remember the last time she woke up in his arms; she couldn't recall when. She did remember, however, having to work to feed her children, having to labor hard without Randell to build them a house, while their daddy was buying furs and cars for his women, humiliating her, because everyone in town knew.

Feeling nauseous, she rolled out of Randell's arms and off the bed. She looked down at his sleeping face and vowed she wouldn't lay down with him again. No promises of a better life or sweet words could erase the years he treated her like dirt. A small voice in the back of her mind that sounded so much like her mama said, "You just wait. He'll show his true self." Mozelle didn't have to wait long. When Randell woke up—full of him-self—he said, "You gon' always want me to do it to you 'cause you know I do it good." She couldn't even look at him. She left him alone in the room to wallow in his victory over her.

That one night was her undoing, and it was her own fault for again letting her flesh get weak. Her life turned upside. She was three months pregnant before she even let herself believe it was true. What's worse, her belly was growing neck-in-neck with Cora's again. Cora was getting ready to have her fourth child. As for herself, having a baby at forty-one was her worst nightmare come true. She took one look at four-year-old Nell rolling around on the floor and jumped up and ran all the way to Miss Hattie's house, pounding at her front door like her life was at stake.

Miss Hattie took her time opening the door. She looked at Mozelle over the top of her glasses in that slow, unexcitable kind of way she had. "The world ain't ending," she said. "Take it easy."

"Please, Miss Hattie," Mozelle said, huffing to catch her breath. "I need to be fixed right now."

"Child, you breathing like the devil hisself was chasing after you. What you running from?"

"I need you to do me right now. I can't have this baby."

Miss Hattie pushed her glasses up on her nose. She looked at Mozelle's stomach.

"Please, ma'am. I can't have this baby."

"Child, why don't you c'mon on in and sit a spell. You need to think about what you asking me to do."

Anxiously slipping past Miss Hattie, Mozelle hurried inside. "I don't need to think about it. I know what I gots to do."

"Mozelle," Miss Hattie said, pushing her door closed, "I done handed you two of your babies. I seen the way your eyes light up when they was born. You ain't the kind of woman that can live with having your baby snatched outta your womb. That's for a girl whose life ain't worth living if she birthed a bastard child. Your life is worth living, ain't it?"

Mozelle sat heavily down in the chair near the door. It was true. Every time she saw one of her own babies being born, she was amazed. Even the babies she didn't want were just as amazing as the birth of Cora. Still, "Miss Hattie, I don't want this baby. The way I feel right now, my life ain't worth living no mo'.'"

Miss Hattie pulled up a chair and sat down close enough to Mozelle that her knees touched Mozelle's. "How come, child? Folks all over town talking about how good you built your house. It seem to me, you got a lot to live for."

Mozelle sighed. "Maybe I do, but I don't need another baby. My husband ain't never helped me take care of the children I got. And U'm gettin' old, and my body is tired. I jest can't start all over again with another baby, Miss Hattie. It's jest too hard."

"U'ma tell you something about me, Mozelle," Miss Hattie said, again pushing her glasses up on her nose. "I learned to deliver babies from my mama, and she learned from her mama. Though I was the first one to go to school and get some real learning about medicine—I'm a nurse by trade, you know. U'm an educated midwife. I worked as a nurse for twenty-eight years."

"Oh," Mozelle said, "I didn't know that, Miss Hattie."

"Not many folks in these parts know that about me. I keep my own life private. I came back to Gadsden because young girls were dying after backwoods, so-called midwives were taking babies out of their bodies with rusty clothes hangers. At the very least, girls were getting tore up inside and getting bad infections. Later on they couldn't have babies when they wanted to."

Mozelle squeezed her thighs together.

"Let me tell you something else about me, Mozelle. I'm particular. I take babies out of folks that have no business having babies. I know that's not for me to say, that's God's business. He decides who's gon' have a baby."

Mozelle nodded in agreement.

"Now those babies that I snuff the life out of, I take because the mamas say there is no place in this world for them, that they will never love those babies. They have their reasons that's all their own. They pay me to free them of them innocent little babies, and it's probably for the best because they might not raise them up right if they don't want them in the first place. But every time I take a baby, I wonder if that baby had been born who that baby could've become, or whose life that child could've made a difference in."

Guilt began to creep up on Mozelle. This was her child she wanted to kill.

"Sometimes I have nightmares about taking those babies. I've been kept awake plenty of nights thinking about all those babies. Truth to tell, I'm not so sure St. Peter is going to open up those pearly gates for me when time come. As you can see, I got a lot on my soul. It don't help that some girls use me much as four or five times over the years. I can see one time, 'cause it was a mistake, but over and over again," Miss Hattie said, shaking her head.

"Miss Hattie, is it a sin to kill your own baby even though it ain't been born yet?"

Miss Hattie took a breath. "Well, Mozelle, I'll tell you what I know. More than a handful of girls have come back to see me over the years. Some say they wanted to make their peace and put their mistakes behind them. Others have said that they wanted to just talk to me. See, a guilty conscious eat away at people until they ask God to forgive them, or until they tell somebody. Sometimes I'm the only one they can talk to; some of them girls ain't never told their folks what they did."

"Then it is a sin?"

Peering over the top of her glasses, Miss Hattie locked eyes with Mozelle. "Well, I guess it depends on your relationship with God. If you think you're about to do something that God isn't going to like, then it just might be a sin."

Mozelle hugged her stomach. "Oh, my Lord," she said, beginning to rock.

"Listen to me," Miss Hattie said, tapping Mozelle on her knee. "I'm telling you this 'cause right now you can only think about not having another baby."

"But I can't afford another baby."

"I understand, child, but later on you might regret what you did."

"To tell the truth, Miss Hattie, I regret what I did to get this baby," she said, looking down at her stomach. "I don't want another baby with my husband."

Miss Hattie laid her hand on Mozelle's stomach. "No matter who's responsible for making a baby, whether the daddy's there or not, it's always going to be the mama's baby. It's mama's heartbeat that that baby feels for nine months, it's mama that brings a baby into the world, and it's mama's milk that makes that baby grow. It don't know nothing about daddy until somebody tell it so. If it's your husband you bothered about, don't. It ain't his baby, it's yours. And if he ain't helping you out like a daddy supposed to, then you better off without him."

Sadly, Mozelle nodded in agreement. All her children were hers. Hadn't Randell denied them all except for Brother? And wasn't Randell hardly in her life as it was?

"Mozelle, I bring babies out dead or alive, but the worst part for me, is killing babies of good women like you. If you want me to, I'll take your baby. It's up to you."

In the end, Mozelle couldn't do it. She couldn't take the life of something that was growing in her, sharing her body, feeling her heartbeat. She left Miss Hattie, still mad with herself, but accepting of having another baby. But with God as her witness, this was the last. When she told Mamie she was pregnant, Mamie said right off that she was crazy. The fact that Mamie didn't speak to her for two days didn't bother her; it was better than being scolded. They never did talk about it again.

There was no need to tell Randell—an ant would've been more interested. She saw no need to flaunt her pregnancy. Like other times before, a big, loose dress and an apron when she was home hid her growing belly well. Since Randell had his way with her, he didn't bother her about laying down with him again. He went back to laying up with his whores and not paying her much mind.

It was early July, two weeks before she was due, Mozelle was sitting on the front porch with Cora looking down on the children playing in the yard.

Cora patted her stomach. "Mama, I think we gon' have our babies just 'bout the same time again."

"I think so, too," she said.

"Woman, you knocked up again?" Randell asked, stepping out onto the porch.

Mozelle looked at Cora, who was looking bug-eyed at her daddy. They both thought he was asleep in the back room, which was what he did when he got in from work, resting up before going out again for the night. Mozelle rolled her eyes slowly up at him. His eyes were blazing with anger.

"You was worrying about trusting me?" he snarled, pointing his finger at her. "I shoulda been worrying about trusting you. You done gone and got pregnant again."

Mozelle saw no reason to argue with him, it was a waste of time. No matter what was said, she was going to be the one supporting this baby right along with the rest. There was nothing to discuss. Mozelle turned her head and looked straight out over the valley at the forest of weeping willow trees bunched up so tightly together, she couldn't tell where one tree began and the other ended. Every year they seem to grow wider, taller, and thicker. It was rare to even see a dead one though there were other trees around them standing naked of their leaves while the weeping willow trees were fat with green leaves.

"Daddy," Cora said quietly, "Mama didn't get pregnant on purpose."

"How you know? You don't know what your mama was trying to do."

"But, Daddy, Mama—"

"Hush up, child," Mozelle said, placing her hand gently on Cora's full, round belly. "This 'tween me 'n your daddy."

Cora cut her eyes up at Randell. "U'ma go down in the yard with the children," she said, pushing herself, belly first, up off the crate. She waddled past Randell to the stairs.

Mozelle calmly watched Cora go down to the yard. Inside, she was seething with anger at herself, not Randell. She had been the stupid one to lay up with him in the first place.

"She's nasty just like you," Randell said, looking at Cora.

Ignoring him, Mozelle again looked out over the valley.

"You may as well have babies, you ain't good for nothing else," he said, starting down the steps.

She whispered softly to herself, "Go to hell."

He stopped halfway down the stairs and turned around. "What you say?"

Still looking out over the valley, Mozelle was tight-lipped.

Leaning on the banister, Randell pointed his finger threateningly. "Mess with me, woman, I'll put you off my property."

Sighing and hoping that he'd hurry up and go away, Mozelle continued to look straight ahead. Off in the distance, she saw someone walking down the road leading to the Clays' farm. She wondered who it was.

"You hear me, Mozelle? Don't mess with me."

She didn't bother to look at him as he went on down the stairs talking some nonsense she didn't need to hear. She kept her eyes on the weeping willow trees down off the road. They were gently swaying in the soft summer breeze. Despite the breeze, because of her pregnancy, she began to sweat. Down on the road, Randell started up his car and pulled out, kicking up a light spray of dust. Only Cora seemed to notice that he was gone. She stood in the yard with her hands far back on her hips supporting her lower back. Her stomach stuck far out in front of her—her baby would come any day.

The second week in July 1954, six days after Cora had her fourth child—her second son—Mozelle had her sixth child—her second son. She had made it to the hospital on her own, and she made it back home on her own as well.

Early spring 1955, Randell came down with a cold that would not ease up. His hacking cough brought up blood, weakening him. His chest pains brought tears to his eyes, and fever kept him in bed away from his job and his women. Mozelle sat back and watched him suffer, often with a cold smug smile on her face, though she didn't stop the children from waiting on him. She worried that they might catch whatever he had, so she made them wash their hands after waiting on him.

Although he was weak and claimed that he felt every day of his sixty-three years, Randell didn't think twice about going up against Mozelle when she tried to keep Randie in school. He told her, "There wasn't nobody that could make me stay in school, if I didn't want to."

Never mind what Mozelle said, that was all Randie needed to hear. She stayed out of school, and there wasn't much Mozelle could do about it—she had to go to work. To keep her from forcing Randie to go back to school, Randell sent Randie to stay with Bernice, who was now living in Gadsden with Nathaniel a little ways up the road. Mozelle figured Bernice only took Randie in to spite her. Her opinion didn't much matter until a few months later when Randie turned up pregnant. Then Bernice wanted to send her back home, but Mozelle wasn't having that. If she let Randie come home, then people would think she got pregnant at home, making her look like a bad mother. She made Randie stay put.

Because he was getting sicker, Randell couldn't do a thing to make her let Randie come back home. By the time he went to Doctor Lester to see about himself in the fall, Randell was told that his lungs were full of tuberculosis. That scared him. It didn't take much talking for Doctor Lester to convince Randell that his life depended on his going into the sanatorium up on the mountain at Noccalula Falls on the outskirts of Gadsden. Going to the sanatorium wasn't a problem until Doctor Lester explained to Randell that the treatment could take as long as two years.

"He must be outta his damn mind if he think I'm gon' go to some sanatorium for two whole years! Naw, I'm not doing it. I got things I got to do. I got a job. I can't leave my job for two years."

"Randell, you got to go," Mozelle said. "You sick. You stay here, you could make all of us sick. Randie and Cora both pregnant. You could make them sick. Randell, you got to go."

"Yeah, you want me to go, don't you? You probably the one that gave me TB."

"You got TB, Randell, not me."

"Well, I . . . I don't know how I got it then. Maybe you put a hex on me."

"Fine," she said, "you go on, blame me. I don't care." She let him have his say. After all, he wasn't going to be bothering her for a long time. The day he was admitted to the sanatorium was probably the darkest day of his life, but it was the happiest day of Mozelle's. Especially after Cora told her that Henry told her that Randell had gotten TB from a woman in town who had died. It would be fitting if Randell stayed in the sanatorium for the rest of his life.

For the first time since she moved into the house, Mozelle felt like it was hers. Finally, the heavy burden of Randell Tate was loosened from around her neck. No longer was she filled with anger or dread that Randell would come home and eat up the food she bought for her children. No longer did she have to worry herself with the thought that Randell was going with some woman up the road or that any of his whores were laughing at her while Randell spent his money on them. It was a good feeling knowing that he was out of her life for a long while. She was going to be all right; she wasn't going to be any worse off than when he was home. He didn't give her his money anyway, and now that she wasn't setting aside money to buy land or to build her house, she had plenty of money to feed her children and put clothes on their backs. God, she felt like she could breathe again. Coming home after a hard day of work was a pleasure. There still was no furniture in the house, but it was home, her home. It was also the first time since Mrs. Mitchell gave her the lace curtains for the front windows that Mozelle felt like putting them up. They had been stored under the bed for too long. The sunlight did indeed look pretty through white lace.

Twenty-Nine

1955

Gordon Ross said he just happened by and thought he'd take a look at how the steps he built were holding up.

"They holdin' up jest fine," Mozelle said. "I figure they strong as the rest of my house."

"You did a right fine job, Miss Tate. You did yourself proud."

"Thank you, sa," she said, feeling real good about herself. "I thank God every day for the blessing of this house."

"Amen," Mr. Ross said.

Looking the house over, Mr. Ross moseyed across the yard. "Mighty fine job," he said, nodding every now and then.

Mozelle watched him inspecting her house, all the time wondering why he was really there.

He came back to the bottom of the steps. "I hear tell that your husband is shut up in the sanatorium."

So that was it. Mr. Ross had heard about Randell. But what did he want? She hoped that he was not calling on her. She didn't want menfolk to be just happening by. It wasn't proper.

"Miss Tate, you got yourself a shotgun?"

"A shotgun? Why no. I ain't got no use for no shotgun."

"Believe me, you got use for one. You a woman living alone with a houseful of children down in this here valley. It ain't safe."

"Mr. Ross, we jest fine. Ain't nobody gon' bother us down here."

"You don't know that for sure, Miss Tate. White boys back up in the hills behind your house have been known to come down and trouble good colored folks for the fun of it."

"I been down here goin' on ten years now. I ain't never had no trouble outta nobody."

"Maybe not before, but now you ain't got no man at home. Everybody knows that."

"Well, truth to tell, Mr. Ross, Randell wasn't home a lot of nights when he was home, and me and my children was jest fine on our own."

"You been lucky, Miss Tate. Jest the other day, I was coming outta the woods. Shot me a good-size rabbit. Had me a taste for some rabbit stew. The wife cooked it up pretty good, too. Anyhow, two of them white boys tried to take that rabbit right out my hand."

"What did you do?"

"I got the drop on 'em 'cause I had my shotgun."

"I declare."

"I made them boys get, but they was waiting for me a little ways up the road."

"Oh, my," she said. "What they do?"

"They tried to throw a snake on me."

"Oh, Lord." She had never worried over white folks bothering her before, but if Mr. Ross heard about Randell being away, maybe other folks—colored and white who was up to no good, might've heard about it, too.

"Now, I ain't stupid," Mr. Ross said. "I know if they had they guns, that snake woulda been bullets, and nobody woulda knowed what happened to me."

"Ain't that the truth. I wonder how come they didn't have guns. I hear tell that them white boys that live back up in the hills, always got them a gun."

"That's the truth. I figure they wasn't figuring they'd come up on me that far back in the woods."

"You think they woulda bothered you if'n they had a gun?"

"Sho'nuff. That's how come me and my wife decided to talk to you about a gun. See, Miss Tate, with you living down here by yourself with them children, you oughts to have a shot-gun to protect yourself, if need be. Now, I got one of my shotguns in the back of my car. You can have it for fifteen dollars if you want it."

"I want it," she said eagerly, "and I know how to use it, too. My daddy taught me when I was jest a girl."

"Well, then, I'll go get you your gun."

She bought the shotgun and tucked it safely against the wall behind her bed. There was nothing she had to worry about now.

One whole month had passed since Randell went into the sanatorium, and she was getting tired of Brother and Essie begging her to take them to see him. Lord knows she did not want to see him herself, and for the life of her, she could not understand why they did. But she was running out of excuses. Giving in, finally, she took all the children, including Cora's, that could walk on their own, though it turned out that children weren't allowed inside. They stayed outdoors while Randell waved to them from an open window. That in itself was odd to Mozelle. It made her sick to see him acting like he was happy to see them when he wasn't ever happy to see them when he was at home. When he tossed them his loose change, she turned her back—there was only so much hypocrisy she could stomach. But all the children had a good time. Maybe Randell's TB was a blessing. Maybe it was God's way of making him be good to his children. They stayed a half hour. From then on she took them every Sunday. She even took Randell some of her fresh-made pan-fried apple pie and peach cobbler. By the fourth visit, she noticed that every time she went inside to let Randell know that they were there, he was always sitting in the lobby with the same woman. The woman would get up and go off somewhere after she got there.

"Who's that woman?" she asked.

"What woman?"

"That woman you always sittin' with when I get here."

"Oh, her? She's a patient here like me. She ain't got nobody visiting her so I talk to her so she don't feel like she by herself. She worse off than me. She got TB real bad."

"Poor thing," Mozelle said, feeling sorry for the woman. She had thought the woman was a visitor. "You can give her some of your pie and cobbler, if you want."

"I will," he said, lifting the cloth off the cobbler and smelling it. "I can't wait to eat some myself."

Mozelle didn't think anymore about the woman and whether or not Randell was whoring in the sanatorium. As sick as he was, she knew that that couldn't be.

At work, Tom would ask how she was getting on. Like everyone else, he knew that Randell wasn't home—Mamie had told him. Mozelle could tell that Tom was sweet on her and avoided being alone with him. She didn't want the look in his eyes to awaken the lust that once stirred in her heart for him. Managing to not be alone with him at work was easy enough to do, they didn't work at the same job. It was what she imagined when thoughts of him invaded her mind at work and at home that worried her. She didn't think that she'd ever yearn to be with a man again, especially since that yearning was what made her forget her vow to never marry in the first place, and the reason she ended up with six children. No, she could never let herself yield and get weak again. That's why each day, as soon as the workday was over, she hurried out of the mill.

"Mozelle!" Tom called, rushing to catch up with her. "Hold up."

Hold up? It was him she was running from.

Tom caught up with her. "Let me walk with you."

"I thought you went the other way."

"Usually. Today U'm going your way."

"Oh," she said, afraid to look at him for fear that she would weaken. She walked faster.

Tom matched Mozelle step for step. "Listen, I been wanting to talk to you about something that's been on my mind for some time now."

Oh, God no, she thought.

"You got time to stop off at the cafe up the road?"

"I can't, my children waitin' on me. I gots to get home and fix supper."

"Then I guess we got to walk and talk fast, huh?"

"What you wanna talk to me about, Tom? Do you need me to help you build a house?" she asked, nervously, though she tried to make it sound like she was funning.

He chuckled. "I guess you could say that. See, Mozelle," he said, seriously, "ever since I spent that little bit of time with you building on your house, I ain't been able to stop thinking about you."

Mozelle's legs suddenly felt rubbery under her. This was what she was scared of. As long as Tom hadn't told her how he felt, she was able to halfway face him, even though in her dreams about him, he had long since said that he wanted her. It was wrong now, and it was wrong in her dreams. She tried to walk faster, but her legs were betraying her. She stumbled.

Tom caught hold of Mozelle's arm and kept her from lurching forward. "Mozelle. . .Mozelle, just hold on a minute."

She tried to keep walking. Tom held her back. Against her will, she slowed down. She eased her arm out of his grasp as she looked around, guiltily, to see if anybody had seen his hand on her. "Tom, U'ma married woman. Folks talk.

"Mozelle, it's okay. Nobody's close enough to hear what we talking about."

"But you had your hand on me. People can see us."

"Mozelle, relax. We ain't doing nothing sinful on this dusty road."

She inhaled sharply.

"I was just funning. Don't go getting upset," Tom said, seriously. "Look, Mozelle, I know you're a married woman, and I been knowing for a long time that your husband ain't nowhere near good enough for you. Now that he's in that sanatorium, it's—"

"Mamie, can't hold water, can she?"

"It don't matter. I'da found out anyhow. But I was thinking, this is as good a time as any for you to leave your husband."

Stunned, Mozelle's eyes widened. Her mouth opened.

"Just hear me out. Mozelle, you can leave—"

"No, Tom, I can't leave Randell."

"You can. There ain't nothing stopping you."

"Yes, there is. I got his children. I. . .no, I can't talk to you 'bout Randell. It ain't right. It ain't proper. I gots to get home." She took off walking as fast as she could.

Tom caught up to her again, and again taking hold of her arm, stopped her from going on. "Mozelle, listen to me. I don't know exactly how you feel about me, but I know you feel something."

She looked around nervously. No one was close by. "No, Tom, I—"

"Mozelle, just hear me out. I know there's something going on between us that ain't been talked about, and I believe you know it, too."

Mozelle quickly looked away. Had how she felt about him been that obvious?

"Mozelle, how you feel about me ain't nothing to be ashamed of. Me and you is just two people who—"

"Tom. . .Tom we ain't got no business—"

"Mozelle, I know U'm being forward, and I know you a good Christian woman, but your husband ain't good enough for you."

"But he's my husband all the same."

"That's true, but he don't deserve you. I been waiting all my life for a good woman like you. I—"

"But what about your children's mama, Tom? Ain't she a good woman?"

"She's. . ." he began but stopped. He kicked at a rock, sending it farther down the road. "Mozelle, we got to talk. Let's go sit over there under that tree."

"I can't. I got to fix—"

"Just for a minute," Tom insisted. "I won't keep you long."

She wanted desperately to run. The devil was tempting her and she was weak because a part of her yearned to be with this man. She would be lying if she didn't admit to herself that it felt good to be wanted by him, but it was wrong.

He tugged on her arm. "Just for a minute," he said again.

She let him take her over to the tree. They both sat down. Tom sat with his back up against the tree, only after she said that she didn't want to sit there herself. She didn't want to get comfortable. For a minute they didn't talk. Words not spoken, she felt in her heart. Tom was a good man. He was most likely a good daddy, at least Mamie said that he was.

"You ever see your children?" she asked.

"I quit my boys' mama over five years ago. She done got herself a husband and another baby since then. They don't stop me from seeing my boys though."

"That's good."

"Laverne is a good woman. I ain't got nothing bad to say about her. It's just that me and her ain't never wanted nothing together. That is besides our boys. Until I met you, I ain't never known a woman to want something, 'cepting a man, as bad as you wanted that house built. When you said you was going to build that house by yourself," he said, shaking his head, "I could not believe it. Bob said you had to have a lot of boy in you to want to do man's work. But I told him, he was dead wrong."

"Truth to tell, Tom, for a while when I was buildin' on my house, I forgot I was a woman myself," she said, pulling out the blades of grass that touched her legs.

"I didn't. I told Bob you got more woman in you than any woman I ever seen."

Blushing, Mozelle kept pulling out blades of grass and dropping them where she pulled them from. She knew he was looking at her, so she didn't look up. At that moment, she felt like a young girl courting for the first time.

"What U'm getting to, Mozelle, is I want to marry you when you divorce your husband."

Inhaling softly, Mozelle looked at him. This was just like her dream, but what Tom wanted, she could not make real.

"I know you wasn't expecting me to say that, but that's how I feel."

"Tom, I can't. . .I got to stay—"

"No you don't," he said abruptly. "Mozelle, it's not a sin to divorce your husband. Especially one like the one you married to. I'll be a good husband to you."

The heat seemed to rise up from her chest and cover her face, making Mozelle feel like she was not sitting under a big shade tree but under the scorching sun. As embarrassed as she was, she could not tear her eyes away from Tom's pleading dark brown eyes gazing upon her sensually, seducing her into wanting to say yes. She wondered if that look would be there ten years down the road after he got used to being with her every day. He touched her knee, sending chills up her spine.

"Mozelle, I think you oughta give us a chance, lessen U'm wrong about how you feel about me."

No, he wasn't altogether wrong, but at that moment, Mozelle didn't know how she was supposed to feel. If she let herself feel good, feel happy, and say yes, then she was breaking her promise to God; but if she said no outright, then she was turning her back on possibly the best man she had ever laid eyes on next to her daddy. She went back to pulling at the grass.

"Mozelle, I promise you, I'll never hurt you or your children. I'll always treat you right. I'll give you half my pay every week for yourself, and I'll pay the bills. I got me a bit of money salted away, I can help you out a lot. I know we ain't courted or nothing, but what I feel for you, I believe is true."

Covering her mouth with her hands, she closed her eyes. Her dreams didn't even come close to this. As much as she wanted to be loved, as much as she wanted someone to take care of her, she had to hold strong to her vow to never be with another man. It wasn't going to be easy, but she was going to have to say no. *Help me, Lord. Don't let me yield to temptation.*

Tom eased closer to Mozelle. He put his arm around her waist. When her back stiffened, he slowly slid his hand down her back to the ground. He saw the tears roll down her cheeks.

His touch was like fire. She felt like her very soul was burning to be loved. She did not want to feel this way. "I can't marry you, Tom."

He looked deep into her eyes. "Is it 'cause you don't feel the same way I do?"

"U'm shame to say, I do feel the same way."

"Why you shamed of how you feel, Mozelle? Ain't nothing bad about two people loving each other."

"Love? Tom, U'm married to Randell Tate. I—"

"Not much longer if you divorce him."

"But I can't be talkin' love with another man. And even if I divorce him, I can't marry you," she said, wiping away her tears with her fingertips.

"Why not?"

Looking at a blade of crabgrass that had a white bud shooting out of its side, Mozelle pressed her lips together. Only when she was about sure that she wouldn't cry, she said, "I promised God that if he got me free of Randell, I would never ever marry another man."

Tom gently lifted her chin and turned her face to him. "God ain't gon' hold you to that, Mozelle. He know why you made that promise."

"U'm holdin' myself to that promise. No matter what it take, I got to keep my word to God."

Tom's eyes shifted and looked across the road just as a bus passed, heading toward Gadsden. He, too, started pulling out blades of shiny green grass, but he tossed them aside in bunches.

Fingering a blade of grass, Mozelle felt the limpness that was not there before she pulled it away from its root. It felt as she did—limp, drained of life. More than her promise to God, she was afraid to let herself fall in love again. It was too painful.

Tom took Mozelle's hand. "I ain't surprised you feel this way," he said. "I know you're scared 'cause you had a bad time of it with your husband. But if you never let yourself trust another man, or let yourself be loved by a real man that don't mean you no harm, you ain't doing nothing but hurting your own self. Every man ain't out to do you wrong, Mozelle. Every man ain't trifling."

Again tears filled her eyes. "I believe you is a good man, Tom. I believe you might jest do right by me, but I got to keep my promise to God. He brought me through the worst times of my life. When I was starving, He kept me alive. When I asked him for my house, He showed me how to build it. I owe Him everything. I cannot break my promise. I know you understand that, don't you?"

Tom let go of her hand. He pensively rubbed his brow. "Mozelle, a part of me understand what you're talking about. See, my mama never had another man after my daddy died; said God was all she needed. It made sense to me at the time that she felt that way, that's probably 'cause she was my mother, and I knew that her and my daddy was good together, and by the time he died, she was a old woman. I could see how she didn't want to be with anybody else. But that ain't the life for you, Mozelle. You ain't old. You got a lot of living to do yet, and I want you to do it with me."

She had to say what was in her heart. "U'm gon' tell you straight out, Tom. I want to be with you, too," she said softly.

"Then—"

"But I can't, Tom. God might smite me for breaking my promise. I—"

"No. God don't work like that. He—"

"But, Tom. Suppose we got together. Maybe things might turn bad for us 'cause I broke my promise to God. I might not do right by you, Tom. I can't let that happen."

Tom shook his head. "I don't see God hurting you or me. But you know what? You feel that strong about your promise, U'm gon' respect it 'cause you want me to. Just the same, I wish I had been the man you married."

To herself she was wishing that he had been, too, but wishing wasn't going to change the past. At first hesitant, Mozelle timidly reached over and lay her hand on top of his. Tom in turn lay his hand atop hers, and rubbing it for a minute, smiled sadly at her. For a long time they ignored passersby and sat holding hands knowing that it was most likely the last time they'd talk or hold hands. Before he helped her up, he kissed her chastely on the cheek.

"You can always count on me," he said, letting go of her hand.

Tom walked her the rest of the way into Gadsden, and then

all the way to Plum Street. They didn't discuss anything more along the way, not even the weather. At the top of the road, he tipped his hat to her then turned and walked off. She watched him go up Short Vine Street past Cora's house until he turned up Fifteenth Street. A little voice in her head shouted, *Run after him! Don't let him get away.* That she couldn't do.

She saw Tom only fleetingly from that day on. Her yearnings for him subsided with time, but there were those moments when she wished that she had given in. Mamie thought she was out of her mind.

"Mozelle, ain't no promise worth giving up on life for," she said. "God ain't holding you to no promise."

"I ain't givin' up on life—I got a lot to live for. I got children to raise up."

"You sho'nuff do, but having a good man at your side can make life a whole lot easier and a lot more fun. What you gon' do when you get hot and bothered?"

"The same as I do now. I ask God to take it out my mind and my body."

"How in the world do God take horny feelings out your body when—"

"That's 'tween me and God, and I ain't gon' talk about it with you."

Mamie sucked her teeth. "Well, don't. It's the craziest thing I ever heard anyhow."

"That's fine. Then we ain't got to talk about it no mo'."

"That's fine with me," Mamie said, flippantly. She hushed up and took a big bite out of her apple.

"Good," Mozelle said, and that was that. They never talked about Tom again and, in fact, she and Mamie didn't talk as much as they use to. That saddened her because Mamie was probably her best friend. Three weeks went by, and Mamie brushed past her and told her that Tom had left the mill. It was for the best. Mozelle couldn't deny the feeling of loss that snuck up on her but she had to live with that.

The sudden death of Henry's mother, Rosa Lewis, added to Mozelle's sadness. If she could have afforded to, she would have taken in Rosa's three boys and her one daughter left at home as Rosa had asked her to. Henry wasn't able to support them either, and after staying with Miss Maggie Bell up the road on Short Vine for a piece, Rosa's oldest girl, Lillie, who was living in New York City, sent for them. Rosa's little house on the other side of the branch was empty now; no one else moved in. Mozelle missed passing the time of day with Rosa on the road in the shadow of the big weeping willow tree that sat out in front of her house.

With Rosa gone, Cora was the only person left to talk to besides Mamie. At times, Cora was more like a friend than a daughter. The time she could spend with Cora on a Saturday afternoon and Sunday was shared with Cora's five babies and Mozelle's own children. Between the two of them, they had a houseful.

When Randell didn't come home by the end of 1955, Mozelle began to believe that he wasn't coming back at all. That was, until she started getting letters from him, in between visits, promising her that he had found God, and was now a changed man. Even while the letters were being read to her, she doubted if that was true. He claimed that he had plenty of time to think and reflect on how badly he had treated her. He quoted bible scriptures and vowed that when he got better, he'd make up to her all the years he didn't do right by her. She figured he'd need another twenty-five years to even begin thinking about ways he could make up for all the misery he caused her.

In January 1956 when Randie was six months pregnant and showing big, Mozelle let her come back home. None of the neighbors could whisper behind her back now that a child of hers had gotten knocked up while living under her roof. That was all well and good, though Randie held it against her that she wouldn't let her come home when she wanted to. That didn't much bother Mozelle though. If Randie didn't want to listen, then her lessons in life had to be learned the hard way. Wasn't that what her folks taught her?

Thirty

March 1956

"Grandma. . .Mama say. . .come quick!"

"Child, what's wrong?" Mozelle asked, rushing from the kitchen while drying her hands on a dishrag hanging from her skirt waistband. Six-year-old Junior's tear-filled eyes startled her. He never cried. Even when he fell off her front porch twenty feet to the ground and cut his leg, he didn't cry.

"Junior, close that door," Randie ordered, "it's cold out there."

Wiping his runny nose with the back of his jacket sleeve and looking only at his grandma, Junior said, "Mama head hurt."

Essie got up off the floor where she had been sitting shooting marbles with Nell and Brother. She pushed the door up and went back to her game.

"She got a headache?" Mozelle asked, wiping Junior's face with the dishrag.

Junior nodded his head repeatedly.

"You go on 'n tell your mama U'm comin' soon as I finish cookin'," she said. She'd had a hundred headaches over the years herself, and though Cora rarely got a one, they eventually went away after she took an aspirin.

Junior slowly turned back toward the door. He put his hand on the knob, but he didn't turn it. Mozelle watched his little body seem to droop before her eyes, his head fell limply to his chest as his shoulders began to shake.

Suddenly she was afraid. "Boy, is your mama that bad off?"

When he turned back to her, a flood of tears poured out of Junior's eyes. "Mama's head made her cry," he said, sobbing.

Essie and Randie both stared at Junior. Mozelle wasn't all that worried before, but Cora had to be real bad off to have scared her child like this.

Mozelle dropped the dishrag on the chair. "Essie," she said, taking her coat off a nail near the door, "bring me that tin of aspirins outta that bowl on the table in the kitchen." She pulled on her coat.

Essie ran to the kitchen and rushed back with the aspirin.

"Essie, I want you to watch Joe and Nell, you hear me?"

"Yessum."

"U'm gon' go check on Cora. Randie, if I ain't back in a little bit, y'all eat the beans and corn bread on the stove."

"Okay, Mama," Randie said. "Mama, Cora's gon' be all right, ain't she?"

"She's gon' be jest fine," she said, trying to reassure herself more than her children. "Brother, I want you to bring in some more wood for the stove."

"Yessum."

Mozelle took Junior's hand, and together, practically running, they made their way quickly up the hill out of the valley onto Short Vine Street. The cries of Cora's eight-month-old baby, Sheila, could be heard halfway down the road. As soon as she stepped inside the house and saw Cora groaning and withering in pain on her bed, her hands pressed against her temples, her face drenched with sweat and contorted almost beyond recognition, Mozelle knew that this was unlike any headache she herself had ever had. She rushed over to the bed. Sitting down alongside Cora, Mozelle lifted Cora's head and cradled her against her bosom. She wondered if the aspirin in her hand was strong enough to stop the kind of pain her child had in her head.

Cora opened her eyes. Their bulging redness startled Mozelle.

"Lord a mercy, child. What kinda headache is this?"

"Ma. . .Mama," Cora said pitifully, "it. . .hurt."

"Junior, go fetch me a glass of water," she said, drying

Cora's face with the hem of her dress.

Junior ran toward the kitchen at the back of the house. Mozelle looked over at her grandbabies as she gently, but firmly massaged Cora's forehead. Sheila lay on the floor on her back kicking, her mouth wide open, hollering. Twenty-month-old David was not crying at that moment, but his face was tear-stained, his nose runny. He was sucking on his snot and pulling on a shoestring in his daddy's shoe. Betty was just four and Ann almost three years old, but they sat quietly together on the couch, their faces tear-streaked, staring wide-eyed at their mama.

Junior came running back with an over-full glass of water, splashing it on himself as he ran.

Mozelle pushed one small white tablet at a time into Cora's mouth and held her head up so that she could swallow the water from the glass. She gave her three tablets. Cora lay back against Mozelle, her eyes squeezed tightly together. The pain was carved into every inch of her face.

Tenderly touching Cora's head, Junior said softly, "U'ma run away if Mama die."

"Boy, how you say such a thing?" Mozelle asked. "Your mama ain't gon' die."

Tears welled up in Junior's eyes anew.

"Junior, listen to Grandma. Your mama ain't gon' die," Mozelle said again, trying to quiet his fears. "She just out of sorts for a minute."

Her words didn't stop his tears.

"Be a big boy and take this glass back to the kitchen," she said, wanting to give him something to do.

Junior took the glass and walked quickly out of the room. He came back just as fast.

"Pick up the baby for grandma and bring her here."

"Yessum," he said, right away turning toward Sheila. He first got down on his knees, then he awkwardly gathered Sheila in his arms. She cried louder as Junior picked her up.

Mozelle took Sheila into her right arm while still holding Cora's head in the crook of her left arm. She didn't have to feel Sheila's bottom to know that her diaper was wet and full. She kissed her on her round, wet cheeks. Sheila stopped wailing and rubbed her face against Mozelle's neck. Now she whimpered. Junior went and sat down on the couch with Betty and Ann.

"Mama," Cora moaned.

"Yes, child."

"Mama," Cora whispered in a strained, controlled voice with her eyes still squeezed shut, "feed. . .the. . .children."

"They ain't ate all day?"

Cora slowly rolled her head from side to side once.

"How long you been like this?"

"All. . .day."

"Do Henry know you this bad off?"

Rubbing her forehead, she managed to painfully say, "Work."

"How come you didn't send for me sooner?"

"Work."

Sheila started wailing again.

She tried rocking Sheila. "Cora, you try 'n sleep. U'ma be back soonest I feed the babies." Gingerly, she slipped her arm from under Cora's head. "Junior, come get some soda crackers for y'all to eat 'til I make supper," she said, carrying Sheila with her to the kitchen. She found the soda crackers. She took two from the pack and gave the pack to Junior to take to the other children. The two she had taken, she broke off a piece of one and put it in Sheila's mouth. Seeing how hungrily Sheila took the cracker and sucked it, Mozelle decided that changing her diaper would have to wait until supper was cooking. All of the children must be just as hungry.

Even after the children had hungrily eaten their sugar-sweetened rice and fried chicken, Cora's headache hadn't eased up a bit. Mozelle cleaned up all the children and put them down to sleep. All accept Junior. He was too worried. At nightfall, Henry pulled up into the yard on the side of the house. At first, he didn't think Cora's headache was serious enough to worry about. He changed his mind, however, when she opened her bloodshot eyes.

"U'ma take her to the doctor," he said, gathering Cora in his arms.

Mozelle draped Cora's coat over her limp body, covering up her cotton nightdress, as Henry carried her out to the pickup. Long after he drove off, Mozelle stood on the porch shivering in the cold crisp March air. She was going to be forty-two on Thursday—but that was in two days, wasn't it? In her bones she felt every one of those forty-two years. Hugging herself, Mozelle stepped back inside the house. The heat from the fireplace felt good.

"Dear God, please let Cora be all right," she said aloud. While her mind was on Cora, she didn't forget that she hadn't seen her own children in hours, but it was her grandchildren that needed her now. Brother was old enough at thirteen and Essie at fourteen to take care of the little ones. Randie had her hands full taking care of herself as she was expecting her baby in a month's time. Mozelle was still not use to the idea of Randie having a baby and not being married, but Randie was strong-willed and followed her own mind. She was going to have to be ready to be a mama.

It was ten o'clock before Henry brought Cora back home.

"The doctor say she just got a bad headache," he said, helping Cora down onto the bed. "She got to take two of these pills every four hours. He say she'll be better in the morning."

Relieved, Mozelle let out the breath she seemed to have been holding on to since Cora went off to the doctor. "Thank You, Lord."

Laying on her back, Cora looked wearily up at her mama. Mozelle could still see the awful pain that filled Cora's eyes as tears welled up and spilled down the side of her face to the pillow. With her hands, Mozelle wiped at the tears on her child's cheeks. "Try to sleep, child. You'll be better tomorra," she said, kissing Cora on the forehead, wishing that she could kiss away the pain. "U'ma come by and check on you befo' I go to work tomorra, and U'ma come by afterward, too."

Cora closed her eyes. Mozelle pulled the covers up over her body up to her neck.

"Want me to walk you home?" Henry asked, standing

behind Mozelle.

"I'll make it jest fine," she said, going to the door. "You come 'n get me if she don't get better."

"I will."

Out on the porch, in the cold opaque darkness with only the light from the front room letting her see his face, she turned to Henry. "You been sneakin' around with Inez Bullock up the road?"

Frowning, Henry pulled back. "No, ma'am."

"I hear tell you is."

"No, ma'am, I ain't," he said, defensively. "I ain't got time for stepping out. I got children to feed."

Mozelle stuck her tongue in her cheek and slowly rolled it around. Her mother-wit told her that he was lying, but she had no real proof other than what she had heard. "That woman bet' not harm my child, and you bet' not make her miserable," she warned.

"No, ma'am, Miss Tate. I ain't never gon' hurt Cora."

"Make sure you don't," she said. She stepped off the porch into the faceless darkness and started off down the road, praying that Cora's headache would go away. Folks had been talking about Henry and Inez Bullock for weeks, and Mozelle had said nothing because she hadn't seen Henry but two times and both times he had been with Cora. She hated to think that Cora was most likely married to a cheating man. Lord knows Mozelle didn't want Cora to know that kind of misery. If Cora had to come back home, she could. Her house was big enough for Cora and her five children. What bothered her just the same, if not more, was the fact that folks said that Inez messed with hoodoo. Henry's cheating could hurt Cora's heart and pride, but hoodoo could make her sick. Maybe even kill her.

Though she couldn't see her hand in front of her face as she trotted down the hill into the valley, Mozelle wasn't afraid of the blackness that engulfed her. She was afraid of the pain that was hurting her child.

Cora lay on her bed asleep, while Sheila was content to be sitting on the bed next to her playing with her feet. Joe and David sat on the floor rolling a ball between them, while Nell played with Betty. They had been fed, and as usual, they were clean. Cora took pride in how well she kept her children.

While Cora slept, Mozelle sat alongside the bed braiding Ann's hair. She had been at the house since mid-afternoon, and ever so often she studied Cora's face to see if she was in pain. Her brow didn't crease as often, so Mozelle figured that Cora was not suffering as much as she had been the night before. By the time Cora stirred and opened her eyes, Mozelle had started on Betty's hair.

"How you feelin'?" she asked.

"U'm better," Cora said, resting her hand on Sheila's plump little thigh. "My head still hurt a bit though."

"You want somethin' to eat?"

"I ain't hungry," she whispered. "I ate on a cracker a while ago."

"When's the last time you ate a full meal?"

"I ate some knuckles and collard greens up at Inez house day befo' yesterday."

A mighty fear gripped her. Mozelle dropped the comb. "No."

"What's wrong, Mama?"

Betty picked up the comb and held it out to Mozelle.

Mozelle, didn't take the comb but instead raised her hands prayerfully to her mouth. "Please, Lord, don't let it be. Heal my child, Lord. Take away her pain. Lord—"

"Mama. What's. . .wrong?"

Mozelle continued to pray to herself. *Lord, Cora's a good girl. Please, Lord, don't let no harm come to my child.*

"Mama."

Staring up at Mozelle, Betty held on to the comb tightly as her bottom lip pushed forward.

"Mama, you scarin' the children," Cora said, grimacing, trying to raise her head. "What's wrong?"

Mozelle lowered her hands. Seeing Betty's wide-eyed gaze,

she gently held her face in her hands. "Me and your mama's jest fine, child," she said, wrapping her arms around Betty and hugging her close. Lord knows if she could believe that herself, maybe her own heart would stop pounding, maybe her own fear would go away.

Cora struggled to sit up. "Mama. . .you—" Cora couldn't go on. She closed her eyes and lay her head back on her pillow.

"You jest lay still, Cora. Don't trouble yourself," Mozelle said, letting go of Betty, who looked even more scared. She took the comb from Betty's hand and went back to combing the front part of her hair.

Cora lay quietly, staring up at the ceiling. After a while, she cleared her throat. "Inez is all right, Mama."

"Child, you don't rightly know that. What I done told you 'bout eatin' other folk's cookin'?"

"Inez wouldn't do me no harm, Mama. Besides, there ain't nothing you can do to greens. They just leaves."

"Cora, when a woman who wants your man give you some of her cookin', it ain't safe. She'll do anythin' it take to get your husband, even if it mean takin' your life."

Now Cora did raise her head up off the pillow. "Mama, what you talkin' 'bout?"

Mozelle dragged the comb through Betty's hair. Betty squirmed and hunched her shoulders, but Mozelle didn't pay her any mind, though she knew that the child was tender-headed.

"Mama?"

"People talkin', Cora. They say Henry been sneakin' around town with Inez."

Cora squinted from the pain. Again, she lay back down. "That ain't true."

"Cora, there's always a bit of truth in what people say. Besides, you say yaself that Henry go out his way to tote Inez to the store."

"But that don't mean nothin', Mama. Willie up the street give me a ride from town the other day. It didn't mean nothin'."

"Maybe not 'tween you and Willie, but it might mean somethin' 'tween Henry and Inez."

Slowly rubbing her forehead and squeezing her eyes shut, Cora said weakly, "Mama, you useta to tell me don't trust folks who talk out the side of they mouth."

There was nothing Mozelle could say to that. That was what she said about folks always ready to bring bad news—they didn't mean anybody no good. Anyway, it wasn't any use in bothering Cora about gossip when she wasn't in any condition to talk without suffering. Mozelle could see how tightly Cora's brows were knitted together.

Sheila started twisting her body, rolling toward the edge of the bed. Cora opened her eyes and quickly grabbed Sheila by her chubby little leg and pulled her back against her side. But Sheila didn't want to stay put. She started to kick her legs out and wave her arms, hitting Cora on the hip.

"Mama, put her down on the floor," Cora said, her head throbbing.

Lifting Sheila off the bed, Mozelle set Sheila down on the floor alongside her chair and said to Junior, "Watch the baby."

He picked up Sheila and set her down in-between his legs, but then he reached over and took the ball out of David's hand, making him cry.

Trying to lift her head, Cora grimaced. She let her head settle back into the pillow. She cried out.

Scared for her child, but not knowing what else to do, Mozelle began to gently massage Cora's forehead.

"Mama, it feel like a butcher knife in my head."

"My God. Cora, you want another pill?"

Painfully, Cora turned her head and squinted over at the clock on the dresser. "I can't take no mo' for a hour."

David cried louder.

"Junior—" Cora began, frowning deeply with her eyes closed. "Mama, make that boy behave."

"Boy, give him back that ball befo' I whop your tail."

Junior pouted, but he rolled the ball back to David, who grabbed it with both hands. Turning his attention to Sheila, Junior started playing with her, tickling her. She giggled in a gurgling sort of way.

Turning back to Betty's hair, Mozelle said to Cora, "Why don't you take a nap. When you wake up, it'll be time to take some more pills."

Cora appeared to be thinking. Her eyes were looking up at the ceiling. "Tomorra's your birthday, Mama," she said. Then she quietly rolled over onto her left side facing the wall. Her body relaxed as she exhaled softly.

Though her eyes were on Cora, Mozelle slowly dragged the comb through Betty's hair, this time being more gentle. Her own birthday was the last thing on her mind. Cora's birthday was coming, too. But right now she was worrying about Cora's headache. Fact of the matter was, she was scared, real scared. She had never heard of a headache lasting this long. She prayed that it would be gone when Cora woke up.

"What you want me to cook for supper?"

Cora was quiet.

"You ain't sleepin' already, is you?"

Cora didn't answer.

"Cora," she said, beginning to feel uneasy, "you playin' possum?"

Cora was still.

Mozelle stopped combing Betty's hair and stared at Cora's head. She listened for sounds of her breathing—there were none. Fear gripped her soul. She stared at Cora's back to see if she could see her breathing—she couldn't. She touched Cora's shoulder and gently pulled her onto her back. There was no frown on her face; she looked peaceful.

Mozelle's breath caught in her throat as she shook Cora. "C'mon, child, wake up. Don't play with Mama like this."

Cora was as limp as a rag doll.

Standing up, Mozelle reached down and lifted Cora up by her shoulders. Her head flopped back. Lifeless. The breath that Mozelle wanted so badly to be able to give to Cora, again caught in her throat. She stared in disbelief.

"My God," she cried. "My baby."

Betty went to hollering.

Cora had fallen into eternal sleep.

Thirty-One

Not since she was sixteen had Mozelle given much thought to her own birthday. In all her years, it was usually just another day to work, another day to earn a dollar. That was, until today. It was the day she had to get her firstborn ready to be put in the ground. It was the saddest and hardest thing she ever had to do. It hurt her to her heart. A flood of tears rushed down her cheeks no matter where she was and no matter what she was doing. She couldn't get the vision of Cora's little head falling lifelessly back down onto the pillow out of her mind.

Nobody thought Cora was sick enough to die. Nobody thought that Cora's baby would ever stop crying. Although there was not a moment that Sheila was not held or coddled, the arms that held her were not her mama's, the voice that cooed her, was not her mama's, the bosom she nestled in, was not her mama's.

Junior did like he said he would—he ran away minutes after Cora died. Hours later when he was finally found down the road at little Billy's house, he was not spanked. He was taken by the hand and brought back home, back to where his mama was to be laid out. He cried late into the night until sleep hushed him.

Betty had gone to hollering when she saw her mama's head drop back onto the pillow. Now she whimpered endlessly.

Ann and David didn't cry, they didn't know what it all meant. They sat on Henry's knees, while he wrestled with the reality of Cora's death. During the wake, in his arms he held one baby or another, sometimes two, while sitting off in a corner of his front room looking lost. Every time he looked over at Cora asleep in her casket, he cried. Sometimes he shook his head like he couldn't believe that she was gone or that any of this was even happening.

None of Cora's sisters or brothers could believe that she was dead. They hadn't known the coldness of death before and couldn't quite understand why Cora would not wake up. Randie had been closest to Cora and took her passing the worse. She had not been able to stop crying.

After company left them, and all the babies were put down in Cora's bed, Henry turned to Mozelle. "What U'm gon' do with five babies?"

Bone-tired, Mozelle sat heavily. "You ain't by yourself, Henry. U'm gon' help you with Cora's babies," she said. "That's what Cora want me to do."

Henry began to pace. "My sister up north say I oughta think about moving up there."

She shook her head. "No, you can't take them babies up north."

"Miss Tate, my sister say they got plenty of jobs up there, and she can help me with the children."

Mozelle felt like something was pressing against her chest. She couldn't lose Cora and Cora's babies, too. "Henry, how you gon' take them babies way up north away from they home? Away from me?" She looked over at all five children sleeping soundly and then over at Cora's closed casket just a few feet away. "You can't. I won't let you."

Henry saw that he had upset Mozelle. "Miss Tate, I ain't going nowhere right now."

Mozelle got up and went to the casket. She opened it. Cora looked like she was sleeping and would wake up at any minute. If only she would. "Mama's always gon' love you," she said, gently stroking Cora's cold, lifeless cheek. "Henry, you can't take them babies away from the home they mama made for them."

Henry let out a troublesome breath and walked out of the house.

Randell claimed his TB was still contagious. He didn't come to Cora's funeral. When Mozelle thought about it, it was only fitting that he didn't come. He was no where to be found when Cora was born into the world. When he was told of her death, he wanted to know how she died, but he didn't ask if she was going to be put away proper. He offered not a dime of the disability money he got monthly from his job, while Henry didn't have an extra dime to his name. If it wasn't for the burial policy she had on Cora, Cora would have had to wait to be laid to rest by the county. But Henry did round up the menfolk who dug the grave.

Doctor Lester came to the house to show his respect. He, too, could not believe that Cora had passed. For lack of a better explanation as to why Cora died, he said that her headache had to come from a busted vein in the brain. On her death certificate, he called it "a possible brain abscess." To Mozelle it only meant that Doctor Lester really didn't know what killed Cora.

"I'm deeply sorry, Mozelle. I just didn't think she was that bad off."

"Well she was, Doctor. I think she was poisoned."

"No, it wasn't poison that killed Cora, Mozelle. She wasn't sick in her stomach, she had bad pain in her head. She had a brain abscess."

While Mozelle didn't believe that, she didn't blame Doctor Lester for not seeing that Cora was poisoned. Mozelle blamed Inez Bullock. Sweet, trusting Cora thought nothing bad about anybody. It never crossed her mind that Inez and Henry could be sneaking around together, not even when the two of them were spending too much time off by themselves. When Inez started coming by the house, Cora didn't think that Inez was pretending to be her friend, she thought Inez was for true. Being around Cora was how Inez came to know that Cora was crazy about collards and never turned down a plate of anybody's greens. The last thing Cora ate before she come down with those bad headaches was collard greens that Inez cooked up.

Mozelle figured that Inez put something in the water. "I know she killed my child."

Henry shoved his hands down inside his coveralls. "You can't keep sayin' that, Miss Tate. Inez say she ain't did nothing like that."

"You believe her 'cause you been messin' with her."

"No, ma'am! I wasn't never messin' with Inez Bullock."

"Don't you be lyin' to me, Henry," Mozelle said, threateningly. "I'll go get my shotgun and shoot you as sure as U'm standin' here."

Beads of sweat popped out on Henry's forehead. "Miss Tate, I swear befo' God, I ain't been with Inez."

"Don't go swearin' befo' God when you know you lyin'."

"I ain't lyin'. I ain't never had nothin' to do with Inez Bullock. Cora know I was a good husband to her."

"Then how come folks talkin' like you was hoin' around?"

"'Cause folks like to start trouble. I was good to Cora. I swear on my mama's grave, I ain't never done nothin' with nobody since me and Cora married."

Mozelle squinted at him. She had never seen Henry with another woman, but she didn't believe him. She backed down only because she couldn't say that she had; it wasn't because Henry swore on his mama's grave. He and Inez, both, had God to thank for their lives, though. If it wasn't for her love of God and her worry about who'd raise up her own children and Cora's children, Mozelle would have shot Henry and Inez the day Cora died. Only through prayer did God give Mozelle the strength to forgive them but not forget what she believed in her heart Inez did. Henry must have also believed that Inez did something to Cora's greens—he stayed clear of her from the day Cora died. Mozelle didn't know what was on his mind, but her mind got no peace thinking about how Cora died. She couldn't let it go.

Mozelle stood in front of Inez' house on Plum Street, her hands on her hips. "Boy, tell your mama to come out here."

Little Bobby ran into the house. Mozelle didn't know what she was going to say but something was going to be said.

Inez came to the door. Seeing Mozelle through the dark torn screen door, she slowly opened it and stood with her whole body inside the house. Only her head was stuck outside. Her hair was uncombed and stood on top of her head.

Mozelle glared at her. Inez looked nothing like Cora. She was plump in her behind and wide in her hips. Her bosom was full whether she was with child or not. Menfolk liked looking at her and didn't care that she had six children and a husband who didn't spend much time at home.

"You want me, Miss Tate?"

"You poison those collard greens you give Cora?"

"I ain't did nothin' like that! How you say that?"

"'Cause I know you and Henry was hoin' around on Cora."

Inez' oldest boy came to the door and stood next to her. "Don't talk to my mama that way, Miss Tate."

"Boy, this ain't none of your concern," Mozelle said to the sixteen-year-old.

"Joshua, you stay outta this; this grown folk business," Inez said.

Joshua hushed up but he stayed at the door.

"Miss Tate, I promise you, I ain't never been with Henry. I got my own husband."

"You ain't never act like it. You killed my Cora so's you could have Henry to yourself."

"That's a lie! Miss Tate, you ain't gon' put Cora's death on me. I ain't had nothin' to do with her dyin'."

"My mama didn't kill Miss Cora!" Joshua shouted. He started to push on the screen door but Inez held on to the frame. Two more of Inez' children came to the door.

"Joshua, hush up! Miss Tate—"

"Cora was jest fine 'til she ate your poison greens."

Inez stepped out onto the porch. Joshua and his two brothers followed her out. They stayed close to her.

"Miss Tate, my greens wasn't poison. Besides, Cora ate my greens plenty times befo', and she ain't never got sick."

"That's 'cause you was tryin' to get her to trust your cookin'."

Next door, Mr. Bill came out of his house. Inez saw him. "Mr. Bill, you ain't never got sick from eatin' my cookin', ain't that right?

"I can't rightly say that I ever got sick, Inez," Mr. Bill said. "Your cookin' jest fine. Miss Tate, U'm sure sorry your girl is gone, but I don't think Inez did nothin' wrong."

Mozelle waved Mr. Bill off. "Mr. Bill you ain't got nothin'

Inez want. Cora had Henry, Inez wanted him."

"I swear befo' God, Miss Tate. I ain't did nothin' to Cora."

"Swear all you want, it don't mean nothin'. You a heathen," Mozelle said, pointing at Inez. "Sure as U'm standin' here, I know you killed my child. God know it, too. You can lie to me, but you ain't never gon' get away with lyin' to God. You gon' pay one day, Inez Bullock. Mark my word."

Bobby tugged on Inez' dress. "Mama, Miss Tate sayin' you killed Miss Cora?" he asked. "Did you?"

"I ain't killed Cora!" Inez shouted. "Miss Tate don't you go sayin' that I killed Cora. I didn't! Don't you be tellin' folks that."

Mozelle slowly nodded her head. "You killed her. I know it," she said, calmly. She stepped back from the house then and walked off.

"Miss Tate, I didn't do nothin' to Cora. I ain't killed Cora!"

It didn't matter that Inez denied killing Cora, Mozelle never expected that she would tell the truth. She would always lay Cora's death at Inez' door, where it belonged. Every now and then, she thought about shooting Inez, but her good sense always stopped her. She talked about killing Inez with Mamie but Mamie warned her that "an eye for eye" stained her Christian soul and made her just as bad as Inez. At times Mozelle doubted God for letting Cora die, although she knew better. If it was God's will, then he must have known best, but leaving five babies without a mama surely could not have been for the best. That she could never believe, but she didn't want to doubt God in His infinite wisdom, so it was Inez she blamed. She had stolen Cora's life. Cora was only twenty-three, just days before her twenty-fourth birthday. Cora was supposed to see her children grow up. She was supposed to live longer than her own mama and see to it that she was properly buried. Yes, Inez was to blame, although Inez started telling folks that Cora had died because she was having babies too quick, that her frail little body never got a chance to heal before she was pregnant again. Nobody believed that, especially Mozelle. Her own mama had twelve babies right after the other and birthing babies never killed her.

Some folks did believe that Inez poisoned Cora. Their

shunning her made it hard for Inez to hold her head up around town. Most days Mozelle came through Short Vine she passed right by Inez' front door. Rarely did she see Inez, but she saw one or the other of Inez' children. Always they stopped what they were doing and glared her way but they never dared say a disrespectful word to her. It wasn't that way when her children and Inez' children met. Rocks would be thrown and ugly fighting words would be said. The feud between them was Cora's legacy.

It was two long weeks after Cora was put in the ground before Sheila stopped crying. Mozelle found herself still crying on the long walk back and forth to work. That was her time to let herself give in to her tears. Not a minute, not a day went by that she didn't mourn for her child. She couldn't sit on her front porch looking out over the valley up to Cora's back door without realizing that her firstborn, her best friend, was not there. Many a night she looked out at Cora's kitchen window to see if the light was on. When Cora was alive, she knew that she was settling down for the night once her kitchen light went out. That light was rarely ever on now. There was no need. The children stayed at her house most nights whenever Henry worked late. If he came home earlier than nine o'clock, he would stand on his back porch and whistle loudly across the valley. That was his signal for Brother, who was not afraid of the black night—although the children were—to bring them home. On those nights that she had them, Mozelle couldn't get enough of looking at them. Having Cora's children close by was the only way Mozelle could shut out the vision of her being covered over by dirt that quickly grew grass and hid any hint of Cora sleeping there. There was no headstone.

At the end of April, five weeks after Cora took her last breath, Randie brought her curly head baby boy, Kenny, home to Plum Street. Soon after, Randie left Kenny behind to move to New York to find work. Johnnie Mae, a girl Randie knew from school, wrote telling her that there were jobs a plenty to be had up north. Mozelle let Randie go because, hopefully, it meant a better life for her than the one she had.

Thirty-Two

When Randell came home Thanksgiving Day, Cora had been in the ground eight months. How Mozelle wished that it was Randell that she had buried, and not her child. Randell was not only alive and well, he was at least twenty pounds heavier, and looked ten years younger than his sixty-four years. She noticed right off that he was even more particular about his clothes and his hair. He looked in the mirror at himself often enough to leave his reflection behind even when he wasn't there. She knew that every time he went into the bedroom, he was looking at himself to make sure his shirt was still tucked in or to comb his already combed thinning, graying hair.

Randell's letters had been a lie. Nothing about him had changed when it came to being a husband and father; he still cared only about himself. Mozelle held her tongue as long as she could, but when he had been home a day shy of thirty days, she asked him to help her buy food since he was eating more than all of them put together. It wasn't like he wasn't getting a check. He was. He came home with a pocketful of money.

"I shouldn't've never come back here," he said.

"No, I guess you shouldn't've," she agreed, glancing over at the children at the table quietly and slowly eating their pig knuckles and butter beans. She didn't like that they were listening. "Children ain't got no business listening to grown folks talk," her mama used to say.

"All you ever wanted from me was my money," Randell said.

She looked at him and remembered the feelings she had for him before he went into the sanatorium. She could feel the hate deep in her gut and that hate was about to tell on her, but seeing that the children's eyes were on her, she walked out of the kitchen. She went into her bedroom with Randell close on her heels.

"You ain't never gon' make do on your own, Mozelle. You ain't worth salt."

"That's jest it, Randell, I been makin' do on my own. Since you been gone, we done got electric lights on in the house and we got our own runnin' water. So you go on, say what you want. Me and the children got on jest fine without you. You should've gone on 'bout your business."

"Don't you worry. Soon as I get myself together, U'ma do just that," he said, slicking back his hair with both his hands. "I got me a real pretty woman waiting on me."

She looked at him and again remembered how low he was. It didn't matter that he was sick in the sanatorium, he could have been in a black hole in hell, and he would have found himself a woman to go with. Smiling to herself, Mozelle realized that she wasn't even angry about it. It wasn't like she didn't know.

"Randell, you best hurry up and pack your bags, you don't want that pretty woman to have to wait on you a minute too long."

"Oh, she'll wait on me long as need be," he bragged, sticking out his chest. "We was closer then two peas in a pod the whole time we was in the sanatorium. She know how to satisfy me just right."

Suddenly it occurred to Mozelle that he was talking about the made-up woman that was always sitting in the lobby with him. "You know somethin', Randell? It don't surprise me none that you was tomcatting even whilst your old body was full of TB. You'll be tomcattin' on your deathbed 'cause that's how low your old lying ass is."

"You damn right, but my baby like this old stuff I got," he said proudly, palming the weight of his manhood through his britches. "Anyhow, I'd druther lay up with a woman with TB than be with your ugly ass any day. You was here by yourself the whole time I was away, and it seem to me nobody wanted you even in good condition."

Thoughts of Tom Shott leaped into her mind. It no longer mattered how ugly Randell's words were, they couldn't hurt her anymore. Tom had wanted her. She looked at Randell and smirked. "Go to hell."

"Soon as U'm finished having a good time, I might just do that. By the way, all them years I went back and forth to Jacksonville, I was with Gail."

Though she tried not to show it, she felt like he stabbed her in her heart.

He sneered. "She was the only woman I ever loved, and you ain't never been able to hold a candle to her. If she wasn't dead, I'd be with her right now, husband or not," he said, turning and strutting out of the bedroom leaving her shaken.

Hearing the front door slam, Mozelle slumped down on the side of the bed. She figured all along that he was with a woman, just not with Gail. Too bad he hadn't died right along with her.

Taking a deep breath, Mozelle felt better. Not much Randell said bothered her anymore, not for long anyway; but she didn't know how much more she could take. He hadn't gone back to work yet, and she didn't think he ever would again, but she couldn't have him laying around the house every day making her life miserable. While she was at work, he told the children that she was out whoring. They told her everything he said, and of course they didn't believe him, but at times, they found it easier to listen to him, especially when they didn't want to do what she told them to do. Randell made it impossible for her to ignore him when he manipulated her children. Arguing, fussing, and fighting all the time was killing her. Somehow, she had to get him out of her house.

Just when Mozelle was at her wit's end, and she was planning on asking Mr. Conley what to do the next time he came to collect her policy money, she came home from working at Mrs. Mitchell's to find Randell loading up his car with the last of his clothes. Brother stood watching him.

Randell glanced over his shoulder at her. "I ain't never coming back."

She couldn't believe her own ears. The answer to her prayers had been a long time in coming, but Randell was finally leaving her.

Brother whispered to her, "He say he going to live with a woman in Talladega."

"Thank You, Lord," Mozelle said, hugging Brother to her. They both watched Randell's car climb out of the valley and, hopefully, out of their lives. She almost wanted to wave.

Thirty-Three

She thought about getting a divorce, but changed her mind when she heard that she had to pay a lawyer. Extra money was something she didn't have, at least not to spend on Randell. She figured if he wanted to marry his whore, he'd pay for the divorce himself. The only thing Mozelle could afford to do was change the lock on the front door.

She was no longer afraid of being put out of her house since Mr. Conley told her that Randell had lied to her—colored women could legally own property in Alabama. That alone angered her enough to want to kill Randell with her bare hands for making her suffer through those last five years.

Every night on her knees she prayed hard that he would stay gone. A month had passed and not a word had come from him. The only other thing Mozelle asked God to do was take the anger out of her heart. It was making her bitter in her soul and disturbing her mind. For a while she couldn't sleep through the night until she figured out that sleeping on the same bed Randell had slept on was keeping her awake. The cologne he had taken to wearing was all in the mattress. She solved that problem by turning the mattress and putting Essie and Nell in her bed. Brother slept on the floor on a half-size mattress she bought secondhand, while she slept on the half-size bed in the front room with Joe.

Again, after a while, her and the children got used to Randell not being there, though she worried herself to death wondering if he was going to try and come back.

Six weeks later, after Mozelle had turned in for the night and the children were all sleeping soundly, there came a knock at the door. She didn't get up after the first knock because often sounds of the house settling or the wind blowing made her think it was something that it wasn't.

The knock came again, louder.

Mozelle sat up in bed. There was no one she would expect to be knocking on her door after dark. Before she had lain down, she had looked across the valley at Cora's kitchen window. The lights had been out. Henry had turned in early.

The knock at the door was now a pounding.

Mozelle reached down on the floor behind her bed and picked up her shotgun, it was already loaded. In the dark she tiptoed to the front door.

"Who is it?"

"It's me."

She froze.

"Open the door."

She started shaking her head no.

"Hurry up, it's cold out here."

"What you want, Randell?"

"I come by to see how you and the children is doing."

"You ain't never cared befo' how we was doin', don't go botherin' yourself carin' 'bout us now. We jest fine."

Bang! Randell hit the door. "Woman, I said open up this damn door!"

"You can't come back here, Randell!"

Bang! Again he hit the door.

Mozelle jumped back.

"Open this door!"

"Mama, who is it?" Brother asked, rubbing his eyes.

She didn't turn away from the door. "You go on back to bed."

Bang! Bang!

Mozelle peered at the door like she could see right through it. "You can't come back here, Randell! You got to stay gone."

The light came on overhead. "Mama?"

"I paid for this land, too. I got a right to stay here!" he

shouted, hitting the door harder.

Mozelle stepped back from the door. She raised the shotgun, aiming it dead center of the door. She cocked the hammer. "You paid twenty dollars at the end. U'm figurin' you done lived out that twenty dollars a long time ago."

"You figured wrong. You ain't putting me out my house."

"This ain't your house, Randell. You a heavy burden that's finally been lifted off my shoulders, and I ain't lettin' you back in to weigh me down."

"The law'll make you open up this door."

"No, they won't. This is my property, you lyin' bastard."

"Woman, this is my property just as much as it is yours."

"Randell, you ain't got no legal claim on my property. Both of us can't stay here no more. One of us got to go, and it ain't gon' be me. Now, I got my shotgun pointed at where I think your black heart is. If'n you don't get off my porch and off my property faster then I can bat my eye, U'ma fill you with buckshots."

All of a sudden, it was quiet on the porch, but she didn't hear his footfalls going down the steps, so she knew he was still there. She figured that he was checking the windows, but they were shut tight and the curtains were drawn.

"You ain't gon' get away with this," he said, the sound of his voice coming from the left of the door.

She aimed the barrel of the shotgun to the left. "Oh, yes I will. 'Cause if I ever see you on my property again, U'ma blow your damn head off. Then U'ma bury your triflin' ass in the woods with the worms."

Bang! "Heifer! Open this goddamn door!"

His banging at the door no longer startled her. Her only concern was that she didn't want him to knock the door down. That she wasn't going to let him do. Mozelle held her breath and pulled the trigger.

Boom! The kick knocked her back. She stumbled but she didn't fall. Screams from the children were nearly as loud as the blast from the shotgun. When the smoke cleared, she looked at the door. Her jaw dropped. There must have been more than twenty buckshot holes in her door.

"Mama!" Brother said, staring at the door.

"God. . .damnit! You trying to kill me!"

It sounded to her like Randell's voice was more to the left of the door than it was before. She aimed the shotgun again. "If you don't get, Randell, U'm gon' blast them holes in you the next time I pull this trigger!"

She didn't know if he was hit, and she didn't care, all she knew was that if she had to kill him, she would. She tried to look through the holes but only blackness was on the other side of the door. She crept closer to the door to see if she could hear him move. She listened hard.

"Mama," Nell said softly, "you kill Daddy?"

Bang! Randell hit the door. "Heifer! U'm gon' beat your black ass!"

"No, I didn't," she said, answering Nell. "Randell, U'm gon' blow your head off if you don't get your triflin' tail off my porch."

"I always said you was a crazy bitch."

Mozelle's finger was firm on the trigger.

Nell and Essie cried, holding on to each other. "Mama, don't kill Daddy," Essie cried.

Brother stared at Mozelle's finger. "Daddy, go on before Mama kill you."

She glanced at Brother. "Brother, y'all hush up. I got me a wild dog with rabies out on my front porch. U'm gon' shoot it dead for sure!" Mozelle shouted, wanting Randell to hear her clearly.

Behind her there was crying; in front of her, there was silence out on the porch. She glanced at the windows, but she could see nothing there either. She waited. Then suddenly she heard Randell's footfalls running down the steps. She let her breath out real slow as she carefully released the hammer and lowered the shotgun. She listened with her ear pressed to the door until she heard his car start up. From the sound, he gunned the engine before he peeled out. The sound of the car disappearing up out of the valley told her that Randell was gone. For good, she hoped.

Mozelle turned around to see Brother, Nell, and Essie staring at her. Their faces were wet with tears. She saw no need to explain why their daddy could not cross her threshold ever again. They already knew. "Y'all go on back to bed. U'm done with your daddy." And this time, she knew for certain that she was.

Thirty-Four

It wasn't but a day before word got back to Mozelle that Randell and his woman, Carrie, had moved into a house sitting on the bluff overlooking the meadow a little ways up the road on South Sixteenth Street—just a stone's throw from Cora's front door. As big as Alabama was, Mozelle couldn't understand why Randell had to settle so close by. While she was at work, he got Nell and Brother to let him into the house so that he and another man could carry out his wardrobe. He told them where he was staying, but he didn't welcome them with open arms. He would not let them stay past a handful of minutes when they did go over there. If he didn't want to be bothered with them, he should have kept his mouth shut. Mozelle wanted to keep her children away from him, but then her children would be miserable. Randell was their daddy, and they were always going to want to see him. Brother visited him most often because Randell bought a brand-new television. Essie and Nell had not seen a television before, but Brother had watched over at the Clays' farm because he was sweet on thirteen-year-old Lois, and he was over there a lot.

Mozelle never asked Brother about Carrie, and she never let him tell her much about her either. She didn't want to know. A little while after Randell had the television, Lois told Brother that the *Three Stooges* were coming on television. Essie, Brother, and Nell all wanted to rush over to their daddy's to watch them on his television.

She didn't feel right about letting them go. "How y'all know his woman gon' let y'all sit up in her house?"

"She'll let us," Brother said. "Miss Carrie say we like her own children."

"Hogwash."

"That's what she say, Mama," Brother defended. "Can we go?"

She really didn't want them to go. "I ain't sure about this."

"Please, Mama," Nell pleaded. "I want to see the show."

Brother, Nell, and Essie were all pleading pitifully with their daddy's eyes. Mozelle never understood how none of her six children got her eyes. They all looked more like Randell than her. Since she wasn't going to be able to put up with looking at his eyes three times over blaming her for missing out on the show, she gave in and let them all go.

"Y'all go on, but y'all best behave y'all self."

Joe started off behind them, but she pulled him back. "You don't even know what a television is," she said, ignoring his hollering.

"I'll watch him, Mama," Essie said.

"No, you go on. He's too little to watch television." Truth to tell, she didn't want her baby near Randell or his woman. No telling what they might do to him. Joe couldn't understand that. He hollered. It wasn't until she put a short piece of succulent sugar cane in his mouth that he settled down. Joe greedily sucked four pieces bone-dry and dropped off to sleep in her lap. Glad for the quiet, Mozelle put him down in her bed and tiptoed out of the house. For a long moment, she stood on the front porch looking out at the weeping willow trees swaying in the warm, gentle breeze. They looked like they were dancing to slow, soft music that only they could hear. Looking at them, she began to feel sleepy herself. She eased her weary body down onto the old straight-back wooden chair Brother found and fixed up. He did a good job. The chair was solid.

Mozelle lifted her tired legs up on a milk crate. She folded her arms across her stomach and closed her eyes. Her head felt heavy. It slowly dropped; her chin touched her collarbone. Nothing in life was ever as sweet as needed sleep.

There was crying; loud, hard crying. It sounded far off, but she could hear it. Mozelle lifted her head but she didn't open her eyes. Was she dreaming or was she wide awake? It seemed so real. The crying seemed to draw closer. Her children were crying. She opened her eyes. Feeling sluggish, she got to her feet. She went to the far corner of the porch and looked off up the road. It was her children. They were all coming down the road. She had heard them even while they were still up on Short Vine. She couldn't imagine what had happened. A full forty-five minutes hadn't gone by since she sent them on their way. Whatever had happened must have been real bad because they were hollering, crying their hearts out, even Brother.

"What y'all cryin' for?" she shouted, not knowing if they could hear her. She looked them over as best she could from where she stood high up on the porch. From what she could see, they didn't look hurt. They were walking all right. She waited on the porch for them to come into the yard. She couldn't imagine why all of them would be crying at the same time.

"What in the world is wrong with y'all?"

"Daddy beat us," Essie said.

She couldn't believe it. Randell had never laid a hand on any of them before. "He beat y'all?"

"He beat us with his belt," Nell said, following Essie up the steps.

"What for?"

"'Cause we wanted to watch television," Essie answered.

"Was y'all bad?"

"No, ma'am."

She looked at Brother as he came up the steps. He looked angriest of all. "He beat you, too?"

"Yessum,"

"What fo'?"

"'Cause we was cryin'," he said.

"Well, how come y'all was cryin'?"

Essie came up onto the porch. "Daddy beat us 'cause we asked him to let us watch television, and he said only if Miss Carrie wanted to watch television."

"Well, didn't she want to?"

"No, Mama," Essie said, "she didn't want to. When we went in the house, Miss Carrie was watching the *Three Stooges*. When we sit down to watch, too, she got up and shut the television off."

"What she do that fo'?"

"She say she didn't want to watch it no more," Brother said. "That's when we went and told Daddy, but he say only if Miss Carrie wanted to watch television then we could watch it, too."

"And she didn't," Nell said. "She say she was tired."

"Then what happened?"

"We started cryin' 'n Daddy got mad, and he beat all of us with his belt."

"I ain't never goin' over there again," Essie said.

"Me, neither," Nell said, pouting and folding her arms across her chest.

Mozelle shook her head. "Well, I ain't never told y'all that y'all couldn't go over there, but that woman ain't never gon' want y'all in her house. Y'all may as well stay home from now on."

"But, Mama, most everybody got a television 'ceptin' us," Brother said, sitting down on the floor under the railing. He let his legs dangle over the edge of the porch.

"Well, Brother, we jest can't afford to buy a television jest yet. One day we gon' have one, too. It'll jest take a bit longer, that's all," she said, looking down at Essie sitting at the top of the steps. It saddened her to see her children so hurt because they didn't have what other children had, but she didn't make enough to buy extras like a television set. She looked at each of their sullen faces before gazing out over the valley. The sun was setting over the Clays' house. Come tomorrow, they would be even more hurt once their friends in school told them about the show, but there was nothing she could do about that either.

"Y'all ought to go on and get ready for bed."

Essie and Nell didn't protest, they went on in the house. Brother continued to sit.

"Brother, you all right?"

"U'm fine, Mama. I jest want to sit a minute."

Mozelle lifted her legs back up on the crate. It worried her that Randell had beat her children when he had never beat them before. Her children had never been bad, not bad enough for their daddy to beat on them.

"Mama?"

"Yes," she said, looking at Brother. He didn't seem like he could pull his eyes away from the bright orange sun.

"You know what Daddy did after he beat me?"

She pulled her legs off the crate. "What he do?"

"He pet me."

She just stared at Brother. That was odd, but wasn't everything about Randell odd? "Did he pet Essie and Nell, too?"

"No, ma'am. How come you reckon he pet jest me?"

Darned if she knew. "I guess he was sorry he beat you."

"Jest me, Mama?"

"I guess," she said, not knowing any other way to explain Randell to his son.

Brother went off to bed, confused and sore. Mozelle stayed on the porch until the sun sank in the sky. She wanted to go and cuss Randell out for beating on her children, but it meant looking him in the face, and she never wanted to be that close to him again. Though she had a mind to tell him that he ought to buy a television for his children to watch in their own house. But who was she fooling? If she couldn't make Randell do right by his children in all the years that he lived with them, now that he lived in another house with another woman, he surely wasn't going to do right by them at this point. The best she could do was keep her children at home. For herself, if she never laid eyes on Randell again in life, it would be too soon. She did her level best to not bump into him up on South Fifteenth Street. If she had to go that way, she found herself looking way up the road for him. His house on South Sixteenth couldn't be seen from the road, so she was able to quickly go on by without seeing him. Most days she just didn't bother. She went the long way around out Plum Street.

She enjoyed every single day of the twelve weeks that had passed since she got Randell out of her life for good. She felt as if she had been born again. Every morning she was grateful for the peace of mind she went to bed with and opened her eyes to. It was a pleasure to be able to sit out on her front porch looking out over the valley, basking in the warm sunshine after finishing up the week at the cotton mill. As far as she was concerned, her life could not get any better.

"Mama, look," Essie said, pointing up the road at the two big red-and-white moving trucks slowly making their way down into the valley. "You reckon somebody moving into Miss Rosa's old house."

"It look like," Mozelle said with interest. She watched the trucks stop on the road. Nobody had lived in Rosa's house since she died. After a minute, the trucks came on down the road and stopped in front of Mozelle's house.

Essie stood. "They must be lost."

One white man and two colored men climbed down out of each of the trucks. The white man with a piece of paper in his hand shouted up to her, "You Mozelle Tate?"

Surprised that he knew her name, Mozelle stood with Sheila still asleep in her arms. "Yessa."

"Well, ma'am, we got your furniture."

Confused, Mozelle looked at the white man. "Say again."

"We got your furniture."

Mozelle stared at the men. "Mister, y'all got the wrong house. That ain't my furniture."

Nell and Cora's children ran out onto the road to the trucks.

"Mama, what you buy?" Essie asked.

"I ain't bought nothin'," she answered. "Mister, I ain't bought nothin'. Y'all got the wrong house."

"This nine thirty four Plum Street, ain't it?"

"Yessa."

The white man turned to the two colored men from his truck. "Jasper, Cleon, y'all go on and take care the inside of the house. We'll start unloading out here."

From the other truck, the white driver climbed down. The two colored men with him went to the back of the truck. The first two colored men came into the yard heading for the steps.

"Where y'all goin'?" Mozelle asked, beginning to get

scared. She had no idea what they wanted with her.

"Ma'am, you best keep your children back out the way," the big muscular man coming up the steps said.

"I said, where y'all goin'?" she asked again, rushing over to the door and blocking it just as one of them was about pull open the screen door.

"Ma'am, we gotta move your stuff out the house."

"Oh, my God," she said, thinking that Randell had gotten her thrown out of her house after all. "Y'all throwin' me out my house?"

The tall, lanky man sighed and rolled his eyes at her like she was dense. "Ma'am, we gotta move the old stuff out befo' we can bring the new furniture in."

"Mama, look," Essie said, pointing down at the trucks.

Down on the road, the other men were unloading big, long colorful rolls of linoleum.

Confused, she said, "I didn't buy none of that."

"Ma'am, can you please get out the way so we can do what we was told to do," the tall, lanky man at the door said. "If you didn't buy the furniture, somebody bought it for you."

"Who?"

"Ma'am, I don't know," he answered, sounding annoyed.

Wringing her hands, Mozelle's heart trembled in her chest. "We ain't got to move out?"

"Look, ma'am. We was told to deliver furniture to this house. Ain't nobody told us nothing about you moving out."

"You sure it ain't a mistake?"

The big, muscular man folded his huge arms across his chest. "Ma'am, why don't you look at it like this. Somebody thought good enough of you to buy you some nice furniture. Don't go askin' no questions. Take it."

"Ma'am, can we go in now and do what we gots to do?" the tall, lanky man asked. "We ain't got all day."

Essie rushed over to the door. "Y'all go on in," she said, nudging Mozelle from in front of the door. "Mama, I'll go get Kenny off the bed befo' they wake him up." She hurried into the house; the two men followed behind her.

"I declare," Mozelle said, switching Sheila to her left hip. Taking a hold of the back of the chair, she dragged it to the far end of the porch away from the door. Dumbfounded, she sat down and watched the furniture coming off the truck. It was the darndest thing that had ever happened to her. Who in the world could've done this for her?

"Y'all get out the way," Essie yelled down to the children in the yard, waving her hand at them to show them how far to move over from the walkway. "Brother, get David back from the road."

Brother scooted over out of the way.

Carrying Kenny in her arms, Essie pulled her crate over next to Mozelle and sat down. Mozelle looked to see where the children were. They were all far over to side of the yard next to the branch watching the men carry a new brown couch into the yard.

The men in the house came out carrying the old mattresses. They dropped them over the railing to the ground. The headboards and the kitchen table they carried down to the ground themselves. Everything was taken from the house, even Mozelle's lace curtains.

"Don't take my curtains," she said, standing up.

The man balled them up tight and threw them over the railing to the ground. "Ma'am, you got something better going up to them windows."

"I declare," she said, making herself sit down again. Her eyes bulged when she saw the men carry from the trucks two big chairs to match the couch, two end tables and a coffee table with glass the color of the blue sky in the center, a big dining room table with six matching chairs, four headboards, one full-size mattress and boxspring and three single-size mattresses and matching boxsprings, the wooden slats and frames for the beds, four dressers, a black wood-burning stove; and a big white refrigerator. She didn't know what the large boxes they carried inside held.

The children screamed, "Mama! A television!" when the big floor-model television framed in a dark wood cabinet was set down in the yard.

"Who you think bought all this for us?" Essie asked, as the colorful rolls of linoleum were carried into the house.

Bewildered, Mozelle simply shook her head. Tears rolled down her cheeks onto Sheila's head. She didn't have the slightest idea who could have done something as grand as this. She turned around and watched through the window as the men rolled out blue-and-white linoleum onto the front room floor. In every room they laid linoleum before they started moving in the furniture. From the boxes came curtains, pillowcases, sheets and spreads and pillows enough for all the beds.

When the men finished, they loaded the old stuff onto their truck. "You gotta sign that you got your furniture," the white man said, handing Mozelle a pen.

Though her fingers were trembling, Mozelle signed. As soon as the last man walked off the porch, she and Essie and all the children rushed into the house. They were all amazed. Mozelle couldn't believe her eyes. Her house no longer looked like her house. All the furniture was placed in the right rooms. All the floors were covered in pretty, colorful linoleum. While all the windows had cotton curtains, the living room had pretty white lace curtains. As a smile touched her lips, tears kissed Mozelle's cheeks. She never dreamed that her house could look like this. Everything was pretty; everything was new. The first thing Essie, Nell, Brother, and Junior wanted to do was watch television. So did she, but she couldn't stay put long enough. She went from room to room looking at all she had, while the children sat stiffly on the new couch gawking at a feisty-talking cartoon rabbit walking upright like a man, being chased by a funny, squat little pig half-dressed like a man with his round bottom showing. Nary a one of the children blinked an eye.

Mozelle circled the house, ending up back in the living room. "My God," she kept saying to herself.

"Mama, how much you reckon all this cost?" Essie asked, sitting in one of the living room chairs and sliding her hands back and forth on its stuffed arms.

"I don't know," she answered, touching the fabric of the

chair herself. It was natty yet soft. She leaned down and sniffed the fabric. It smelled clean. "It sho'nuff smell good in here."

"That's new smell," Essie said. "That's how it smell in Daddy's house."

She didn't want to think about Randell or what he had. "I wish to God I knew who paid for all this."

"Maybe it's Miss Mitchell. She got lots of money."

"She do, but I don't expect she woulda bought me a houseful of furniture."

Essie shrugged her shoulders. "Maybe it was somebody else then."

"But who?" she asked, going over to the television. She carefully turned the knob to shut it off.

"Aaah, Mama!" Brother and Nell both cried out.

"Y'all hush up. We got to thank God for our blessing before we can use anything," she said, kneeling down in the center of the room.

None of the children complained about that. They all gathered around Mozelle and bowed their heads while she gave thanks to God.

That night, like her children, Mozelle nestled cozily in her new bed with her crisp new white sheets, the first she had ever lain on. That night she wouldn't have to dream her dreams of old; all of her long-ago dreams had finally come true.

By Sunday evening, Mozelle had stood in the doorways throughout her house a dozen times over looking at her new furniture marveling at the wonder of it all. She couldn't help but think that Cora would have loved everything in here. In the front room she had rearranged the furniture three times and dusted the tables just as often. Any moment she expected someone to knock at the door and ask, "How do you like the furniture?" No knock ever came.

In church, earlier, although she had been happy in the Lord and praised him for the blessings he had heaped on her, Mozelle suspiciously eyed the people around her, looking for the slightest hint that someone knew something about the furniture.

At work, Mamie concluded, "Only God knows."

Essie thought that maybe Randell had bought the furniture, but Mozelle knew that he wasn't even worth considering. Randell never even bought a roll of toilet paper to wipe his own tail. So a stick of furniture was out of the question. Though when he found out, Randell said what she expected him to say. He told Henry, "Mozelle paid for that furniture on her back." She paid him no mind. There was nothing Randell could say anymore that could hurt her feelings. Not anymore. His bad ways had hardened her heart, and his ugly words had closed her ears to him.

Every day after work she rushed home to see her beautiful home. Then, on Wednesday, she got an unexpected caller.

Through the screen door Mrs. Mitchell smiled at Mozelle. "I been hearing talk about your new furniture. I thought I'd come see for myself."

Surprised, Mozelle quickly opened the door. "Well, sa, you jest come right on in," she said graciously, stepping aside to let Mrs. Mitchell in.

Mrs. Mitchell didn't wait to be shown through the house, she went on ahead of Mozelle like she knew the way. Walking slowly behind Mrs. Mitchell, Mozelle tried to sneak peeks at her face to see if she could tell whether Mrs. Mitchell was already familiar with the furniture or not. Nothing in her face gave her away, but it seemed to Mozelle that Mrs. Mitchell was inspecting everything. She circled the house.

"Would you like to sit a spell?" Mozelle asked.

Back at the front door, Mrs. Mitchell gently dabbed at her upper lip with her frilly white handkerchief. "Thank you kindly, Mozelle, but I got to get back. I just wanted to come down and take a look-see for myself. You got yourself some right pretty furniture now. Your house look just fine."

"Thank you, ma'am."

Again, Mrs. Mitchell dabbed at her upper lip. "Well, I got to be going. I'll see you come Saturday."

"Yessum." She followed Mrs. Mitchell out onto the front porch. The one question that had been nagging Mozelle was itching to be asked. "Mrs. Mitchell, ma'am—"

"It's right pretty down here, ain't it?" Mrs. Mitchell asked, starting down the steps.

"Mrs. Mitchell, ma'am, did you buy this furniture for me?"

Mrs. Mitchell stopped and looked back at Mozelle. She smiled. "You are truly blessed." She went on daintily down the steps holding on to the rail with one white-gloved hand and carrying her big white shiny leather pocketbook over her other arm.

A warm feeling came over Mozelle and filled her heart. "Thank you, ma'am. Thank you."

Just as she figured, it was Mrs. Mitchell. She was never going to be able to repay such kindness, but she would make it her business to take even better care of Mrs. Mitchell's house. She was going to keep on cleaning it as good as she cleaned her own.

With Randell out of her life, Mozelle's blessings were growing in leaps and bounds. The house and land were free and clear, the bills were manageable, the children were clothed and fed, and her house was furnished. What's more, she had at least two good dresses for every day of the week. She found plenty of bargains on everything from spoons and forks to clothes at yard sales. Yes, God was good. She no longer worried about what her mama and daddy would have thought about her ending her marriage. Somehow she thought that maybe they would be proud of her for making it on her own.

Thirty-Five

The news of Randell's death on Tuesday, January 19, 1960, was not altogether unexpected, yet it numbed Mozelle anyway. It took more than a minute for it to sink in that he was truly dead. He had gone into the hospital Sunday afternoon because he had been unable to turn his head or lower it to his chest. Brother went to see him that Tuesday, the day his neck snapped.

"Mama, when I went in Daddy's room, he couldn't turn his head to look at me. He heard me, though. He said, 'Is that Daddy's boy?'"

"My word. He asked you that?"

"Yessum, but then he died, Mama."

Mozelle raised her hand to God. She closed her eyes. "My Lord," she said, opening her eyes again. Randell had never denied Brother, but knowing that his last words, "Is that Daddy's boy?" were on his lips gave her some satisfaction. She listened intently as Brother told her how old Randell looked sitting stiff as a board in agony alongside his bed, his head back, his mouth open like he was gargling. She knew that if Randell had been able to see his whole self in the mirror like that, that alone would have killed him.

Unlike with Cora's death, the doctors knew right off what took Randell's life—meningitis and pneumonia, and something about his spine drawing up and pulling his head back she never understood. She wondered if someone had put a hoodoo curse on him after all, because she had never before heard of anybody's neck snapping like a dry twig. Maybe that was Randell's due.

For some time Mozelle had dreaded the coming of her birthday because it reminded her of Cora's death, and each year she mourned her anew. But for Randell, she wasn't going to weep or mourn his passing. She was no hypocrite. True enough she loved him deeply when they first married and for a long time after he stopped being a good husband. But by the time Cora died, Mozelle wanted nothing more to do with the man she vowed to love until death parted them. Now that Randell was dead, there would be no occasion that would make her yearn to see him again. She was at peace with how she felt about him. While she had never divorced him, and to her knowledge he had never divorced her, word was that he had married Carrie over in Georgia. But Mr. Conley told Mozelle that her marriage to Randell was the only legal one. That meant that she could lay claim to whatever he owned. If it had been her who had died, Randell would not have waited for her body to grow cold before he came to lay claim to her house and land.

Carrie didn't have a leg to stand on when Mozelle, along with Brother, went to her house. "I want whatever Randell got in this house."

"You can't have nothing out my house," Carrie said, her hands on her narrow hips. "Me and Randell got married in Georgia two years ago. Randell was my husband."

"You dead wrong 'bout that. Me and Randell never divorced. The law say he can't marry nobody else long as he's married to me. Randell was my husband when he was alive, he was my husband when he died."

"That ain't true. Randell told me he got a paper that say he divorced from you."

"There ain't no such paper. He lied to you. Me and Randell, we ain't never even talked about divorce. The law say U'm his one and only wife on this earth, but you bury him. I ain't spendin' a dime on him."

Carrie's arms dropped like a sleeping possum out of a tree. She stared blankly at
 Mozelle.

"I don't want his clothes, you keep 'em. I want his car and that ladder he used when he went out to paint."

It seemed that Carrie had no will to protest. She stood aside and let Brother go around the side of the house and get the six-foot ladder. He tied it to the top of the car. Mozelle was rusty in her driving, but Brother wasn't. He was seventeen-years-old and was on the road to being a good mechanic. Brother got behind the wheel of the '47 Plymouth while Mozelle sat back and enjoyed the ride back home to Plum Street. She was not going to wear out another single shoe walking those long, dusty roads a day longer. That was her due.

Carrie sent word for the children to attend their daddy's funeral. Mozelle thought it only right that they say good-bye to the man that was their daddy. She sent all the children to the funeral with nothing bad said against Randell. As for herself, she said her good-byes the night she wanted to shoot him full of buckshots. Randie sent money, but didn't make it home. Essie took Cora's children—Junior, Betty, David, and Sheila—to the funeral, but Ann refused to go without her grandma. Together, Ann and Mozelle sat out on the front porch looking down at the naked weeping willow tree branches dancing wildly in the January wind. It was a breezy day, but it wasn't too cold. Strange, although she hadn't seen Randell in more than three years, until he died, she had always felt his presence. Now, she only felt the fresh air caressing her face.

Thirty-Six

"Mama, there's a lady at the door wanna see you."

Mozelle dropped the last dumpling into the pot of boiled-down chicken parts. "Who is it?"

"I don't know," Nell replied, starting back through the front room.

"Nell."

"Yessum."

"I can't leave my pot. Tell that lady to c'mon in," Mozelle said, slowly stirring the pot to keep the dumplings from sticking together in the thick, creamy sauce.

"Yessum."

Leaning over the pot, Mozelle inhaled the delicious aroma of stewing chicken, celery, and onions. Chicken 'n dumplings was everybody's favorite, and she didn't expect there'd be a drop left over.

"Afternoon," the lady said.

Straightening up, Mozelle turned and looked at the woman standing in the doorway of the kitchen. She was dressed in a beautiful dark blue suit made out of a better, heavier cotton than any Mozelle had ever worn, though she had wound yards and yards of it on bolts at the mill.

"How do?" she asked, giving the dumplings one good stir before putting the top back on the pot and laying the spoon down on the middle of the stove.

"Mrs. Tate, I won't take up but a minute of your time. By the way, your chicken 'n dumplings smell quite good. It's a favorite of my husband's."

"Thank you. You from the county?"

"No, ma'am. I'm from Jacksonville."

"Jacksonville?"

"Mrs. Tate, I am Mrs. Gail Webber. I don't know if you know about me, but I was a friend of your husband's."

Mozelle's mouth dropped open slightly. She stared although she knew better. This was the last person she ever expected to see standing in her house.

Gail Webber looked down at her hands. "I know I'm the last person you expected to come to your door."

"Randell said you was dead, but I see you're not," Mozelle said. She boldly took a good look at the supposed-to-be-dead woman. Although Gail Webber looked to be much older than her, she certainly wasn't dead, and she was very attractive. Her hair was straightened and hung in curls to her shoulders. She wore red lipstick and a pretty strand of pearls around her neck to match the earrings on her ears. The prim-and-proper way she held her gloved hands clasped together in front of her while her navy blue leather pocketbook hung from her arm, showed clearly that she didn't work in the fields picking cotton or scrub anyone's floors for a living. Gail Webber was the type of woman that must have looked good standing next to Randell, the type of woman he should have married.

"Please forgive me, Mrs. Tate, I would have never come if I had any other choice."

"U'm sure, Mrs. Webber, that you had plenty choices other then to come here," Mozelle said, turning back to her pot. Lifting the top again, with trembling hands, she stirred the dumplings. She didn't know what to think. This was the woman Randell had put her up against. The woman that she could never hope to be like. She prayed that when she turned around again that Gail Webber would be gone. Mozelle's mama didn't tell her how to deal with her husband's "friend."

"I understand if you don't want to speak to me, Mrs. Tate, but I—"

Slam! Mozelle slammed the top back down on the pot, making Gail Webber flinch. She took her dishrag and lifted the big, heavy pot to the back of the stove onto a cool eye.

"S'cuse me," Nell said. "Mama."

She turned around. Nell was standing next to her daddy's "friend."

"Mama, U'm going up the road to the store. You want something?"

"No. Where's Joe?"

"He went up the road with Essie."

"Stop by Cora's house and see if they're there. Bring all them children back with you. Supper gon' be ready soon."

"Yessum."

Ignoring Gail Webber, Mozelle turned back to the stove. She didn't know what the woman wanted with her, but she for sure didn't want to talk to her. She felt herself growing angrier by the minute.

Gail Webber waited until Nell left the house. "Your daughter looks like Randell."

She turned abruptly back to face Gail Webber. "That ain't somethin' U'm proud of."

"Oh, I'm sorry," she said, pulling off one of her gloves. "Mrs. Tate, I'm not here to upset you or to cause you harm."

"Then why is you here?"

"I'm here because I can't close my eyes at night without thinking about you and your children."

"That ain't my concern. If you feelin' guilty, that's 'tween you and God."

"I know, but Mrs. Tate, truly, I feel bad about the way Randell treated his children."

"He didn't jest treat his children bad, he treated me bad, too."

"I know, and I'm sorry."

"Are you?" Mozelle asked, glaring at the woman that had Randell's heart way before he married her.

"Yes, I—"

"Mrs. Webber, all those years you was with Randell, was you closin' your eyes at night in peace and thinkin' about me and my children when Randell left us all by ourselves so you and him could lay up? Did you rest when I was eating dirt and walkin' holes in my shoes, or feedin' my babies grits and mush, and puttin' ugly, scratchy sack dresses on my girls? Did you sleep good when me and my children was put outdoors more times then I can count while Randell was with you not even carin' about us?"

"I didn't always know about you and your children, Mrs. Tate. Not until Alice told me a few years ago when I stopped off in Royston. I didn't know. Randell told me you couldn't have children."

"Randell lied quick as he blinked," Mozelle said bitterly. "I had six children that lived and buried four that didn't. Randell was daddy to them all."

"I'm sorry. I only knew what Randell told me."

"Well, he told me you was dead."

Gail Webber sucked in her breath.

"Randell always lied to suit hisself."

"I see," Gail Webber said, barely above a whisper. "I guess Randell felt that I was dead to him because I told him that I'd never leave my husband."

"You don't say," Mozelle said, flatly. It didn't surprise her one bit that Gail Webber had cheated on her husband to be with Randell. Weren't she and Randell one of a kind? "U'm surprised that Randell didn't get everythin' he wanted."

"Mrs. Tate, I could never leave my husband for Randell, and he knew it. He was angry with me for that."

While she felt sick to her stomach, Mozelle was growing angrier by the minute. "So Randell told me you was dead 'cause his pride was hurt?"

"I don't know about his pride, but I did hurt him when I didn't mean to."

Mozelle couldn't believe how coolly this woman was standing in her house telling her how she didn't mean to hurt Randell's feelings when he was not even her husband! As mad as she was, she could only laugh. "Ain't that somethin'? I was the one he married but you was the one he loved, and you the one that hurt him."

"Mrs. Tate, me and Randell wasn't good together. I wasn't

trying—"

"Oh, that's what it was? You wasn't good together?" she asked, amazed at what she was hearing. "You cheated on your husband for years with Randell, and he cheated on me with you from practically the day we got married, and you wouldn't leave your husband and he was gon' leave me only if you was free, but you wasn't good together?"

Gail Webber pressed her lips tightly together. She lowered her eyes.

"Humph! Ain't that somethin'?" Mozelle asked, realizing that Randell had lied to her from the very start. Randell never, ever had any intention of doing right by her. All along he loved this woman. No wonder he was so hateful to her. "He punished me 'cause of you, didn't he?"

Wringing her hands, Gail Webber looked down at the floor.

"Why didn't y'all jest spare me and your husband the trouble and run off together?"

"I'm going to be truthful with you. My husband never knew."

Mozelle threw her hands up in exasperation. "So U'm the only one y'all put through hell?"

"No, I wasn't—"

"I don't know how your husband didn't know, considerin' all the times Randell disappeared on me."

"Most times he came when my husband was out of town. Other times we met only briefly. But it wasn't—"

"You knew about me," Mozelle said, thumping her chest with her finger. "Didn't you think I was hurtin' knowin' that Randell was somewhere with somebody else. I didn't know it was you, he had so many women, but I knew it had to be somebody in Jacksonville, most times, 'cause he didn't want me in that town but a minute."

Gail Webber pulled her glove on. "Mrs. Tate, it took a lot of soul-searching for me to get up the nerve to come here. I—"

Mozelle suddenly brushed past Gail Webber, not caring that she pushed her into the doorjamb on her way through the living room to the front door to get some air. She opened the door and inhaled the cool, fresh air, relieving the nausea she felt. When she felt the queasiness leave her, she said loudly without turning around, "I don't want you in my house. It's like lettin' Randell back in, and he wasn't ever welcome here."

Stone-faced, Gail Webber began walking slowly across the living room. Adjusting her pocketbook on her arm, she stopped in the middle of the room. "Please, Mrs. Tate, hear me out," she pleaded. "I won't take up much more of your time."

"What's done is done. Randell is dead. There ain't nothin' mo' you have to say that I wants to hear."

"You have every right to be angry with me. My relationship with Randell started twenty years before he married you, and as many times as I tried to end it, I never could until the day my son died."

"So he told the truth about your son," Mozelle said, looking down onto the road in front of the house. The red-and-white car sitting there looked brand-new. A surge of hate shot through Mozelle all over again for Randell. He was tormenting her with his sordid life even from the grave.

"My son—"

"U'm sorry about your son," Mozelle said, folding her arms across her chest. "But please, jest go."

"Mrs. Tate, you have to hear me out."

Mozelle turned around. "No I don't. I don't want to hear no mo' 'bout Randell."

"It's not about Randell. It's about your children."

That stumped her. Mozelle stared at Mrs. Webber. "What my children got to do with you?"

"Mrs. Tate, my son, Richard, was my only child. He never married so I don't have any grandchildren. When he died, I let go of Randell because he reminded me of my loss."

"You shoulda let go of Randell the day you married your husband."

"I know that now," she said. "My husband has always been good to me. He knew all along that Richard wasn't his flesh and blood. He was there for me when Richard was born, and when he died. It was then I realized how much I loved him and how wrong

I was to have cheated on him."

"So why did you?" Mozelle asked, feeling no sympathy for the woman who was partly the cause of her miserable life with Randell.

Gail Webber sank down onto the living room chair. Pensively, she lowered her head and pressed her gloved fingertips to the bridge of her nose.

Feeling hateful of the woman, Mozelle looked at her and grinded her teeth, refusing to let her heart soften.

"When me and Randell got together," Gail Webber began, looking dejectedly down at the floor, "I was young, headstrong, and head over heels in love with a man that my father did not like. He would not hear of me marrying Randell. When I got pregnant, my father made me marry Harris to keep from shaming the family, but it was Randell that my heart wanted. We didn't see each other for more than a year. When we started seeing each other again, one time turned into ten times, and one month turned into a year and so on until it was thirty-two years. I'm ashamed to say, it was natural to keep on seeing him."

"Sneakin' around ain't natural."

"No, it isn't, but—"

"There ain't no *but*, Mrs. Webber," Mozelle said angrily. "Randell married me knowin' that it was you he wanted. I didn't need to know that. Why did he even have to bother me? I was jest fine befo' he come along and ruined my life."

Gail Webber didn't answer. She wouldn't even look at Mozelle.

"I need to know from you, Mrs. Webber, how come Randell married me?"

Finally looking up at Mozelle, Gail Webber did not raise her head. "To spite me."

By now Mozelle thought she would have been immune to feeling such pain. She wasn't. She could feel her heart shrivel and draw up tight in her chest. Turning back to the door, she thought about all the times she let Randell take her body while hoping that he'd not only pay the rent but perhaps start to care for her even a tiny bit.

"I'm so sorry," Gail Webber said sadly. "I told Randell not to do that to you, but he wouldn't listen. And honest to God, Mrs. Tate, I tried to stop seeing him then, but he kept coming back, and I'm ashamed to say that I kept backsliding. I hated myself for it. I swear before God, every time me and Randell got together, I tried to tell myself that it was going to be the last time."

"You lied to yourself and God."

"It wasn't all my fault. Randell wouldn't stay gone. He was in my blood, and, I guess, I was in his."

"I don't wanna know none of this. Do you hear me, Mrs. Webber? It is your fault and Randell's, too. Your flesh was weak jest like mine was. You and Randell—"

"Mrs. Tate, I know what I did was wrong. That's why I wanted to try and make it up to you. That's why when I heard about your children and how Randell wasn't taking care of them, it bothered me."

"Didn't it bother you about me? My life was miserable."

"I'm ashamed to say I never thought about you like I should have."

"So what do you want with me now? You want me to help ease your shame? I can't do that. You got to talk to God about it."

"Believe me, I have. That's why I wanted to talk to you about your children. Maybe I can help you in some way."

"It's a lot too late for that, Mrs. Webber. My Cora needed food, a roof over her head, and her daddy to love her. She never got any of them things. She's dead now. There ain't nothin' you can do for her."

"I'm sorry."

"Don't be. Cora wasn't your child."

"I am truly sorry."

Mozelle couldn't stand to hear another "I'm sorry," nor could she stand the sight of Randell's well-dressed whore a minute longer. "I want you to leave my house."

"Please. I have a check for thirty-five hundred dollars. It's yours," Gail Webber said, pulling it out of her pocketbook. "Randell made me beneficiary on a policy he took out years ago. It's not a whole lot, but it might help you in some way."

Stunned, Mozelle stared at the check. If Randell was alive, she'd kill him. He'd paid on a policy and had the nerve to not even leave the benefits to her or her children, but to his "friend." She slapped the side of the doorjamb hard with her hand. God, how she hated that all the hate she had buried deep on the day Randell was put in the ground was again so alive and strong inside her. "I hate him," she said, "and U'm gon' hate him till the day I draw my last breath."

Gail Webber held the check out to Mozelle. "Please take this. My son is dead. It's only right that you should have it for your children."

Looking at the check, Mozelle again felt like laughing. Her laugh was bitter and raw, but it kept her from crying. It was funny how life had a way of bringing to light things done in the dark.

Gail Webber looked down at the check she held in her hand. Her eyes batted repeatedly.

Mozelle stopped laughing. "If your son was alive, Mrs. Webber, U'm figurin' I wouldn't know a thing about that check."

"I would've—"

"No you wouldn't't've," Mozelle said, quickly. "Mrs. Webber, there was a time when I prayed on rusty, bended knees and a empty stomach for a single dime so I could buy a piece of fatback or a pound of flour. I use to beg Randell to feed his children, but he wouldn't. That man that was in your blood, ate the last crumb off my table but wouldn't put five cents worth of beans in the pot or a pound of cornmeal in the cabinet. Most times, he wouldn't even keep the rent paid. This house you standin' in, I built with my own two hands. Randell didn't do nothin' to help me."

"I swear to you, Mrs. Tate, I didn't know Randell was like that. I never saw that side of him."

For some reason, Mozelle wasn't feeling quite so angry anymore. "No, I guess that's not the Randell you knew. You had a different man from me."

Gail Webber looked bashfully at Mozelle. "Randell was never cruel to—"

"I don't want to know how he was with you, Mrs. Webber.

To me, Randell was the worst man I ever laid eyes on. Every day I was with him was like wrestlin' with the devil. That check, I don't want it," she said, shaking her head. "In life, other than my children, Randell gave me nothin' of his own free will. U'm sure he wouldn't want me to have any of his money now."

Standing quickly, Gail Webber went over to Mozelle. She held the check out to her. "I'm giving you this money. I want you to have it. It belongs to you."

"No, you keep it. You buy yourself some peace of mind so you can sleep at night."

"But. . .don't you need this money?"

She chuckled. "Mrs. Webber, that money could buy my children a whole lot of earthly things, but I been makin' do all my life without Randell's help. No, you keep the money."

Her shoulders slumped; Gail Webber's eyes watered.

"The way U'm figurin' it, if you had kicked Randell out your bed some thirty-odd years ago and been faithful to your own husband, you would be able to lay your head down on your pillow and sleep like a baby. You can't use me or my children to get rid of your guilt. See, I sleep real good at night. I got my children and my grandchildren, I don't have to buy peace of mind," she said, pushing open the screen door. "You take your check and get out my house. Go on back to your husband and do right by him."

Pressing her trembling lips together, Gail Webber slid the check back down inside her pocketbook. She straightened her back but as she started past Mozelle, her shoulders dropped. Their eyes didn't meet, though Mozelle recognized the scent of the perfume she had on. Randell had brought it home so many times on his body and clothes. Just smelling it reminded her of those awful nights when he crawled back in her bed after being gone for a while. As soon as Gail Webber's foot cleared the screen door, Mozelle pulled it closed. She should have been feeling good knowing that Randell left Gail Webber in as much pain as she, herself, suffered all those years, but she didn't. She did, however, feel good that she no longer needed Randell's money to make do.

Thirty-Seven

Christmas, 1965

She wasn't quite sure of what Essie was trying to tell her on the other end of the telephone; she was crying so hard. It was the kind of hard crying that left a body weak and plumb wore out. It was the kind of crying that didn't come from a spanking or a scolding, but from a hurt deep in a person's soul. Mozelle was scared.

"Child, what's wrong?"

"Mama. . .Mama," Essie cried.

"Essie, you gots to stop cryin'. What's wrong?"

"Mama, it's on fire."

Mozelle's heart fluttered. "What's on fire?"

"The house is burning down."

Mozelle didn't want to believe that Essie was saying that her house was on fire, but she knew that her child was not a liar and was never one for funning. *Fire.* The word struck her like a bolt of lightning. She could feel the jolt, but instead of feeling hot, she could feel her blood run cold in her veins. It couldn't be. Not fire.

Her legs began to tremble. They gave way under her as she sank to the floor clutching the telephone to her chest. For a brief, insane minute she didn't realize that the gut-wrenching wail that rang in her ears was coming from her own throat. She forgot about where she was—that she was cleaning house for the Comstocks. That was until she saw the pale frightened face of Mrs. Comstock in front of her. Until then, she had not been able to stop screaming. Even after the receiver was pried from her hands, she clenched her fists tight, digging her nails deep into her palms to keep herself from screaming again. Although she was hurting herself, any other pain was bearable to what she was feeling in her heart. Besides her land, her house was all she had to show for years of backbreaking work. As she got to her feet with Mrs. Comstock's help, Mozelle clung desperately to her words, "Perhaps it's not that bad."

But she knew what fire could do to a house made of wood. The flames wouldn't die down until it had nothing else to feed on. Praying to herself, she begged, *God snuff out the flames. Please, Lord, don't let the fire take my house.*

Even now, as Mr. Comstock was driving her home, she couldn't stop praying. God had to hear her. She couldn't imagine her house smothering or singeing, or bursting with glowing flames like the logs of wood she tossed into the fireplace over a hundred times in her life. Not the house she had prayed and sweated for. Not the house she had built with her own blistered hands. Until she saw it for herself, she wouldn't let herself believe that she was losing everything.

Turning into onto Plum Street, Mr. Comstock's headlights alone lit the way. This was the second time he had to drive her home to this part of West Gadsden where only colored folks lived. The first time was during the day when Joe stepped on a rusty nail and would let no one else pull it out but her. The shot the doctor gave him seemed to hurt him more than the rusty nail. Joe dropped his head back and cried his heart out, the way she wanted to let go and cry now. But she kept her head up and her eyes on the road as Mr. Comstock crept along easylike because he was unaccustomed to the long, dark, narrow dirt road that sloped downward before it steadily began to climb upward again before overlooking the valley.

At the top of the road where Short Vine and Plum Street touched, and before the road dropped down into the valley, Mozelle's heart suddenly stopped beating. Tears rushed from her eyes. She believed.

Mr. Comstock said softly, "My God."

The sky over the valley was ablaze with light from the leaping flames from the house. It was as if the sun had forgotten to set. Halfway down into the valley, Mozelle could see clearly her children standing on the road with so many other people looking up at the ball of fire that was their home. Her own eyes began to burn, but the tears that swelled and brimmed over didn't soothe them.

Stopping his car on the road before it crossed over the branch to the front of the house, Mr. Comstock said again, "My God." He climbed out of the car while Mozelle stared trancelike up at the flames, unable to move.

"Mama!"

Hearing Nell scream, Essie, Joe, and Kenny took off running behind her.

Mr. Comstock rushed around to the passenger side of the car and pulled open the door. He held out his hand to Mozelle. She put her hand into his without concern that she had never touched a white man's hand before. However, the softness surprised her—her own had never been that soft. But then, her life, had not been soft. When she climbed out of the car, she stepped into Essie's arms.

Crying, Essie asked, "Mama, what we gon' do?"

Mozelle could only shake her head. She didn't know what to do. With her children crying and clinging to her, Mozelle crossed over the path above the branch and stood frozen staring up at her burning house. She didn't want to look, but the flames drew her and held her transfixed. It was a sight like none she'd ever seen. It burned into her mind and soul. The roof she had hammered on so solidly was exposed to the sky like an open pit. The walls she had raised she could not see. There was nothing not burning. All her pretty furniture, all her pretty dresses, all the things that she had been proud of owning, the flames were burning, leaving her nothing to hold on to. There would be nothing left to show for all her years of picking cotton, of cooking for hundreds of hungry folks, of working in the cotton mill, and of scrubbing floors for white folks.

Her tongue was thick and would not let her speak, but her

mind screamed, *Lord, my God! How is it that the same murdering flames of fire that's burning my house down to the ground and turning it to ashes can look so bright and pretty against the night sky? How is it that my eyes can stare in wonder at the red, orange, and yellow flames leaping to touch the stars above, yet empty stinging, bitter tears for the house I built with my own two hands? Lord, those burning walls know my anguish and my frustration. The roof that's no more was like a worn field hat shielding me and my children from the blistering sun and the pounding rain. I raised five children in that house, Lord, in these fifteen years. I dreamed of leaving it behind for their children. This house and this land is all I own in this world, Lord. Why did fire have to take it from me? Why, Lord?*

"Mama, the tree's burnin'!" Joe shouted. He grabbed hold of her and hugged her tightly about the waist.

Indeed, the giant water oak that had shaded the front porch was burning. Mozelle quickly glanced over at the weeping willow trees along the road. She sighed when she saw that they were at least safe.

"Can't we try 'n put out the fire?" Nell asked. "We kin tote water from the branch up to the house and throw it on the fire."

"Child," Mozelle said, tasting a sourness in the back of her mouth, "there ain't nothin' we kin do. The branch is low, and if we could get water from it, the house is sittin' too far up on the hill. It's too far gone for us to save it."

Nell, holding on to Kenny, began to cry anew.

Mozelle's heart weighed heavier than the weight of Essie and Nell clinging to her arms and Joe clutching her about the waist. But it was their bodies that kept her from falling to the ground.

"Mama, where we gon' live?" Essie asked, tearfully.

"And what about our clothes, Mama? They all gone!" Nell cried. "What we gon' wear?"

Although the fire held Mozelle's gaze, fear was choking her. She battled to hold on to her faith in God. "The Lord'll provide," she said, softly.

"Mama, how kin you say the Lord'll provide when He let

our house burn down?" Essie asked.

"Child, God loves us. He wouldn't put more on us than we could bear."

"But, Mama, we can't bear this," Nell cried. "God is lettin' our house burn down."

Abruptly shaking Nell off her arm, Mozelle grabbed her face, and squeezing her cheeks hard, said, "Child, don't you ever let me hear you question the Lord again. It is because of the Lord we got our house in the first place. He the one that give us all that furniture. God do love us, but He is testin' our love for Him." She let go of Nell.

"But, Mama," Nell said right away, crying. "All our furniture is burning up. All our clothes. We been good. We been going to church. We been praying to the Lord every night. How come we got to lose our house to prove we love the Lord?"

For a minute Mozelle stared into Nell's angry, questioning eyes. In her own mind, she wanted to ask God that question herself, but she had to trust in His wisdom. "Lord," she said, looking up at the sky past the flames, "please give me the knowledge to help my children keep their faith in you." She looked at Nell. "Child, we all got our life. Nobody got burned, nobody got killed. Tonight, God gave us life for our house. I don't want none of y'all to worry." This time she looked at Essie and Joe. "We gon' be jest fine. I got insurance. The Lord'll give us another house and more furniture."

"When?" Nell asked.

"Mama, you said you built our house," Joe chimed in.

"I did, with the Lord's help. He showed me what to do."

"Oh," Joe said, not fully understanding what she meant.

"When we gon' get another house, Mama?" Nell asked, impatiently.

"Nell, you just sixteen, but you know well as I do, the Lord works in His own time. Believe in the Lord, child. He'll make a way for us. Didn't He make a way for me to find steady work so y'all children could eat and have clothes on your back?"

"Yessum," Essie answered.

"Well, then, he'll see us through this, too."

"U'm sorry, Mama," Nell said, "but U'm scared."

"I know," Mozelle said, drawing Nell to her and hugging her tightly. She could never admit to her children that for a minute she had questioned the Lord herself. When she saw that there was no saving the house, she wanted to shake her fist at the sky and blame God for forsaking her. But that was something that she could never let her children see. They had never seen her weak or beaten down, and this fire would not bend her back now. She had to trust God for another house.

"Mama?" Joe said.

"Yes, child."

"We gon' call Brother and Randie and tell them?"

She nodded. Brother was working up in Detroit in the car factory. "Tomorra."

"Mozelle! Mozelle!" Mr. Jake shouted, out of breath from running down the road from his house up on the hill on Short Vine. He was old, but his seventy-two-year-old legs were having no trouble keeping up with his two sons. "My God in heaven! What happen'd? Everybody all right?"

"We jest fine, Mr. Jake."

"What in God's name happen'd here?"

"Lord knows. Essie called me at work, and Mr. Comstock brung me home right quick, but by the time I got here it was too late."

"Ain't nobody call the firemen?"

"I called them," Essie said. "They on the way."

"How come one of y'all didn't come up the road and get me and my boys? We might've been able to put out the fire befo' it got real bad."

Nell looked at Essie; Essie shrugged her shoulders; Joe and Kenny, both, stared at Mr. Jake.

"It happened so fast," Nell said, quietly.

"I guess they wasn't quite sure what to do, Mr. Jake," Mozelle said in defense of her children. "U'm jest glad they got out."

"Praise the Lord," Mr. Jake said.

They all stood gazing trancelike up at the crackling flames.

"What you think started it?" Mr. Jake asked.

"Coulda been the Christmas tree. I told them children not to leave the lights on when they go out the house, but Essie said they was on."

"Tree musta been dry."

"Musta been," she agreed. "If I didn't have to work late, this might not've happen."

"Mama! Here come the fire truck!" Joe shouted. He and Kenny ran off to meet it.

Mozelle wiped at the tears beginning to seep out.

"Damn shame fire kin destroy a house so fast," Mr. Jake said, staring up at the fire.

"Mighty shame," she said. "You know, Mr. Jake, I built that house practically all by myself."

"I recall when you built it back in fifty. Folks was talking about you doing menfolk work. Nobody thought you could build a house, but you showed 'em."

"I sho'nuff did. I built it strong, too, didn't I?" she asked, though she wasn't really expecting an answer. She didn't need anyone to tell her how good a job she had done. She had lived in that house, she knew how strong it was. Fresh tears washed down her cheeks. All was lost.

The fire truck came to a stop a little ways up the road. The firemen took their time getting down off the truck. They, too, could see that the house was too far gone to be in a hurry for. They stood watching the fierce flames hungrily devouring the house.

Joe anxiously rushed up to the white firemen. "Ain't y'all gon' put out the fire?"

"Boy, we ain't got enough water for that there fire. We may's well let it burn itself out. What we are gon' do is wet down them trees around it so it don't spread."

"What 'bout our house?" Kenny asked. "Ain't y'all gon' wet it down, too?"

"Y'all can't let our house burn down," Joe said.

"Boy, your house already done burned down."

Joe and Kenny stared hurtfully at the firemen. They didn't

understand.

The fireman's words just confirmed for Mozelle what she knew the minute she saw the fire high up in the sky. Hearing those words, however, hurt her like an open sore. She tried to shut out that pain, but she wasn't strong enough.

"Joe! Kenny!" Essie called. "Y'all come back over here."

Kenny started back at a trot, but Joe, slowly began backing away from the firemen. "Y'all jest don't wanna put out our fire," he accused.

"Boy, what you talking 'bout?" one of the white firemen asked.

"Joe!" Mozelle called. "Get over here!"

Turning, Joe ran back to Mozelle's side. "Mama, they ain't gon' put out the fire. They—"

"Hush, child. There ain't nothin' they kin do."

"Mama, they can put out the fire. They jest don't want to."

"No, Joe, it's too late. The fire is too big."

"But, Mama, they ain't even gon' try."

She embraced Joe and pulled him to her. "Joe, it look bad for us right now, but I don't want you to worry. We gon' get us another house. You'll see."

Joe hid his face in the warmth of her bosom and cried. Mozelle gently rubbed his back.

"Mozelle, what you gon' do?" Mr. Comstock asked.

"I declare, Mr. Comstock. I done plumb forgot you was here. Thank you, sa, for carrying me home."

"What you gon' do?"

"Well, sa, right now, U'ma go sit down back yonder on that there big rock near the branch and wait for the fire to die down. By then I'll know what to do."

"Do you have a place to go tonight?"

"I believe I do," she said, although she didn't know that for sure. She said she did because she didn't want him to know that her house was all she had to her name, and though she had insurance on it, it might not be enough to build her another one.

"All right then. I don't expect you at work tomorrow. You come back when you're settled. Don't you worry about your wages. Me and the Missus gon' do all we can to help you."

"Thank you, sa," Mozelle said, her arms still around Joe. With Essie holding on to Kenny, and Nell still clinging to her, Mozelle walked over to her favorite rock and sat down. This time, the rock seemed hard and unyielding under her weary body. Although the night was frigid and the smooth stone was cold, the chill in her body quickly vanished when she looked again up at the flames dancing against the sky.

Sitting at Mozelle's feet on the cold, dry ground, Joe lay his head on her lap and stared up at the burning house, while Essie and Nell stood on either side of her, their arms around her shoulders. Many a day she had sat facing the branch, watching the sparkling water run on its way downstream into the woods. This night, she sat with her back to the branch, watching her house burn down. Years ago, she had sat thus and watched it take shape. It had been backbreaking, exhausting work when she was thirty-six and had the drive and the strength. But now, at fifty-one, it was not in her to build another house. If Randell was alive, he'd be having a good laugh. He'd probably even come down and laugh right in her face. Maybe in the end, he had gotten the better of her anyway. She felt like dropping down on her knees and crying to God to put out the fire, to help her. But she knew that wasn't going to happen, the house was gone. Her eyes again filled with bitter tears. All of her hard work was gone.

"I can't believe this," Essie said.

"Me neither," Nell agreed.

Mozelle believed. Her eyes were wide open, there was nothing to doubt. She glanced over at the naked weeping willow trees swaying by the side of the road, then back at the flames. It seemed to her that the long, willowy branches and the flames, though they were not close enough to touch, were partners in a dance. She kept looking back and forth between the two. While the weeping willow trees gave life and the fire took life, they seemed to dance as one. If they did dance in each other's arms, the fire would surely burn down the willows and take their life, like Randell had taken hers for so many years. If they had never come together, she would have never been burned so badly.

Without Randell in her life, she would have surely lived her life differently, but they had come together, and her life was now what it was. She had come through with her head held high but she had always been scared. She was scared now, but she was counting on her faith in God to help her to rise above this fire. She knew that come late spring, the land where her house burned down would have healed and be overgrown with weed. Even if she didn't build another house there, one day, her children or their children would. Since 1960, Cora's children had been living up in New York with Henry and his sister now, but her land was heir property and would always be there for them, too. She would make sure of that.

Thirty-Eight

In the early morning hours when the last of the flames had died out because there was not a stick of wood left unburned to feed on, and the black smoke was no more, Mozelle bent her back and rested her head on her folded arms atop her knees. Through the night she stayed that way, not really sleeping, not really awake, her lungs full of smoke, her body cold, sitting on her rock, too numb, too distraught to go with her children to Mr. Jake's house. She wanted—no, needed—to be alone to mourn her loss and calm her worried mind. Though she was bone-tired and her body was as cold and as hard as the rock she sat on, she would not have been able to sleep peacefully in a house that wasn't hers after having had her own for such a long time. Cora's death had filled her heart with a pain she had never known and had never since known, but losing her home left her feeling empty with nothing to show for the blisters on her hands and on her soul. Lord, she had no doubt that her weary bones could not carry the load of building another house, not by herself or, for that matter, with a hundred hands helping her. It was all just too hard.

As much as she feared what she would see in the light of dawn, slowly, with her eyes still closed, she straightened her stiff back and raised her aching head. The heavy smell of smoke overwhelmed her. She coughed. Her chest and throat tightened, and for a fearful moment, she held her eyes shut and prayed, "Lord, give me strength." She opened her eyes. She gasped. What she saw was worse by far under the morning sky than she had seen in the darkness of night. It was as if her house had never been. There was no porch, no stairs, only a black mess of ashes and charred, smoldering wood left to say that it had been.

Then the tears that suddenly chilled her cheeks reminded her that her sorrow could have been worse—her children could have died in the house she built and their bodies part of those ashes. Just the thought of it scared her. Their lives' breath could never be given back to them with the insurance money that she would surely use to buy a house, maybe not as grand, but a house none the less. Despite the fire, she truly had something to be grateful for. God hadn't forsaken her. Now that she thought about it, she wasn't all that bad off. Not like she used to be. She no longer worked at the cotton mill, but she had two good jobs with good white folks, and she had enough money socked away for hard times. It was going to be a big help that Brother and Essie earned their own keep. More clothes and more furniture could be bought—it wasn't going to be that hard. As soon as she made her way up the hill and out of the valley, she'd find a place for them all to stay until she got her insurance money. She was feeling a mite better, she was feeling stronger, and although her body was weary, she realized that she could more than make do. She bowed her head and covered her face with her hands; she couldn't leave without saying a prayer of thanks to God.

"Mozelle."

She recognized Tom's voice. She uncovered her face and looked up at him. He was a beautiful sight to behold.

"U'm sorry about your house. I know what it meant to you."

Mozelle could feel herself about to cry again, for seeing him was like a dream come true. She had wanted to see him for a long time, but always put thoughts of him out of her mind. She wanted to stand up, but her stiff knees and prickly legs didn't act like they wanted to. So she stayed put.

"It's all over town about the fire. Is there anything I can do?"

For a little while, she let herself take him all in. She deserved that. She hadn't seen him in years, yet, he looked just about the same, though he was a bit more handsome with the gray hair at his temples.

He crouched down in front of her. "Mozelle, are you all

right? Did anybody get hurt?"

His eyes were now level with hers. That old, almost forgotten fluttery feeling in her stomach rushed back at her. "We all right," she said, her voice a hoarse whisper.

"U'm here to help."

"Mighty obligin' of you, Tom. Thank you kindly, but we gon' be jest fine."

He took hold of her hand. "You're freezing. Here, take my coat." He hurriedly unbuttoned his coat and took it off. He put it around Mozelle's shoulders on top of her own coat and then went about rubbing both her hands to warm them.

It wasn't just his coat, but his touch took away the chill that filled her body. If only he had been the man that had come to Royston all those years ago.

"Mozelle, I got a house over on the east side that I live in by myself. It ain't got much furniture, but I can get some in there by the end of the week without a problem. I can replace everything I bought for you back in fifty-seven with something better."

Her eyes popped wide open. Her jaw dropped. "Come again."

Tom nodded.

"That was you that bought my furniture?"

He nodded again.

Folding over and dropping her head to her lap, she cried . . .she cried. . .she cried.

With his hand on her back, Tom stroked her and let her have her cry.

When she could, Mozelle sat up again.

"Mozelle, I want you and your children to come live in my house."

"Oh, Tom, we can't do that."

"Yes, you can. You need a place to stay."

"But that's your home."

"Yes, it is, and if you don't want me there, if you feel it ain't proper, I'll leave."

Her stomach fluttered. She felt like she was a young girl being courted for the first time. Tom was still everything that

Randell had never been. "Tom, I 'ppreciate what you tryin' to do for me, but a man should never be put out his own house. Besides, I can get me a house."

"I ain't got no doubt that you can, but for some time now, I been wanting my house to be our house."

They held each other's gaze for a long, loving moment until Mozelle bashfully lowered her eyes. "Tom, I can't."

"I know you made a promise to God, Mozelle, but He ain't holding you to that promise, you are."

"But a promise to God is—"

"Mozelle, listen to me. I ain't never been able to get you out my mind. None of the women I come across was anything like you, and I wasn't settling for less. I started to come see you after your husband died, but I remembered your promise."

"Then, how come you bought me all that furniture?"

He smiled. "'Cause I wanted to. When I heard from Mamie that you put your husband out for good, I started to come by. Then I felt like if I gave you something that you wanted and needed, it would make me feel like I did something for you. Long as I was sure that your husband wasn't gon' use none of what I bought, I went on and bought the furniture."

"Oh, my God," Mozelle said, amazed that he would do something so grand for her.

"When Mamie told me how happy you was, just knowing that made me feel good."

"I was happy, Tom, but now all your pretty furniture is gone."

"That's all right. Furniture can be replaced. Your life can't."

"Praise the Lord," she said, wiping her eyes. Suddenly it dawned on her. "Did Mamie know that it was you who bought my furniture?"

"Mamie helped me pick out everything."

"Oh, God," Mozelle cried, clasping her cold hands to her bosom and slowly rocking back and forth. "I love you both from the bottom of my heart. I ain't had a best friend since Mamie died two years ago. I miss her so much."

"Well, she loved you just the same."

"Tom, all these years, I thought it was Mrs. Mitchell who bought me that furniture. How come you let me think that somebody else did somethin' that good for me when it was you?"

"Like I said, knowing that you was happy was good enough for me."

Remembering the day the furniture arrived, she smiled. "Tom, you got to know, I ain't never forgot about you. You always been on my mind."

Again, they looked deep into each other's eyes, deep into each other's souls. Words were not needed to tell each other how they felt. This time when Tom took her hands into his own, he lifted them to his lips, tenderly kissing the palms of each.

Mozelle didn't draw back or pull her hands from him. She felt no shame. In fact, a surge of heat seemed to flow from her hands, straight up her arms into her chest the minute his lips touched her skin. A yearning that she hadn't had in her body in years was suddenly awakened, but it frightened her. At a time like this, she was reminded how weak her flesh was. Tom began to rub the back of her hands with his thumbs. She eased her hands out of his and lowered them to her lap.

He saw that she was uncomfortable. "What are you planning on doing, Mozelle?"

"I was thinking a while ago, before you come up, about what U'm gon' do," she said, aware that a part of her wanted to throw herself into his arms and warm up altogether. But it was wrong. God was watching her. "Tom, the fire took my house, and for a terrible minute, it took my faith. But I know now that God is gon' bring me and my children through. U'm gon' make do."

Tom shook his head. "Mozelle, I don't think God intended for you to make do by yourself for the rest of your life. I don't even think He intended for you to build that house by yourself. Didn't you ever think that maybe God wanted me to help you? That maybe that's how come I was here in the first place? It was your husband that didn't want me helping you, not God," he said, standing. "Now, we're both getting up in years. I figure God is giving us another chance to be together. I know He won't mind."

The temptation to let go of her will to stay true to God was strong and pulling at her, so she tried to avoid looking at Tom so that she wouldn't weaken. But she was remembering that day way back when they sat under the big oak tree along the side of the road. The same feelings she had for him that day were at this moment just as strong. No, she didn't think God would mind, and He might even forgive her if she broke her promise to him, but she wasn't of a mind to break her promise. Breaking a promise to anybody was bad, but breaking a promise to God was a sin. She could not outright sin when she knew better.

"Tom, I hope you don't ever hate me for what U'm about to say."

"Just don't say it."

"I got to. To tell you the truth, it would be nice to not have to jest make do."

"You don't have to, U'm here," he said, putting his hand out to her.

Tearing, Mozelle put her hand in Tom's and let him pull her to her feet and right into his strong, warm arms. She didn't notice the tingly ache in her legs. Her arms circled his body. Tom's embrace was a sweet temptation that tested her faith. She lingered a little longer in his arms than she intended because it did feel good. She savored his strength and his love; she was going to have to remember them as long as she drew breath. A soft morning breeze brushed past them, and the swaying of the weeping willow trees caught her eye. The fire that had not touched them but had badly scorched the giant water oak, had given her a second chance at love, but she was going to have to say no. Gently, she pulled back out of his arms and eased Tom's coat from around her shoulders. Her eyes were blurry as she handed it to him.

"Thank you, Tom. I ain't never gon' forget you."

"Mozelle," he whispered. "Don't do this. I—"

She put her fingertips to his lips. "Tom, U'm married to God now. I gots to keep my promise. Please, help me to keep my promise."

It was Tom's eyes that now filled with tears. He tenderly kissed Mozelle's fingertips. It was the sweetest kiss she had ever

had. She closed her hands and folded her arms. There was nothing more to say. Tom knew that he would not be able to sway her.
Mozelle watched him walk away. As was his way, he did not look
back. It was all for the best. Although her heart was heavy, her
mind was at peace. She was going to be all right. God was going
to see to it.

Epilogue

Sunday, December 10, 2000

As I sit here in this grand church, overflowing with a host of family members, from near and far, and with hundreds of well-wishers, young and old, black and white, all here to pay their last respects to a humble soul, I can't help but think back on the life of Mozelle, my grandmother. I am Ann, one of Cora's children.

After the fire that took her house in 1965, Mozelle did go on and "make do." She moved out of the valley, away from the branch, away from the weeping willow trees, but she held on to her land. She bought herself another house on the east side of Gadsden and there, continued to raise her children and many of her grandchildren. As was her way, she devoted her life to her family and to the children of the families she worked for. She treasured her friends and her church family, and always warmly gifted us all with her hot apple pies. Her caring and devotion touched us all.

Mozelle continued to work hard and long, well past her retirement and long after her aging body cried out to be rested. Throughout her life, she kept her promise to God—she never did take another man as her husband. In God she put her trust and said often, "When he calls me, I'm ready."

In the early morning hours of Sunday, December 3, 2000, a cold, unforgiving dawn, a fire that long ago blazed and burned down Mozelle's house on Plum Street came again to touch her life. This time, however, the flames embraced her and two of her great-grandchildren. This time, the sun set on the noble life of

this beloved woman, and on the tender lives of four-year-old
Kandance and six-year-old Jamichael. To us, Mozelle's five children, twenty-three grandchildren, twenty-seven great-grandchildren, and five great-great-grandchildren, Mozelle was either
Mama or Grandma. And on all of their behalf, I honor her.

Mama, Grandma, it's been seven days since we last laid
eyes on you, it's been seven days since we last heard your voice.
But right now we feel your warm smile, we feel your sweet love,
and we feel your gentle spirit hugging us, oh so close. Although
we know that you have gone on to your glory, we're missing you
all the same.

Mama, Grandma, we know the backbreaking struggles and
the hard-earned achievements of your life. We know the strength
of your convictions, we know the selflessness of your character,
we know the righteousness of your morals, we know the correct-
ness of your principles, and we all know the depth of your faith
in God Almighty.

While your eighty-six years stole your precious independ-
ence and tested your stamina and patience, those trying but
blessed years also gave you wisdom and tolerance beyond measure, and gave us a mother's unconditional love beyond reproach.
For all that you were, you knew that no one was perfect. Please
forgive us for, at times, not being worthy of your special love.

Mama, Grandma, we know that Kandance and Jamichael
are nestling in your loving arms, and that you will be with them
and care for them throughout eternity. We will miss the radiant
light in their eyes, the exuberance of their playfulness, and the
sounds of their joyous laughter. We will try to not think about the
lives they might have had, we will think only of the joy they have
in being with you, with God, and with each other.

Rest easy, little ones. Rest easy, Mama. Rest easy,
Grandma. We will never forget you.

We're missing you, we're missing you, but we will be loving you all our livelong days.

Weeping Willows Dance

The seasons of our lives are ever changing and everblooming. As one life ends, another life begins. Throughout our lives, at any given age, we know with spring comes rebirth and another chance to go after what we want most. We set our sights and sway like the weeping willow tree on a breezy day, standing our ground against all obstacles that come our way, always proving that we're strong and will let nothing or no one keep us from our goal. The Lord never promised us an easy life, he only promised us life. What we do it, is on us.